War on Christmas

A Steamy Enemies-to-Lovers
Holiday Romance

ELLE CAMPBELL

Copyright © 2023 by Elle Campbell

All rights reserved.

No part of this publication may be reproduced, distributed, or transmitted in any form or by any means, including photocopying, recording, or other electronic or mechanical methods, without the prior written permission of the publisher, except as permitted by U.S. copyright law. For permission requests, contact Elle Campbell through www.authorellecampbell.com.

The story, all names, characters, and incidents portrayed in this production are fictitious. No identification with actual persons (living or deceased), places, buildings, and products is intended or should be inferred.

Cover illustration by Chelsea Kemp

First edition: 2023

To my husband.
For loving my light and my dark in equal measure.

content warnings

I understand that, as readers, we come to stories with unique experiences, values, and personalities, and it's important to me that readers can make an informed choice about what type of content they'd like to engage with or potentially avoid. If you'd like to review the content warnings for *War on Christmas*, please visit authorellecampbell.com/content-warnings. However, please be advised that the content warnings contain spoilers.

Prologue

Let me set the scene.

A Chicago coffee shop. Monday morning. Not early morning, before the 9-to-5ers go to work. Regular morning, when the freelancers and tourists and trophy wives have peeled themselves out of bed and are propping open tired, sandpaper eyes with a solid hit of caffeine. It's cold—because *Chicago*—and windy—because *Chicago*. Personal bubbles are jealously guarded by giant paper bags from Macy's and Saks, filled to bursting with sweaters that won't fit, perfumes that will cause hives, and toys that will break before Christmas lunch.

A red-and-green pestilence has hit the city. Storefront window displays, streetlights, benches. Nothing is safe from the bows or the holly. Giant gold horns erupt from historic department stores, hovering ominously over the sidewalks and passersby. Evergreen trees that once lived quiet, peaceful lives in snow-shrouded forests and rural tree farms have been sacrificed to the holiday fervor. Now, instead of sheltering bushy-tailed squirrels and wise, blinking owls, they're encased in the menacing glow of tiny, twinkling lights made half a world away in sweat shops powered by poverty-stricken children.

Christmas is here.

ELLE CAMPBELL

The line shuffles forward, everyone—consciously or unconsciously—stepping in time to the jazzy beat of Pentatonix' "Let It Snow! Let It Snow! Let It Snow!" even though what they're all really thinking is: *Please, please don't make me shovel again.*

And that's when it happens.

At the front of the line, a middle-age man with a long overcoat and slicked-back hair grabs his sixteen ounces of coffee, corn syrup, and artificial flavoring from the harried barista, his mouth twisting lecherously as he says, "Did you put some extra sugar in there for me, honey?"

"Ex—excuse me?" the barista squeaks. She's young. Probably a college student struggling to make rent, and a pink flush of panic crawls up her neck. "You ordered a peppermint mocha, right? We don't add extra—"

He chuckles as he leans forward onto the counter, the sound grating. "I didn't mean *literally*, sweetheart. I meant, did you make it extra sweet? Just for me."

Her large, hazel eyes go round behind red, heart-shaped glasses, but before she can answer, a new voice, biting and aggressive, enters the fray.

"Take your coffee and go."

Halfway down the line, a customer steps to the side and narrows dark eyes at the man. Between the black knit hat pulled low over her brow and the gray-and-black plaid scarf wrapped over her chin, only a five-inch slice of her face is visible. Pale skin, thick black eyeliner, and bright red lips.

He scoffs. "Don't get your panties in a twist, sugar. I'm just getting her number then—"

"One," the dark-eyed woman spits out, "I'm not wearing any panties. So joke's on you. Two, she's just trying to do her job. Stop harassing her. Sound good, *sugar*?"

WAR ON CHRISTMAS: A HOLIDAY ROMANCE

Silence stretches as the man bristles. On a small end table next to the frosty window, the fake tree sheds a plastic needle, and everyone can hear it whisper to the wet, slushy floor. Finally, with a dirty look at the woman, he grabs his disposable cup and stomps out the door into the wind and blowing snow.

In the coffeehouse, a wave of relieved chuckles and "Oh my gods" circulates. Someone lets out a celebratory "Woot!" and the song changes to "Hard Candy Christmas" by Dolly Parton. Meanwhile, the dark-eyed woman steps back into line. Her eyes squeeze shut, her lips press together, and mentally, she's counting down the days until this holiday-season nightmare is over.

That's me. The angel of vengeance who circumvented the harassment of an innocent coffeehouse employee by announcing to everyone that I'm going commando.

I'm the heroine of this syrupy, sappy, bullshit Christmas romance.

one

FREYA

22 days until Christmas...

"Auntie Freya!" Abi screeches as I pick up her video call. Her eyeshadow flows seamlessly from neon purple to shimmery black, and I smile at her earnest, angsty face as I flop onto my green velvet couch, my "Witchy Woman" coffee cup in hand. I kick my bare feet onto my coffee table, and a stack of junk mail slides onto a pile of shimmery fabric, a costume I'm altering for Tuesday's performance.

At The Sphere, the theater I manage, my job encompasses everything from handling the utility bills and payroll to playing the roles of impromptu seamstress, stagehand, nurse, and master of ceremonies, all depending on the day. What my job lacks in pay and health benefits, it makes up for with variety. I am, in short, a professional theater nerd.

Except for the first Tuesday of the month. The first Tuesday of the month, I'm so much more.

Not that I'm going to tell my fifteen-year-old niece about that.

"Your eyes look amazing," I tell Abi, my gaze shifting to my bedroom door to make sure it's still closed. "Have you reached out to D.G. about doing makeup for the musical yet?"

Abigail—or Abi to those who actually listen to her—is a dark, mysterious creature who holds my family in constant suspense, waiting for her next drama to unfold. Or, more accurately, explode. A shaved head? A hunger strike for endangered bats? They live in fear of the day she finds a tattoo artist who doesn't check ID.

Obviously, I adore her, and, given her talent with a makeup brush, I've been encouraging her to connect with the high school drama teacher, Mrs. Davis-Green. (Affectionately known to the theater kids of Northview, Wisconsin, as D.G.)

"More importantly," Abi says, as if I won't realize she's changing the subject, "Grandma says you're coming home for Christmas. Please tell me it's true. Pretty, pretty please."

I choke on my coffee. There is no way in hell I'm going home for Christmas. My plans are the same as they've been for the past four years: cozying up and drinking mulled wine while binge-watching *Chilling Adventures of Sabrina*. It is, objectively, the perfect Yule/Winter Solstice celebration.

I blink at the screen as I wipe coffee off my chin, trying not to get drawn in by the hope in Abi's large, almond-shaped eyes. Eyes such a dark shade of gray, they sometimes look black. Eyes like mine.

"I...wasn't planning on it," I hedge.

Usually I love crushing people's dreams; it builds character. Both my twin brother, Thad, and his girlfriend, Sam, have been texting me for weeks begging me to go home for the holidays, and I've thoroughly enjoyed telling them no. But Abi is my kryptonite. When her lower lip begins to tremble, I sigh and lift my gaze to the black crystal chandelier hanging above me. This shouldn't be on me. It *isn't*. What was my mom thinking getting Abi's hopes up like that?

I'm also, if I'm being honest, a little impressed at Mom's sneakiness.

Somehow, despite her unerring ability to never understand me at all, she zeroed in on my biggest weakness: Abi. It was the dart, thrown wildly in the pitch dark, that miraculously hit the bull's-eye.

I look to my framed poster of Frida Kahlo hanging on the exposed brick of my living room wall. Her clear eyes and thicket of unruly brows cheer me on: *Stand your ground! No excuses! No apologies!*

"*Please*, Auntie Freya. It's been forever since you've come home from Chicago. I miss you. Things at school have just been—ugh, the *worst*. And Mom is *Mom*. You're the only one in this family who gets me. I've got all this stuff going on with my friends, and her advice is all like, 'Try out for cheerleading! Join the newspaper! Have you thought about yearbook?'"

As she talks, Abi impersonates my older sister, her voice lifting with fake cheer like she's giving herself a pep talk. I know she's trying to make me laugh, but it triggers too many memories. If anyone knows what it's like to not live up to my older sister's expectations, it's me. I'd say I grew up in Bethany's shadow—prom queen, cheerleader, teacher's pet—but it was more like growing up as some cave-dwelling, primordial creature thrust into Bethany's unrelenting sunshine.

That said, I don't talk trash about Bethany to her kids. That's what therapy is for.

"I'll think about it, ok?" I lie. Then the bedroom door squeaks open to my left, and I jump to my feet. "Gotta go, Abs."

"But wait!" Her eyes go wide. "What about my tarot read—"

"I'll call you later this week!" I rush to say, hanging up just as a quiet, timid voice behind me says, "Freya?"

"Hey..." I drawl as I spin to face Tim, who is standing in my bedroom doorway, shifting from side to side. He pushes his thick, black-framed glasses—the only thing he's wearing other than plaid boxers—up his nose. "Do you want a cup of coffee before you go?" I ask over my shoulder as I walk into the kitchen. Then I'm slammed with a stroke of genius. "Or I have paper cups. So you can take it with you."

Was that too obvious? I wonder, then decide I don't care.

Tim smiles a sweet, crooked smile and comes to give me a kiss on the cheek, his fingers wrapping around my hip. *Or...not obvious enough*, I conclude, as I lean away from him with a grimace, my back pressing into the edge of the countertop behind me. My silky robe gapes, and I pull it closed. Tim grabs a ceramic mug and fills it with coffee.

"Do you have creamer?" he asks.

"No."

"Oh." His forehead furrows for a moment, but he bounces back quickly. Like an overeager puppy. With another hopeful smile, he settles into a stool at the kitchenette island. "So, was that your mum?"

Damn his cute British accent. It's what finally broke me. After months of him hanging around The Sphere, he caught me during post-performance drinks with the cast and crew and serenaded me with English slang: "So, I had a cuppa," "I was gobsmacked," "Cheers." Combined with a months-long dry spell and the fact that he's totally my type—artistic, emotional, easily manipulated—I guess it was inevitable that we ended up messing around. I only resisted for so long because I knew this awkward morning after would be just as inevitable.

I ignore his question and take a long drink of coffee, staring him down until he blinks and looks away. Good. He knows who the alpha is. I established that the night before, of course, but sometimes they rebel. Best to be sure.

As if sensing the need to exert dominance, Hecate leaps onto the island and positions herself next to Tim, lifting her tail to present him with her butthole, a small pink starburst in her sea of inky black fur. Feline behaviorists claim this implies trust, but I know better. Supremacy through humiliation is her modus operandi. Tim's face contorts with disgust, and he pulls back, looking to me for help. I take another drink.

"I'm allergic to cats," he reminds me.

"Oh."

I can tell the moment it sinks in. His face, usually the startling white of a consumptive Victorian poet, grows ruddy. Hecate takes a strategic step backwards, wiggling her furry behind closer to his nose.

"So, it's going to be like that?" he asks.

I raise my eyebrows—*Yes, it's going to be "like that"*—and feel grateful that I rolled out of bed and immediately put on my full makeup, complete with bold winged eyeliner and classic red lips. Crusty eyes and smudged lipstick just don't command obedience the same way. With a sigh, Tim pushes away his coffee and walks briskly through the apartment, collecting his belongings. Socks from the couch. Wallet and phone from the coffee table. By the time he's wrapping his scarf around his neck and pulling on his coat, a muscle jumps in his jaw. I sip my coffee as I watch, and Hecate leaps gracefully from the island to the countertop next to me, rubbing along my arm.

"You're going to end up alone, you know."

I chuckle into my mug. "One can hope."

WAR ON CHRISTMAS: A HOLIDAY ROMANCE

He's half bent over, wrestling his feet into suede, lace-up boots. "Don't you get sick of it? Of hanging out with the latest crop of Sphere actors until they move onto bigger, better things and leave you behind?"

Whaddya know, Tim's turning out to be more interesting than I gave him credit for. Not interesting enough to keep around, mind you, but I stay silent to see what he'll say next.

"I'd say to call me when you're ready to grow up and have a real relationship, but you know what? Don't. I don't care if you *do* have amazing tits."

"Aww," I singsong, "you think my tits are amazing?"

He rips open my front door, and when it bangs off the wall, I finally allow myself to smile. Imagine if he'd been this passionate in bed. (To be fair, he didn't get much of an audition. We only messed around a little.) He steps into the hallway, chest heaving and dark hair mussed, and I cross the apartment to stand in the doorway.

"Take care, Tom," I say as I close the door in his face, almost laughing out loud at his expression when I deliberately call him by the wrong name.

I'm still smiling to myself ten minutes later as I drift around my apartment picking up dirty laundry and coffee mugs. My phone is squished between my ear and shoulder as I relay Tim's magnificent exit to Leo, my best friend from work.

Leo and I are close. We bring each other take-out pho when we're sick, and before he started dating Todd, we spent the past four Christmases together. But Leo is my third "Leo." Jolie was my first. She showed me the ropes around Chicago until she left for LA, where she now plays a supporting role in a popular sitcom. Rebecca, my second Leo, relocated to New York after being discovered and has been in several popular Broadway musicals.

Now, our interactions consist of occasionally liking each other's Instagram posts. Still, Leos are nice while they last. I've simply learned to accept that, with the exception of Thad—because there's no escaping your twin—I'm on my own.

My current Leo guffaws with laughter.

"'You're going to end up alone, you know,'" he imitates with a perfect London accent. "Jesus, Freya, what did you do to him?"

"Nothing I'm proud of," I say, then add, "but nothing I'm ashamed of either."

That's when I look up to see Hecate perched on the coffee table, shiny fabric hanging from her teeth. My heart gives a painful thump at the flash of silver in her mouth, and my phone crashes to the hardwood floor as I leap for her.

But it's too late. She swallows the needle before I can stop her.

TWO

JEREMY

20 days until Christmas...

"I'm telling you, man, you're going to be so glad you came." Wes, a friend from work, bounces on his toes, hands shoved into his pockets.

It's cold. Winter in Chicago cold. The people standing in line with us huddle and shiver in pea coats and puffy coats and parkas that envelope them from neck to snowy boots. Still, they seem in good spirits as we wait for the doors to open at The Sphere, the hole-in-the-wall theater that hosts these once-a-month, off-beat burlesque shows. Wes discovered them last summer and has been bugging me to come with him ever since. According to him, they're becoming a cult phenomenon. No advertising. Word of mouth only. First come, first served, tickets at the door. Each month there's a new theme, and nobody knows in advance what it's going to be. When Wes came in June, it was summer solstice themed, with the performers dressed as fairies and flowers.

I've been looking forward to this little adventure. I moved to Chicago a decade ago when I started working at Andersen & Sons Architecture, and all of my theater experiences have been work related. Which is to say, mainstream. *Phantom of the Opera* and *Wicked*. Maybe *Hamilton* when out-of-town customers are feeling extra spicy. But The Sphere? This place is different. As we filter inside to its dozen rows of moth-eaten seats, I pick up the scents of weed, body odor, and patchouli, a nostalgic reminder of my college days.

Wes grins as we shrug out of our coats and get seated. He's got that blond, blue-eyed, prep-school look. Like he spent his adolescence in blazers and ties eating meals that require four forks. He's an all right guy, though.

"Glad you get to be fun again now that Elaine's out of the picture," he quips.

I roll my eyes. I'm not going to badmouth my ex. But he's not wrong. Elaine *was* the reason I didn't come to one of these shows sooner. She would've spent the entire night nagging that it didn't go with her "Instagram aesthetic" and that we should've gone to *The Nutcracker* instead.

Personally? My eyes flit around, taking in the hipsters and black-clad college students as the house lights dim. I like this place. It's unique and artsy. Something out of my routine.

And I think I need that.

Over the past couple of years, I've completely paid off my student loans, bought my condo, and got a big promotion at work. I've done all the right things to feel secure and safe, but to what end? So I can stick to the same boring routines? Daily gym, work, TV. Drinks on Friday or Saturday. Over and over again. Have I been busting my ass for the past seventeen years so I can keep spending Christmas alone with takeout and *Die Hard*?

A dragon in an orange, shimmering costume wanders onto the circular stage, dragging a long, stuffed tail, and I shrug off my dark thoughts, grinning with anticipation.

Shit is about to get weird.

"Welcome, welcome," the dragon says, lifting his arms in greeting. The crowd goes wild, hooting and hollering. It's the same fun, frantic energy as the showing of *The Rocky Horror Picture Show* I went to in my early twenties. The dragon beams a Cheshire-cat smile as he waits for the cheers to die down.

"Do we have a treat in store for you tonight, folks," he continues. "Especially for the freaks and geeks out there. You know who you are. While the rest of your classmates were worried about the school dance and who was going to be named captain of the basketball team, you were locked up in your room..." He pumps his hand like he's jerking off, then rolls his hips. My surprised laughter gets lost as the theater goes berserk again. "Daydreaming of a faraway galaxy. Fantasizing about mythical creatures and epic quests. Tonight, my fellow dorks, is for you. Welcome to our original burlesque performance of *Hardcore Nerdcore*."

Knockoff *Game of Thrones* music pumps through the theater, and, with one graceful motion and a sudden rip of Velcro, the dragon tears off his costume to reveal a shiny, skintight bodysuit. Hands clap. Feet pound the floor. Wolf whistles and catcalls echo. Then the dragon turns to strut offstage, and laughter—mine included—erupts as the audience catches sight of his bare ass hanging out of his bodysuit.

The next scene—two gyrating elves shedding leaves from their costumes faster than a tree in October—begins to unfold, and I'm pleasantly surprised at the memories that bubble to the surface. Not sexual ones, just...happy ones. Innocent. Afternoons off school eating frozen pizzas with cardboard crusts while watching *The Lord of the Rings* in Thad and Freya's basement. Long nights of laughter as we played out rambling Caves & Conquerors campaigns. My sketchbook filled with fantastical creatures: ax-wielding dwarves and busty fairy queens and craggy, bearded wizards. Nowadays, my sketches are...less interesting. Mostly blueprints for strip malls and office buildings, all straight lines and right angles. Square, literally *and* figuratively.

My phone vibrates, but I ignore it. In a theater this small, there's no inconspicuous way to check it. Around me, awed whispers circulate: "So meta" and "I love the interplay between high fantasy and our gritty, urban setting." I scoff at the commentary but clap politely when the elves take off their tops to expose marijuana-leaf-shaped pasties. Wes hoots along with the rest of the theater.

The third number, starring a tall, skinny troll, is just getting started when my phone vibrates again. I wince and dig in my pocket, fully intending to power off my phone and return my attention to the stage, where the troll just tossed off his tattered robes to expose a two-foot-long fake schlong bouncing happily between his knobby knees. I'm laughing, giving my screen only a cursory glance, then my eyes catch on the number on the caller ID. A number I haven't seen in ten years.

Home.

I shoot to my feet, apologizing as I stumble over legs and purses on my way down the aisle. My fingers fumble to answer. Wes stands to follow me, but I wave him off. I push my way outside, barely noticing the frigid night air.

"Mom?" I choke out.

And then I hear her voice. Thinner than I remember. More fragile. But it's her.

"Jem?"

My breath leaves my body, leaving me dizzy. I try to respond, but I can't speak over the lump rising in my throat.

"He died," she says. "Gary just died. Keeled right over."

THree

FREYA

17 days until Christmas...

I'm in my office at The Sphere, catching up on paperwork. Everyone else is in rehearsal, their voices echoing faintly in the background, when Thad's text comes through.

The Good Twin: Jeremy will be driving up from Chicago Sunday morning to help his mom out with Gary's funeral. Any interest in catching a ride with him?

I stare at my phone, unable to stifle a loud groan, then my eyes flick to the $1,500 vet bill on my desk.

Hecate didn't even pretend to be sorry about eating the sewing needle and throwing my finances into disarray. She hissed and spit at all the vet techs until they sent her home early after surgery, then as soon as I let her out of her carrier, she proceeded to knock my "Witchy Woman" mug onto the kitchen floor, where it smashed into thousands of pieces.

One piece for each dollar I now owe.

Is it worth it? Of course. I've loved the little furball since the moment I first saw her photo on the shelter website, a little blob of midnight fur amid her tabby striped brothers and sisters.

However, I'm officially on the verge of being broke.

Which means that, combined with the unpaid two-week break The Sphere always takes over the holidays, my bank account is looking more pathetic than Hecate's shaved, stitched belly.

Which means that when Joe, my favorite bartender, offered to pay me a great nightly rate if his in-laws could stay at my apartment for a couple weeks—like an off-the-books Airbnb—I couldn't exactly turn him down.

Which means that I need a place to stay.

Which means that—rub me down with crystals and douse me with incense—I'm going home for Christmas.

Still, I have *some* pride left. I fire off a reply to Thad.

Me: How do I put this delicately? Fuck no.

The Good Twin: Come on, Frey. It's been 17 years. What did he ever even do to you?

What did Jeremy Kelly do to me? I scowl at my phone. Jeremy Kelly had been my best friend. A sweet, creative goofball of a kid who, other than Thad, was the only person to ever truly understand me. To really *see* me. Then, freshman year of high school, he grew eight inches in eight months, discovered he could throw a football, and traded in his clunky, Jeffrey Dahmer-style glasses for contacts, thus completing the most astounding "glow up" since Neville Longbottom transformed into Matthew Lewis, certified hottie of the Harry Potter universe. *Then* Jeremy went on to date a string of popular girls who called me Freaky Freya for the remainder of high school. That's when he and I fell into a rivalry that encompassed everything from petty squabbling to competing over grades.

Me: He exists.

The Good Twin: Your a pain in the ass.

Me: *You're*

The Good Twin: Ha! I only did that to bug you. What are you going to do? Drag that hellion of a cat on a 20-hour bus ride? Will they even let you bring her?

See? This is what happens when you let your guard down and love something. People use it to manipulate you.

Me: Let the record show that I am not happy about this.

The Good Twin: Let the record show that you're never happy about anything.

Touché.

Me: Fine.

The Good Twin: Good choice. Sam and I will be there in a week. It's all going to be ok.

Four

JEREMY

15 days until Christmas...

I stand outside Freya Nilsen's building and give myself a chance to breathe. To collect myself.

Since my mom's call Tuesday night, life has been a blur. Filling out HR forms for family leave. Handing off projects to coworkers. Contacting clients to let them know I'll be out of the office for a couple weeks. It was all sliding together, fuzzy and indistinct, until Thad's video call a few nights ago.

"He's dead?" Thad frowned at the screen, his forehead wrinkled with concern. In the background, I could see his girlfriend, Sam, puttering around their kitchen.

"Yup." I popped the final consonant and took a long swig of warm beer.

"Well...good," Thad said after a long pause.

"Yup," I repeated, like it's the only word I know.

We're not assholes. At least we're not assholes for being glad my stepdad is dead. Now *there* was a real asshole. Gary Cassidy is—well, *was*—as mean as a rattlesnake and gave less warning before striking. That sorry-excuse-for-a-man's only redeeming quality was that he stuck to words as his weapon of choice.

For whatever that's worth.

I'm not sad about Gary. My biological dad ran out before I was born, and whatever hopes I had for a normal father-son relationship with Gary died not long after he married my mom when I was eight. It was Thad's dad who taught me how to throw a baseball. My chemistry teacher, Mr. Diedrich, who showed me how to tie a tie for Honor's Night. My high school football coach who taught me how to drive. I had to rely on a patchwork of father figures. Neighbors and teachers and mentors who took pity on a fatherless kid trying to figure things out.

No, I'm not grieving Gary.

It was Thad's last question, as we were about to hang up, that felt like a drop-kick to my stomach.

"Any chance you can give Freya a ride to Northview?"

I haven't seen Freya since our high school graduation, where she and I stood shoulder to shoulder on stage as co-valedictorians. The auditorium was filled, every seat occupied, and I knew I should feel intimidated or humbled—something that fit that milestone moment. Instead, all I could focus on was every breath Freya took, every rise and fall of her shoulder against my ribs, and that peppery floral scent she used to wear. Freya, on the other hand, refused to acknowledge my existence, surveying the crowd like a witch on a pyre. *You tried to break me*, her gray eyes accused them, *but you failed.*

The next day she got on a plane for New York, where she had a summer internship at a small, off-Broadway theater.

As children, we'd been close. Freya, Thad, and Jeremy: the trifecta. Always together, always in trouble. Like triplets, people joked. I never liked the triplets comments, though. I didn't mind people calling Thad my brother—he's as close as I'll ever get to one—but Freya never felt like a sister. She always summoned a secret sense of awe in me, something magical and wondrous that I never sensed between her and her twin. I always got the impression that to Thad, Freya seemed as ordinary and familiar as breathing.

But Freya was never ordinary to me.

Now I haven't heard a word about her since we were eighteen. At a party on graduation night, half-drunk and more than a little desperate about Freya taking off across the country, I'd harassed Thad for information. Would she really be gone the *entire* summer? Did she have someplace safe to stay? Weren't big-city guys creeps? Was he sure she'd be ok? How could she ditch out on her last summer vacation before college? Finally, Thad had turned away from making out with Molly Turner and told me, "Dude, I'm done playing middleman. I mean it. If you want information about Freya, ask *her*. I'm not gonna be the sad kid stuck in the middle of your divorce anymore."

And to give Thad credit, he's stuck to it. I knew she lived in Chicago. That much slipped because Thad always spends time with both of us when he visits from Minneapolis. (He and I jokingly refer to it as our "shared custody" arrangement.) But other than that, I know nothing. The handful of times I broke down and asked, Thad's answer was always the same: "Why don't you pick up the phone and ask her?"

I roll my shoulders, as though I could physically shake off my nerves, and head up to Freya's unit. It's a small, older building that smells like cooking spices, laundry, and the warm, musty smell of pets. It's got character. Probably ghosts, too, which makes me smile. The Freya I knew would love living in a haunted building.

My knuckles rap against the thick wood door. At the shrill slide of metal on metal, my heartbeat accelerates from its usual throb of bored indifference to a quick, heavy trip of anticipation.

I'm about to see Freya for the first time in seventeen years, and I know *nothing* about her. Not anymore.

I once knew her favorite color. (Black, obviously.) Her favorite foods. (Tie: Broccoli and frozen Snickers bars.) Her one giveaway when she was lying. (A twitch in her right eyelid.) Her favorite movie moment. (Éowyn declaring "I am no man" in *Lord of the Rings: The Return of the King*.) I knew she was secretly self-conscious about the tiny mole next to her nose, even though it was super cute. And I knew that when she was six years old and her parents gave her a Barbie Dreamhouse for Christmas, she locked herself in her room and cried because she'd really wanted *The Nightmare Before Christmas* on VHS.

The door swings open, and my polite smile freezes. Because standing in the doorway of a small, neat apartment is a bombshell. Sophisticated and sharp. Dramatic curves and poise.

A bombshell I've never seen before but would recognize anywhere.

This isn't the little girl who ran through the neighborhood wearing her mom's panties and bra over her clothes, pretending to be Princess Leia in a gold bikini. And this isn't the silently seething teenager I stood next to at graduation. This is someone new. Someone who took all the versions of the Freya I'd once known and transformed them into a woman. A woman with the confidence to meet my shellshocked gaze with an ironic tilt of her eyebrow.

When I knew Freya, too many people couldn't see past her black clothes, her black hair, her black eyeliner. Some even said her black heart.

But when I was with Freya, the world went from black and white to technicolor. It's always been that way, and it still is. Because right now, all I can see are her red lips. They're the luscious lips of a 1940s pinup girl. Full, bowed, and inviting. The bright, intoxicating color of poppies. Of fresh, shiny apples. Or, as Freya would probably prefer, *poison* apples.

I finally drag my gaze away from her mouth. You know the color of those lips? Forbidden fruit. Those lush, pouty lips gave me my first kiss, and all *that* did was get me permanently kicked out of Freya's good graces.

A black sweater and dark gray jeans mold themselves to her full hips and breasts and highlight the tiny curve of her waist. No more baggy band T-shirts then. And instead of dusty, dilapidated Vans, she's wearing cute black ankle boots. To top it all off, a black cat lies draped across her forearm like a living accessory, staring at me with bright, golden eyes.

My heart thumps painfully, but I ignore it, giving Freya my most charming smile as I finally meet her gaze. Why? Because I know it will drive her nuts. And nothing—I mean *nothing*—makes me feel alive like driving Freya Nilsen out of her goddamn mind.

"Hey, Sunshine. Is this everything?" I nod at the two suitcases next to her. "Or do you need anything else?" I purse my lips and pretend to think. "Extra coat? Purse?" I pause. "Broomstick?"

She stares back, deadpan. "If my broomstick was working, why would I need a ride from you?"

Five

FREYA

He whistles while he carries my suitcases to the car. I give him my best death glare, and he winks back. Because he knows it will drive me nuts.

That's how it was between us. He became Mr. Popular, the happy-go-lucky, friendly guy who everybody loved. I doubled down on Freaky Freya, the little emo theater geek who steadfastly refused to smile. We poked and prodded each other relentlessly, like canker sores we couldn't keep our tongues away from. But whereas Jeremy's barbs came across as innocent and cute ("Oh, he said, 'Good morning, Sunshine'? So adorable!"), mine always got me cast as a grade-A bitch ("You told him that Zac Efron called and wants his ugly-ass haircut back? That's just mean, Freya.").

But he's not that teenage kid anymore. His eyes are the same shade of blue-green, but they have smile lines around them now. His hair is still sandy blond, but he traded in his *High School Musical* shag for a stylish crew cut with some length on the top. He still towers above me, but the lanky, boney awkwardness of adolescence is gone. In high school, his shoulders were too big for the rest of him, like shoulder pads he forgot to take off after football practice. He fits them now, moving with easy, athletic grace as we walk down the snowy sidewalk.

I roll my eyes. Of course he's gorgeous. Nothing like the pale, passionate, artsy types I usually favor. Just objectively, undeniably handsome.

Annoying.

However, I didn't miss how his jaw dropped when he first saw me, and I'm vain enough to really, *really* appreciate that little victory.

As awkward and emo as I was in high school, I discovered my style quickly once I was immersed in the New York theater scene. And, not to brag, but guys dig it. Dramatic eyes, red lips, dark wavy hair. The costume designer at the theater where I interned taught me how to thrift for clothes that show off my pinup-girl curves, and I ditched my baggy jeans and T-shirts and never looked back. I've attracted a lot of male attention since then, but that look on Jeremy Kelly's face just now? That might be the best.

He's parked half a block away, his car a silver hybrid sedan that I eye with interest while he stows my bags in the back seat. Hecate mews plaintively from her carrier—she's not a fan of the stiff, December wind—and I open the door opposite Jeremy and strap her carrier into a seat, sneaking a glance at him as I fiddle with the seatbelt.

I know nothing about him anymore. My summer in New York, Thad got fed up with me asking my snarky questions ("And how is Mr. Popular?") and told me in no uncertain terms he was done being our go-between. "I don't know, Frey, why don't you pick up the phone and ask him?" So, aside from knowing that Jeremy also lives here in Chicago, his life is a mystery to me.

As I slide into the passenger seat, I look around the car for some clues, anything that will give me insight into this enigma of a man who can still make my blood boil. However, there's not so much as a crumpled receipt telling me what takeout he likes.

"Did you rent this?" I ask, running my hands over the upholstery next to me. There's not even a speck of dust on the dashboard. If Abi were here, she would call it "Sus."

"No, it's mine." He glances down at my hip, checking I'm buckled before putting the car in drive and pulling into traffic. "I have colleagues and clients in here pretty frequently, so I like to keep it clean." I nod, intrigued by that "colleagues and clients," and, like a mind reader, he asks, "So, how should we do this? I ask you all my questions? You ask me yours? We take turns? Ooh, I know—Truth or Dare. That could be fun. You pick. But no daring me to wear frozen underwear again. That was a once-in-a-lifetime experience."

I stare at him, horrified, and barely refrain from patting my bra to double-check for the garnet and snowflake obsidian gemstones I tucked away for protection. If they are there, they're definitely not working.

My plan had been to spend the three-hour drive in contemplative silence while pretending to be a rich lady with a chauffeur. One of those "one-percenters" all my communist theater buddies want to eat. Outside the window, a wintry Chicago speeds by, and I consider jumping out at the next stoplight. Or maybe I can do one of those fancy, action-movie rolls while the car is still moving? If I break enough bones, I can stay at the hospital for the next two weeks. I have a high tolerance for pain.

Jeremy takes his eyes off traffic to look at my face, and he breaks into a wide grin that makes me curse his straight, white teeth.

"All right," he says, reaching to turn on the radio. "Christmas music it is."

He's going to drive me out of my goddamn mind.

SIX

JEREMY

She breaks between Kenosha and Milwaukee. The playlist—combined with my enthusiastic and entirely off-key singing—was carefully curated for exactly this result. It starts out with oddball artists for Christmas music—Snoop Dogg, Weezer, Bad Religion—designed to give her false hope she might be able to withstand it. Then, an hour in, I hit her with Dave Matthews Band. Her musical nemesis. The first bluesy notes fill the car, and she slams her hand into the stereo's power button. I swallow my smile and admire her long, slender fingers stretched across the clock, her fingernails a dark, glossy purple.

She always did have pretty hands.

"Fine," she grunts. "What do you do?"

We spend the next two hours catching up. It's the big stuff. Nothing too personal. College and jobs. Career highlights and vacations. When she says she's single, something constricted relaxes in my gut, a clenched fist releasing its hold, but I ignore it. Because as attractive as I find the woman sitting next to me—as much as my attention keeps flitting to the long sweep of her lashes and the way her dark hair grazes the pale skin of her cheek—I'm determined not to make the same mistakes again.

She stays guarded. Which isn't surprising. The only time Freya's cool, indifferent mask cracks is when I recognize the name of the theater she works at.

"The Sphere?" I echo, a note of excitement creeping into my voice. "I was just there for the burlesque show. This past Tuesday."

Her gray eyes flash, just for a moment.

"Oh?"

My smile falters. Maybe she doesn't care for the burlesque shows? But now that I know Freya works there, I can *see* her in it. Not on stage, obviously. In high school, she'd always preferred working behind the scenes. But the show's quirkiness? Its dark humor and its drive to subvert expectations? They all carry Freya's witchy fingerprints, her unique brand of magic.

"Yeah," I admit, turning my gaze back to the road.

"And..." She pauses. "What did you think?"

For a moment, I consider making up some bullshit Puritanical answer about the evils of sexuality, just to see her reaction. But I don't. Art is vulnerable. It's a vehicle for our deepest truths, and I want to honor her question with an honest answer.

"I thought it was brilliant," I say. "What I saw was funny and smart and plowed right over the edges of decency. Like good art should."

Her lips twitch into a brief smile. If I'd blinked, I would've missed it.

"What you saw?" she asks.

"Yeah…" Now it's my turn to look uncomfortable. The conversation has been easy so far. Light and surface level. I don't want to bring up Gary. "I only got to stay for the first three songs."

She nods, then changes the subject to my job. Unfortunately, I don't have anything half as interesting as fantasy-themed burlesque to talk about.

When I exit Highway 41 and drive through Northview's historic downtown, we both fall silent. Chicago gets really decked out for Christmas. It's an urban winter wonderland. But even the evergreen-draped stores of Michigan Avenue can't hold a candle to Northview at Christmastime.

Legend has it that on the eve of its founding in the 1870s, the town was gifted with a dazzling performance of the northern lights, inspiring the town's planned name, Springtown, to be replaced with Northview. (Ironically, the exceptional views of the aurora borealis were a one-time fluke.) Then, through the generations, a process of association took place that went something like this: northern lights come from the North Pole; the North Pole equals Christmas; Northview equals Christmas.

That's right. Freya and I grew up in a town that's the next best thing to the North fucking Pole.

In the passenger seat, Freya sighs as we drive past brick storefronts drowning in garlands. The ice rink crawling with families. Old-fashioned lampposts twisted with white and red ribbons to look like candy canes.

For most people, Northview must seem downright magical during the holidays. For a kid like me, whose stepdad made a point of not "wasting" money on decorations or presents—"not dropping my hard-earned cash on another man's bastard"—it felt…not so magical.

I ease to a stop at a crosswalk, allowing shoppers to cross with piles of bags, and notice how white my knuckles are against the steering wheel. I stretch my fingers.

"How long since you've been back?" I ask.

"Four years," she says, her voice flat. Her answer catches me off guard, but before I can press for more information, she asks, "You?"

I'm surprised at the way my guts twist at her question. I've replayed my last night in Northview over and over so many times that I thought it had lost its sting. But the hurt is still lodged in my chest, like a pill I had to swallow without water.

I can still recall that night before I left for college with perfect clarity. Every single word: "I'm done supporting another man's bastard." (Notice a theme?) "Take all your shit with you tomorrow. Because you're not coming back." Every godawful expression: Gary, purple-faced with rage. My mom, clutching her bathrobe and sobbing. My initial reaction? Stupid, naïve kid that I was, I felt hope. I'd been so sure that if he forced her to choose between us, she'd pick me. She'd be out. *We* would be out.

I was wrong.

My mom didn't like him kicking me out. I knew that much. But when I left for UW–Milwaukee the next morning, it was with the clear understanding I'd stay out of their lives for good. Sure, her face was red and puffy from crying all night, but she'd stood on that curb and waved goodbye. *It's been real, kid. Have a nice life.*

"Seventeen years," I answer. Freya starts, her eyes wide with surprise, and I fight down the urge to blush. Look, I know it wasn't my fault, but there's a shame in being rejected by your own mother that's hard to kick, logical or not. I force my voice to stay light as I continue. "Gary kicked me out when I left for college. Thad never told you?"

She shakes her head. "That's why you were never here for the holidays?" Her brows draw together, forming an adorable little V in her forehead. "I always assumed you were traveling or…I don't know. With a girlfriend or something."

"Nope."

I keep my eyes on the road as I turn onto our street. I don't like to think about those first Christmases on my own. The clumsy, blundering conversations with dorm friends: "Any chance I could crash at your place over break?" Their panicked responses: "For the whole month?!" Luckily, by my junior year, I'd figured out how to leverage the system. How to volunteer for odd jobs and projects that would keep me on campus year-round. I always could have stayed with Thad's family, of course. However, the idea of being next door to my mom and Gary, but unable to go home, felt unbearable.

When I finished grad school and finally got a real job, I tried one final time to convince my mom to leave. My job at Andersen & Sons was good. I wasn't going to be rich, but I could take care of us. That's why I'd pursued architecture, even though part of me would've loved something more creative like art or graphic design. Architecture could provide security. Never having to wonder, ever again, if there'd be a couch for me to crash on. More importantly, I could finally get my mom out. So, I'd swallowed my pride, called her up, and begged her to come to Chicago with me.

She picked Gary, of course. Again.

My thoughts skitter away from that memory like it's an open wound, too painful to touch even ten years later.

Instead, I focus on Freya. "Did Thad tell you he died?" I ask her.

She nods curtly as she, too, looks out the window. "It was like Christmas came early."

I snort, not at all shocked by her honesty. Everybody else—neighbors, teachers, friends—turned a blind eye to Gary's behavior. "It's not like he's hitting the boy," I overheard so many times I lost count. But Freya? She had never hesitated to call it out. Because Freya, unlike everyone else in our Midwest-nice town, wasn't afraid to look directly into the shadows. All those unseemly things that lesser humans turn their gaze away from...Freya stares that shit down.

And when you *live* in the shadows? When your life doesn't fit the sunshiny narrative everybody wants to see for a nice, athletic, book-smart kid? The one person who's willing to acknowledge your reality, to stare at it unflinching, can feel like a lifeline. *I'm not crazy. This is really happening, and it's fucked up.*

It's why it hurt so fucking bad to lose her.

I clear my throat. "That was pretty much Thad's response," I say, dread settling heavy and hard in my stomach as we approach our block. "Well," I shrug, "mine, too."

We grew up in a middle-class neighborhood, a row of 1950s and '60s ranches, simple and well-kept. My mom bought our house from her grandma, and it's a boring gray box. One long rectangle with front door, two windows, and square garage door. No trees to add interest to the front yard. No gardens or even bushes to liven up the plainness of the property. Just grass and that ugly gray box of a house.

The Nilsen house, by comparison, is cute. Tan brick with a setback garage and a little porch protecting the front door. The birch tree we climbed as kids still stretches across the front yard, and the bushes lined up in front of the living room window glow with multicolored lights. (Mr. Nilsen always did get into holiday decorating. Every year, the day after Thanksgiving, you could find him on his ladder, stapling and cursing.) Long fingers of icicle lights trail from the eaves, and a projector shines on the white garage door, covering it in tiny, blue snowflakes.

I pull into their driveway and put the car in park, focusing on Freya's face. She's staring at her house with a pained expression, her forehead pinched. I need just one more minute before facing whatever's waiting for me next door. I rack my brain for something, *anything*, to say that might keep me in her cool, steady presence a little longer.

"I play golf now," I blurt out. She turns her dark gray eyes to me. This is different than the careful, perfunctory conversation that's gotten us through the past two hours. This is a confession. "I hate it. The grass looks fake. The conversation with my boss feels fake. Pretending to enjoy swinging a big stick at a stupid little ball is fake. It's like I've been trying so hard for so long to do the right things—make the safe choices—that now I don't even know what's *real*."

If I'm stunned at my outburst, I shouldn't be. Freya pursues the truth ferociously, and while most people find that intimidating, I've always found it liberating. I might twist and bend myself to meet the expectations of coworkers and friends and lovers, but I've always been myself with her. She's always had that effect on me.

I sit with the words that just spilled out of me, and for a second, I feel...free.

Freya stares at me, her expression giving away nothing. It rarely does.

"Sounds like something you should figure out," she finally says, reaching for the door handle. Without thinking, I spring into action, jumping from the driver's seat and jogging around the car to open her door and help grab her bags. When we have everything unpacked, we stand shoulder to shoulder in her driveway for a moment, our warm breath mingling as it freezes in the cold air. She glares at the blinking "Happy Holidays!" sign on the front door and mutters, "Welcome to hell."

seven

JEREMY

I stand at my front door, suitcase in hand, and debate whether I should knock. It's my childhood home. The place I grew up. There are notches on my bedroom doorway tracking how much I grew each year. *Knocking would be weird...right?* Counterpoint: I haven't set foot on this property since I was eighteen. George W. Bush was President. Donald Trump was just a reality TV star. Steve Irwin was still happily hunting crocodiles. A lot has changed. *I should knock...right?*

Suddenly, I wish I hadn't come. I wish when I'd seen "Home" on the caller ID, I'd let it go to voicemail. I wish when she'd asked me to come back to Northview, I'd said no.

Because I'm afraid. I'm afraid of stepping into this house and feeling like a scared, helpless kid. I'm scared of seeing my mother's face and feeling the sting of rejection all over again. Worst of all, I'm afraid of not being able to contain the anger I can feel simmering beneath the surface. I'm afraid of giving voice to every horrible, shameful thing I'm feeling and directing it at a woman who's spent the past twenty years being made to feel small.

After all, I know better than anyone what she put up with. For years, it was her and me, together, tiptoeing around Gary's moods like they were shards of glass. When she and Gary first got married, she tried to shield me, throwing herself on his sharpest barbs to protect me, but it didn't take long to figure out that interference only escalated his temper. So, we both learned how to make ourselves quiet. How to anticipate Gary's triggers and avoid activating them as much as possible.

There's an intimacy in that. In haunting the shadows together. Maybe that's why I felt compelled to come back. To see if there's enough of our relationship left to stitch back together.

I'm starting to shiver, still unsure what to do, when the front door swings open. My mom, wearing jeans, a plain pink T-shirt, and a matching cardigan, offers me a hesitant smile.

"It's freezing out there," she says quietly. "Come on in."

Was she always this small? I wonder as I step into the living room. Clearly, I got my height from my father. She's so tiny, her shoulders so narrow and boney under her thin sweater, that I suddenly feel giant and awkward. Like my freshman year of high school, when I grew so quickly my shins throbbed like a toothache. We stand a few feet apart, and she looks skittish, her eyes never meeting mine. I try not to stare, but it's impossible not to.

Somehow, in my mind, she's been ageless, immortalized as that sad, soft-spoken woman who waved goodbye to me from the curb. That day, she was only a few years older than I am now, thirty-seven to my thirty-four. Now, she's fifty-four. In our time apart, she slid firmly into middle age. Her hair, once the same dirty blond as mine, is mostly silver now. And her face is wrinkled—narrow lines crisscross her forehead and deep grooves run from nose to mouth—but it's more than that. There's a softness to her features. The slow, gentle toll of gravity tugging at her eyelids and chin and mouth.

I open my mouth to say something, but nothing comes out. I clear my throat.

I'm usually *good* at defusing awkward situations. Really good. Without a family system to fall back on if I get ditched by my friends or fired by an irritable boss, I've learned to be adaptable and agreeable. I know how to celebrate Thanksgiving with families I've never met and get invited back the next year. ("Do you remember how he insisted on doing the dishes?") I know how to treat my friends' grandparents like my own, kissing old ladies' dry, powdery cheeks and calling them things like "Meemaw." I know how to break up with a woman so gently that I'm guaranteed an invitation to her wedding a couple years later. ("Congrats! The better man won.") I'm a fish, slipping and sliding through every sticky situation until I find a win-win solution, and I do it with a smile. It's my specialty.

I can do this.

"Um. Hi," I choke out, fighting the urge to hunch over so I don't feel so huge.

"Hi." She talks to my feet, which also feel too big. "Thank you. For coming up. Taking off work, too. I—I know you didn't have to do that. Thank you."

I stare at her. *Thank you? Thank you?! I ruined your life. If you hadn't been struggling to take care of me, you never would have married him. And, speaking of him, how could you choose him? How could you choose him over me?*

"Sure. No problem," I mumble. "I mean, you're welcome."

She nods, her eyes still lowered. "You can take your things to your room. If you want. All your old stuff is still in there."

"Really?" A surprised flutter of excitement ignites my belly, easing the knots.

There was no way I could take everything with me to my dorm. I'd hitched a ride to Milwaukee with an acquaintance from school, and his parents' minivan was already full of all the things I couldn't afford. A futon, a microwave, his own desktop computer. I'd feverishly stuffed as much as I could into a few duffle bags and resigned myself to Gary trashing everything I'd left behind.

"Uh-huh," she says, and for the first time, she smiles. The barest quirk at the corner of her mouth. "I told him I'd put rat poison in his dinner if he set so much as a finger on it."

"Um, thanks," I say, grabbing at the back of my neck. Suddenly, I notice my leather boots melting snow onto the old tan carpet and step aside to toe them off on the doormat. "Sorry about that."

My mom shakes her head—*No problem*.

It was *Gary* who'd been waiting to criticize every mistake I made. Ready to fly off the handle at every inconvenience.

I swallow. "I—I guess I'll go get settled then."

***

FREYA

"Give your auntie a hug," Bethany instructs Andy. She grabs him by the shoulders and steers him toward the couch, where I'm clutching a Tom

& Jerry like my life depends on it. Because it does. Alcohol is all that's sustaining my will to live right now.

After greeting me with shrieks and hugs, Mom had informed me that Bethany, Drew, and their four kids were coming over for a family dinner. "To welcome you home," she'd said, running her hands over my hair like I was her personal sensory toy.

I'd say Mom is an older version of Bethany, but that isn't exactly true. She *looks* like an older version of Bethany. Blonde, slender, way too smiley. But whereas Bethany is all type A, Mom is less controlling. She's also less aware. Her attention just...goes where it wants to. She sees what she wants to see. Growing up, it was usually focused on the little floral shop she and my dad run. So, when she was cursed with a brooding, stoic daughter, she simply didn't pay attention. She plastered on her signature smile and pretended she could mold me into Bethany 2.0 with princess dresses and Barbie Dreamhouses. Our conversations usually went something like: "Detention again? What hap—Ope! I forgot—can you help unload the poinsettias from the van? Welcome to Fox Valley Floral and Gifts!"

I, in response, grew closer to Thad and Jeremy, who were happy to include me in their daily regimen of mud fights and blowing up green plastic army men with firecrackers.

I watch Andy as he approaches, hands tucked behind his back. He's dragging his feet as he walks. He wasn't quite two the last time I saw him in person. He was round cheeked and baby faced, still wearing diapers and smelling of spoiled milk. Now he's in kindergarten, about to turn six next month. When he arrives before me, round belly leading the way, his eyes fall to the carpet.

"Hey, Andy." I lean forward so I don't have to shout to be heard, and Bethany narrows her eyes suspiciously. She's a drill sergeant, demanding perfect obedience, but I refuse to hug a kid who's not comfortable with it. "I like your Spider-Man socks," I whisper.

His button nose wrinkles as he smiles. Like Abi and his big brother August, he has my dark hair and slate-colored eyes. Only Aiden, Bethany's second, shares her blond-haired, blue-eyed fairness. Do I find this amusing? Yes. Yes, I do.

"Thanks, Auntie Freya," he whispers back. "They're my favorite."

Across the living room, standing in front of the Christmas tree decorated with four decades of school craft projects, Bethany makes aggressive hugging gestures at me. I ignore her.

"How about this?" I ask. "Why don't you sit on the couch for a minute and tell me something *new* about you. Something I don't know."

He peeks up through long, dark lashes. "Really?"

When I nod, he climbs next to me and sits with his legs crisscrossed, bouncing on the cushion. Bethany is still swinging her arms—"Hug, *hug*," she mouths—when Drew makes his way to her side and drapes his arm over her shoulders. Drew, Bethany's husband, is the opposite to her in every way. Dark to her fair. Easygoing and relaxed to her uptight. I've always liked him. I just wish he would rub off on Bethany a little more.

"I," Andy whispers, his eyes darting to Bethany like he's assuring himself she can't hear him, "have a *monster* under my bed."

"Really?" I ask. Leave it to the almost-six-year-old to initiate the most interesting conversation of the evening. "What does it look like?"

On the other end of the couch, Aiden, eleven years old and wearing a preteen perma-scowl, looks up from his Nintendo Switch to scoff at Andy. "Dummy. Monsters aren't real."

"Are too!" Andy says.

"Are not."

This goes back and forth a few times, volume escalating with every round. I take a fortifying gulp of my Tom & Jerry before jumping into the fray.

"Ok, if you're going to fight about it, let's make it a real debate. Are monsters real?" I grab my phone and open the Notes app so I can record their points. When I look down at Andy, he's biting his lip. "What's up?"

"What's be-bate?" he whispers, and I almost smile. Almost.

"A *de*-bate is where we look at both sides of a question," I explain. "What evidence is there that monsters are real? What evidence is there that they aren't?" I pause, letting him absorb this information. "Do you *want* to have a debate with Aiden?" Aiden watches us curiously, his game player forgotten in his lap. Andy appears to think it over for a second, then nods.

"Let's be-bate."

"Yes!" Abi says from the chair next to me, then leans forward to smirk at Aiden. "I'm on Andy's team."

EIGHT

FREYA

Hecate purrs next to me as I curl up in my papasan chair and contemplate how pissed my mom will be if I count my days at home by scratching tally marks into the plaster walls.

Like a prisoner.

Half a day. Half a day is over, which leaves fifteen more. I take a long drink directly from the brandy bottle. The hot burn of alcohol stopped a while ago. Now it's just warm, comforting numbness.

But honestly? Today could have gone worse.

Seeing Abi and her brothers was...kind of fun. (Not that I would admit it out loud.) They really got into the monster debate—much to Bethany's horror, which made it even better. They spent the entire meatloaf-and-mashed-potatoes dinner getting into gritty, existential questions: What *is* a monster? Does it have to be evil? What *is* evil? Can one person's monster be another person's hero? Ultimately, they'd concluded that, yes, there are monsters, but, no, probably not like in the movies (or the Roblox game that apparently inspired Andy's monster under the bed). However, just to be sure, Andy's older siblings recommended leaving a pillow and blanket under his bed because, they reasoned, if his monster is comfy enough, he'll sleep through the night and leave Andy alone. By the time they left, Andy seemed ready to tackle bedtime fear-free. *Suck it, Bethany.*

He'd also given me a very sweet, very *voluntary* hug on his way out the door. His older brothers, on the other hand, had opted for fist bumps. "Night, bruh," they'd drawled in unison.

Seeing Jeremy, on the other hand, was annoying. He'd been too handsome. Too chatty. Too charming. Not that I expected anything less.

However, I did dodge a bullet with the whole burlesque thing.

I signed up for my first burlesque class after a string of bad breakups in my mid-twenties. By that point, I was figuring out that I am *not* what guys are looking for in a relationship. Do I have admirers? Sure. Guys who want a down and dirty fuck or a booty call on speed dial? Yeah.

I'm just not the girl they want to take home to their mothers...or their fathers.

"You're kind of...intense," my first college boyfriend told me, his eyes flitting nervously around his dorm room. Ok, when fourteen-year-old me read about Angelina Jolie and Billy Bob Thornton wearing vials of each other's blood, did it stir my romantic heart in a way cartoon princes and princesses never have? Yes. Can I objectively understand that's a little too much for most men? Also yes. That's me—a little too much. A little too intense. A little too honest. A little too opinionated. A little too moody.

Then, when I was twenty-five, Ryan Taylor happened. Ryan was a straight-laced investment banker who treated me like I was his salvation. It was classic opposites attract, but somehow, I started to hope. To dream.

For a few months, I thought I was on my way to marriage, babies—the whole shebang. Because there had been a part of me that wanted those things. I mean, I'm a Scorpio; I crave intensity. And what's more intense than swearing yourself to another person for life and spawning miniature versions of yourselves? But the Ryan situation taught me pretty damn undeniably that I am *not* the marrying type.

After that, I was over it. "It" meaning relationships. Love. Emotions. Romance.

So, I nursed my broken heart by signing up for a burlesque class, and from my very first day, I loved it. Because when the rest of the world says, "Too much," burlesque says, "More." Burlesque doesn't only welcome my curvy ass and big tits; it welcomes my drama, my dark sense of humor, my drive to undermine authority. For the first several years, it was just for me. Classes at the studio with occasional public performances. Then, a few years back, The Sphere went through a tough financial streak, and we started the monthly shows as a fun, low-cost way to stir up excitement and get new people through the door.

And for one night a month, I ditch my cozy office for center stage.

I'm not embarrassed by my stints as Scylla Wilde. I love them. Scylla is bold and empowered and sexy. Everything I needed to feel when I was brokenhearted.

I just don't need my parents—or anybody back in Northview—to know about her.

A scratching noise at the window draws my attention, and I narrow my eyes, trying to focus on the darkness outside. To my astonishment, a tiny figure starts hopping and swaying along my windowsill. I try to blink it away. Did the monster debate go to my head? And if, hypothetically, I *were* to hallucinate a monster, wouldn't I come up with something scarier than the four-inch elf dancing outside my window?

Holy fuck, I'm way more drunk than I thought.

I grab Hecate and roll out of the papasan, nearly knocking it off its platform. I tuck her under my arm and do an awkward, one-arm crawl—*arm-leg-leg, arm-leg-leg*—across the room. I slowly raise myself up until my eyes are at window level and peek outside. The first figure—Legolas?—is joined by a second one. I squint. Arwen?

My eyes go wide as recognition dawns. I'm staring at the collectible *Lord of the Rings* toys I'd earned, one Burger King kids meal at a time, so I could give them to Jeremy for Christmas when we were in eighth grade.

I reach up to unlock the window and open it a quarter-inch.

"Go away, you crazy-ass stalker," I hiss.

A pair of blue-green eyes appears opposite mine, and I jump. I blame the brandy; I'm not usually so excitable. Those tropical-water eyes crinkle at the corners, and I scowl back.

"Or what?" I can hear the smile in his voice, and my blood pressure spikes accordingly. "You'll hex my prom date?"

Ah, the prom date hex. The stuff of legend at Northview High. Our junior year, there were widespread rumors I hexed Jeremy. When his first prom date broke her ankle playing basketball, everyone shrugged. When his second date came down with mono and missed a month of school, my classmates got suspicious. When his *third* date concussed herself playing pickle ball in gym class, all bets were off.

To this day, I have neither confirmed nor denied the hex.

"Can you prove it?" I force the words through gritted teeth, and he laughs. A man's laugh, but it carries echoes of the boy I knew. Movie nights and Caves & Conquerors and kick-the-can on sticky summer nights.

"Come on, Frey," he pleads. "For old time's sake. It's cold as balls out here, and things are fucking awkward with my mom. Please?"

I slam the window shut and roll so my back is to the wall, my knees propped up in front of me. Hecate mews from where she's tucked in my armpit, and in my other hand, I'm still clutching the brandy bottle. My heart races uncomfortably, and the combination of my rapid pulse and too much brandy leaves me feeling vaguely dizzy. Fiona Apple and Pete Wentz stare back at me from my bedroom wall.

This—whatever Jeremy is trying to do right now—is a very bad idea. Right up there with flavored Mountain Dew and *Star Wars* episodes one through three. We've both been doing perfectly fine before today. I have *my* life in Chicago. And Jeremy has *his*. That doesn't have to change just because I needed a ride home for Christmas. We listened to music. ("He assaulted me with music" feels more accurate.) We chatted. The end. Now we can go back to hating each other and not talking again for another seventeen years.

Simple.

Next to me, the window squeaks open an inch, and I curse myself for not remembering to lock it. Fucking brandy.

"What are you afraid of, Frey?" he whispers, and I can hear his teeth chattering.

"Afraid of?" I scoff. I set Hecate on the Pepto Bismol pink carpet I've always loathed and kneel so I'm looking out the window again. Jeremy, his nose pink, stares back from inches away. I glance down. He's wearing gray sweatpants and a Green Bay Packers hoodie. No hat or gloves. He must be freezing. "I fear nothing."

"Is that brandy?" His eyes light up when he sees my bottle, and I squeeze it to my chest. "Are you *drunk*?"

"Jealous?" I ask.

"Extremely." His teeth chatter again. "There's booze at home, but I don't want to drink in front of my mom." I tip my head in question, and Jeremy explains, "Gary was a dick when he drank. *I'm* not, but she doesn't know that, and I don't want to stress her out." He looks longingly at my bottle. "Just for a minute? Unless you're scared, of course."

I roll my eyes. "I'm not an idiot, Jeremy. I'm not *that* easily manipulated."

He grins. "Aren't you?"

He has a point, and I hate him for it. Whatever weird game we'd played through high school, he'd undeniably played it better. The meaner my comebacks, the funnier he found them. Not engaging would have been the only way to defeat him, and it was the one thing I couldn't do. He always knew how to draw me out, guns blazing. But I'm older now. Maybe even wiser. I slide down the wall and bite my lip.

I am *not* smiling.

"Ok..." He drums his fingers on the windowsill. "How about this? Isn't letting me in the more *interesting* option?" Still definitely *not* smiling. "*I may make safe, boring choices. But never you, Freya Nilsen. You never, ever settle for boring.*"

Dammit. I reach above me and push the window open. Just one drink. One *sip*.

With a quiet chuckle, he ducks through the window and closes it behind him. Then he slides to the floor next to me, long legs stretched out in front of him. My room isn't especially tiny—Bethany and I shared it until she moved out—but it's not big either. Those wide shoulders of his, the ones that fit him just right, seem to eat up space, but I won't give him the satisfaction of shifting away. He's wearing unlaced sneakers with no socks, and I wince when I see the snow melting inside his shoes.

To my surprise, he doesn't immediately say something annoying. Instead, he leans his head back against the wall and closes his eyes, giving me plenty of time to study him in a way I never felt comfortable doing in the car today. He's always been beautiful. At least to me. His nose is long and straight and turns up the tiniest bit at the end. His cheekbones are high and always covered with a faint spray of freckles, even in winter. And, my personal favorite, the small, deep dimple in the center of his chin. Like an elf pressed her teeny-tiny finger into it.

Things were already strained between us when he ditched his glasses for contacts freshman year. The tension was my fault. I can admit that now, at least to myself. Then his glasses were suddenly gone, and this secret I'd been keeping my whole life—"Jeremy Kelly is *cute*. Jeremy Kelly has dreamy eyes and a smile that can make your knees weak."—was out. And I hated every one of those insipid girls who were noticing it for the first time. *Could they really not see past a dumb pair of glasses?* I remember thinking. *It's Jeremy for fuck's sake—not Clark fucking Kent!*

He turns his head toward me and cracks open one eye.

"Wanna' talk about it?" He keeps his voice low. It's not like my parents would care if they knew he was here. They *love* Jeremy. Everybody does. Besides, I'm thirty-five now. I'm pretty sure I'm allowed to have boys in my room with the door closed. But we keep our voices soft, like we did when we were kids and Jeremy would sneak over to stay with Thad or me on particularly bad nights. Usually when Gary was drinking.

"Talk about what?" I whisper back.

His gaze sweeps the room, and my breath shudders as I realize what he means by "it." The last time he was in my room. Christmas break 2002. The night I lost my best friend.

I shake my head, and he smiles, but it's sad. Like he'd been hoping to rehash something that I know can't be fixed. Then he grabs my brandy bottle, and as he raises it to his lips, I hear something that sounds suspiciously like, "Coward."

NINE

JEREMY

The brandy burns in the best way possible. A baptism by fire that may not burn my sins away, but may distract me from the heat of Freya next to me. She's wearing tight black leggings, and they embrace every curve of her legs, from her rounded thighs and ass to her muscular calves and dainty ankles. Even her feet are pretty, graceful bones with rounded toes pointing like a dancer. A gray wide-neck sweater sits unevenly on her shoulders, revealing the delicate lines of her collarbones and the upper swells of her breasts. Her makeup is still in place, but she's swept her long, wavy hair into a messy knot on top of her head, and I have to force myself not to stare at the stray curls at the nape of her neck.

I take another drink.

"It was only a kiss," I mutter.

That's always been the worst part. At least to me.

WAR ON CHRISTMAS: A HOLIDAY ROMANCE

We'd been best friends. Freya and Thad and me. Then, the summer between eighth grade and high school, something began to shift. It was like an unexpected sequel to your favorite movie—*What? There's more?!* It happened bit by bit, moment by moment. Freya stepping out of the public-pool dressing room in her first bikini, and my eyes jumping out of my face. The way she smiled in response, even though she tried to hide it. My stomach contracting whenever our hands brushed as we passed the sunscreen or a soda can. The way the apple scent of her shampoo would distract me into making ridiculous mistakes during Monopoly games. Each little moment felt like it was leading somewhere. Somewhere amazing.

It dragged on like that for months. Both of us trying to pretend that things were the same. The tension climbing. Then, a few days after Christmas, Gary had his holiday work party and came home in a foul mood with a fouler mouth. So, like countless times before, I'd "gone to bed" then snuck out. I used to go to Thad's room, but once Bethany moved out, I was climbing more and more through Freya's window and spreading blankets into a makeshift bed on her floor. This time, though, instead of staying in her own bed, she stretched out on the floor facing me, her gray eyes wide and luminous. It felt natural to cup her face in my hands, her skin soft, like the silky edge of my favorite blanket as a kid. My thumbs brushed along her cheekbones, and I breathed in the soapy scent of her face wash.

It all felt so innocent. The obvious next step we'd been waiting for.

When she bit that full bottom lip of hers, I was lost. I've revisited that moment so many times, that final half-second when we could still pretend to be "just friends." Every time, I want to scream at my fourteen-year-old self: *Don't do it, buddy! Just don't.* But I couldn't resist her. I couldn't fight that unspoken pull between us anymore than I could stop my voice from changing or my feet from outgrowing their shoes for the second time that school year.

Just like that, I outgrew the old version of us.

My heart jackhammered behind my breastbone, my pulse thundered through my ears. But I could still hear the throaty sigh she released against my lips when they met hers.

It was awkward at first. As awkward as any first kiss, I guess. We were normal, awkward kids. Noses bumped. We pressed close, pulled away, pressed close again. But I never felt embarrassed. Not at the time. It was Freya. *My* Freya. Bold and serious and earnest. I could do anything with her. There was no rush, no urgency. Just the feel of her lips on mine as we lay side by side in her familiar room—a clash of Bethany's pink and Freya's black—dimly lit by the glow of white Christmas lights. It was Freya who deepened the kiss. Freya who tentatively stroked her tongue against my lips. My whole body jerked like I'd been shot—an arrow, straight to the heart—and her mouth curved against mine in a smile. We both knew in that moment that she owned me. And did I care? Not a bit. I already would have given her anything.

We must have kissed for hours. Innocent and sweet and wondrous. And that's what changed everything.

By the next day, Freya had already started to pull away. By the end of January, feeling heartsick about Freya and determined to recover, I started going out with Tiffany Ebner. And by the end of freshman year, Freya and I had the most infamous rivalry in the class of 2006.

"If you were just going to ignore me, why did you bother asking if I wanted to talk about it?" she asks, her voice chillier than the frosted window next to us.

I shrug. "It was twenty years ago, Frey. I think we probably have the emotional resiliency to tackle this one by now."

Silence. Then, "Like you said...it was just a kiss. There's nothing to quote-unquote tackle."

She jerks the bottle back from me and takes a long pull. God, she's feisty. Always has been. Her red mouth turns down at the corners, and I want to kiss that sullen scowl off her face, but I resist. *Forbidden fruit*, I remind myself.

"Good." I smile broadly. "Then we can be friends again."

That idea took hold while I was in my childhood bedroom, taking inventory of everything I'd left behind. Board games, action figures, CDs. All of them carried Freya's imprint. Even the things she'd hated. The Dave Matthews Band T-shirt I bought at his Alpine Valley concert in the summer of 2005? I'd stood at that merch table with my football friends, surrounded by pot smoke and music I could barely stand, and thought, "I need to get this ridiculously overpriced T-shirt because I want to see the look on Freya's face when I wear it." And every time I wore the shirt and her lips curled into a disgusted sneer, it was totally fucking worth it.

Because even back then, as a dumbass teenager bumbling my way through high school, I'd known that life was better—more vivid, more interesting, more nuanced—with Freya Nilsen in it.

That's what I want now. I can't get back the years we've lost, but we live in the same city. I can have her back in my life. I can go to opening nights at her weird theater. She can introduce me to the underground art shows I don't hear about sitting in a corporate office all day. She can help me remember who I was before I went down the rabbit hole of popularity and workplace ass kissing: that quirky kid who spent hours sketching magical creatures and kept an immaculate collection of all nineteen Burger King *Lord of the Rings* collectible toys.

"Friends?" Her eyes narrow on my face. "Why?"

"Because I've missed you," I say honestly. She turns her attention to her purple toenails, and I fiddle with the plastic elves sitting on the carpet next to me. "Because I have no one in my life who'll call me out on my bullshit golf habit, but I know you will." I bump my shoulder into hers. "Do you want more confessions? About how vanilla my life has become? I've got plenty. My too-clean car. My business casual wardrobe—lots of chinos. My gym schedule. My 401(k)."

"Spare me," she mumbles.

"See, you're doing it already." I give her a thumbs-up, and she rolls her eyes.

"There's just one problem," she says.

"Hmm?"

"I don't want to be your friend."

I fight to keep the grin off my face as I lower my head closer to her ear and drop my voice to a suggestive growl. "If you wanted to be more, Freya, why didn't you just say so?"

My legs tense, ready to block the elbow to my ribs I'm sure is coming. However, instead of pummeling me, Freya scooches back and gives me an assessing look, her eyes traveling from my snow-damp hair to my ice-cold toes and back again. There's a long, drawn-out silence, and the muffled intonations of the ten o' clock news float from the living room. Teenage Freya had been a wild, reactive creature. All honesty and no strategy. Not this Freya. As the eerie quiet stretches, I can see her calculating, rapidly trying on and discarding ideas like shirts in a dressing room, seeking out the perfect fit.

I blink, all pretense forgotten, and try not to swallow my tongue.

What the hell is happening?

"To be clear," she says finally, "nothing serious. Obviously. We'd break things off when we get back to Chicago. But it would make the next couple weeks more interesting." She reaches over to give my bicep a considering squeeze, and my muscles twitch beneath her fingers. "It's not like you're hard to look at."

"Are you...serious?" I choke out.

All these years, I'd prided myself on staying one step ahead of her. But as her gaze falls, and then lingers, on the crotch of my sweatpants, my gut tells me she is sincerely suggesting a holiday sex fling with a two-week expiration date. And I...I did *not* see this coming. My cock starts to harden, and when my pants tent, Freya meets my gaze and raises a perfectly arched brow.

"Of course I'm serious." She shrugs, then leans back on her hands. Her sweater slips down one shoulder, revealing decorative swirls of black ink. Of course she has tattoos. My breath leaves my body in a *whoosh*. I want to lick her. I want to unwrap her like the world's sexiest Christmas present and run my tongue along every line of ink on her perfect, glowing skin. "Why not?" she asks. "We're both single. There's been some...chemistry between us for a long time. Why not get it out of our systems and try to make this weird-ass holiday break somewhat tolerable? You know, get some exercise while you're away from your gym."

She licks her lips—*forbidden fucking fruit, Jeremy*—and I stare at her, slack jawed, as I try to figure out what the fuck is going on. Am I interested? Hell yes. But...

"Why not just enjoy ourselves and see what happens?" I ask. "What's up with the time limit? It's a relationship, not a carton of milk."

"But what we would have"—she reaches out and taps me on the nose like a naughty puppy—"would not be a relationship. It would be a"—she purses her lips as she searches for the right word—"distraction."

I don't even need to think about it.

"No deal." I shake my head, and her eyes widen with surprise. *Good.*

"No deal?" She glances pointedly at my pants, where my cock is vehemently protesting, but I raise an eyebrow back at her.

"No deal." I shrug. "I'm an almost-thirty-five-year-old man, Freya, not a teenager. And while I'm sure sex with you would be enjoyable—" *phenomenal...it would be fucking phenomenal* "—I don't have a problem finding sex. What I've missed is you. So, friends it is."

"Friends with benefits," she negotiates, "except not friends."

I grin. "Nope. Friends."

She glares. I smile wider. Fiona Apple and Pete Wentz watch our silent showdown from the wall above the glass vanity.

I think Freya's about to kick me out of her room, but then her face softens and she leans closer. Alarms blare—*You're in trouble, man. Abort, abort!*—but I stand my ground, even when she plants a pale hand on my chest and runs her nose up the length of my jaw. She wears a different scent now. More mature. Still floral, but with earthy overtones of musk and patchouli. *Fuck.* Sweat breaks out on my forehead.

"Why are you pretending you'll be able to resist me?" she whispers, and my head spins as my blood races to my cock. It's disorienting. Not just the lack of oxygen but being back here in her room. Same setting, but different characters. This Freya is confident. Experienced. She's not some trembling girl waiting for her first kiss. She's in control. Every word, every touch is carefully plotted. "I'll make them all come true, Jeremy." Her finger trails from my chest to my stomach, and every muscle jerks at her touch. "Every horny, teenage fantasy you ever had. For two wonderful, blissful weeks, I'll be all yours."

She is severely underestimating how many fantasies I had about her; two weeks would *not* be long enough. Her fingers, light and teasing, toy with the drawstring of my pants. Every sweep of her fingers brings her closer to my erection, and my eyes fall shut for a moment as I let myself imagine those pretty, purple-tipped fingers wrapped around my cock.

But I'm not a kid anymore either.

I grab her chin between my thumb and forefinger and tilt her head so she can see the promise in my eyes. Her breath catches, and her tongue darts out to wet her poison-apple lips. Down the hallway, I hear her parents turn off the TV.

"I'm going to friend you so hard, Freya," I say softly. "I'm going to drink stolen liquor on the floor with you and be here to listen when you need to vent about Bethany. Because you will. I'm going to make you watch all the movies we should have watched in high school but didn't because you were too fucking stubborn. I'm going to tell you why all your ex-boyfriends were morons while you paint my toenails. I'm going to friend you so hard that when we get back to Chicago, you'll be giving me your extra apartment key and asking me to water your plants when you leave town for the weekend."

Her dark eyes glitter in the shadows as she stares back at me, then something totally unexpected happens.

Freya smiles.

"Game on, Kelly."

Ten

FREYA

14 days until Christmas...

The Good Twin: So...how did the drive go? Is Jeremy still alive?

I pause outside the flower shop, staring at my phone. How did it go? I think of the sizzling battle of wills that took place on my bedroom floor last night. The way Jeremy's pulse raced when I made my proposition. How his pupils dilated, taking over his blue-green eyes. How his fingers flexed against his thighs, like he was fighting for self-control. I want to smile, but I have a reputation to maintain. However, I do allow myself a smirk as I send my reply.

Me: He's alive. I'm going to seduce him.

WAR ON CHRISTMAS: A HOLIDAY ROMANCE

An elderly woman in a bright red coat with giant black buttons scoots around me on the sidewalk, and the giant wreath on the front door swings as she goes inside. I wait for Thad's response. *One...two...thr—*

The Good Twin: And this conversation is officially over.

My work here is done.

With a sigh, I turn to Fox Valley Floral and Gifts. Located in the historic downtown neighborhood, it's a cute, brick storefront with a large front window that's always seasonally decorated. Two weeks before Christmas, that means pungent evergreen garlands, red and white poinsettias, and a collection of garden gnomes repainted to look like they're wearing holiday-themed sweaters.

I've always liked the gnomes. They have black, beady eyes that follow you in the dark, and Thad and I have a tradition of stealing them from the shop and hiding them around the house. Nothing beats the anticipation of waiting to hear his terrified scream when he throws back his covers or opens a dresser drawer so I can yell, "You got gnomed!"

"Hello, Edward," I mutter to the roundest, squattest gnome as I enter the shop.

Fox Valley Floral and Gifts (better known as "the shop" in my family) was my parents' dream. Or, more precisely, my mother's dream. My father had always wanted to own a business and be his own boss; he just hadn't been particular about what *type* of business. Then he fell in love with my mom, who'd known exactly what she wanted. "A little flower shop," she'd say with a faraway look in her light-blue eyes, "in a little brick building. With flowers like a rainbow, in every shade. We'll get to surround ourselves in happy moments. Weddings and new babies and anniversaries." At which point, I would interject, "And funerals."

In some ways, the shop is home as much as our house. We'd all grown up here, playing tag around five-gallon buckets of long-stemmed roses and helping Mom and Dad restock the coffee mugs and trinkets they carry as easy add-on gifts. And all of us—Bethany, Thad, and I—worked evenings and weekends here throughout high school. It was a bit cheery for my tastes, but I'd enjoyed the creative outlet of arranging flowers, and Thad was usually there to interact with actual customers. It hadn't, now that I think about it, been all that bad.

As I step inside, I'm expecting the shop I'd always known. Exposed brick walls and distressed tin ceiling tiles. Cutesy wall art with plant and flower puns: "I'm so excited, I wet my plants!" Bright but traditional flower arrangements filling the coolers.

Instead, I stop short, thinking for a moment I've entered the wrong building.

"Freya," Bethany calls from behind the counter, giving me an overly bright smile as she finishes checking out a customer. "I'm so glad you dropped in."

I blink. "What—what *happened*?"

Our mom-and-pop floral shop is...well, *gorgeous*. Lush and bursting with color. The old shelves are painted a trendy, earthy green. Rows of tiny, round lightbulbs swoop from the ceiling. Small, indoor trees—weeping figs with braided trunks and rubber trees and money trees—line the walls. And the flower arrangements are...well, they're different. My mom always had a decent eye for arranging, and she'd taught us all the basics, but the vases now crowding the coolers are edgy and eye-catching. Mixed textures and complementary colors that draw your attention from across the room.

Bethany sighs as she steps out from behind the counter, her hand resting on her hip. She's wearing jeans and a flowing marigold top, a patterned scarf wrapped loosely around her neck. With her golden hair, she looks like a literal ray of sunshine. "Well...I thought we needed some updates."

After getting married right out of college and having Abi at twenty-five, Bethany spent several years as a stay-at-home mom. And she'd been good at it. (Like she's good at everything.) She'd done crafts and taken her kids to playdates and made home-cooked meals. She'd been on the cusp of returning to work when Andy had arrived—surprise!—and set back her professional plans another five years. When he started kindergarten this past fall, she'd shocked all of us by choosing to work at the shop again. It's not like she'd hated working here as a teenager. I'd just always assumed she'd want to do something "bigger"...like world domination.

Mom and Dad had been thrilled. Of course. Their favorite daughter working at the shop? What could be better? And Mom *had* mentioned that it was going well. She just hadn't mentioned *this*.

"It looks really good," I say. "Like *really* good."

The inventory of gifts has been updated too. Instead of generic, run-of-the-mill coffee mugs and coasters, the shelves are loaded with artisanal, hand-poured candles and organic bath bombs. An entire section features products—jams, salsas, and teeny-tiny bottles of maple syrup—from other local small businesses. If I brought friends up from Chicago—which I wouldn't—this is a place I'd bring them to show off my hometown. Quaint, charming, and a little bit hip.

Bethany, to my amazement, tosses her hair with a huff. "Come on, Freya. If you don't like it, just say so."

I stare. Bethany's always been high-strung. Ready to snap like an overstretched rubber band at the first sign of criticism. It's my favorite thing about her. How easy it is to reach out and pluck her nerves, to send her shaking and vibrating with insecurity. But this seems excessive. My eyebrows knit together as I consider how concerned I should be about my big sister.

"Um...I said it looks 'really good.'" I choose my words carefully. "What exactly did you hear?"

"What *I* heard," Bethany says, blowing her bangs out of her eyes, "is that I've made too many changes to an already successful business, and clearly I'm going to mess things up and tank the value of the shop right when Mom and Dad are getting ready to retire. And what was I thinking? It's too much! But also—"

When a boisterous laugh bubbles out of me, Bethany sputters to a halt. I'm as surprised as she is, and I press the back of my hand to my mouth to stop it.

"Are you insane?" I ask once I've regained control.

Bethany shrugs, agitated. "I have four kids. Probably." Then her attitude drops as quickly as it appeared, and her eyes turn hopeful. Like my approval means something to her. "You're saying you like it?"

Part of me wants to say something cutting and witty. The instinct is there to bring her down to size. Maybe I could point out the excessive number of "Live Laugh Love" tchotchkes? But much to my surprise, Bethany seems invested in this. She didn't just come back to the shop to get out of the house and make some cash. She has a vision.

"Yeah," I tell her. "I like it." Then I circle back to something else she said. "So, are you going to take over then? When Mom and Dad retire?"

Her eyes flick around the shop. It's a Monday morning. Only a few customers are milling around, but you have to be careful what you say in a small community like ours. Word travels fast. I join Bethany behind the counter and settle onto the empty stool, so we can talk without being overheard.

"They started talking about selling the shop last summer. Right as Andy was getting ready to start kindergarten." She keeps her voice low. "I wasn't really sure what to do. Where to work, I mean. I'd been teaching yoga a couple nights a week, but I don't really want to do that full time. The shop just seemed...I don't know"—she shrugs—"right. And Mom and Dad have been great about letting me try out some new stuff. My degree was in business, and I've been taking some online classes on flower arranging. You know, trying to update things a bit. It's been..." Her smile is hesitant, as if she's waiting for my reaction. "It's been fun."

"I'm happy for you," I say.

There was a time when this situation would have chafed—*Well look at that. Bethany stepping up to be the perfect daughter. Again.*—but all I feel is a quiet sense of satisfaction for my parents. While they'd never pushed any of us to take over the shop, we'd always known they would love for it to turn into a multigenerational business. And it seems like a good fit for Bethany. I've got my own career that I love. There's no reason for me to begrudge Bethany having the same.

And that, as my therapist would say, is what we call progress.

Bethany reaches out like she's about to hug me, but I'm saved when the bell on the door chimes and a cold gust of wind blows through the store. I'm momentarily distracted by one of the customers, a woman with a large, snow-white bouffant who looks vaguely familiar, but when I see Bethany's eyes flare, I turn to the front of the store to see what—or who—piqued her interest.

Eleven

FREYA

I bite back a smile, my stomach fluttering pleasantly. Standing in the doorway wearing a formal gray suit and black overcoat is Jeremy. Yesterday morning I'd been filled with dread as sour as spoiled milk at the thought of seeing him, but everything shifted last night. In high school, he'd held all the high-value assets: popularity, the favor of the teachers, athletic ability. But what do those things matter now? I never cared that he could throw a football. What I *do* care about is the way he undressed me with his eyes when I answered the door to my apartment and the way his pulse tripped drunkenly when I touched his chest.

I'm not at a disadvantage anymore. Jeremy Kelly and I are finally going head-to-head in a fair competition.

And I am going to crush him.

Moreover, once I've won, I'll finally know what category to put him in. For years, he's been stashed away in his own little storage container with its label scratched over and rewritten so many times it needs to be replaced.

~~Best Friend~~

~~Crush~~

~~First Kiss~~

~~Guy I'm Awkwardly Avoiding~~

~~Arch Rival~~

However, once we have our little holiday sex spree, which I'm sure will be highly enjoyable, I can move him over to my Sexual Conquests bin with my other ex-lovers and move on.

Ta-da! Closure.

"Um, when did Jeremy Kelly get *hot*?" Bethany murmurs.

"A while ago. You were just too wrapped up in Drew to notice," I answer. Then, not really sure why I'm sharing this with Bethany of all people, I add, "He wants to be my friend again, but I'm going to seduce him instead. Don't worry. I've already informed him."

Jeremy looks around the shop curiously, and when he finds Bethany and me behind the counter, his eyes stop on me and his face lights up with a warm smile. Bethany titters next to me—*Really, can't she get a grip?*—but I keep my own face carefully blank as he approaches. His Jedi mind tricks won't work on me.

"Bethany, it's good to see you." He inclines his head, indicating the shop surrounding us. "The shop looks amazing, by the way." Bethany giggles—*Jesus Christ*—then Jeremy turns to me. "Freya." His smile widens. "My dear, old *friend*."

"Mmm." I purse my lips and take my time perusing him, not even trying to hide the deliberate slide of my eyes over his body. He had liked that last night. Me looking at him. Showing my interest so openly. The gray fabric of the suit clings to his thick thighs—no emaciated poet here—and his shoulders press into his coat. "Nice suit," I finally say. "What's going on? Hot date? Important business meeting? Funeral?"

I mean it as a cool, flippant joke. Pretty on-brand for me, really. But when his eyes widen and he chokes back a laugh, I belatedly remember that his stepdad just died.

He's literally going to a funeral.

"Jesus Christ, Freya," Bethany mutters at the exact moment that I grimace and say, "Holy shit. Are you going to the funeral *right* now?"

I'm rarely ashamed of my dark humor. It's my thing, and I own it. But that was a bit far. Even for me.

He's trying to hold back his laughter. His eyes are apologizing even as the chuckle drags out of him in fits and starts, like a cat that started swallowing a string and has it forcibly removed from its mouth. Bethany rolls her eyes and mutters, "I'll go grab those flowers for you. We would have delivered, you know," as she strolls to the back of the shop where we keep pre-ordered arrangements. My face is growing hot—Good gods, is this what *blushing* feels like?—when I realize that snowy bouffant lady is standing directly next to Jeremy and has heard our entire exchange.

And now I recognize her. Fucking perfect. If I was going to run into someone, couldn't it be Mrs. Davis-Green? I'd welcome a visit with D.G., but no such luck. Instead, I get Mrs. Milton, the front office secretary from our high school who definitely hated me.

"Jeremy Kelly," she singsongs, her mauve-colored lips lifting in a smile. Struggling to gain control of his laughter, Jeremy turns to the tiny older woman and wraps her in a hug. His big frame swallows her for a moment, so all that's visible is the white puff of her hair through the circle of his arms.

"It's so good to see you, Mrs. Milton." And damned if he doesn't sound like he means it. "How have you been?"

They exchange pleasantries about Mrs. Milton's retirement and Jeremy's job, and the entire time they're chatting, I frantically rearrange myself behind the checkout area, trying to hide from Mrs. Milton's eagle eyes. I'm half crouched behind the short, spinning display of florist cards when I hear her flinty voice spit out, "Freya Nilsen." I straighten, like she called me out during a game of hide-and-seek, and she adds, "I'm glad to see you."

I guarantee you she is not. My rivalry with Jeremy drove her crazy, and she was not an unbiased observer. Whenever we got sent to the office for whatever spat we were having that day—"accidentally" spilling red paint on his Dave Matthews Band T-shirt comes to mind—she'd roll her eyes at me and huff a "You again." Then she'd turn to Jeremy with a sympathetic smile and say, "I'm so sorry, dear."

No, she was never my biggest fan. I gather my dignity around me like an elven cloak and give her my most regal nod. "Likewise, Mrs. Milton."

She narrows her brown eyes at me, and I'm tempted to stick my tongue out at her, but Bethany comes rushing out of the back room with a large blue-and-white funeral wreath. Lilies, roses, mums, carnations, and blue delphinium. She hands it off to Jeremy, then gives him a skinny metal stand as well. Mrs. Milton gives me one final glare before slinking off to do her shopping.

Jeremy sets down the wreath stand to grab for his wallet, but Bethany waves her hands at him. "No, no. Mom and Dad want to cover this."

"Are you sure?" he asks, brow wrinkled. "I'm happy to—"

"Nope," Bethany cuts him off. "They just want you to come by while you're home. Especially for Sunday dinner if you can make it."

"Well, that's kind of them," he says, then adds, "They've always been kind to me."

That would be because my parents are, at heart, kind people. The reminder has me tugging at my scarf for extra air. They're kind, simple people who've just never quite known how to interact with their black sheep of a daughter. So, I've been stuck in limbo, never really fitting in with my family (except for Thad) but not kicked out either.

Jeremy looks up from the wreath to smile at me. "Well, *friend*, I'll see you la—"

"Can I come?" I blurt out. "To the funeral?"

Jeremy assesses me for a long second, like he's trying to analyze my offer. *Does he think I'm going to jump him in the cemetery in my quest to seduce him?* I wonder. Even *I'm* not that depraved. I just don't like the idea of him facing it alone. Not that he's upset about Gary, but it *is* a weird situation with his mom and everything. He could use a—I sigh. Well, he could use a friend.

"That's ok," he says. "I know you weren't planning for a funeral and—"

"But Jeremy, that's the best thing about having me as a friend," I interrupt, hopping from the stool. I unzip my black winter parka to reveal my black jeans, black sweater, and black boots. "I'm *always* dressed for a funeral."

TWELVE

JEREMY

As adamant as Freya was about coming to the funeral, she's silent on the drive to the church, her breath misting over the cold window as she stares outside. I've always liked that about her. Her comfort with silence. Since childhood, I've been valued for my ability to chat and prattle, to fill moments of quiet with amusing anecdotes and harmless observations. Because lesser mortals are desperate to fill that void, afraid of what demons we might find there.

Freya, on the other hand, pulls up a chair and makes friends with them.

I park across the street from the church, a traditional stone behemoth with two steep gables and a towering spire. When I turn off the car, we sit for a minute, saying nothing. The last time I was inside this building, I was eight years old, and my mom and Gary were getting married. I still remember Freya's collared, purple dress flying around her knees and her lacy socks drooping down her ankles as we raced through the church basement before the ceremony.

"So," I finally turn to her. "Coming to my stepdad's funeral...that's downright friendly, wouldn't you say, Sunshine?"

Sunshine was my nickname for Freya in high school. It was guaranteed to get a rise out of her—pretty much my raison d'être sophomore through senior years—and teachers felt silly punishing me for a name that was, essentially, complimentary.

They severely underestimated how conniving I was when it came to Freya.

"Just playing to my strengths," she says and twists to grab the wreath stand from my back seat.

I grin. During Freya's years working at the shop, she was the de facto funeral expert. Friendly, fun-loving Thad would practically break out in hives when he had to make funeral deliveries—"Seriously, dude, look at my back. Can you see 'em? I feel itchy all over."—and the rest of the sunny Nilsens weren't much better. Funerals were an unfortunate but necessary task of owning a flower shop. But Freya, according to Thad, was a natural. Calm, quiet, unperturbed. She never, as Thad had, fucked up by asking people how their day was going or cheerily commenting on the gorgeous weather.

Grabbing the wreath, I follow her inside, my eyes glued to the swing of her hips as she walks. I have no clue what to expect from her after last night, and a pleasant anticipation thrums through my veins at the novelty of this little game we're playing. Whatever it is.

We drop off the wreath in the church sanctuary, setting it up next to the closed cherrywood casket, and I pause for a moment to watch Freya fiddle with the blue flowers scattered among the white. She prods and pokes them into position, her full red lips pursed with concentration, but when she catches me staring at her, she pulls back.

"What?"

I can't very well tell her how mesmerized I am by her mouth. That would definitely be a point in the Seduction column, and she'd use it against me. Ruthlessly. Learning to live with that mouth is the price I'll have to pay if Freya and I are going to be friends, and I'm prepared to pay it. So, I smile and glance pointedly around the church.

"Just pleasantly surprised you haven't burst into flames or been struck by lightning."

I'm not sure what reaction I expected. Probably an eye roll or an angry snort. What I'm not prepared for is the full-belly laugh that erupts from her. It's husky and warm, and her meticulously lined eyes heat from gray to deep, shining silver.

My body's reaction to that laugh is so strong, so instantaneous, that I know in my bones I am helpless against it. It's my Achilles heel. That laugh wraps around my cock like crushed velvet and demands I fall to my knees, prostrate before her. There is nothing, literally *nothing*, I wouldn't do to hear that laugh again.

Then I'm about to panic because—holy shit—I'm going to lose this friends-versus-benefits standoff, and part of me thinks that's the best, most amazing thing that could ever happen to me.

"Is that little Freya Nilsen?"

Like a ghost, my mother materializes at my elbow. For the first time since I've been home, I'm happy to see her, and without thinking, I wrap my arm around Mom's slim shoulders. She doesn't shrug me off, but when her muscles tense underneath my arm, I remove it and tuck my hands into my pockets.

"Yup," I choke out. "Little Freya Nilsen."

***

In the hour before the service starts, Freya throws herself into "theater manager mode." Gary's funeral is a performance that, under Freya's watch, will go off without a hitch. My mom and I watch in awe as she double-checks details with the church receptionist and pastor, then adjusts the handful of flower arrangements. She's efficient, thinking of details that never would have occurred to me. When she discovers that the sign directing people to the service has a typo—"Garry Cassidy" instead of "Gary Cassidy"—she gets one reprinted in the office right before the first attendees arrive.

When her parents show up, she comes over and rests a hand across my forearm. If she notices my muscles jump at her touch, she doesn't show it.

"Is there anything else you need?" she asks.

I swallow, a little overcome with gratitude. I'd been relieved when she asked if she could come along. If nothing else, I knew I'd appreciate having a buffer so I wouldn't have to be alone with Mom. But Freya went above and beyond. Not only was she undaunted by the circumstances, but she was also helpful.

"No. You were—well, you were perfect." I clear my throat. "Thank you."

She nods and joins her parents a few rows behind where Mom and I will sit.

It's a small service. There's a handful of Gary's relatives as well as his boss and a few of his friends from the factory where he worked for almost thirty years. His union buddies call him "Big Gare" when they talk to my mom, and I look to the rafters to stop myself from rolling my eyes.

"Big Gare" is a guy who plays catch with his stepson at halftime during Packers games. "Big Gare" takes his wife to the supper club for Friday night fish fry and sometimes forgets their anniversary but is overall a nice, steady husband. "Big Gare" ruffles his kid's hair and tells him it's ok when he spills his milk.

Gary—the real Gary—had a nightly practice of cataloguing every minor mistake his wife made throughout the day, from parking three inches too far to the left in the garage to not adding enough salt to the tuna casserole. *Gary* made his stepson scrub the floor with his toothbrush when he spilled his milk.

Luckily, I had two friends who walked the half-mile to the drugstore with me to buy a new one, even though we weren't technically allowed to cross the streets with stoplights. They even gave me the two dollars to buy it, since I didn't get an allowance.

I don't listen to the service. Common wisdom says "Don't speak ill of the dead," but I'm tired of pretending. Instead, I watch my mom, sitting next to me in a black dress that's too big for her frame. I'm not sure what her reaction will be. Sad tears? Happy tears? Which one, I wonder, would be better? Maybe it will hurt less if she's overcome with grief. If she truly, deeply loved him, at least it would be an explanation, however disturbing, for why she picked him over her own son.

However, she remains dry eyed and quiet. Her hands lie folded in her lap, and she doesn't so much as shift her weight or rearrange her legs until the service is over.

When I was little, she was always fidgety, hopping around from one thing to the next, like an overly excited bird. Dancing to the radio as she scrubbed dishes at the sink, up to her elbows in bubbles. Bouncing over to the vintage Formica table where I was drawing to *ooh* and *aah* over my pictures, her wet hands dripping dishwater down my neck and making me laugh. She was a cyclone. A single mom in her mid-twenties trying to hold it all together.

God, her mid-*twenties*? I shake my head, disbelieving. I'd had more responsibility than most at that age, being completely on my own, and there had been moments when it felt crushing. Moments when I had to talk myself down from the ledge. What if I lost my scholarships? What if I lost my position as an RA? Where would I live? Where would I go? To have that kind of pressure but with a *kid* I was responsible for, too? It was unimaginable.

Maybe the wildest part is that those early memories, before Gary, were *happy* ones. Chaotic, sure. A lot of drawing or looking at books in the corner at the diner where she worked. Or frantically running errands in her rusty, cherry-red '79 Chevy Nova. But the *feeling* of those memories? It was fun. Life was an adventure, and we were in it, for better or worse, together.

Had she truly been so full of energy? I wonder now, watching my mom's eerily still posture. Or had it been the flailing of a drowning woman? A single mom desperate for anything, any*one*, to rescue her?

When the service ends, everyone drifts out, pulling on winter coats and bundling into scarves, hats, and gloves. A few pause to shake my mom's hand and offer some final condolences, but it's mostly quiet. Subdued. The only ones who pay any attention to me are Freya's parents. Mrs. Nilsen folds me in a warm hug, and I lean into it.

"It's so good to see you home," Freya's mom whispers, and I smile into her shoulder as I pull her close.

"Thanks, Mrs. Nilsen. It's good to see you, too."

She pulls back. Her eyes, furtive, slide to my mother, who's standing across the aisle from us listening to a cousin of Gary's.

"Please, call me Mary," she says, then pats my hand. "I wish—" Her voice drops even lower, so I bend over to hear her, close enough that her breath tickles my ear. "I wish we could have done more. I was never sure what to do."

I shake my head. "Mrs. Nilsen, you were..." My mouth twists to the side. Words seem inadequate for the role the Nilsens played for me. The sense of normalcy and stability they provided. It's because of Thad and Freya's parents that I know what a healthy marriage looks like. What a real family looks like. "...you were wonderful," I say. "I've never thought anything different."

Mr. Nilsen hugs me next. Everything about Mr. Nilsen is big. He's only a couple inches shorter than me, and his round face, his bushy beard, his belly that pushes against his belt—all of it is big. He's got a big heart, too. He always played father to me, right alongside Thad, whenever I needed it. Boy Scouts events. The puberty talk at school. Learning how to fix a broken bike chain. He showed up, over and over again.

"Good to see you, son." He's aged. Unlike Mrs. Nilsen, who I'm sure colors her hair to match Bethany's, his salt-and-pepper has faded to almost white in our years apart. But his voice is still gruff and familiar, and I work to swallow back the lump in my throat at his words. When I nod, unable to speak, he pats me on the back. "Don't be a stranger, ok? We expect you at supper on Sunday when Thad comes home." His eyes flick to Freya, who's standing to the side. "And, of course, you should visit Freya whenever you want."

I clear my throat. Did he hear Freya and me talking in her room last night? Then I feel ridiculous because I'm thirty-four years old. Mr. Nilsen isn't going to track me down with a shotgun for hanging out in Freya's room. After all, Freya and I are going to be friends again. Friendly friends. Friends who have a friendly competition over whether or not she can seduce me.

Yup, friends.

"Yes, sir," I mumble.

To my surprise, Freya doesn't leave with her parents. Instead, she hangs back, and as the final attendees straggle out, she collects stray funeral cards and programs, then quietly directs the men who arrive to take the casket to the cemetery.

I'm pretty sure I'm the only one who sees her flip off Gary's casket with a purple-tipped finger as they roll him away on the trolley, and I press my lips together to hide my smile.

THIRTEEN

FREYA

I'm lying in my double bed, staring at the swirls in the ceiling plaster and plotting how to seduce Jeremy, when my phone dings.

Abi: Auntieee. I need a favor..Z

I frown as I squint at my phone, willing the letters to make more sense. For all her drama and her Gen-Z membership card, Abi usually texts with the grammar of a middle-school librarian. When her messages leave me confused, it's usually due to some mysterious new acronym. ADIH (Another Day in Hell) or SSDD (Same Stuff Different Day) are two favorites that come to mind. At my hip, Hecate turns to look at me over her shoulder, her gold eyes flashing in the glow of the Christmas lights.

Yes, this morning my mother decorated my room with Christmas lights like she did when I was a kid. She even put up my miniature Christmas tree with the black ornaments I collected as a teenager.

Me: Who is this and what have you done with my niece?

As I wait for a reply, I mentally sift through my recent conversations with Abi, and a peculiar sinking sensation weighs down my stomach. Sad, leaking gray eyes and "Things at school have just been—ugh, the *worst*."

Fuck, fuck, fuck.

Abi: I needs ride. Please. I'll text you address. Plese..

She's drunk. I know it. Sweet little Abi Banana whose stomach I used to raspberry until she'd spit up is drunk. I can see it all playing out in my head like a bad movie: Bethany going goddamn ballistic, Abi spending her winter break grounded, and this incident forever being remembered in Nilsen family lore as the Christmas that fifteen-year-old Abi snuck into some unsuspecting parent's liquor cabinet. Unless she was doing more than drinking. My stomach cramps. *Fuck, I wish Thad was here.*

Me: Text me the address. Are you safe?

I'd been lounging in yoga pants and a beloved Fall Out Boy T-shirt that I refuse to throw out despite the gaping hole in the right armpit. While I wait for Abi's reply, I quickly dig through my suitcases for some extra layers. I shrug into a cozy, lined hoodie, my scarf, and black fingerless gloves, then unearth my old Sorel boots from the back of my closet. By the time Abi texts back with the address and, *Yes safe. At a freinds houss*, I'm ready to come to her rescue.

Except, I realize, I don't have a car, and a quick search for my parents' car keys is unsuccessful.

For any other mission, I'd wake them up and ask them where they are. But then they'd ask where I'm going, and I'm not sure yet what I'm going to do about Abi. To be clear, I know what I'm *supposed* to do: dutifully report all the details to her loving parents, etc. But I also feel like she might need someone to confide in, and how can she trust me if I narc her out to her mom?

WAR ON CHRISTMAS: A HOLIDAY ROMANCE

Want to know what kind of holiday celebrations *don't* lead to dilemmas like this? Drinking on the couch and watching *Chilling Adventures of Sabrina*.

When the solution comes to me, I groan. Just last night, I boldly declared my intention to seduce Jeremy. And now we'll have spent a day together staging a funeral and rescuing a drunk teenager.

Sexy, Freya. I sigh. *So sexy.*

***

I tap my fingernails along the frosted window, *tap-tap-tap*, then wait for a response. It's freezing. The kind of freezing that transcends the spectrum of heat-versus-cold and goes straight to painful. As my fingertips start to tingle and go numb, I almost feel sorry for how long I made Jeremy wait in the cold last night before letting him in. Almost.

"Hey, Asshat, open your window," I hiss. *Tap-tap-tap!* Then I make a mental note to think of nicer endearments before I actually try to seduce him.

A series of bumps and thumps tell me Jeremy has heard me, and a minute later the window slides open.

"Hey, Sunshine." He leans out the window, grinning. His hair sticks out in all directions, and there's a line from the sheets across his cheek. He looks adorable. Sleepy and rumpled. I can tell just looking at him that he smells like dryer sheets and toothpaste. Something pleasant and warm stirs low in my belly. "Come on in. It's freezing out there."

I swing my leg over the windowsill and hoist myself into Jeremy's room, except I manage the maneuver with all the coordination of an aardvark on shrooms and stumble as I land. Immediately, strong hands reach out to grab my elbows, and he helps me regain my balance as I straighten.

"Thanks," I breathe. Then, as his hands slide away, my eyes adjust to the dark and I make out Jeremy's form standing a couple feet away from me. "Umm, wow."

Jeremy is shirtless. Jeremy wasn't lying when he said he takes his gym routine *very* seriously. I vaguely remember making a snarky comment about this gym routine, but I was wrong. Very wrong. Whatever Jeremy is doing at the gym, I wholeheartedly approve. Two thumbs up. Five stars. Yes, I would recommend this experience to a friend.

I remind myself to breathe.

There is no amount of money or torture that could get me to admit this to Jeremy, but as a teenager, I wasn't above watching out my bedroom window for him to return shirtless and sweaty from his morning runs. He'd had a nice body, tall and lean, and he had a clearly defined six-pack that I'd loved to hate.

He was very cute.

But grown-up Jeremy? Grown-up Jeremy could *crush* teenage Jeremy. Not "crush him" in the figurative, he'd-beat-him-in-a-friendly-competition kind of way. Like, he could *physically crush* teenage Jeremy.

His arms, his chest, his stomach. They're all wrapped in thick, heavy layers of muscle, not as defined as they used to be, but more powerful. This isn't a boy training for high school football. This is a man who's been preparing for war. A man who could swing a broadsword or a battle ax. A man who could singlehandedly push a pickup truck out of a mud pile. (That's a real-life thing, right?) A man who could, at any moment, pick me up and fling me to the bed to—

"I've gotta admit," he says, crossing his arms over his beautifully sculpted chest, "I don't know how 'friendly' it is, but I don't entirely mind you randomly showing up in my bedroom to eye fuck me. It's pretty hot, actually."

My gaze lingers on his torso. The only light in his tiny bedroom comes from the glow of streetlights filtering through the window, and I can just make out the faint texture of hair across his chest and stomach. No manscaping for him. This man is a straight-up Viking, and I *love* it. My heart thumping in my chest, my blood rushing through my veins, my breath tickling past my open lips...arousal heightens these usually unnoticed bodily activities into a pleasurable hum that could easily drown out every other thought.

But...Abi.

"Um, I definitely want to talk about *this* some more later"—I swing my hand in a circle that encompasses his body, getting lost for moment in the Eighth Wonder of the World that is Jeremy's black joggers dipping down his waist to reveal the jut of his hip bones—"but I actually have a very friendly favor to ask."

"Oh." He sounds surprised, but not upset. Maybe even a little eager. "That's what friends are for, right?"

"Friends for an hour," I concede with a sigh. *Dammit, Abi.* "Abi's drunk. She—"

"Bethany's oldest?" he asks. When I nod, his thick eyebrows fly up and his lips twitch. He's already grabbing a T-shirt out of the dresser as I continue.

"She texted me that she needs a ride home, and I can't get my parents' car keys without waking them up." I wince. "Are you up for a rescue mission?"

Fourteen

JEREMY

If my years as an RA in the dorms prepared me for anything, it's drunk adolescents. Belligerent ones. Sick ones. Silly ones. I've seen them all. I have the presence of mind to grab the tiny plastic garbage can from my room—just in case—but as I climb into the driver's seat, I'm more excited about a late-night lark with Freya than I'm worried about being able to handle one drunk teenage girl.

Freya's only been my friend again—albeit an *unwilling* friend—for twenty-four hours, and she's already shaking things up.

Freya, unlike me, is clearly stressed. The cool, take-charge professional who jumped into coordinating a funeral at a moment's notice is gone, replaced by an aunt who's been put in an impossible position. I don't envy the conversation she'll need to have with Bethany, who is 100 percent, no questions asked, going to go berserk.

As Freya reads me the address and I put it in my phone's GPS, she bites at her red lower lip.

"Did you put on lipstick just to pick up your drunk niece at eleven at night?" I ask as I start the car, and her eyes flick to my face. *Good, I've distracted her.* I double-check that she's buckled in and back out of the driveway.

"You like the lips," she says.

She's wrong. "Like" isn't a strong enough word. I'm *obsessed* with her lips. *Mesmerized* by them. I want to *worship* them. I want them to worship *me*. But I nod.

"If we're going to have two weeks to indulge in whatever this is"—her fingers point back and forth between herself and me—"then I'm going to fill it with the things you like, Jeremy."

I swallow, my fingers drumming on the steering wheel as I try to review 1990s Packers stats to keep my blood in my brain, where it belongs.

"Although..." Her beautiful red lips draw down into a frown. "We're going to be down to thirteen days now. Pity."

"Ok, what's up with that?" I ask. If she's going to be so up front about it, then so can I. "That whole 'let's have a two-week fling with a predetermined end date' thing? Why are you so opposed to seeing where things go?"

The streets are empty this late on a Monday night, so I can take my eyes off the road to watch her face for a few seconds. Just long enough to see her incredulous look.

"See where things go? Like...date?" Her lip curls, and her obvious distaste has my previously hardening semi wilting like a sad flower. *Jesus, she drives me fucking crazy.*

"Yeah, like 'date.' Why not?" I grip the steering wheel harder. "Like you said last night, we're both single. We're attracted to each other." I'm not sure that "attracted" covers the desperate way I needed to jack off when I got home the night before, my mind continually skipping like a broken record to the feel of Freya's breath along my jaw. But I'm going with it. "Why not date? Worst case scenario, it doesn't work out and we go our separate ways. Right? We're no worse off than we were before."

Ok, the whole "going our separate ways" part sounds shitty. That's where my "let's be friends" plan has merit—less likelihood of messy fallout. However, if we were going to give dating a real shot, it's a risk I'd take. This whole two-week fling bullshit, though...

"Jeremy, we *hated* each other through almost four years of high—"

I'm so shocked, I nearly slam on the brakes.

"Whoa, whoa, whoa, whoa." I turn to Freya, shaking my head. "Hold the fuck on. Did you just say we *hated* each other in high school?"

"Um, yah." Not *yes* or even *yeah*—she said *yah*, which everyone knows has an automatically implied *dumbass* tacked onto the end of it. "Jeremy, we couldn't *stand* each other. We were at each other's throats practically every day. They tried to add a 'Most Likely to Murder Each Other' category to the yearbook for us our senior year."

"Freya!" Her eyes widen, and I realize I may have yelled. She doesn't look afraid. *Does she look excited?! Heaven help me, she looks excited right now.* Still, I lived with a man who liked to yell, and I promised myself I'd never be one. I take some deep breaths—in my nose, hold, out my mouth—and when I feel reasonably certain I can speak at a normal volume, I try again.

"Freya," I say more calmly, "I spent all of high school absolutely, positively, *fucking desperate* for you to pay attention to me. I get that I was always going out of my way to annoy you, but that was the only way you would even look at me. Wait—" My jaw drops open. "Are you saying *you* hated *me*?"

Her answer is immediate and unexpected.

"Why did you wear that fucking Dave Matthews T-shirt, Jeremy? I know for a fact that you *hate* Dave Matthews." She points a finger at me, and her voice is cold and scary. "Now tell me: Why did you wear that shirt?"

Fuck, if I'd known she would hate the shirt *this* much, I would have bought two.

"Because I knew it would drive you crazy. And it did!" I pound my palm into the roof of my car in triumph. God, I know her so well. "Now answer the question: Did you hate me in high school?"

My pulse is zipping with electricity, like her answer to my question is of life-or-death importance—right now, this instant. Not like it's about something that took place almost twenty years ago.

To my delight, Freya howls with frustration, a raw, guttural sound that rips out of her. "Yes, I hated you! I hated your stupid, preppy clothes and I hated your stupid, preppy girlfriends and I hated your stupid, preppy football team. I missed *you*—the *real* you—and it was like you were taken over by some goddamn Abercrombie & Fitch zombie!" She throws herself back in her seat, chest heaving.

I blink, giving myself a moment for her words to sink in. Next to me, Freya stares outside, her face folded into a mutinous glare.

"So, what I heard," I say, "is that you missed me."

"Honest to god, Jeremy, you won't be able to date *anyone* if I murder you."

And despite all the drama, all the adrenaline, all the revelations, I find myself smiling.

"I don't want to date just anyone." We're only a block away from Abi, and I have so much more to say. "I want to date *you*. But if you're not open to that—which you've said you're not—then I want to be friends again. You *just* said you missed that, Frey."

"In *high school*." She rolls her eyes. "I missed it in high school. My bigger point is that I've made it through the past seventeen years without you, and I'm fine. If you want to mess around and have some fun for the next couple of weeks while we're stuck in Northview, then great. I'm game. But I'm not setting myself up to be hurt again when we get back to Chicago and have our own separate lives to live. I'm not signing up for that."

A long lock of glossy black hair has escaped between her hat and scarf and is curling along the shoulder of her sweater. Holding my breath, I reach out and let my fingertip trail down its length, gently capturing the ends between my thumb and forefinger so I can rub the silky strands. Her eyes close, and her eyelashes fan out across white cheeks. I stretch my fingers and cup the smooth line of her jaw, my skin tingling at the warmth of her. For a moment, I think she presses into me.

"I never left you, Freya," I say. I try to keep the pain out of my voice, but it's there. "*You* left me. *You* were the one who pulled away. Not me."

A long silence stretches between us, my eyes flicking away from the road to glance at her face. She glances at anything *but* me.

"I just needed time," she finally says. She presses her lips together. "I was scared of things changing between us. I was scared of something happening and losing my best friend. I'm not saying I handled it well, but I was *fifteen*. I didn't know what the hell I was doing. I just needed some time to adjust, and then I blinked and you were dating Tiffany fucking Ebner."

She *blinked*? I look back at the three weeks between our kiss and when I started dating Tiffany, and it feels like one of the longest, most interminable times of my life. An entire fucking era of fear and self-doubt.

"You don't think I was scared?" I ask. "I was terrified, Frey." I check the rearview mirror to make sure nobody's behind me, then pull the car to the side of the road and throw it into park. Then I reach for her, my fingers sliding into the hair at her nape, and I drag her to me. Meet her halfway. Her surprised, black-lined eyes widen, and her breath accelerates. But dammit, I'm not signing up for her stupid two-week rule, and until she takes it off the table, I'm damned if I'm going to kiss her. No matter how much I want to. So, instead of letting myself taste her, the way my body is screaming for me to do, I press my forehead into hers. "I just thought you were worth the risk."

Fifteen

FREYA

Those words—*I just thought you were worth the risk.*—echo through my head for the rest of the silent drive to pick up Abi.

Silence is different in winter. Deeper. It's one of the things I like about these slow, frozen months. I don't know if it's the snow or the cold, but it absorbs sound differently, taking it in and swallowing it whole instead of bouncing it back to you in that sharp, crisp way summer does. Right now, the silence is an echo chamber, a blank, barren space that returns Jeremy's final words to me over and over again.

We pull up in front of a brick, two-story Cape Cod, and I roll my eyes at its cheery wreath and light-draped bushes, then grab my phone and shoot off two rapid-fire texts. The first to Abi.

Me: Here.

The second to Thad. (Don't judge. He once texted me at two in the morning on a Wednesday because he was having a brain block about Pippin the hobbit's real name. It's Peregrin. Peregrin Took.)

Me: Jeremy hated me in high school...right?

The lights are on in the house, and the front door swings open to reveal the outline of a wobbly Abi, bundled up in her winter coat and supported at the elbow by a tall teenage boy in shorts and a T-shirt. I frown. For whatever reason, I'd assumed that Abi was with girlfriends. When she talks to me about her friends, it always sounds like the same three or four girls who've been hanging out since middle school. My eyes narrow as I throw open my door and run to help her. Jeremy is close behind me, shoes crunching on the snow, and despite my reeling thoughts about the conversation (*argument?*) that just took place, I'm glad to have his giant, Viking physique at my back.

"What happened?" I ask the boy, sliding in next to Abi and displacing him at her side.

Abi, as always, looks like a perfect combination of Bethany and me. She's willowy, like Bethany was at that age, with long legs and none of my curves, and she has Bethany's cute, button nose. But her hair, pulled into a thick, elaborate braid that trails down her back, is black like mine, and her dark jeans and the black-and-white studded belt are definitely reminiscent of me, circa 2005.

I've always loved Abi. From the first moment I saw her squishy, wrinkly newborn face as she howled herself purple in her hospital bassinet—like she already knew this world was a bullshit place and she wanted a refund—I loved her. But I've never needed to feel *protective* of her before. Bethany was always there to do that. Now, for the first time, I feel the sharp side of maternal instincts. The instinct to rip and claw and destroy anything that could possibly harm her. Kill-first-ask-questions-later kind of instincts.

Mostly directed at this dumbass teenage kid who's shivering on the porch.

I wrap an arm around Abi's shoulders and turn to glare at him, and his brown eyes go wide with alarm at whatever he sees on my face. He's cute in a young, cocky way, but if I had to guess, he's a few years older than Abi. I spot some stubble on his chin—*He shaves? Abi was under the influence with a guy who shaves?*—and I'm not sure, but I may bare my teeth at him.

"Woah, Abi." He takes a step back. "I thought you said your aunt was cool."

"Hey, man." Jeremy steps forward, his demeanor relaxed and friendly. "We're just here to take Abi home. But it will help us out if we know exactly what she had. Just alcohol, or—"

"Oh! Yeah, yeah." The kid's eyes go round, and he waves his hands in front of him. "Abi came over to study with my little sister." He gestures toward the front window, and I sigh with relief as I spot a teenage girl standing there, nose pressed to the glass as she watches us. "We may have...gotten into my parents' stuff? My parents are out of town, so I was supposed to be in charge and"—he grabs at his curly brown hair—"and I guess I didn't do a great job. Abi just had a few drinks. I'm honestly shocked how drunk she is."

I want to grab him by the shirt and shake him down—just to make sure he's telling the truth—but Abi slumps into me, and I know we need to get her to the car. Jeremy, however, reaches out and claps the kid on the back.

"Thanks for calling us," he says in a casual, man-to-man voice. "It was the right thing to do. Are you ok taking care of your sister?"

The boy nods his head, frantic. "Oh, yeah, bro." *Jesus, what is with boys these days calling everybody bro?* "I'm good. You gonna be ok, Abi?"

Secured in the crook of my arm, Abi nods miserably and raises her hand in farewell. "G'bye, Tay-ler," she slurs.

As far as I'm concerned, Taylor is dismissed. I turn my back on him and wrap Abi's arm around my neck, and without missing a beat, Jeremy comes around to her other side and takes most of her weight. We start navigating the icy walkway and driveway, and I hear myself growl low in my throat. Jeremy counters with a soothing *shushing* sound, whether for me or Abi, I don't know.

Blinking, Abi turns her head to look up at him, then turns to me. "Hoosthat?"

"Jeremy." Her foot slips on a patch of ice, and I tense, but Jeremy has already steadied her.

She looks at him again, then back to me. Her voice goes breathy, like she's trying to whisper, but her volume is way too loud. "Heeees hooooot," she slurs into my ear, and I shake my head. Drunks are the worst. However, I'm oddly comforted by the fact that she's this wasted from a few drinks. If her tolerance is this low, I don't think this is a regular habit.

"Yup," I agree. Because what's the point in pretending? Thirty minutes ago, I was openly ogling his half-naked body.

I sneak a peek at Jeremy. I hate myself for it, but I can't help it. He's looking back at me over the top of Abi's head, and when he winks, I quickly turn away. *Asshat.*

We make it back to Jeremy's car, and I'm just opening the back door to tuck Abi inside when she makes an ominous glugging sound. Before I can react, Jeremy pulls her away and keeps a hand on her shoulder as she doubles over and pukes, staining the white snow a startling, neon pink. He even holds her long black braid out of the way.

It's not until five minutes later, when we're a couple blocks from Bethany's house, that I remember to check for a reply from Thad. Abi is passed out next to me in the back seat, her head on my shoulder, and I shift her weight to reach my phone in my jacket pocket. Sure enough, a text is waiting for me.

The Good Twin: You thought he HATED you?!? I always told you I got the brains.

sixteen

JEREMY

13 days until Christmas...

"Knock-knock."

I blink awake. I'd been sleeping in after my late-night adventure, and my head is squished between two pillows to block out the morning light. But even muffled, I know that low, husky voice. I grin, enjoying a few more seconds of darkness before throwing the pillow off my face and squinting into the too-bright sunlight.

My gut twinges with guilt about feeling so happy. Last night had, after all, been a total disaster for Abi and her distraught parents. But despite all that, it had felt like a win when it came to Freya and me. The raw emotion? The truth bombs? The eye fucking?

Definitely a win.

I stretch my arms above my head as I climb out of bed. For a second, I play with, then discard, the idea of putting a shirt on. Because, friendly or not, there is no part of me that doesn't enjoy Freya checking me out.

Smile in place, I open my bedroom door and lean against the doorway, arms crossed over my chest.

"Morning, Sunshine."

"Morning, Asshat."

Yeah, the teachers and principals hadn't been as fond of Freya's nickname for me. It had earned her more than a few detentions. But there's no heat in it this morning. As anticipated, her gray eyes travel over my arms and torso, and I soak up every second of her attention on my bare skin.

I don't usually consider myself vain. The gym routine started as a coping mechanism when I got to college and suffered nearly constant anxiety after being unexpectedly cut adrift. When what-ifs and worst-case scenarios pulled me into darker moods, I found that my only way out was to take things moment by moment, and exercise helped me do that. One muscle-screaming lift, one pound of my sneakers on the pavement, one tricep-burning push-up at a time.

Now? Now I would do every single rep all over again just to have Freya's eyes eating me up like this. As an experiment, I scratch at a pec, then smirk when Freya's gaze follows. Fascinating.

Not that I'm any better, mind you. I've always found Freya attractive. She was constantly reinventing herself in high school, floating between emo, goth, and even grunge. Any style that accepted her heavy black eyeliner and flipped a giant middle finger at the mainstream kids. Whether she was rocking cut-off denim shorts or T-shirts and flannel, I'd been unable to keep my eyes off her. I'd loved her drive to challenge and subvert.

WAR ON CHRISTMAS: A HOLIDAY ROMANCE

Maybe because once I started getting noticed by the Tiffany Ebners, I lost that ability myself.

If she's staring at me now, I'm staring back just as hard.

"I owe you," she says finally, her expression giving away nothing. I bite the inside of my cheek to stop from smiling too big, knowing full well she'll snatch back her olive branch if I act like a dick about it. She sighs. "I was thinking a friendly brunch?"

***

I tuck into my food, attacking the French toast I drenched in real Wisconsin butter and maple syrup. Wren's Café, a greasy spoon diner in downtown Northview, is an institution. It's been owned by the same family since the Great Depression, and it hasn't been updated since. A long counter that stretches the length of the restaurant. Overstuffed napkin dispensers that make the single-ply paper rip every time you try to grab one. Old-timey cholesterol and saturated fats.

It's glorious.

"So, you haven't been home in four years." I take a drink of stale coffee. "Why?"

For a second, Freya balks, her nose wrinkling as she takes a bite of pancakes. The question, as planned, busts through the polite barriers I'd allowed her to keep in place during our drive from Chicago. She owes me big right now, and I'm not squeamish about capitalizing on it.

"Uh-uh, *friend*." I talk around a mouthful of food as I point my fork at her. "I dragged my ass out of bed at eleven o'clock last night to help rescue your precious little niece. You can pretend to be nice for an hour and have a friendly conversation over this heart-attack-on-a-plate. So talk. Why haven't you been home in so long?"

It's not like I don't know the gist of Freya's family dynamics. Freya has always been on the outside of the Nilsen crew. Misunderstood. A black sheep, even. With Thad, their opposing dispositions felt complementary. Maybe it was their twin bond. Maybe it was the nerdy hobbies they'd shared. Whatever the reason, Freya was the yin to Thad's yang, and it worked for them.

The other Nilsens, however, have always seemed bemused by Freya. Not angry or aggressive that I ever saw. There were never any major falling outs. At least not while I was still around. Just a cautious receding to the sidelines, where they participated in her life as quiet observers, watching a game with rules they didn't quite understand.

But four years away from home...that feels more like a full-on estrangement.

I watch her across the booth as she contemplates whether to answer the question or tell me to fuck off. It's a 50/50 shot, I'd guess. The coin toss seems to fall in my favor, however, because she rolls her eyes and huffs.

"Fine." Setting down her fork, she leans back and wraps her hands around her coffee cup. "You know how things have always been..."

I nod as I shovel more French toast into my mouth.

"It's just been more of the same." She snags a piece of my bacon, and I let her. She takes a bite before continuing. "A few years ago, my friend Leo from work didn't have anywhere to go for the holidays, so I stayed in Chicago to celebrate with him. And the distance from my parents...and Bethany—" she shrugs. "I felt like I could breathe."

WAR ON CHRISTMAS: A HOLIDAY ROMANCE

My forehead wants to furrow into a scowl, but I pull a page out of Freya's book and keep my expression guarded as I casually stab a forkful of her pancakes.

It's there. The instinct to criticize her choices. The urge to resent her for not trying harder with a perfectly nice family. I would have given *anything* for parents like the Nilsens.

But this isn't about me. My goal is to understand Freya better. So, I push my personal judgments aside.

"And then..." I prompt, stealing another bite of her pancakes as she grabs another slice of my bacon.

She sighs. "Look. I get it. You had a truly shitty situation. I don't expect this to make sense—"

"I didn't say that." I shake my forkful of pancakes at her. "I want to understand. So, tell me, *friend*."

She thinks for a minute as she chews. "The theater where I work...it's like its own little family," she explains. "Family where we all have something in common. We love art and performance and looking at things from new angles. Sometimes creepy or uncomfortable angles. We all love pushing the limits, and every production is a chance to do that. Spending holidays with my Sphere family—" she sighs. "It's so simple and uncomplicated. I never feel like I don't fit in with them."

Something a little shameful heats my chest. I get along with my coworkers. Some of them, like Wes, have even become friends. But I would never describe them as family. I've been without family since I was eighteen, and apparently Freya has *two*. I try to quell the sour taste of envy with more pancakes.

"So...you're just checking out of Team Nilsen?"

Her eyes narrow. "I'm here, aren't I? But here's the real question: Have I ever *really* been on Team Nilsen? I don't exactly fit with the rest of the team."

Now it's my turn to sigh. Despite my jealousy, I get why Freya feels that way. Mrs. Nilsen was adamant about attending every single one of Bethany's cheer performances, even if it meant having to pay someone to watch the shop. She was equally dedicated to Thad's track meets and math team competitions. But I never saw her at the school plays and musicals that Freya dedicated countless hours to. (I'd know. I was at all of them.) Sets, lighting, sound...Freya was the force behind the scenes, the beating heart of the theater department. I'd asked Thad once why his parents never attended the performances, and he'd shrugged. "I don't think she *wants* them there. And they'd go if she had an actual part."

"What about you?" Freya asks, ruthlessly redirecting the conversation. "How are things going with your mom?"

I had that coming. I was, after all, the one to bring up family drama. I set down my fork, suddenly feeling full. In the background, the music switches to the Burl Ives version of "Holly Jolly Christmas," happy and upbeat, and it feels out of sync with this conversation. Some "Blue Christmas" would fit the moment better.

"You were at the funeral yesterday." I watch her carefully, curious about *her* impressions of my mother, but her face gives away nothing. As usual. "More of that, basically. Tiptoeing around each other. Being so polite it feels like an extreme sport." I force a chuckle as I scratch at the back of my neck, even though there's nothing funny about the situation. "I don't know that I can expect more than that. Right?"

"It's only been two days. After seventeen years." Freya opens her mouth to say more, but our waitress, Wanda, returns, resting a hand on her boney hip.

"And how is everything?" she asks. She's about my mother's age, I'd guess, with dyed copper-red hair that doesn't match her thin, black eyebrows. When she catches my eye and winks, I'm mortified to feel myself blush. Freya snorts.

"It's great," Freya says. "Could I get more coffee, please? We're trying to unfuck his life, and it's going to take a while. And a lot more caffeine."

"Right on it, sugar." Wanda winks at me again, and Freya sinks further into the booth with a throaty laugh. But she doesn't hesitate to dig right back into my fucked-up life as soon as Wanda leaves.

"Do you *want* to have a relationship with your mom?" she asks. "Nobody would judge you if you needed to move on. Or even if you just wanted to. The ball is in your court, and I bet your mom's waiting for you to make the next move."

I groan. That's the problem. I have no clue what I want. I know what I *wanted*. I wanted her to be a mother—a real mother—and refuse to let me go.

But now that he's dead, she'll never get a chance to pick me.

It's fucked up. *I'm* fucked up. How can I be so pissed at a woman who spent the past almost thirty years in a shitty marriage, having her confidence undermined at every turn? I know how horrible it felt to be the target of Gary's moods, and I had my mom doing what she could to intercede. Nudging me out of the house, either to the Nilsen's or football or whatever escape presented itself. *She's* the one who took the brunt of it.

And what do I want now? Now that I'm forever and always the consolation prize, permanent second place to Stepdad-of-the-Year Gary Cassidy?

I thought I'd know once I came back, but I just don't. The time I've spent with my mom so far doesn't feel loving or nostalgic. It doesn't fill the invisible hole I've been living with. It feels tentative and awkward, like being stuck in a broken-down elevator with someone you had a nasty breakup with.

"I *am* fucked up," I say. Freya's clear, gray gaze unlocks something, and without planning to, everything comes pouring out of me. All the things I couldn't say, even to Thad. My head drops into my hands. "I'm so pissed at her, Frey, and I get how fucked up that is. She's so...fragile. You saw her." Freya gives a single, jerky nod of acknowledgement. My mom's overly quiet voice. The way she jumps at anything unexpected. "She's obviously dealing with trauma, and I get it. Rationally, I can step back and recognize it. Gary was abusive, and it changed her, deep down. I can't judge the choices she made. Or I *shouldn't*, at least. But—"

"Here you go, honey." Wanda returns, filling Freya's cup and topping off mine. She obviously heard some of what I said, because her flirtatious glances morph into something maternal and soft. Pity.

I drop my gaze to the Formica tabletop until she's gone. Her white sneakers recede, but I stay silent. I'd told Freya I wanted to be friends, and friends confide in each other. However, the situation with my mom seems a little intense to unload on anyone. People choose to stay in my life because I know how to be pleasant, entertaining. Not because I word-vomit my deepest fears over pancakes and bacon.

"But..." Freya urges, sipping calmly from her coffee, and that single word is all the permission I need.

"But how could she do it? *How?* How could she let him just cut me off like that? I still feel so"—a loud exhale rips out of me—"so *angry* with her about it."

I swallow, and it tastes bitter. Rancid. My stomach churns, every drop of grease I consumed suddenly swishing and rebelling in my guts. It disgusts me, this anger. It makes me feel small and weak, like the scared, powerless kid I used to be, and I want to get away from him, but I can't because I *am* him. My eyes drop again, tracing the red-and-white swirls in the tabletop, because it's bad enough knowing how gross *I* find this anger. I can't bear to see Freya's revulsion.

There's a long silence, filled only with the clattering of silverware and the hum of conversations around us. And, of course, Christmas music. A few tables down, Wanda's "Right on, sugar" breaks through as she takes another customer's order. For a second, I wonder if Freya will get up and leave. This was supposed to be a "friendly brunch." Fun and casual. The stuff I'm usually good at. Instead, I turned it into a goddamn therapy session. This is enough to send anyone running in the opposite direction, high school rival or not. I wait to see Freya's cute black ankle boots scurrying away, like Wanda's white sneakers.

Freya's hand slides across the table, palm up with fingers open and loose, curling gently. Not a gesture of disgust. A gesture of invitation. Acceptance.

My chest tightens, my Adam's apple bobbing as I reach out and lay my hand on top of hers. Mine is much bigger, my wide palms engulfing her pretty, tapered fingers and pale skin. She's soft and cool—she's always had cold hands—and something primal unfurls in me as my heat soaks into her, warming her palm.

This. This quiet recognition of the darkness that lives in each of us—the anger, the shame, the hurt—this is Freya's unique magic, shadowy and magnetic. All those thoughts and feelings that make most people duck their heads in embarrassment...Freya takes them in. She doesn't celebrate them. She doesn't push or prod you into them. She just...accepts.

For a second, with her skin against mine and a thrum of electricity connecting us, I'm thirteen again, the thrill of feeling so totally accepted by her pulsing through me. During those nights when I crawled through her bedroom window, I could tell her anything—fears about Gary, frustrations with my mom, my silly, fantastic ideas about drawing and art—and she'd listen, quiet and absorbed. Sometimes she'd sit beside me, my head next to her lap, and glide her cool fingers through my hair until my eyes drifted shut and we'd sit in silence, simply enjoying each other's presence. Not because we were happy and shiny and perfect, but because we were, both of us, human and warped and a little bit broken. Because our jagged edges fit.

Outside, snow starts to fall, giant, wet flakes coating everything in a fresh layer of white. Inside, Freya's fingers tighten around mine, grounding me, and I squeeze back.

seventeen

FREYA

Tonight is a new moon.

Pop culture reserves its excitement for full moons, blaming them for everything from werewolves to overwhelmed labor-and-delivery units. For those of us who embrace magick, full moons are a time to let go. To unclasp your grubby, greedy fingers from what no longer belongs to you.

Personally, I prefer new moons.

I like the darkness of them. How the moon is a whisper of a shadow in the night sky. I like the mystery of them. Full moons look back at a completed cycle; they carry the comfort of 20/20 hindsight. New moons look forward to an unknown future. What do you want for yourself? What are you willing to *do* to make it happen? Each new moon is an inky little pocket carved out of the month, a place to hide and dream.

I'm sitting cross-legged in my papasan, Hecate purring loudly from my lap as I shuffle my tarot cards in the dull glow of the Christmas lights.

Most months, my new moon tarot readings are mundane. Practical. I take a deep breath, enjoy a moment of stillness, and soften my senses so I can approach a current challenge with fresh eyes. How can the theater scrounge up enough money for a new sewing machine? What should the theme be for the burlesque show? How can I navigate the romantic drama between Greg and Robby?

Tonight, as the cards flutter through my fingers, my thoughts circle back to Jeremy. He's a bad penny in my psyche, insistent on resurfacing no matter how much I try to concentrate on my life—my *real* life—back in Chicago.

There's not even a question for me to ask, because I already know how our story ends. We'll play out this little charade of being "friends" for a while. Jeremy will try to ignore the chemistry between us. Because he's foolishly optimistic. I'll wait him out until the chemistry between us wins. Because I'm tragically realistic. The sex will be good. (Fine—better than good.) And then it will be over. Finished. Done.

I have zero interest in creating false hope for myself. I refuse to waste time or energy daydreaming about a future I know will never come to pass, and I'm being up front with Jeremy about that. I may be a lot of things, not all of them nice, but I'm not a liar. The "two-week rule" isn't some imaginary power struggle I'm needlessly stoking. It's a matter of honesty. Integrity.

I try to drag my thoughts back to the theater. I imagine myself as a huge, bumbling troll—complete with warts and crooked teeth—violently clubbing my own thoughts over the head and tugging them back where I want them to be. The Sphere. My *real* friends. Life in Chicago. But when the memory of Jeremy's large, warm hand wrapping around mine interrupts *again*, I blow out a frustrated breath and resign myself to a generic question: What do I need to know right now?

A tiny, barely perceptible pull in my solar plexus tells me when to stop shuffling, and I rest the deck on my knee, cutting it with my left hand. When I turn over the top card, I snort. Not a little ladylike one either. Hecate turns to me with an irritated glare, and I run my hand along her bony spine until she settles back into a soft, contented lump.

Then I turn back to the card I pulled: The Hermit. Upside down. Of course.

My deck is black, with spooky, ethereal images sketched in white. The Hermit is a lone man, old and weathered, his back bent as he carries a lantern before him. Upright, it's a call to solitude, encouraging you to take some space and turn inwards for the answers you seek. Reversed, like it is for me, it's a warning. Don't get lost in your solitude. Only retreat mindfully, with intention. Don't retreat to avoid something.

My teeth grind as I shove the card back into the deck. Even tarot is against me today. Fiona Apple eyes me coolly from my bedroom wall, and I stare back as I contemplate drawing a new card. A do-over. However, if I pull the Hermit again, I can't pretend it was a bum card. I bite at the inside of my cheek as I wage my internal debate: *To pull? Or not to pull?*

A soft knock at my door saves me from deciding.

Thank the gods.

"Enter."

The door cracks open, and, to my surprise, not one, but *two* blonde heads poke through. My mom and Bethany. I must have been more lost in thought than I realized, because I didn't even hear Bethany arrive at the house. I'm not surprised, though. I'm sure she's here to get advice or just vent to Mom about what happened with Abi last night. She's always turned to Mom for comfort in a way I never have.

"Why are you sitting in the dark?" Bethany asks, pushing her way through.

She reaches to flip the light switch on but pulls her hand back at my muttered "Don't."

My mom, more timid, tiptoes in Bethany's wake, looking cautiously around the room. But aside from some dirty laundry and the tiny altar of amber, lapis lazuli, and onyx I've set up on top of my dresser, it's the same as it's always been. Hecate jumps from my lap and pads across the nightmarish pink carpet to greet our visitors, sniffing them both until they each scratch behind her ears. She's the troll under the bridge, and her currency is ear scratches.

"It's a new moon," I tell Bethany as she and my mom walk to the bed and sit side by side. In the shadowy light, they could easily pass for sisters, their straight, careful postures identical. "I like some quiet and contemplation on new moons, and I find it easier to contemplate in the dark…and the quiet."

I watch them both for a reaction. My spiritual practices—tarot cards, crystal magick, and astrology—aren't for everyone, and I'm used to people jumping to conclusions. It's why, until now, I've never discussed my magickal beliefs openly with my family (other than Thad and Abi, of course). Not that I expect them to race to the garage for pitchforks and tiki torches. I just figured it would be one more tally in the "Ways Freya Is Weird" column, and really, aren't there enough of those already?

However, my brunch conversation with Jeremy is lingering, and not just the impromptu hand holding. His quiet anguish as he discussed his mom haunts me. Feelings aren't a competition; the pain of his family experience is different from mine. Apples and oranges. Still…when I voiced my own family complaints next to his, the situation with the Nilsen crew didn't seem quite so insurmountable. As different as I am, I've always known I have a place to go if I need it. A safe home and food on the table. A family to spend the holidays with when my cat wipes out my savings account. Hearing Jeremy's story has me taking these things a little less for granted, and if I want to make more of an effort with my family, being more open about my life seems like a decent first step.

There is also, of course, the specter of that reversed Hermit card hanging over me. I should isolate myself less? Fine. Take *this*, tarot deck.

My mom's eyes widen slightly, and her voice straddles between awe and nervousness. "Are you like...a witch?"

Above all else, my spiritual practices are solitary. If I *am* a witch, I don't want a coven; I want to be left alone. My only interactions regarding my craft come from watching #WitchTok videos and occasionally commenting on my favorite magickal blog, *Hope & Stardust*. A lot of the *Hope & Stardust* readers refer to themselves as Hot Mess Witches, but labels have always seemed unnecessary to me. However, if I *am* going to be saddled with a label...I don't totally hate this one.

I shrug. "I guess so."

"Ooh!" Bethany coos.

If I'd been expecting shock, I would have been seriously disappointed. It reminds me a little of Leo's coming out story, which consists of his family staring at him incredulously until his mom finally whispered, "Oh, honey, we've known for years."

Bethany shoves a bottle of wine, which I just notice, into my mom's lap, and hops from the bed, eyeing my tarot deck with excitement. My mom, for her part, doesn't have much reaction at all. She's already focused on unscrewing the wine bottle as Bethany grabs my deck.

"Oracle cards," Bethany says, nodding. "I want to order some decks to carry in the shop."

My lips tilt into a smirk. "Not oracle cards. Tarot."

Truth? I've been pulling cards for Abi since we started video calling each other regularly a couple years ago. I never explicitly told her she couldn't tell her mom, but I assumed she wouldn't because we didn't know for sure how Bethany would react. As I watch her flip through the deck with avid curiosity, though, I realize I should have given her more credit. Then her face scrunches up with horror, and I hear myself cackle, knowing *exactly* what is coming.

"Tarot is just so *scary*," she says, holding up the Death card, which features a leering, skeletal face. "I really prefer my angel oracle deck."

"One," I say, holding up a finger, "life is scary. Two"—I flip up a second finger—"it's not about literal death. It's about reaching the end of a cycle or stage. So, chill the fuck out."

I'm pleasantly surprised, though. Bethany is the poster girl for "Positive vibes only!" which isn't my thing, but her spiritual beliefs are still way more interesting than I anticipated. Like good Midwesterners, we've avoided talking about anything close to religion since my junior year hexing incident. I'm now realizing that I don't know anything about Bethany's spiritual beliefs.

My mom hands me the wine bottle, and I grab it, watching Bethany as she continues to flip through my deck. I don't see any cups at this impromptu party, so I tilt the bottle to my lips.

"So how is my favorite niece doing after her grand adventure?" I ask, handing the bottle to Mom. Bethany returns my cards with a deep moan.

"Oh, you know, it's basically all my fault," she says, flopping back onto the bed. "I'm too overprotective. All the other kids do it. I'm turning her into a social pariah."

I cringe. I felt like a total asshole busting Abi by taking her home to Bethany and Drew last night, but she didn't leave me a choice. She was too far gone for me to cover for her if she came here. And ultimately, hiding it from Bethany didn't feel like the right thing to do.

"Can you do one for me?" my mom asks, her hands clasped in front of her chest.

"Can I do a what?" I ask, confused.

"A card? Or is it called a reading?" Mom's lips twist to the side. She's nervous. Not about the tarot cards, but about getting the words right. She's worried about offending me.

"Are you sure? You don't have—"

"Oh, I know I don't," she assures me, then takes another drink of wine before handing it to Bethany. "I had one done at a fair as a teenager. It was interesting."

"Ooh, me too," Bethany jumps in, sitting back up with a jerk. "Tell me whether getting Abi through high school is going to literally kill me. Or maybe it will be the boys. It's gonna be one of those little punks, just you watch."

And that's how we end up cross-legged on the floor, my favorite tarot deck between us. Hecate settles into my mom's lap, leaving a layer of stray black hairs on her stonewashed mom jeans, and the wine bottle travels between us as I give a brief lesson on crafting tarot questions. By the time I'm shuffling the cards again, my head is swimming pleasantly and Mom and Bethany's cheeks are stained pink. My mom, like me, opts for the old *Hope & Stardust* standby question, "What do I need to know right now?"

When I ask her to cut the deck, her eyes meet mine and her shoulders shrug toward her ears. She's excited. I almost—*almost*—smile at her enthusiasm, but I manage to keep my face solemn as I turn over the top card and she leans forward to see it, her lip caught between her teeth.

It's Justice, a robed, blindfolded woman standing over meticulously balanced scales.

"Hmm," I mutter, and Hecate purrs in agreement. We all stare at the card, and I notice that Bethany is squinting to focus. She has definitely had more than her fair share of the wine. "The Justice card is like the karma card of tarot," I explain. "The two sides of the scales are past and future. You receive the results that you set in motion with your past actions. So, if there's a situation that's bothering you *now*, look to your past actions for answers."

Reading for other people always results in one of three reactions. One: They are utterly confused, and they look at you like you're a crackpot. (This is usually accompanied by an "Oh my god, I get it now!" phone call a week later, when the pieces fall into place.) Or, two: They immediately make a connection and look at you like you're a fucking wizard. That one's fun. Or, three: They make the connection—you see the moment of illumination flash across their face—then they pretend that they haven't. They go all cagey, like a dog that's just eaten a plateful of Christmas cookies.

Number three is my absolute favorite. It means you hit on a secret.

It's also the exact reaction my mom has.

"Oh! Oh." She pats nervously at her blonde bob, schooling her features from surprise to a bland smile. "I'll have to think on that one, honey."

"Mmhmm." I raise my eyebrows, and she clears her throat.

"Ok, my turn." Bethany bounces and pats her knees in a drumroll. "For my question, I'm going with—with—" Her head tips to the side, her ponytail swaying, and her brow wrinkles into deep furrows as she stares over my shoulder. "What the fuck is *that*?"

With a sinking sensation, I turn to follow Bethany's gaze. On the windowsill outside, tiny figures of Frodo and Samwise Gamgee are trekking through the snow.

"And that," I sigh, accepting that this new moon has gone off the rails, "would be Jeremy."

EIGHTEEN

JEREMY

I grin as I hear the window sliding open, anticipating Freya's stern, serious gaze. Instead, I'm stunned silent as Mrs. Nilsen's blonde head pokes out and she looks down at me with wide blue eyes.

"Jeremy?"

I clutch Frodo and Sam to my chest with one hand, and the bottle of Jack Daniels I swiped from above the refrigerator with the other, staring back at her as my stomach bottoms out. Part of me always assumed that Thad and Freya's parents knew about my late-night visits and looked the other way because they felt sorry for me. Judging from Mrs. Nilsen's shocked expression, though, we'd been way stealthier than I thought.

I clear my throat, still crouched in the snow. "Hey, Mrs. Nilsen."

Bethany, to my shock, sticks her head out next.

"Hey, Jeremy McHottie," she says too loudly. "Ooh, and you brought booze." Then she grabs me by the hoodie and pulls me through the window, where I land in a heap on Freya's favorite pink carpet.

I'm still sprawled on my stomach—luckily Bethany relieved me of the glass bottle during my journey through the window—when I hear Freya's bored voice next to me. "Hey, Jeremy McHottie."

I scramble into a sitting position, trying to shake the sensation that I traveled through a portal into some bizarre alternate universe. Mrs. Nilsen plants her hands on her hips, leveling me with an expert-level mom look.

"How long have you been sneaking into my daughter's room, Jeremy Kelly?"

My face heats, an almost painful contrast to the freezing cold of a few seconds ago, and next to me Freya chuckles darkly. I shoot her an annoyed look, which only makes her laugh harder, and I'm hit with simultaneous urges to shake her and kiss that sassy smirk off her red lips.

"Um, well..." I keep looking at Freya, hoping for some guidance, but she just shrugs. The little minx is enjoying this. I sigh and mentally add this to the list of things I'd like to bend her over my lap and spank her for. "I guess it started a little over twenty years ago now?"

"Oh. My. *God.*" Bethany says, her gaze swinging wildly between Freya and me. "You two were..." She pauses to make an obscene hand gesture, and I frantically turn to Mrs. Nilsen as Freya breaks into more laughter. Yesterday, I thought I'd do anything to hear that laugh again, but now I find myself hauling her to my side and clamping my hand over her mouth. She wiggles next to me, trying to break free, and I squeeze her tighter.

"*No.*" I shake my head at Mrs. Nilsen, who looks like her eyes are about to pop out of her head. Freya bites my thumb, and I grunt but keep my hand in place. "It wasn't like that. I stayed in Thad's room too. It was just when things—well, when things were bad with Gary. They'd let me camp out on the floor."

"Oh." Her face falls, and she instantly transforms from bad-ass disciplinarian to sad, hovering mother figure with her hands fluttering helplessly at her sides. "Oh, honey. And we didn't know?"

"Wait." Bethany flops onto the floor next to me, and I watch Freya for signs that she'll bite me again as I gently ease my hand away from her mouth. But instead of teeth, this time she brushes the pad of my thumb with a quick dart of her tongue. The velvety stroke goes straight to my dick, and I know she sees the flash of panic in my eyes, because she gives me a flirty wink before turning back to the cards she's shuffling. "So you were coming in her room a bunch of nights—while you were both teenagers—and you two never..." She makes the hand gesture again, as if we wouldn't understand her meaning without it.

"Somebody's a perv when they drink," Freya mutters, and she sounds impressed. Maybe even pleasantly surprised.

"Everyone is a perv when they drink," Bethany corrects her, taking a long pull of Jack straight out of the bottle. I glance at Freya, who winces and shakes her head at me, so I ease the bottle from Bethany's fingers. She doesn't seem to notice as she pats my knee. "Guess what?" she asks.

"What?"

"Weeeeee"—she circles her finger around the room—"are Freya's coven now."

"Oh." I blink. "So, Freya's a—"

"A witch, yes." Bethany nods, a drunken sage. "We were helping her with her new moon ritual."

"*I* was minding my own damn business and quietly contemplating, and they wanted me to pull tarot cards for them," Freya explains, the corners of her lips pulling down as she shoots Bethany an exasperated glance. Then she turns her scowl to me. "You should probably go home."

"And miss all the fun?" I bump my shoulder into hers.

I'm not surprised Freya was called in this direction. She did, after all, possibly (probably?) hex all three of my prom dates. My own spiritual beliefs are more practical—aka practically nonexistent—but her old Ouija board is likely still tucked under her bed, and she had a sizeable crystal collection by the time she got to high school. She also made Thad and I watch *The Craft* with her a couple dozen times.

"Yeah, don't make McHottie go and miss all the fun," Bethany says, flinging an arm around my shoulders. Mrs. Nilsen, who is now sitting in the circle with us, *tsks* quietly, but Bethany ignores her. "Now do my cards," she orders Freya.

"You heard the woman," I echo, smiling at Freya. "Do her cards."

Nineteen

JEREMY

It's an hour—and several swigs of Jack Daniels—later, when Mrs. Nilsen closes the bedroom door behind her with a tiny wave goodnight. Bethany, who is in no condition to drive, is tucked away safely in Thad's old room, snoring next to a garden gnome named Edward that Freya planted there for her twin. And I'm sitting against the wall, legs stretched out in front of me. Freya's cat lies on my thighs, gently rumbling as I trail my fingertips through her soft midnight fur.

"She doesn't usually like men," Freya says, her voice low, "but she likes you."

"Good. Because I like her." At my words, two golden eyes blink at me through the near dark. She'd put me through some weird butt-in-my-face ritual, but once I passed that gauntlet, she immediately plastered herself to my lap.

WAR ON CHRISTMAS: A HOLIDAY ROMANCE

Freya's sitting next to me, eyes closed and head tipped back to the wall, and I take the opportunity to stare at her, to drink in the sight of her flawless face mere inches from mine, relaxed and contented. The tilt of her nose, the strong chin that's probably a little too pronounced to be feminine but fits her perfectly, the graceful arch of her brows. They're all familiar, etched into countless memories from my most formative years, but they house a new, unknown creature. A woman whose calm and unshakeable confidence fill me with such an acute wanting, it makes my bones ache. Even now, sitting in the silence, I have to concentrate on keeping busy, tickling along Hecate's spine, so that I don't reach out and grab Freya's hand. Again.

The impromptu tarot party was fun, and not just due to the whiskey. Freya took charge, guiding us newbies through the intricacies of each card, pointing out the symbolism behind every sketched detail. I'd marveled at the artwork, drawings that managed to be both ethereal and chilling, all while encapsulating centuries of tradition and meaning. Do I believe in the cards? I don't know. But I'm mesmerized by Freya's expertise. It's another layer of her, rich and complex, and I can't shake the feeling that getting to know her again is like watching a flower bloom, each row of petals revealed more gorgeous than the last.

"You looked like you were having fun tonight. With your mom." I pause for dramatic effect. "And *Bethany*."

Freya chuckles and turns her head toward me, hitting me with that steady look that makes my stomach tighten.

"And *you*," she adds. "Jeremy Kelly. Prep. Academic rival. Captain of the football team." Her pert little nose wrinkles. "*Ew*. What is happening?"

The corner of my mouth twitches as I watch her, her face animated with feigned shock and disgust. Twenty feet away, in my mom's house, everything is confusing. Awkward and fraught. But here with Freya…it's not that everything makes sense. It's that everything outside of her and me ceases to exist. It reduces my world to a bubble of wide, slate-colored eyes and poison-apple lips and the fundamental need to be close to her. I shift my weight so my shoulder and hip brush against hers, and the ache of wanting her subsides a bit.

"Maybe it's the booze," I suggest. "It didn't work so hot for my family, but it seems to loosen things up for yours."

"It certainly appears to ease the stick out of Bethany's ass," Freya murmurs, eyes twinkling.

I'd been worried after brunch—and the friendly hand-holding—that she'd retreat, pulling into herself and shutting me out. I spent the afternoon and evening laboring through small talk with Mom as I helped her sort through Gary's things, and the entire time, I had to fight the instinct to come to the Nilsen's and glue myself to Freya's side. I was an enemy army, desperate to hold on to the precious inches of territory I'd gained. Of course, there was the alternate strategy I'd tried in high school: giving her space to process. The result? Twenty years of "space."

It's not an outcome I'll risk repeating.

My phone dings in my sweatpants, and I curse myself for not silencing it before I came over. I grab for it, fully intending to ignore the message and simply turn off the volume. Hecate gives me a grumpy look as she jumps off my lap.

"You can check it," Freya says, breaking her gaze from mine.

"Thad," I say as soon as I see my screen. My phone is just recognizing my face and automatically unlocking when Freya's fingers sneak over and pluck the phone from my hands. The instinct to grab it back is automatic, but she's quick, and when she slides away from me, shuffling her butt along the floor out of my reach, I let her go. There's nothing on my phone I need to hide from her. Instead, I focus on reading her expression, which goes from curious to amused, her red lips curving.

"What?" I ask, and her eyes crinkle as they meet mine.

"He wants to know if I've seduced you yet."

"You *told* him that?"

She must have because *I* definitely didn't. Rule number one of the Bro Code is "Don't fall for your friend's sister." I'm a miserable failure at that one, and Thad knows it. Keeping the ugly, pathetic details to myself has always seemed like the least I can do, so I was hardly going to tell him about Freya's intention to seduce me.

She shrugs. "I like freaking him out. It keeps him on his toes."

Her fingers start to fly over the keys, and, too late, I recognize the glint of dangerous glee lighting up her face. I lunge for my phone in earnest, one hand grabbing for her hip to keep her in place, but she wriggles away and scrambles to her feet, sprinting to the other side of the room. There's no place for her to go. I'm too fast and the room is too small to offer any kind of real escape. But she doesn't need to escape. She just needs enough time to finish whatever horrendous message she's typing and press "Send."

Which I'm pretty sure she does.

She's giggling—*giggling!*—when I trap her against the wall between a bookcase and a wicker hamper, and the sound sends chills of horror down my spine. My heart races, the adrenaline of the chase pumping through my veins, and when she looks up at me and bites her lower lip, I plant my hands above either side of her head and lean in close. The floral scent of Freya spiked with whiskey makes my head reel.

"Freya Estelle Nilsen." She's clutching my phone to her chest, shaking her head as if even she can't believe her own nerve. "What have you done?"

As if answering my question, my phone emits a series of manic dings. *Ding, ding, ding!* Oh god. It's bad. Whatever she wrote, it's really, really bad. We stare at each other, her eyes going wider as the notifications continue. *Ding, ding!*

"Burning your phone and getting a new one might be your best option," she says, tucking it behind her back.

"Give it to me," I say, surprised at how deep and rumbly my own voice is. God help me, she smiles as she shakes her head.

"That's supposed to be my line," she whispers, the devil in her eyes.

Fuck. Me.

Strategy, strategy, strategy, I remind myself, grasping wildly for some semblance of self-control. I need to play the game—*she* obviously is—and brunch this morning felt like a win. I'd opened up with her, and the gamble had paid off. There'd been a new vulnerability between us. I have no clue whether it had been friendly or romantic. There isn't anything overtly sexual about holding hands, but I sure as hell don't do that with Thad when we talk about hard shit. And the truth is, I don't really care if the morning went in the Friends column or Seduction column; I care that it was real. A moment of genuine connection.

But right now, my body is in the driver's seat, and the connection it's most concerned with is one that would be a hell of a lot easier without clothes on.

Friendly, Friendly, Friendly, my head chants. My head, sadly, is utterly overpowered by my cock, which chants, *Closer, closer, closer.*

I step closer, so my body presses her into the wall. At first, I keep my hips tilted back so she can't feel the hard-on I'm sporting. I'm not, after all, an animal.

Then Freya slides her body against me, one long, slow, feline roll that presses her soft breasts into my chest as her eyes hold mine. And something in me...snaps.

Maybe it's the two decades of wanting. Maybe it's that throbbing in my bones, like the missing her has finally bled over into physical pain. Maybe it's the flash of something hot in her eyes when our bodies make contact. Whatever it is, it tips me over some invisible ledge, and the next thing I know, one arm is wrapped around Freya's tiny waist and I'm pressing closer. Every soft curve of her body is yielding to me, and my hand grips her ass, hard. I'm supporting her weight, dragging her up against me until her toes leave the floor, and without prompting, her legs wrap around my waist.

Her arms are pressed between her back and the wall. The phone is literally brushing my hand. I could let go of her bottom and grab it at any second, but the phone isn't my goal anymore. My single goal is *closer*, and with her legs wrapped around me, she's right fucking there. The heat of her. The core of her. My hips surge forward, pinning her to the wall, and she gasps, a breathy little sound that has my cock twitching against her. I grunt, pushing forward again, and again, and I know that she can feel every inch of me pressed between her legs. Her eyes are closed now, her red lips parted, and with a moan, she presses back, tightening her legs so that she's inching up my erection, only to let herself slide down again.

Fuck. Fuckity fuck fuck fuck.

I'm going to lose this seduction battle eventually—*thank god*—but I need to think. This physical pull we have toward one another...it's not going away, and right now, she's the one using all that momentum while I'm flailing like some dumbass fighting a rip tide.

And I'm flailing because I haven't been honest with myself.

I don't want Freya as just a friend. I want *all* of her. I want her earnest, penetrating looks that see into the darkest depths of me. I want her sassy red lips that continuously taunt me. I want her authenticity, bold and unapologetic, that refuses to bend to societal expectations. I want her passion. I just want...her.

I can see my mistake now. In my desperation to have her back in my life, I'd been willing to compromise. I thought I could play it safe. I thought I could guarantee a relationship with her by going back to before attraction complicated things between us. By being "just friends."

Clearly, I was an idiot.

"What are we doing, Sunshine?" My mouth lowers to her jaw, her throat, then nips along her collar bone. Her scent fills my nostrils, overtaking every short, desperate breath, and the clean, salty taste of her skin is on my tongue. All the while, my hand grips her bottom, supporting her as she rides up and down my cock through our clothes, and I try valiantly not to pass out on the spot.

"I'm about to have a very friendly orgasm," she pants, her cheeks flushed. "From how hard you're friending me right now. What about you?"

I squeeze her ass harder—she's so sassy—and she laughs low and sultry as she wiggles against me. Not good. Not good at all.

My vision goes dark around the edges, and I clench my jaw, my muscles starting to shake. Not from the strain of supporting us against the wall, but from the effort it takes not to strip off her leggings, drop my pants, and sink into her. She's ready for me. I know it. She'd take every inch of me, wrapping me in her wet, silken heat. And I need it. I need it like a drowning man needs air. My hand kneads her ass as she rides me, and she makes a soft, needy sound in the back of her throat as she leans forward to run her tongue along the length of my neck.

Fucking. Think. Man.

I might have made a mistake, thinking I could ignore the chemistry between us. But Freya miscalculated too.

Her head tips back again, her hips working feverishly against me, and I can tell from her pinched brow and the sexy fucking noises she's making that she's right there. She's about to come apart, riding my cock like a favorite sex toy, and I *love* it. I love seeing the pleasure my body gives her. I love watching her use me, watching her take what she needs so shamelessly. She's not calculating how she looks, and she's not worried about messing up her hair. She's *in* the moment, in her body, and I want to fall to my knees and worship her for it, to give her every drop of pleasure she's craving.

But we're also more than just this, and that's *her* error. Thinking we can be just fuck buddies and move on.

If I'm going to win this war, it's going to be because I'm the first one to accept it, the first one to truly acknowledge that Freya has—and has always had—the potential to be my everything.

However, I'm going to lose her if I let her use me as her fuckboy. Looking at the history she gave me of her boyfriends, I can see her M.O. Freya, always in charge, taking what she needs, then moving on before anything gets too messy. Before those big, beautiful emotions of hers can kick in. I can picture exactly the type of guy she targets: sensitive, unwilling to stand up to her. I bet she had a grand old time leading them around by their dicks and running roughshod over them.

But it's going to stop. Now.

My hips ease back. My hand slides to grab her hip bone, slowing the pace of her movements to a lazy crawl. Her eyes shoot open, piercing me, and I see her shock. How unused she is to anybody setting limits with her, fighting her for control. For a moment, I almost feel sorry for the pathetic schmucks she's been leaving in her wake for the past seventeen years.

Almost.

I lean forward, trailing my nose along her jaw and breathing her in, letting myself get intoxicated on her scent. My tongue plays with the soft hollow behind her ear, and my arm tightens as she trembles against me. Then my lips trail over, just inches, until her mouth—that perfect, red, wet dream of a mouth—is almost brushing against mine.

What about you? she'd asked.

"I'm going to kiss you," I tell her.

TWENTY

FREYA

"Wha—what?" I drop Jeremy's phone, and it falls to the carpet with a thud.

Ok, I get it. Five seconds ago, I was riding Jeremy's cock like a pogo stick and happily anticipating an earth-shattering orgasm. I can admit there's a certain intimacy to that. But it all just *happened*. One second, I was sending very poorly thought-out texts to Thad to tweak him out, and the next Jeremy was pinning me to the wall with that big, gorgeous body of his, growling out my name and ordering me to "Give it to him" like the world's sexiest tyrant.

And chaos—very *sexy* chaos—ensued. All in all, it felt like a big old win for Team Seduction.

He could have just *done* it. Kissed me. The energy was there, the impulse to get closer and physically connect. To devour. I would have welcomed his mouth on mine (Fine. I would have welcomed his mouth *anywhere*.) as part of that dizzying frenzy that consumed us.

Now, though...

His eyes bore into mine, his pupils eating up the summery blue-green so they appear almost black, and his pelvis is pushing into mine, holding me in place. He's slamming on the brakes, halting the wild, thoughtless free fall we'd been enjoying, and he's replacing all that frantic energy with something slow. Something still and deep. Something that's the absolute opposite of thoughtless. Because there are all sorts of thoughts going through his head right now. I can see it in the way his gaze is roving over me, taking in my ragged breath and my hot cheeks. I can feel it in the way he brushes a stray lock of hair from my face, the way he cups my jaw.

"I'm going to kiss you, Sunshine," he repeats, as if I hadn't heard him the first damn time.

"But—but—"

What the hell, Freya? My heart, which had already been racing, now stumbles and reels, a puppet ruled by an amateur puppeteer. There's no calling this kiss, if it happens, an accident. He's giving me fair warning. Declaring his intent. Making it slow and...well, sweet. This kiss is a choice, and something about that is throwing me off.

"But what?"

His lips, warm and dry, press a soft kiss to my forehead. His fingers slide back to cradle my skull, and they're moving in my hair, a gentle, hypnotic massage that has my eyes fluttering shut. I wiggle my arms free and wrap them around him, gripping the hard muscles of his back.

"But why?" I ask.

Why? Why?!? What is wrong with me?

His lips curve into a smile against my hair as his fingers continue their slow, steady pressure along my scalp.

"I've been waiting for twenty years to kiss you again, Freya." His lips graze my neck and his tongue flicks into the hollow at the base of my throat. I think I purr, but I'm not sure. Whatever I do, he rewards me with another hot flick of his tongue. "I don't honestly know what base we were just on." He pauses here to press his hips into me, so I can feel him still hard between my legs. "But I'm not skipping first when I've been waiting two decades to get there."

"But we hate each other," I whisper. My body is blazing, and every gentle stroke of his lips and tongue as he works his way slowly toward my mouth adds fuel to the fire.

"Mmm." He kisses the corner of my mouth, the tip of my nose, the tiny mole on my right cheek that I hated as a kid but now think of as my beauty mark. "So you keep telling me."

"We ended up in the principal's office seventy-eight times."

"Seventy-nine."

"The bloody nose doesn't count," I argue. He's nuzzling my neck now, his five o'clock shadow a pleasant rasp against my bare skin. "It was totally spontaneous. Mrs. Johnson just assumed I gave it to you."

"Wanna know what I thought about while we were in the principal's office? While I had tissues shoved up my nose?"

It's a trap. I can smell it as surely as I can smell the warm, spicy scent of his faded cologne. Unfortunately, my fatal flaw is that I'm a total Pandora. Now that he's dangled that little box in front of me, there's no way I'm not going to open it.

"What did you think about?" I ask, hating how soft and breathy my voice sounds.

"Your mouth." His lips brush over mine, barely touching. My legs tighten around his waist. "You were wearing black lipstick that day." I don't remember that. I remember his green-and-white striped polo, dotted with blood. I remember hating it because it marked him as this new and improved Jeremy, popular and trendy. "And I was wondering if you'd taste the same with black lips as the first time we kissed."

"Oh." The single syllable drops from me. Falls between us.

I'm waiting for him to pounce. For his mouth to crash into mine. Instead, his assault is gentle. Subtle. His lips graze mine only to coast to my cheek and chin and jaw before returning to my mouth, each pass marginally firmer than the last. It's teasing. A sexy, flirty "Come play with me" that my stupid body can't resist. My mouth chases his, and we're both smiling, our breathing fast, until I reach up and grab his face, holding him still so I can finally, *finally* press my lips to his.

He jerks, the barest tensing of his muscles, and I puff out a laugh as we kiss. He did that same thing, that little lurch, the first time we kissed, and for a moment I catch a glimpse of the sweet, sensitive boy I knew. That boy who felt electrified by an innocent brush of my lips against his.

Jeremy's arm tightens around my waist, but he keeps the kiss slow and unhurried. A leisurely exploration that taunts me into softening for him, unfurling, my body going loose and lax as my lips part to invite the sweet, gentle invasion of his tongue. He groans into my mouth.

"God, you taste good, Sunshine."

He tastes oaky and sharp, like whiskey, and I can't get enough of it. All of it—his body against mine, the press of his lips, the smell of his skin—all of it is new and exciting but old and achingly familiar. Because it's *him*. My best friend. My worst enemy. The one I'm never going to get over. Not completely. Because maybe I've never admitted it to myself, let alone to him, but I've been waiting twenty years for this kiss too.

That's how I am—pinned to the wall, legs wrapped around Jeremy's waist, hands holding his face, wanting him *way* too much—when the door gives a too-small, too-late squeak of warning and my dad's deep, booming voice fills the room.

"Just wanted to—Oh! Sorry—Oh!"

Jeremy shoots back from me like he's been burned, face flushed and eyes darting frantically. But when my legs give out on me and I stumble, he jumps forward, his hand grabbing my elbow to steady me even as he turns his panicked, guilt-stricken face toward my dad.

"Um, hey there...Mr. Nilsen," Jeremy says, then clears his throat. "Sir."

"Uh, right." My dad looks even more panicked than Jeremy. He's standing there in his plaid pajama bottoms and frayed T-shirt, half in and half out the door, one hand on the knob and the other over his eyes. Then he's clearing his throat too. "Jeremy. Mary mentioned you were here—and I just wanted to say—well...hi. Sorry. Should've knocked. But, you know, locks." Here he stops to inspect the lock on the door, twisting the knob to double-check that it works. It does. He slaps his hand back over his eyes and his moccasin slippers start shuffling back into the hallway. "Well...I'll just let you two—well."

I start to feel it swelling inside me then. A dark well of hysteria that feels an awful lot like a giggle. Giggling is *not* a noise I make. And if I'm honest, it's the second time tonight. Clearly, Jeremy has broken me and I'm suffering some kind of malfunction. I clamp my hand over my mouth to stifle it. Jeremy's hand slides over mine, and he shakes his head at me, looking positively mortified, until the bedroom door shuts with a *click*.

"Shit," he whispers. "I think he thinks we were having *sex*."

I pull his hand down, freeing my mouth.

"Well, if you had given it another minute or two—"

He stops me with a short, hard kiss that instantly has my knees wobbling again. Then he pulls back, his breath short and choppy.

"God, I love that sassy mouth of yours." He grips my chin, his eyes on my lips. "Now I'm getting out of here before it gets me into more trouble."

"You call *that* trouble?" I scoff. "You've gone soft."

He groans out a laugh, running his hand down his face. "Sunshine, I am anything but soft right now."

"Well, better make up your mind how you want to play things." I raise my eyebrow. "As of tomorrow, we're down to twelve days."

Twenty-one

JEREMY

12 days until Christmas...

Thad: I can't believe I'm asking you this, but...has Freya seduced you yet?

Me: You bet your ass she has. best pussy Ive ever had. Ever. Tastes like cotton candy and tight like a bamboo finger trap. Forget ping pong balls..your sister could shoot marbles out of that cooch bro

That's how far I get reading the text exchange between Thad and Freya—on *my* phone—before blowing a mouthful of Lucky Charms across my mom's kitchen table. I haven't eaten Lucky Charms since I got serious about working out in college, but my mom had been so proud to show me that she remembered my favorite breakfast cereal that I didn't have the heart to tell her I don't eat it anymore. So, I've been starting off my day with an amusement-park-level sugar buzz and adding an extra mile to my run to work it off. I might also be trying to run off an unhealthy dose of sexual frustration, but...best not to think about that.

My mom, who's sitting across from me eating a piece of whole wheat toast—like an adult—looks up from her folded newspaper to stare at me. She's in a matching pj's set and wrapped in a gray quilted bathrobe, looking like a magazine version of a mom.

"Is...everything all right?"

I shake my head, staring in horror at my phone.

Thad: Jesus, Frey.

Thad: NOT COOL.

Thad: Seriously. WTF is WRONG with you????? My new memoir title is going to be TWIN TO A PSYCHOPATH.

Thad: And you made Sam shoot red wine out of her nose.

Thad: She says you owe her a new white sweater now.

When Freya suggested burning my phone, I hadn't taken her seriously. Upon closer inspection, however...it probably *is* my best option. I'll have to change my number, too. Would witness protection take me on for something like this? Because a whole new life doesn't sound half bad at the moment, and if I were Thad, I would definitely kill me.

To be fair, Thad immediately knew it was Freya who sent that message. So, I'm probably safe.

I take an extra-big gulp of coffee and scrub my hand over my face. Then I screenshot Thad's response to Freya and text it to her.

Me: Still thinking about that kiss last night. Also...what broke you?

Dots immediately appear on my screen, and despite how horrified I am, I catch myself smiling in anticipation. Because Freya might be terrifying, but she's never boring.

"Did something happen?" Mom asks, setting down the newspaper to give me her full attention.

"Um..." I'm distracted, one eye on my phone. How could I begin to describe the wonderful, weird, erotic, embarrassing events of last night? To my mother of all people? "Freya." I finally say. "Freya happened."

"Ah." She tries to hide her smile with a bite of toast, but I still see it. A flash of dimple and an amused glint in her brown eyes. She's still pretty, beautiful even, when she smiles like that. "I've always liked her."

"Yeah," I sigh, running my hand through my hair. "Me, too."

Mom laughs then, a quiet chuckle that has me doing a double take. There's an easiness to it. Like maybe she's starting to relax around me. A little bit.

"You did spend most of high school prancing around like a peacock trying to get her attention." Mom sips her coffee. It's not the most flattering picture of high-school-era me, but I can't be offended because it's absolutely true. "The calls I'd get from school about you two..." She shakes her head. "Every morning you'd go out for your run like you had the devil chasing after you. And every morning, I'd stand in the kitchen and watch *her* watching you out her bedroom window. Giving you all sorts of attention when you weren't looking."

I grin and settle back into my chair, suddenly enjoying this story. "Oh, really? Do tell."

Her smile turns soft. "Maybe you should ask *her*."

On cue, my phone dings, and my mom nods at it, silent permission to check my messages.

Sunshine: Kiss? What kiss? Ah, that's right. I'd forgotten.

I snort, scraping a hand down my jaw. The poor, unlucky fools she must have eviscerated with that attitude of hers.

Me: Guess I'll have to remind you then. Plans tonight? Helping out my mom around the house today.

Sunshine: I'm free. Helping B at the shop since she's hungover af, but I'm up for something low-key later.

Me: On it. See you tonight.

***

"What's going on?" Freya asks.

I'd been waiting in her parents' kitchen, having an afternoon cup of coffee with her mom, when Freya walked in from the garage only to stop short at the sight of me. Her brow draws down, her eyes narrowing as she watches me. Quickly, I shoot Mrs. Nilsen a smile and jump up to grab Freya's coat and purse and hang them on the coat rack. Freya kicks off a pair of red flats in the back hallway as I grab her hand and drag her toward the basement stairs.

"Thanks for the help today, Mrs. Nilsen," I say over my shoulder, and she waves me away with a smile. Was it a little awkward seeing her and Mr. Nilsen today, given what Mr. Nilsen walked in on last night? Nope. It was *super* awkward. However, they both seemed determined to put me at ease, so I'd let them.

"I told you, sweetheart," Mrs. Nilsen says, "call me Mary."

"Yes, ma'am," I say with a wink, and Freya rolls her eyes. From the basement, a series of giggles and shouts erupts.

"Um, I repeat: What's going on?" she asks, trying to peek around my shoulder down the stairs.

"I'm getting you in the Christmas spirit," I say. "Or is it Yule spirit for you? Solstice spirit?"

Freya's mouth quirks for a second. She's clearly pleased, though she's trying to hide it. "Either works for me," she says magnanimously.

I smile. It took some coordination—phone calls to Mrs. Nilsen, Bethany, and even Bethany's husband, Drew—but once the idea occurred to me, it was a boulder tumbling downhill. I had to roll with it. Rubbing my thumb over the back of her hand, I pull her the rest of the way down the stairs, where Bethany's kids are waiting for us, all grinning with mouthfuls of popcorn and candy. Andy, the littlest, jumps down from his spot next to Abi on the '70s floral couch and runs to Freya, Twizzlers clenched in his chubby fist.

"Auntie Freya!" he shouts, and Freya pulls her hand away from mine so she can crouch. Andy's arms wrap around her neck in an enthusiastic hug, and Freya squeezes him back.

"What are these yahoos doing here?" she asks, her gaze taking in the pizzas, bags of chips, and boxes of movie theater candy. Abi even helped me string up some Christmas lights and set up a hot cocoa station—complete with marshmallows, candy canes, whipped cream, and sprinkles—on an old card table where we used to play out Caves & Conquerors campaigns.

"Well," I grab the back of my neck, knowing I'm giving her a half-truth, "I figured after so much time away from your family, you'd want to see your niece and nephews, and what I planned for tonight was kid-friendly. So, I coordinated with Bethany and had Drew drop them off."

They are also—although I don't say this part out loud—there to keep things *friendly* instead of *frenzied* between Freya and me. Four perfect little cockblockers.

Don't get me wrong—I've accepted my fate. There is no way Freya and I are going to be *just* friends. And I'm looking forward to that. A lot. I'm simply trying to slow things down enough that I can prove to her we're more than just sexual chemistry. That we're friends too. Compatible. That deep down, she and I are made of the same stuff. Dark and dorky and broken but ultimately hopeful.

"We're watching a scary Christmas movie," Andy tells Freya with wide eyes, and she stands, ruffling his dark hair.

"Bruh, it's *not* scary," his older brother—Aiden?—says from a recliner that's older than me. (In seventh grade, I spilled half a can of root beer that's still embedded in that chair's stained upholstery.) "It's like a baby movie. You'll be fine."

Freya turns to me, her gray eyes hopeful. "It's not—"

"Yes!" Abi interrupts enthusiastically from the couch. She was quiet and moody when Drew dropped her off, giving her dad the cold shoulder when he said goodbye, but she's been friendly toward me. Probably because I'm not the one who grounded her into the next millennium. Or maybe because I held her hair back while she puked? Her voice grows big and dramatic as she sings out, "The Nightmare Before Christmas!"

"It *sounds* scary," Andy says, his nose wrinkling.

I wince, rethinking my plan. I know nothing about kids. I don't *dis*like them, but I'm an only child, and my mother's family wanted nothing to do with her once she got pregnant with me with no husband in sight. So, not only do I not have nieces or nephews, I didn't even have cousins growing up. Maybe this is a horrible idea and I'm condemning Bethany and Drew to weeks of Andy's nightmares and sleepless nights, which definitely *isn't* what I'm going for. But before I can walk the entire thing back, Freya sinks down to eye level with Andy again. She pulls his hand toward her mouth and takes a bite off his Twizzlers, making him laugh.

"Tell you what," she says around a mouthful of licorice. "Try it and see if you like it. And if at any point it feels *too* scary instead of *fun* scary, let me know, and Jeremy will take you upstairs to Grandma and Grandpa. Deal?"

Andy looks up at me, questioning, and I nod.

"Just say the word," I tell him.

"What word?" he asks, and Freya smiles.

"Just tell Jeremy if you want to go up by Grandma and Grandpa," she clarifies, and he takes a deep, fortifying breath, his little cheeks puffing out, before nodding. Brave boy.

Within minutes, the lights are out and I'm settling into the corner of the couch, Freya squeezed in next to me with Andy on her lap. He's happily munching on popcorn as the opening music begins, and Freya turns to pin me with a direct, no-bullshit stare.

"What?" I whisper.

"One: Thank you." She smiles, and my stomach somersaults. I'll take one of Freya's rare, hard-won smiles over a fake, dime-a-dozen smile any day. "Two..." Here she raises a single, dark eyebrow. "Using children as human shields?" she asks, tipping her head toward Andy. "Really? Hardly a clean fight."

I smile back. On the other end of the couch, Abi watches us, her expression curious, so I lean in close to Freya's ear, close enough that her dark hair skims my jaw and I'm surrounded by the scent of flowers and patchouli.

"You should keep in mind, Sunshine..." I run my nose along the curve of her ear and feel her suck in a sharp breath, "that I'm always, *always* willing to fight dirty where you're concerned."

Twenty-Two

FREYA

11 days until Christmas ...

"Still cold?"

I look up from the playing cards spread across the amoxicillin-pink carpet to find Jeremy watching me, his gaze on my hands as I try to rub some warmth into my numb toes.

"Mmhmm," I admit.

Before the admission has totally left my mouth, Jeremy is sweeping the cards into a pile—*Game over*—and pulling my feet onto his lap, his big hands taking over the task of coaxing some heat into my extremities.

For the second night in a row, he included Bethany's brood in our evening together. Like a little gang of undersized, eagle-eyed guardians. Tonight's adventure? Sledding. I'm shocked to admit it, but I've been enjoying the little hooligans. Abi and I have always been close, so I knew the time with her would be great. But Andy is sweet, all sincere gray eyes and elbow dimples, and even Aiden and August, with their YouTube bro culture, are growing on me. I don't necessarily appreciate the kids' role in slowing down my seduction plans, but after the years apart, it *is* nice getting to know them better.

Besides, spending time with them lets me feel like I'm doing *something* to lighten Bethany's load. I'm not holding out hope for Sister of the Year or anything—when I go back to Chicago in twelve days, I fully anticipate returning to our relationship of rare and random phone calls to coordinate birthday presents—but I might as well help while I'm here. Bethany is obviously overwhelmed, and while our relationship has been complicated, I don't want her to have an actual breakdown.

So, the time with Abi and the boys is fine, but these late-night visits from Jeremy? They're all about one thing: Mission Seduction.

"Wine, please." I hold out my hand, an imperious queen, and Jeremy hands the bottle over.

I consider him as I take a swig. Tonight, so far, is turning out a lot like last night. After we watched *The Nightmare Before Christmas* under the doting gazes of Bethany's children, Jeremy went home. Then, at bedtime, he showed up at my window with a bottle of wine and an old fantasy card game we loved as kids. We traded whispered insults as we battled—for old time's sake—then as the card game ended, we gravitated closer, until his fingertips dangled along the curve of my spine and played with the loose wisps of hair at my nape, his touch always light and steady. Always electrifying.

I watched his eyes taking me in, and I thought *This is it—it's finally happening*. And I leaned in and pressed my lips to his, drinking in the warm, masculine taste of him. He gave that involuntary shudder and pulled me closer, his fingers fastening onto my hips like anchors. Like he was never going to let me go. Then we kissed until I felt woozy and drugged. Until the heat between us flared from an ember to a five-alarm fire. At which point, he pulled away with a groan and snuck back out the window with a wink and a raspy, "See you tomorrow, Sunshine."

Tonight, though...tonight, I think I've got him.

After getting home from sledding, I changed into a pair of silky pajama shorts and a loose, off-the-shoulder T-shirt that reveals a lot more skin than I've exposed to Jeremy before. From the moment he climbed through the window tonight, I could feel his gaze eating me up. Especially my tattoos. As soon as I noticed the way his eyes kept dragging back to them, I swallowed my smile and carefully positioned myself so the soft fabric of my pj's fell away from my shoulder and hip, playing peek-a-boo with my ink. His fascination has been addictive. Every mistake he made during our card game made me feel like a goddess.

His hands, warm and firm, are surrounding my feet, and I wiggle free so I can crawl to him and straddle his lap. He's already hard, his grip desperate as he pulls me to him.

I run my hands through his hair, my need spiking as I trail my tongue up the column of his throat, breathing in the wine and spice scent of him.

"Is this ok?" I ask, nipping at his earlobe.

He half-laughs, half-growls as his fingertips bite into my ass, dragging me forward along his erection.

For as relaxed and go-with-the-flow as Jeremy usually is, he's not—I've been surprised to learn—afraid to take charge. I'm used to setting the pace with my partners, and my sensitive, Victorian-poet types aren't prone to manhandling. But every time Jeremy wraps his big hands around my hips or shoulders and positions me exactly the way he wants for those long, steamy kisses of his, I submit. It's ridiculous. *I'm* ridiculous. If Tim/Tom had tried to maneuver me around like a rag doll, I would have asserted control. Reminded him who was boss.

Getting to see this side of Jeremy, though...I suspect that aggression, that edge of dominance, is something he rarely shows to people. And those shadowy, hidden pockets—those secret corners of a person's psyche that rarely see the light of day—they're an obsession for me. Flecks of bright, golden truth in the inane gray gravel that people show publicly.

So, I find myself going soft around him, warm and pliant, when things turn passionate. I tell myself it's strategy, turning feminine and receptive to draw out the inner Viking I'm convinced he's hiding.

The fact that I enjoy it so much? Well, that's just a bonus.

"What part of me doesn't seem to be enjoying this, Sunshine?" he asks.

"Hmm..." My hands drift between us, down his chest, then his stomach. As soon as I get close to the hard bulge in his pants, however, he grabs my wrist with a hiss, stopping me even though it appears physically painful for him to do so. "The part of you that seems determined not to let us go past first base?" I suggest.

To prove my point, I balance myself on his shoulders and lift myself onto my knees so my breasts are just inches from his face, nothing between my puckered nipples and his warm breath but the thin cotton of my T-shirt. His eyes close, and his tongue shoots out to wet his lips. I know what I'm doing. Not to brag, but my tits are spectacular. They're always the highlight of The Sphere's burlesque shows. Right after my red lips, they're the thing Jeremy can't stop staring at, and judging by his dazed look, I might as well be hypnotizing him with strategically swirling pasties.

"I mean," I sit back so my weight is across his thighs, releasing him from the pull of my breasts in his face, "consent isn't only important for women to give to men. And you *are* kind of giving me mixed signals with your whole 'let's be friends but let's make out until we're on the brink of orgasm' thing. If you want me to stop—"

"Frey." His voice is gritty. Charged. My nipples pull tighter. "Don't you *dare* stop seducing me." I shift restlessly on his lap, and his hands graze my bare arms, pushing up the short sleeves of my shirt and exposing the sprawling tattoo that wraps around my right shoulder and down my arm. "Now." He clears his throat. "Tell me about this."

I love my shoulder tattoo. It looks innocuous to the untrained eye. All black ink, delicate and feminine and pretty. Flowers and herbs, twisted together and joined with the gossamer strands of a spider's web. But to a gardener, or any green witch worth her salt, it's anything but innocent.

"It's a witch's garden," I explain, then take his hand in mine and trace his fingers over the inked lines. "Hemlock." I drag his fingertip over the tiny flower buds. "Belladonna." Round, black berries, each ringed by a starburst of leaves. "Foxglove." Elongated blooms, like little trumpets. "Henbane." Five-pointed stars with dark centers.

"Poisons?" he asks. I let go of his hand, but he keeps tracing, his eyes intent on his task. "Is that how you see yourself?"

I shrug, not bothering to hide my shiver from the sweep of his fingers on my skin.

"One person's poison is another's medicine," I whisper. "In the wrong doses, these plants can be lethal, but used in the right way, they can provide relief. Comfort." His gaze shifts to my face then. Locks onto mine. I swallow before I can continue. "People want to see the world as good or evil. Black or white. But that's not how the world works, is it? We all have the capacity for good *and* evil. We're all both. Poison and cure. Hero and villain. Angel and demon."

The words fall between us, heavy in the silence, but Jeremy doesn't look away. Because as upbeat and easygoing as he's learned to become, he's always liked this side of me. The dark side. The part of me that's a little bit morbid. That never sees the glass as half full. That insists on seeing the world as it is, not as it makes people comfortable to see it.

It's why it was so devastating to lose him.

"And this?" His voice is thick, his hands gentle as he shifts me so I'm lying on my side, my legs sprawled across his lap. I prop my arm under my head like a pillow and watch Jeremy's face as his hand rides up the side of my thigh, pushing up my shorts and the thin lace of my boy-cut panties to expose my hip tattoo. Again, the ink is all black, but instead of poisonous plants, it features two giant chrysanthemums, my birth flower. And in between them lies a shaded scorpion, tail curved and ready to strike. I open my mouth to answer him, but before I can, he whispers, "Scorpio," his fingers already running along the endless curves of ink.

"Scorpio," I echo, my voice a whisper. "You remember that?"

He smiles as he continues to trace the tattoo. "I remember everything, Freya."

Twenty-Three

FREYA

10 days until Christmas...

Sam: You can never tell your brother I asked you this, but...how is the seduction going? (BTW I'm ALL Team Freya on this one. I've heard the Freya and Jeremy stories, and clearly there is some major tension there that needs resolving.)

I grin at the message from Thad's girlfriend and take a quick peek around the store. It's the afternoon slump, no customers, so I lean forward onto the counter, my thumbs already flying across my phone.

*Me: Some great make-out sessions. The first one was interrupted by my DAD. (Talk about high school flashbacks.) I think Jeremy knows resistance is futile, but he's putting up a valiant effort. He's been *using my sister's rug rats as human shields. Kid-friendly movie night. Sledding. Ha. As if some babysitting is going to best me...*

Seconds after I hit send, my phone dings with a reply.

Sam: LOL! Oh no! Poor Papa Mike! Well, keep me posted. I want DETAILS. I've always suspected there's more to Jeremy than that Mr. Nice Guy shtick...DETAILS, Frey.

Me: Fine. You big perv. See you in a couple days. Hopefully I have some DETAILS for you by then.

The shopkeeper's bell chimes merrily, and I slide my phone into my pocket, looking up to greet whoever entered. I stop short when I see a colorful, flowing skirt and hear a familiar jingle of bangle bracelets.

"D.G.?" I ask, straightening from my slouch against the counter.

"Freya Nilsen."

Mrs. Davis-Green, the sweet, soft-spoken language arts teacher who dragged me to my first stage crew meeting, stands in the doorway, her smile warm.

When I made my way through her classroom two decades ago, D.G. homed in on the loneliness behind my brash mouth and brasher fashion choices. I would have told her to get lost when she suggested I join stage crew, but she clearly had a fellow-artist's soul and she was just so kind, with her soulful brown eyes and thick-rimmed glasses.

Even I, at my absolute fifteen-year-old worst, could not say no to her.

By the time I graduated, she was more than just a teacher to me. She was a friend and mentor. We stayed in touch for a while, exchanging emails a few times a year, but like most of my friendships, this one, too, slipped away from me.

Her expression is cheerful and affectionate now—there's no anger or judgment—but as she wanders into the store, I'm acutely aware that it was me who let our correspondence die.

"It's great to see you," I say to D.G., "but shouldn't you be in school?"

D.G. laughs. "I always take a personal day before the holidays. The shops are too crazy during the weekends." She picks up trinkets as she goes, carefully inspecting each one. "Besides, I heard that my favorite student was back in town, and I wanted to pop in and say hi."

My face heats. In many ways, I'd been a great student, smart and driven, often a top performer in any given class. However, despite my stellar academics, my teachers usually remained wary of me. (Probably due to my flip-flopping between endlessly sparking debates and wielding an attitude of bored indifference.) The fact that D.G. was willing to push through my bravado and really see me? That she *liked* me? It meant a lot.

It still does.

We fall into easy chatter as D.G. shops. She's been keeping busy, stepping up as director of the local community theater during summer vacations and even writing some plays. I, on the other hand, have the uncomfortable realization that, even though it's been eight or nine years since we've been in touch, I don't have much new to report. Aside from burlesque, which I don't feel like talking about with my former teacher, my life looks remarkably the same.

As D.G. pays for the considerable pile of items that I carefully wrap in tissue paper and bag, she reaches across the counter and pats my arm, sending her bracelets clinking.

"Don't be a stranger, ok?" she asks. "If you want to grab lunch or coffee while you're in town, give me a call. My number is the same."

I nod, but I know I won't. As much as I love D.G., I don't want to bind myself to yet another relationship I know will fall by the wayside when I return to Chicago.

The door is still closing behind D.G. when Bethany runs into the shop from the workroom, clutching a fistful of white tulips in one hand and spiky globes of purple allium in the other. Her cheeks are flushed, her eyes shining with the near-panic that's always simmering under her surface.

"Freya!" she bursts out.

"Bethany!" I shout back, leaning back on my elbows against the counter.

"I need your help." She bites her lip. "Drew just texted, and his client's flight got cancelled, so he'll have to take him out to dinner again tonight." My stomach sinks like someone filled it with rocks and chucked it in the icy waters of Lake Michigan. "And it's the—"

"Fucking Christmas festival," I mutter, finishing her sentence.

Every year, Northview hosts a big downtown holiday event. Stores stay open late and offer elf-sized cups of hot cocoa with stale marshmallows. Santa's at the plaza next to the ice rink, which crawls with skaters. Mrs. Claus leads crafts. Portable fire pits dot the sidewalks, offering a place to warm your hands or make s'mores. It's cheery, wholesome fun, straight out of one of those goddamn TV Christmas romances Leo's obsessed with. And this year, Bethany helped organize it. She's been talking about it nonstop.

"You need me to watch the store?" I ask. Forget hot cocoa. My cup is going to be filled to the brim with mulled wine.

"No! It's going to be really busy. Like, *really* busy." She winces. "Mom and Dad are already planning to cover the store tonight while I help manage the festival. It's the kids. Drew was going to bring them. They come every year. It's tradition—"

"Fine." I roll my eyes. "I'll bring your demon spawn to the festival. Just don't blame me when I lose one of them."

"I'd be insulted, but I know that coming from you, 'demon spawn' is a compliment," Bethany retorts. I shrug. She's not wrong. "I've also set up help for you. So that you *don't* lose one of them. I texted Jeremy—"

"Of course, you did." I roll my eyes again, but it's not unexpected. Somehow, in the five days since we've been home, Jeremy has insinuated himself back into Honorary Nilsen status. To be fair, *I'm* the one hanging out with him every day. It's mostly my fault. But now Bethany just gave him yet another opportunity to spend time with me while her children chaperone. Perfect.

"Come on," Bethany says, her mood shifting now that I've agreed to her plan. "There are worse fates than spending time with Jeremy McHottie, who is very obviously crazy about—"

"One! You cannot call him Jeremy McHottie when you're sober. It's bad enough when you're drunk." I shake my head, but she just snorts, crossing her arms over her chest. "Two! Jeremy McHottie has been using your children as cockblockers to keep our relationship platonic." (Aside from the first-base-only make out sessions.) "So, yeah, Jeremy McHottie is fucking annoying."

Bethany lights up like a string of fresh-out-of-the-box Christmas lights. "Ooh, so he's been foiling your seduction plans?" She grins. "For whatever it's worth, he's totally into you. It's obvious. Why do you think he's holding out?"

I lean back against the counter, crossing my ankles. "I want a fling. He wants to date. Which is *not* going to happen."

"Um, why not?" Bethany's forehead wrinkles. "He's the total package, Frey. Have you seen him with Andy? The man is going to be a fantastic dad." *Oh gods.* Something in my chest short circuits, and I rub at my breastbone. Maybe it's heartburn. I've been drinking too much coffee to make up for my late nights with Jeremy. "He even likes the same nerdy shit as you and Thad."

"Maybe I'm not looking for the 'total package,'" I respond, complete with air quotes. "Maybe I'm just looking to get my rocks off."

"Jesus, Frey." Bethany's eyes sweep the shop to make sure it's empty. Then her voice drops to a whisper. "Does that even apply to women? 'Get your rocks off'? It seems—"

"Fine." My eyes narrow. "I'm looking to get my skittle diddled. To get my bottle popped. To get my cream churned—"

"Oh my god!" Bethany tries to cover her ears, but her hands are full of flowers. Instead, she dissolves into a laugh, and somehow, I find myself laughing with her. "All I'm saying is that you can do *all* of that, *and* you can date. Pro tip: They're not mutually exclusive."

I sigh. Maybe for Bethany they're not, but as I've established...I'm not Bethany. When Bethany met Drew's parents, they probably brought out their good china and measured her hips to ensure safe passage for their grandchildren. Me? Not so much. It's been ten years since the whole Ryan incident, but I learned a valuable lesson as I stood in the foyer of his parent's fancy house, his mother's lip curling as she took in my red lips and my dress, modest as it was, clinging to my curves. I may be a fantasy to a lot of men, but I'm not the type they commit to. I put my dreams of a happily-ever-after to rest a long time ago, and I have no interest in resurrecting them just so Jeremy "The Total Package" Kelly can bash them to bits.

We're playing *my* game, and it ends at Christmas.

Twenty-Four

JEREMY

"Mom is freaking the fuck oooooout," Abi croons next to me, her face splitting into a wicked grin. I glance around to make sure her brothers didn't hear her f-bomb, but Andy's across the small bonfire roasting a marshmallow with Freya, while Aiden and August are fencing with metal marshmallow-roasting sticks. I reach out and grab the sticks with one swift movement, and for a second it looks like they're about to protest. But when I raise my eyebrows—*Really?*—they give me sheepish grins and stick their hands in their pockets. They're not quite a year apart in age, twelve and eleven, and, according to Freya, it was August's rapid arrival after Aiden that pushed Bethany from high strung to manic.

"Why?" I ask Abi, handing the sticks off to a pair of teenagers. "It looks like everything's going really well."

Freya's eyes flick up to me, and my stomach gives an involuntary lurch. I've been waging a constant war with my inner caveman, who wants nothing less than to drag her off to a hotel room for the next ten days and make love to her until our entire floor is complaining about her screams of ecstasy. We would emerge for a few hours on Christmas morning to exchange gifts with family and nourish ourselves with holiday delicacies—because we would have burned *a lot* of calories—and then I'd take her back to my condo in Chicago and start all over again.

The fact that I'm pretty sure Freya would enthusiastically comply with this plan—right up until Christmas—doesn't make it any easier. So, I swallow the fluttering in my stomach and fall back on my new mantra, which crawls through my mind like a 24/7 news ticker: *Not a fuckboy.*

"I think it might be going *too* well," Freya explains, tipping her head toward the ice rink. "The line to see Santa is *long.*"

Abi nods and goes on tiptoe, leaning toward me so the hordes of small children around her can't hear. I dip my head.

"Mom hired a new Santa this year. She said she wanted to try something different to compete with the mall Santa in Appleton." Abi shrugs. "I guess it worked."

My attention shifts to the ice rink and the line that snakes around it. Children are crying, mothers and fathers are arguing, and all of them are obviously freezing, rubbing mittened hands together and bouncing from foot to foot trying to keep their circulation going. With a grimace, I turn back to Abi, keeping my voice low.

"Does Andy need to see Santa?" I ask.

She nods. "Oh, yeah. It's tradition. My mom doesn't like us going to the mall Santa because she prefers to support local businesses here in Northview when we can."

"Should we get in line?" I ask Freya.

Freya is holding Andy's mittens as she watches him lick sticky marshmallow from his chubby hands. He'd been nervous about roasting his own marshmallow, but Freya had urged him to try it and stayed at his side, ready to help. But no rescue had been necessary. Her mouth is curved into a small smile, but at my question, she turns to me and nods.

The first twenty minutes in line are ok. Aiden and August entertain themselves with some mild roughhousing. For a while, Abi joins them in several rounds of slapsies. Andy dances around the group, brimming with energy from roasted marshmallows and the promise of meeting Santa.

Freya stands shoulder to shoulder with me, and every time we shuffle forward in line, I swear she steps a little bit closer. When her bottom lip starts to quiver, I grin to myself and wrap an arm around her shoulders, hauling her into my side. She huddles in, seeking out my heat, and I unzip my down jacket and pull her flush against me. The cold air is getting in now, but it's totally worth it when her arms wrap around my torso inside my jacket and her face snuggles into my chest. I drop a kiss to the top of her head, take a moment to breathe in her flowery scent, and wrap my jacket around us both.

"You're not wearing a hat," I say, fitting her body more tightly against mine. Her curves mold into me, and I take a deep breath, willing my cock to behave since we're surrounded by approximately a million children, including her niece and nephews.

She tips her head back. "Vanity," she admits, teeth chattering. "I didn't want to ruin my waves."

"Well, they're very beautiful." I smile down at her, and she stares back. "Now that I've properly admired them, do you want my hat?"

"Auntie Freya, when do I get to see Santa?" Andy interrupts, tugging at the edges of her coat. His booted feet bounce back and forth. A sugar crash is coming. I can feel it. I just hope we make it to Santa before it hits.

"Soon," Freya tells him, not letting go of me, and he returns to dancing and skipping. Then Freya's nose wrinkles as she appears to consider my offer, and after a deep sigh, she reaches up and snatches the knit hat off my head, cramming it down over her own. I smile, even though my ears are immediately freezing, and wrap my coat tighter around us.

"Why are you smiling like that?" Freya asks, her voice suspicious.

I shrug. "I like seeing you wear something that belongs to me," I admit. And I do. It makes her look like mine, and it's doing nothing to suppress my inner caveman.

Freya rolls her eyes, but the corner of her lip twitches.

"So, when are you going to ask me out on a date?" she asks, then immediately clarifies, "Like a real date. Without adolescent chaperones?"

I sigh. I'd love nothing more than to take Freya on a real date. But if we go there right now, it's going to end up with us in bed. Or on the floor. Or on the couch. Or all three? *Dammit, Jeremy.* The point is that we'll have sex, and then she'll pigeonhole me. I know it because I know *her*.

I need more time. Time to show her what we could be. So, once again, I find myself chanting: *Not a fuckboy. Not a fuckboy. Not a fuckboy.*

"When you take back your ridiculous two-week rule," I tell her.

She pokes me in the side. "It's a ten-day rule now, mister."

I open my mouth to respond, but Andy's back again, tugging at Freya's coat.

"Auntie?" He bites at his lip.

"Yeah, squirt?" Freya pulls back from me to look down at him, and I resist the impulse to pull her back.

"I need to go potty."

Twenty-Five

FREYA

For the first time in my life, I experience something approaching hero worship for Bethany.

Jeremy stayed with the older kiddos so I could take Andy to the flower shop bathroom, and let's just say the trip has been...illuminating. While Andy takes care of business, I wander the shop, saying a quick hello to my mom and dad, who both wear huge smiles as they buzz around taking care of the influx of holiday customers. Christmas music is blaring (*cringe*) and poinsettias are flying off the shelves, along with the locally sourced candles, bath products, and Christmas ornaments Bethany stocked. It's a great night for business.

I've just circled back to the bathroom and am waiting for Andy to emerge when two women line up behind me. Judging by their overly excited whispers, the cold isn't the only thing responsible for their flushed cheeks, and I'm turning around to ask where this godforsaken festival is hiding the booze when I catch their conversation.

"Stone. Cold. Fox," the blonde whispers, drawing out *fox* suggestively. I lean closer to eavesdrop. Then she adds, "*Silver* fox."

"Fucking brilliant," her redheaded friend responds before burping quietly into her gloved hand. "Seriously, who wants to stand in line at the mall when you can stay in town and see *this* guy? Forget Father Christmas." She snorts. "I want to see *Daddy* Christmas."

Just as the two friends collapse into giggles, the bathroom door opens and Andy steps out, looking much more relaxed. That's when the pieces fall into place: Bethany's nerves over "trying something different" and finding a new Santa…the long line wrapping around the ice rink…the two friends' whispered conversation…

Bethany hired a hot Santa Claus.

Ok, I can admit it. I have severely underestimated my sister and her public relations skills. Sure, Bethany is overly controlling and, I suspect, on the fast track to a nervous breakdown. But hiring a hot Santa for the Northview Christmas festival? This move is legit bad ass. Nope, it's Bad Ass. Capital B. Capital A.

And as I take Andy's hand in mine and lead him back to the line, I'm already planning how to use it to my advantage.

***

The line is moving faster than I thought. By the time we make it back to our group, there are only three or four families in front of us. Jeremy welcomes us back with a smile so bright it makes my heart trip, but I ruthlessly ignore it. He opens his coat, a clear invitation for me to return to the warm cocoon of his body against mine, but instead I squish his hat unceremoniously onto his head and comb my waves with my fingers to combat my hat head. I dig into my purse for my lipstick and compact mirror. I can feel Jeremy's eyes on me, assessing, as I reapply and pop my lips.

"What's going on?" he asks, his eyes narrowed, just as the line shifts forward and Abi pipes up next to me.

"Um, *wow*." Her eyes go wide. "Santa is *hot*."

A silver fox who even a fifteen-year-old recognizes as a hottie? My heart accelerates with anticipation. Even the rousing, off-key rendition of "Jingle Bell Rock" sung by the middle-school choir can't bring me down. I shoot onto tiptoe and bend at the waist to look around the crowd, and that's when I spot him, sitting on a green velvet throne surrounded by white flocked Christmas trees and a pile of giant presents wrapped in silver and gold paper.

Hot Santa.

Instead of the traditional baggy jacket sagging around a bowl full of jelly, Hot Santa sports a sharp, maroon velvet suit that hugs a lean but muscular frame. His shirt is white and crisp, and a green-and-red plaid tie trails down his chest and over what I suspect is a six pack. His hair and beard are the customary snowy white, but his hair is a fashionable crew cut and his full beard is shaped to perfection. His cheekbones are high and sharp. No round, rosy cheeks here. Then, as I stare at him, his gaze slides away from the little girl on his lap, and for one magical Christmas moment, we make eye contact and his wide mouth quirks into a sexy grin.

Daddy Christmas, indeed.

"Did Santa Claus just make googly eyes at you?" Abi asks, her eyes round with holiday wonder. In response, I shrug out of my winter coat, scarf, and mittens and shove them into her arms. The cold air hits me like a slap, but I don't slow down, turning my back on Santa as I quickly undo the top three buttons of my black, scoop-necked Henley and plump my breasts in their push-up bra. Abi snorts out a disbelieving laugh, Andy bounces from foot to foot—"We're almost to *Santa*!"—and Jeremy gawks at me, his mouth slowly sliding open with dumbfounded shock.

"What are you *doing*?" he whispers, stepping closer, almost chest to chest. I have to crane my neck to meet his gaze. Bloody Viking.

"What does it *look* like I'm doing?" I whisper back, adjusting my breasts again because I like the way it makes Jeremy's eyes flare. With lust? With alarm? All of the above?

Jeremy stares down at me, and a vein on the side of his forehead starts to visibly pulse. I want to pump my arm in triumph, but I play it cool, lifting an eyebrow at him.

"Are you doing this to punish me?" he finally asks through gritted teeth.

Why, yes. Yes, I am. Enjoying it? Because I sure am.

I grab his coat and lean in, going up on my toes. The scent of his cologne does something goofy to my insides that I refuse to acknowledge.

"Wow. Not everything is about you, Mr. President of Narcissists Anonymous." He snorts, but I'm not done. "It's real simple. I'm going to go up there, sit on Hot Santa's lap, and tell him what I want for Christmas. Got it?"

My fingers release his coat just as the elf at the head of the line yells, "Next!"

It's not until I turn on my heel, my hand on Andy's back, that I allow myself to smile.

Santa's green velvet throne sits on a dais, and as Andy and I walk the three steps up to him, Hot Santa leans back, all masculine ease, and his eyes track me as I get closer. I urge Andy forward, and he jumps onto Santa's lap without pause, immediately launching into a long, meandering wish list. I stand close by, arms behind my back, and will myself not to shiver as I wait for the opportune moment to make my move. Just when I think I won't be able to stop my teeth from chattering, Andy ends his monologue with an endearing, "Please, please, *please*," and Hot Santa offers him a miniature candy cane as Andy slides off his lap.

And that's when I slide right on.

As I settle onto Hot Santa's lap, wiggling my butt on his hard thighs and wrapping an arm around his shoulders, I'm pleased to see his face, which is even more handsome up close, split into a wide grin. It's a nice smile, reaching all the way to clear, sky-blue eyes that crinkle in the corners.

This is *definitely* a Santa who makes a girl want to end up on the naughty list.

"Hey, Andy?" I don't take my eyes off Hot Santa as I speak. "Go back to Abi, ok? I need to talk to Santa for a minute."

He waits for Andy to toddle back down the dais in his clunky snow boots before giving me his full attention, his eyes twinkling merrily.

"I'm so sorry to bother you, Santa," I start, running my fingers down his silk tie. "You see, I have a little problem that I thought you could help me with. It has to do with a large, Viking-like man who's probably giving me a serious death glare right about now."

His smile doesn't falter as his eyes flick over my shoulder to the line of people trailing down the sidewalk.

"Black coat? Knit hat?" he asks, and I nod, sifting my fingers into the soft hair at his nape.

"That's the one. You see, he *claims* he wants to be just friends, but there's obviously more...chemistry between us than that." Fully aware that Jeremy is watching my every move, I shimmy forward, making sure my chest is on full display. Santa chuckles—I'm sure it looks to Jeremy like I just said something *hilarious*—and his arm curls around my hip. "Now, the way I see it"—I pause to bite my lip, and Hot Santa's eyes follow obediently—"this little talk we're having could really help me out. Because as much as the Viking wants to deny the chemistry between us, I don't think he'll appreciate watching me with another man. Especially one as handsome as you. It just might be enough to put him over the edge."

"Hmm, I see." He nods sagely, reaching up to stroke his beard. "That does sound like a conundrum. I hope you don't mind me saying so, but he sounds like a scrooge. He should be jumping at the chance for a romance with a beautiful young woman like you."

Ok, to be fair, Jeremy is definitely up for romance. *I'm* the one who's setting limits. But I don't think Santa needs to know the finer details. So instead, I focus on his scrooge comment.

I run my hand up the soft lapel of his suit, shaking my head sadly. "I'm afraid *I'm* the one who hasn't been in the Christmas spirit, Santa, and this whole 'We should just be friends' thing he's doing is *not* helping." Santa, on cue, runs his hand up my arm in one long stroke. It's difficult, but I somehow resist the impulse to peek at Jeremy. "I really think he just needs a little nudge—maybe a little friendly competition—to realize that we're missing out on an opportunity to have some...fun."

Santa's eyes flick over my shoulder, and his lips twitch into a merry smile. My only warning that we're no longer alone is the clatter of heavy footsteps as they pound up the dais. The hot flush of pride I feel at my victory is almost enough to thaw my frostbitten nipples.

"Excuse me," Jeremy's terse voice cuts in, and I give Santa a conspiratorial wink. He winks back. "Sorry about this whole—whatever this is. Freya, let's go."

WAR ON CHRISTMAS: A HOLIDAY ROMANCE

Jeremy is standing to my side, every line of his big body taut with irritation, but I'm careful to keep my eyes on Hot Santa.

"I'm not finished here," I reply curtly to Jeremy, then I run Hot Santa's tie through my fingers and lift my gaze to his, open and hopeful. (Honestly, it's a waste I didn't feel called to acting.) "Whaddya say, Santa? Are you free tomorrow night?"

"Oh, for fuck's sake," Jeremy growls next to me, and in a twinkling, his hands are wrapped around my upper arms and he's lifting me off Hot Santa's lap. I peek over my shoulder at Santa, giving him a triumphant grin and a thumbs-up, and Santa's droll mouth lifts on one side as he tips his head into a regal nod. I turn back to Jeremy, waiting for him to put me down, but he's braced his feet and is holding me suspended six inches off the ground so we're face to face.

I've pushed him too far. I can see that now. His nostrils are flared. His jaw is set. But as I dangle in midair, staring into Jeremy Kelly's scowling blue-green eyes, I realize that Whoops! I've Gone Too Far is my new favorite place.

"*You*," he grinds out, "are busy tomorrow night."

"I am?" I blink at him, all innocence, and the muscle in his jaw starts to tick dangerously.

"You are."

"Oh, I must have misread my schedule." I pronounce it "sheh-dule" like a proper British lady, and Jeremy closes his eyes and shakes his head. He's making a valiant effort not to throttle me. So, I do what I do and push harder. "Pray tell. What am I doing tomorrow night?"

His sigh is tortured, ripped from his depths against his will. "You are going on a date. With me."

"Mm..." I nod, appearing to consider this. "And will there be chaperones on this date?"

Jeremy's mouth twitches. "No."

"Then I accept."

Jeremy grunts, then I'm sliding down his body until my feet hit the ground, his eyes burning into mine the entire time. He wraps his hand around mine, like he thinks I might bolt, and turns to leave.

"Hold on a second," Santa interjects, leaning back in his plush, oversized chair. Jeremy and I both turn toward him obediently—he is Santa after all— and that jolly old elf's eyes are on mine as he continues. "If things fall through tomorrow night...I'll be at The County Line bar until ten. Stop by." He gives me a wink of his eye and then reaches down to the bucket at his feet and extends his hand toward me. "Don't forget your candy cane."

Twenty-Six

JEREMY

9 days until Christmas...

Me: Umm...not sure how to say this, but...I'm taking Freya out on a date tonight. Sorry, man. I know it breaks The Code. I just...well. You know better than anyone I've always had my head up my ass when it comes to Freya.

I stuff my phone back in my jacket pocket. Mom and I are standing in the backyard, watching a blazing fire fueled by a wheelbarrow full of Gary's old shit. Mostly dusty models of military ships, airplanes, and tanks that he filled the basement with. Their monetary value is negligible, and there's no point in donating them. So, into the fire they go.

It was my mom's idea, and I sure as hell wasn't going to stop her. Because this is cathartic as fuck. It took some finagling to wrestle the portable firepit out of the garage and into the snowy yard, but watching all Gary's favorite stuff go up in smoke? Worth it.

I bite the inside of my cheek as I wait for Thad's reply. It's hard to gauge how much he knows about what took place between Freya and me when we were teenagers. I never confided in him, but for all I know, Freya gave him all the gritty details just to watch him squirm.

"Did something happen at the festival last night?"

My mom stares me down from across the fire, one hand wrapped around her coffee mug. Her eyes are narrowed, and her mouth twists to the side with concern. I swallow.

"I, uh...I asked Freya out on a date." To give my hands something to do, I grab another model, a World War II airplane, and throw it into the flames. "I was just giving Thad a heads-up."

Mom's worry appears to melt, her mouth spreading into a wide smile that I've been seeing more and more often.

Gary being dead seems to agree with her.

"Oh, Jem, that's *good*," she says with enthusiasm. Then I sigh, and her smile falters. "Isn't it?"

I stare at her. Part of me could really, *really* use someone to confide in. Usually, my go-to person is Thad. But he, for obvious reasons, is out of the question. There's Wes from work, but he would think I'm out of my goddamn mind for saying no to a no-strings-attached fling with a smoke show like Freya. It's hard to admit, but my only available sounding board might be a fifty-four-year-old woman who also happens to be my mom.

Jesus Christ. I rack my brain for how to frame the situation in a way that won't be utterly traumatic for both of us.

"Freya...uh. Well, she doesn't want to stay in touch once the holidays are over. When we go back to Chicago, she wants to"—I hold my pointer fingers together and then tear them apart—"go our separate ways."

The concerned look is back on my mom's face. "But you've been spending so much time together."

"Yeah, well," I clear my throat. "I think she sees it as a necessary evil of being back in Northview. We're friends by default here, I guess."

"But you..." My mom slowly tips her head toward me as she throws a wooden tank into the firepit. "*You* want to stay friends." I nod, but her face folds into a confused scowl. "But wait—are you *just* friends? Because you also said you're going on a date." Her nose wrinkles. "Right?"

Which just about sums up how fucked up and confusing this entire situation is.

"She's just..." I groan and let my head sink into my hands. "I missed her." Missed doesn't seem big enough. I miss my king-size bed and my favorite coffee shop in Chicago. I miss the Italian beef from the sandwich shop on State Street that shut down a couple years ago. But none of those things ache like missing Freya. "At first, I thought we could be just friends, but..."

I'm thinking again about the sight of Freya wrapped around Santa Claus last night.

When Freya crawled onto his lap, her pretty hands running over his chest, my inner caveman won. I knew exactly what she was doing. A distant, logical part of my brain tried in vain to coach me: *She's playing you. Stay strong. Be strategic, Jeremy.* Unfortunately, it came in about as loud and clear as a broken, tinny speaker from half a mile away. Because every other part of me—my bones and guts and some ancient, animal part of me—stomped their feet and yelled, *Mine! Mine, mine, mine, mine, mine.* So, I'd marched up there like the caveman I am and bodily removed her from Santa's lap, torn between kissing her senseless and throwing her over my knee and spanking her luscious ass red.

I groan. I'm not inexperienced. I've dated my fair share of women, and I have *never* been the jealous type. Best friends with your ex? Cool. Mysterious text messages dinging through our dinner date? Whatever. Other men ogling you when we go out? Lucky me, having the prettiest woman in the room on my arm. I respect my partners and their autonomy. I'm a grown-ass adult who can control his emotions.

Until Freya decides to play me like a fucking fiddle.

"But..." my mom wades back into the conversation. "Now you want to be *more* than friends?"

My head jerks in a nod.

"So...isn't going on a date a good thing then?"

Before I can answer, my phone dings and I rush to grab it.

Thad: "The Code?" LOL. Dude. None of my beeswax. You're both consenting adults. (Right? She didn't coerce you into this, did she?)

I stare at my phone for a second, trying to decide if being expertly manipulated by my baser instincts counts as coercion. Probably not.

Me: Thanks for being cool about it. Looking forward to seeing you and Sam tomorrow.

As I set down my phone, I turn my attention back to my mom, who's busy breaking a bamboo fishing pole that belonged to Gary's dad over her knee. And I realize I have a whole new problem to deal with.

"So," I sigh. "Any ideas on where I can take a girl on a date these days?"

***

FREYA

Sam: OMG!!! Thad said you and Jeremy are going ON A DATE!!!!!!!!!!!!!!!!!!!!!!!!!!!!!!

Sam: Where are you going? What are you doing? What are you wearing?

Sam: DETAILS, FREYA!

"Why is your phone blowing up?" Bethany asks, her eyes tearing away from the arrangement she's working on to peek at the phone cradled in my hands.

She spent the morning tutoring me on her new, edgier floral style, which is largely based on contrasting textures and bursts of complementary colors. I was just helping her put together some table arrangements for a local company's holiday party tonight when my phone started chiming wildly on the over-sized butcher-block island where we're working.

"Hmm." I stare at my phone. *I* didn't tell Thad about the date, which means Jeremy must have. I contemplate lying to Bethany. She did, after all, go on that "Jeremy McHottie is the total package" diatribe yesterday. However, she also hired Hot Santa. My perception of her has shifted, and I decide to give her another chance. "It's Sam. Jeremy and I are going on a date tonight—*without* your children—and she's hitting me up for details."

"*I* want details," Bethany says, stabbing a small pine branch into her arrangement.

"I bet you do," I smirk. "Married for a million years…a gaggle of children always pulling you in ten different directions…*I'd* want to live vicariously through me too."

It's a gamble. A few years ago, this comment would have sent Bethany careening into a hissy fit. But things have been...well, they've been better during this visit home. Different. Don't get me wrong, Bethany is still having hissy fits, but so far, they haven't been directed at me. Late night wine and tarot readings...debating the merits of Jeremy McHottie...gossiping while I help at the store. For the first time, I almost feel on even footing with her. And it's only taken thirty-five years.

My comment is rewarded with a snort and an eye roll, and Bethany shoves some holly berries at me.

"I actually have *you* to thank for the date," I tell her, following her unspoken direction to add some red to my bouquet. "Jeremy refused to ask me on an official date until I got all flirty with Hot Santa last night. So...thanks."

Bethany grins, her cheeks pink.

"It was a little brilliant, right?" she asks. "Just a little?"

"A little?" I scoff. "Umm, that was straight-up inspired."

Her grin stretches into a wide, beaming smile of pride.

"Best turnout yet," she tells me. "The Christmas festival committee already asked me to lead operations for next year. And now *you*..." she draws out the word, "get to work your wiles on Jeremy tonight. A real date without my children around. Sounds promising."

I try to keep my expression neutral, eyes on my flowers. But even surrounded by evergreen boughs and bombarded by the classic Christmas music drifting in from the shop, I can't totally swallow my smile. There are still nine days left until Christmas, and I'm pretty sure this date is going to push Team Seduction over the finish line.

Twenty-seven

JEREMY

Not a fuckboy. Not a fuckboy. Not a fuckboy.

I keep up a steady stream of small talk as I drive us to dinner, but in my head, I'm clinging to the mantra like a drowning man to a hunk of wood. If I know one thing going into tonight's date, it's that I cannot let Freya take the reins like she did last night. She's going to come out swinging, and her single goal will be pushing me onto the fast track to fuckboy territory.

And it's the one place I refuse to go with her.

Since our first—well, technically *second* kiss—I've been trying to show Freya that we can be more than just the sexual chemistry between us. We can talk about our lives—our families and jobs and friends. We can hang out with her niece and nephews and exchange bewildered looks at the slang we're now too ancient to understand. (Side note: What the actual fuck is a "yeet"?)

I already know what Freya would say to all of this. *It'll be different when we get back to Chicago. We are too different. Straight-laced architect, artsy theater manager, blah blah blah.* She doesn't get it. I don't want someone who slides seamlessly into my old life in Chicago. If that's what I was looking for, a dozen women I've dated could have done just that. What I want—what I *need*—is someone who will shake me out of the safety zone of mediocrity I've created for myself.

I'd been feeling lost.

But since reconnecting with Freya almost a week ago, I feel...well, *not* lost. Sure, this week has been hard. It's not fun spending day after day sorting through Gary's stuff, every greasy-collared shirt and scuffed up pair of boots a reminder of the man who looms over my childhood like some mythological monster. It's awkward trying to find a way forward with a mother I no longer know. But despite all of that, I'm hopeful. Being home again, having Freya back in my life...it's been like a quest, an epic C&C campaign, where I'm required to face the past I've been running from since I was eighteen. And if I can find the pieces of me that I lost and put myself back together, maybe I can finally move forward. Maybe I can find a way to love my job again. Have a real relationship. Take some risks.

And Freya is at the heart of it. The key to this whole, crazy adventure. Because as infuriating and terrifying as she is, she's always seen me, the *real* me, and accepted me without reservation. The dorky parts. The scared parts. The angry parts. The only time she rejects me is when she knows I'm faking it. When I become the "Abercrombie & Fitch zombie" version of me. Is she ruthless? Hell yeah, she is. But only when she's holding me accountable. Only when she's pushing me to be true to myself.

And that's exactly what I need. Which is why I cannot fuck this up tonight.

WAR ON CHRISTMAS: A HOLIDAY ROMANCE

I eye Freya nervously as I park in front of the Galway Inn. It's a new addition since I left Northview, but according to my mom, it's the most popular place in town. An Americanized version of an Irish inn and pub that serves traditional Irish food with Irish and British drinks on tap. It's busy, but I made reservations, so I'm not worried about getting a table.

I am, however, worried about whatever Freya is wearing under her black dress coat.

The coat itself is cute, accentuating her tiny waist and extending to her knees. But what's underneath is going to destroy me. I could tell from the sassy way she sashayed into the living room when I picked her up. She'd already buttoned it up to her neck so I wouldn't see what's coming.

Whatever she's wearing tonight is her secret weapon in this little war we're waging.

I lead her inside, my hand stretched across the small of her back, and the hostess, a twenty-something redhead with a spray of freckles across her cheeks, appears harried as she shows us to our booth.

A four-piece band plays Irish folk tunes from a small, makeshift stage in the corner, background music for the countless conversations taking place throughout the bar and restaurant. The smell of alcohol and shepherd's pie permeates the air, and a fire crackles in the fireplace. It's warm and welcoming, a cozy contrast to the snow and cold outdoors.

Whatever Freya has on under that coat, I'm safe here. There are too many people around for things to get out of hand. Yet.

Then Freya spins around to face me, dropping her coat to her elbows.

Did I say I was safe? Scratch that.

I am fucked.

Freya's wearing a vintage-style dress that hugs her generous breasts and the slender curve of her waist before flaring out over her hips. It's a deep, classic red that matches her lips, and it cuts into a deep V filled by a scoop of black and white polka-dot fabric. Panels in the skirt echo the flirty polka dots, and a short row of shiny black buttons runs down each side of her ribs. The colors make her pale skin—her slender arms, her neck, her perfectly made-up face— glow, opalescent. Her black hair falls in elegant waves down her shoulders, and the dress is sleeveless, exposing the swirling lines of her tattoo on her upper right arm. Her flowers and herbs. Poison and medicine.

Without the ink, she'd be a flawless illusion. A 1940s lady heading out on the town. With the ink, she's downright dangerous. None of this is a happy accident. Freya's a devil who carefully curated every detail of this look, right down to her shoes, to break me.

My heart pounds, the sound a dull thudding in my ears, like I used to hear when I had to make a big play in football. When the pressure was on and every eye in the stadium was on me. *Thud. Thud. THUD.* Down by six with thirty seconds left, fourth and goal.

Not a fuckboy. Not a fuckboy. Not a fuckboy.

***

FREYA

I try not to smirk as I hand my coat to Jeremy and he fumbles it to the floor. He's usually so at ease in his body that it's impossible not to feel a little thrill at how obviously affected he is by my outfit. He doesn't even take his eyes off me as he bends to pick up my coat. The entire time, he stares at me like I'm an all-you-can-eat buffet and he doesn't know where to start.

Which is exactly where I want him.

The problem is that there are too many layers to Jeremy and me. We're that neglected chain necklace that's been lying in the bottom of a jewelry box, links tangled and locked into a jumbled ball with no hope of being unraveled. The formative years of childhood friendship, of laughter and secrets and fun. The transition from middle to high school, with our growing attraction to one another. High school, with its bitter rivalry that still felt better than not having Jeremy in my life at all. Then...seventeen years of nothing. Seventeen years of wondering, but never knowing, what he was doing.

And now...

Now all I want is to take this opportunity to simplify things. I want Jeremy to finally make sense to me. We're single adults who are obviously attracted to each other. We just need to enjoy each other while it lasts—nine days, to be precise—and go back to our very different lives.

Then there's Jeremy, who—in true infuriating Jeremy fashion—seems intent on complicating things at every turn. If we're a knotted chain, he's grabbing each end and pulling, tightening the snarls into an irredeemable cluster fuck. Hot, steamy, teenage-style make-out sessions. Late-night wine and games, complete with trash talk. Movie nights and sledding and festivals with Bethany's kids. Earnest, heartfelt confessions about his complicated relationship with his mom.

It's messy. And maybe popular, captain-of-the-football-team, I-shoot-rainbows-out-of-my-ass Jeremy can do messy and come out unscathed, but it's never worked out for me. It's much easier (and less painful) to keep my expectations realistic. Whatever game Jeremy's playing isn't going to lead anywhere but disappointment.

Which is why I worked so hard to get my look exactly right for this date. And not just my look. I used every weapon at my disposal. I scoured *Hope & Stardust*'s archives for every seductive morsel I could find. I made a batch of their sexy sugar scrub and exfoliated every inch of my body, my skin soaking up the scents of rose, patchouli, and ylang-ylang. I even have a hunk of carnelian, good for passion and sexual energy, tucked away in my purse.

It's time to get things back on track.

Jeremy swallows. I can see him trying to collect himself. Trying to regain control. He looks good tonight. It's not the same kind of transformation I underwent, but his date-night look offers me a glimpse of who he is in Chicago, fashionable but understated. His black chinos and white button down with a camel-colored jacket are simple. It's an outfit any of my typical beaus might wear. Jeremy, however, fills it out differently, his shoulders and thighs stretching against the fabric, a reminder of how big he is. How powerful. Powerful enough to hold me suspended off the ground last night while he demanded I go on this date with him. The reminder gives me a sudden urge to fan myself, but I ignore it.

I need to stay sharp.

He reaches to hang my coat on the hook behind me, his eyes never leaving mine, and as his arms fall, he grips my hips, anchoring me in place.

"Sunshine…I've never wanted anyone like I want you right now." His voice is low and deep, and at his words, my entire body tightens. My nipples pebble, and heat takes root deep in my belly. "But let's be clear. No matter how amazing you look—and you look *incredible*—I'm damned if I'm going to be your fuckboy."

I smirk, grabbing the lapels of his coat and pulling him closer.

"You're damned either way," I tell him. "But at least fuckboys get to *fuck*."

I draw the word out, long and dirty, and his nostrils flare. The background noise—the band's slow, hypnotic rendition of "My Wild Irish Rose," the clink of silverware, the hum of voices—fades. There's him, his face hard and his pulse beating heavily at the base of his throat, and there's me.

His fingers tighten on my hips.

"I'm not one of those simpering man-boys who let you lead them around by the dick. And *when* I fuck you,"—his voice in my ear is all gravel and grit and promise, and the rough edges of it send a delicious shiver from my nape to my tailbone—"I'm going to teach you some manners."

I hear his words with my ears, but I *feel* them in my core, reveling in the heat unfurling there. When I stand on tiptoe, pressing my chest to his, I'm relieved to feel the hard press of his erection against me. At least I'm not the only one getting turned on by this conversation.

"Aww, do you talk to all the girls like this?" I breathe. "Or am I special?"

His laugh is strangled, like he's in pain. "Never doubt, Frey, that you are the only one who can drive me this far out of my goddamn mind." He pulls back, so he can meet my eye. "You know you've always been special."

His expression is serious, his gaze direct, and I fight the urge to clear my throat. Because he's not just talking about our chemistry, about that throb of electricity always simmering below the surface of our interactions. He's talking about the other stuff too. The whispered conversations. The dark-humor jokes he'd only make to me. The unabashed nerdiness of our two-hour debate about the most recent Star Wars trilogy. He's talking about all of it, and I don't want to hear it.

"You know what else is special?" My smile is too bright, but I push on, desperate to wrestle the conversation where I want it to go. "These *arms*." My hands slide from his chest to his biceps, and I give them a hard squeeze.

But instead of looking flattered, like Tim/Tom would, Jeremy rolls his eyes and eases himself away from me.

I laugh and give his chest a soft push, like it was *my* idea to put some space between us, but he just shakes his head and mutters something that sounds, if I'm not mistaken, like, "Chicken shit."

I can't be sure, though. Because at that exact moment, the restaurant fills with a piercing shriek, followed by a long, high-pitched, "Oh my gawd! It's Jeremy Kelly!"

And the next thing I know, Tiffany Ebner is wrapped around my date.

TWENTY-EIGHT

JEREMY

Clearly, unbeknownst to me, I did something royally awful that made me the flashing-red target of karmic retribution. Because I've just been thrust into whatever circle of hell makes Tiffany Ebner magically appear in the middle of my first date with Freya.

Fan-fucking-tastic.

I puff out a breath, trying to get the strands of Tiffany's long brown hair out of my mouth, and plant my hands on her shoulders, pushing her gently away from me. She's already babbling—"Oh my gawd!"..."So long"..."Where have you *been*?"..."It's been *forever*"—but I'm not listening. I'm watching Freya, whose red lips are pinched and tense. Fuck. I want to turn to Freya and assure her that I didn't know Tiffany would be here, but Tiffany is already trying to wriggle closer for another enthusiastic hug. I keep my arms braced, blocking her from clinging to me, and try to smooth over the situation. Fast.

"Hey, Tiffany. It's good to see you," I lie. "But if you'll excuse me—"

"It's so good to see you, too!" she squeals, trying to throw her arms around my neck.

I duck out of them and step in closer to Freya, holding a stiff arm out to prevent Tiffany from coming too close.

"Becky is here too!" Tiffany enthuses, slapping my shoulder with every word. Then she turns and yells over her shoulder, "Hey, Becky! Look who I ran into!"

"Oh, that's great," I reply, but in my head, all I can think is, *Jesus Christ, please just go away.*

Next to me, Freya mutters a dry, "Of all the gin joints in all the towns in all the world..." and despite the stress of the situation, I find myself chuckling with relief. If Freya is cracking jokes, she's probably not going to hex my testicles. Maybe.

"And who is this?" Tiffany turns her smile to Freya, who arches an incredulous eyebrow back at her. "Sister? Cousin? Coworker?"

Tiffany and I dated for six months. It was twenty years ago, but she knows very well I don't have a sister. I roll my eyes, already sick of the smell of Tiffany's bullshit. She's trying to look friendly, but her dark-blue eyes narrow at Freya, and her hand clutches my arm tighter. It's been less than thirty seconds since Tiffany Ebner came crashing into this date, and I can already remember what I disliked so much about dating her. The double layers to everything she does—what she *wants* people to see, and the hidden subtext. I didn't like it at fifteen, and I sure as hell don't like it now.

I shake Tiffany's hand off my forearm and start to make introductions. "You remember—"

"Freya Nilsen!" Becky Floyd, Tiffany's faithful sidekick, has no problem recognizing Freya. She bounces up to Tiffany's side, carefully balancing a full-to-overflowing pint glass in each hand.

Becky has always been the better half of their dynamic duo. Whereas Tiffany was—and I suspect still *is*—cool and calculating, Becky was warm and friendly, always the first to welcome a new kid to class or check in with you during a bad day.

She hands off a pint glass to Tiffany but never takes her eyes off Freya, looking her up and down. "Girl, you look amazing. Like, ah-mazing!"

Tiffany's jaw opens and closes like a fish gasping in air, desperate for it to be water. She's still sputtering, her eyes fixed on Freya, as Becky studies the three of us and smiles with understanding.

"Oh, shit. You two are on a date," she pieces together. Her hand shoots to Tiffany's elbow, and my stomach unclenches when I realize she's going to drag Tiffany away and put a stop to this nightmare. Thank Christ. I always did like Becky. "It was good to see you, Jeremy. Freya. Maybe—"

"You're on a date with Freaky Freya?" Tiffany sputters, interrupting Becky and ripping her elbow out of her grasp. "But you two *hate* each other."

Her words land like shrapnel, and a moment of silence ensues as I absorb each tiny sting. Next to me, Freya goes rigid at her old moniker, and in response, I feel myself drawing up to my full height. There's no missing the malice in Tiffany's voice or in her curled lip. She's every inch the bully she used to be.

I'm shifting myself between her and Freya, physically blocking off Freya with my body, when Becky erupts into a loud guffaw.

"Hate each other?" Becky snorts, then takes a long pull from her drink. "Tiff, you didn't start the whole Freaky Freya thing because they *hated* each other. You started it because you caught him ogling her in the lunch line that day she wore those cut-off shorts and fishnets." She throws a grin at Freya and me. "They've *always* had a thing for each other. Why do you think he dumped you as soon as he heard you call her that stupid name?"

My chest tightens, and instinctively, I reach back, grabbing Freya's hand. Becky just casually dropped a handful of bombshells like they were common fucking knowledge, and I'm stuck standing in the wreckage as they explode around me.

I knew Freya had a rough time in high school. I wasn't dumb. I knew about the Freaky Freya nickname. But I didn't hear it often. The first time I heard it was from Tiffany, and I broke up with her almost immediately afterwards. She was the most popular girl in our grade, and she'd used her considerable social influence to punch down at Freya. *My* Freya. It was gross. But I never knew that Tiffany had *started* it. That she'd started it because of jealousy. Because of *me*.

Three and a half years of high school race through my memory. Three and a half years of whispers and innuendos and snickering behind Freya's back. And I didn't even hear the worst of it. My new friends—my *popular* friends—knew I was protective of Freya in my own weird way. After all, Thad was my best friend, and Freya was his twin sister. Sure, *I* could argue with her endlessly and tease her into dozens of trips to the principal's office, but it was always in good fun. And nobody else better do it.

But if my friends shielded me, what did Freya endure that I don't even know about?

Tiffany, Becky, the entire fucking bar...they cease to exist. I turn my back on them, so I'm facing Freya, her body trapped between me and the tabletop. I'm reeling, my stomach churning with a sticky, overwhelming guilt, and I cup her face in my hands, tipping her eyes up to mine. Freya's gaze is steady and cool.

"I didn't know, Frey," I say softly, my words only for her. Two minutes ago, we were all games, sparring for the upper hand in this labyrinth of friendship and attraction. Now, all I want between us is honesty. I want to fall on my knees, bury my head into the softness of her, and beg her forgiveness. I need her to understand how sorry I am for my part, however unintentional, in what happened to her. "I didn't know Tiffany was behind all that stuff. I know you and I had our differences, but I was *never*—"

"Shut up and listen to me." Her red lips barely move as she talks, and her hands are on my chest, pulling me close. I go willingly, fitting my body to hers, my thigh sliding between her legs. Behind me, Becky lets out a long, low wolf whistle. "Two options. One: Pretend we're mature grownups, tell Tiffany to get lost, and have our date as planned."

"Or..." I prompt. Because for the life of me, I cannot fathom a second option.

Freya, it turns out, has a better imagination than me. "Two: Invite these two to join us, then you fawn all over me like I'm goddamn Gal Gadot, complete with Wonder Woman costume, until Tiffany's so jealous she *literally* barfs."

I choke on a laugh and cover it up with a cough. Even though I'm thoroughly sick of Tiffany and her mean-girl antics, I've always kept things civil with exes.

"Um..." I run my hand up and down Freya's back. "Doesn't it seem pathetic enough that she even still cares? I mean, shouldn't we be the bigger—"

"She bedazzled 'Freaky Freya' onto a giant pair of granny panties and taped them to my locker during gym class," Freya hisses at me, her eyes sparkling with the thirst for vengeance.

And just like that, I'm all in. Fuck the high road.

"Let's do this, Sunshine."

Twenty-Nine

FREYA

I've always believed in the powers of my own evil genius, and tonight...tonight just proves how very right I was. Because right now, I'm curled into Jeremy Kelly's side, his big, muscular arm draped over my shoulders, and he's staring at me like he wants to rip off my clothes and have his wicked way with me on our tabletop.

And Tiffany Ebner looks positively green with envy.

Look. I get it. I'm a grown-ass woman, and the mature, empowered thing to do would be to move on. Enjoy my nice date with Jeremy McHottie and let bygones be bygones. This little ruse to make Tiffany jealous is petty as fuck, and it should be beneath me.

Except...I'm enjoying every fucking minute.

"So, I heard a rumor about you..." Becky, who's been delightful, leans across the table with a cheeky grin, her dimple flashing. My memories of her mostly involve being lab partners in chemistry and her excitement when I helped her pull an A both semesters. She's still petite and blonde, but the sparse, wiry frame she had as a teenager has softened and rounded, and she's traded her low-rise jeans and crop tops for leggings, an oversized sweater, and boots.

"Don't believe everything you hear," I caution her, then grin back. "But it's probably true."

Jeremy, who's showing an admirable commitment to his role, appears to barely be listening to the conversation. Ever since we sat down, he's been plastered to my side, his hands roving over my curves as we talked over drinks and dinner. *Possessive*—that's what he's been. Fingertips trailing down my arm. Soft kisses dropping along my neck. His hand teasing along my thighs, playing with the edge of my skirt. He even started a game of feeding each other, each of us offering bites of our meal to the other.

If I didn't know he was playing, I would have melted into a puddle on the floor before dessert ever arrived. But if I were a puddle, I couldn't enjoy the way Tiffany is glaring daggers at me. And I'm really, *really* enjoying it.

"Well..." Becky looks over either shoulder to be sure nobody else can hear. Then she leans even closer. "Last year, Jacob Fontaine and Amy Tahlier got married. You remember Jacob, right?" I nod. Jacob was a year ahead of us and played Kenickie in *Grease* our junior year. He didn't have the charisma to pull off Kenickie, but he'd been quick to joke with the stage crew. I'd liked him. "So, his buddies took him for this epic trip to Chicago for his bachelor party. And while they were there, they saw a burlesque show..."

I start for a moment, my shoulder jumping under Jeremy's hand.

A rumor...a bachelor party...a burlesque show...

I'd known being recognized was a possibility, but between my stage name and the costumes and makeup, the possibility had seemed small. And for years, I'd been right.

Until tonight, apparently.

I brace myself, waiting for a rush of embarrassment or fear. Anticipating the itchy, pinprick crawl of guilt beneath my skin. Instead, all I feel is a soft swell of amusement, a laugh I swallow and hide behind a mysterious smile.

Next to me, Jeremy goes still.

"Hmm..." I hum into my pint glass as I sip my Guinness. "And..."

But before Becky can continue, Jeremy, who is suddenly paying *a lot* of attention to the conversation, interjects.

"At The Sphere Theater?" he asks. Becky nods, and he squeezes my hand under the table as he adds, "I caught one of their shows just a couple weeks ago. It was brilliant."

He doesn't offer the fact that I'm The Sphere's theater manager. He's leaving that up to me. It's sweet. It also shows that he does *not* see what's coming.

"Um, the guys said it was amazing," Becky confides, watching me closely. "They also said that the star of the show looked like a dead ringer for Northview's own...Freya Nilsen."

The table goes still. Dead still. Jeremy's fingers, which had been flirting with the sensitive skin along my knee, stop. The breath I'd just inhaled stops. Across the booth, Tiffany's fingers drumming on the tabletop stop.

Jeremy blinks, obviously trying to hide his shock. After all, if he was really my doting boyfriend, he would already know I'm the main attraction of The Sphere's burlesque shows. But underneath the table, his fingers grip my knee a little tighter, and I don't miss the way his pupils dilate or how his body next to mine goes rigid.

Men, in my experience, typically handle this revelation in one of two ways. One: They are threatened. Sure, they might enjoy watching my performance as a casual observer, but it's not behavior they expect or desire from their partner. Two: They are turned on. They *want* to be with the woman who everyone in the room is fantasizing about.

I can't tell which response Jeremy is having. He's tense, every muscle in his body hard and unyielding as the truth rocks through his body like a silent bombshell, but beyond that…

I bring my hand up and cup the back of Jeremy's head, pulling our faces together so Becky and Tiffany can't hear us. "Does it bother you?" I breathe.

Jeremy gives his head a tiny shake, and his fingers on my knee start moving again, soft, sensual strokes that make me want to clamp my thighs together at the rush of warmth between my legs. But I keep my muscles soft, allowing the exquisite torture of his touch. "I bet you're amazing, Frey."

His head dips, and his lips are on mine, warm and sweet and possessive. I don't bother lying to myself that it's for Tiffany's sake when I kiss him back, my mouth opening to welcome the taste of him, the tangle of his tongue with mine. His arm pulls me closer, molding me into him. Every touch, every action he takes, says one thing: *Mine*. And for a moment, I let myself believe it. I let myself get lost in the fantasy. That I'm his.

And, of course, Tiffany chooses that exact moment to find her annoying, shrieky voice. "You're a *stripper*?"

If I thought there was something wrong with being a stripper, I would find Tiffany's words offensive.

Unfortunately for Tiffany, I don't.

I would just ignore her, but Jeremy stiffens. And *not* in a sexy way. I have approximately 3.2 seconds to defuse this situation before he detonates.

Don't get me wrong—part of me is wildly curious to see Jeremy lose his shit at Tiffany. But even I have limits to my pettiness. I put my hand on his arm, an unspoken signal for him to let me handle it, and luckily, he listens. I turn to Tiffany with a corn-syrupy-sweet smile.

"Oh, sweetie." I trail my hand up Jeremy's arm, making sure she sees it. "Unfortunately, I just do the shows for fun. A hobby." Tiffany scoffs, and I add, "I would make *so* much more money as a stripper."

Becky laughs. Tiffany scowls. Jeremy slides out of the booth and pulls me with him, my hand clasped tightly in his as we stand.

"Becky." Jeremy turns to her. "It was really nice to see you. Tiffany..." He turns to his ex, who's glaring at us both. "You owe Freya an apology. For both high school and the way you just talked to her. I hope that someday you're a big enough person to do it." He takes a deep breath. "And on that note, *I* owe *you* an apology."

Now *I'm* glaring at him too. Why is he apologizing to Tiffany? His eyes, that breathtaking shade of blue-green, rise to mine, and his thumb trails up the skin of my inner wrist. He's addressing her, but his attention is on me.

"It was always her, Tiffany." He shrugs oh-so-casually, like he just reminded us of the weather forecast or a sale at the supermarket. Not like those four little words—*It was always her*—just reframed everything I thought I knew about our relationship. "I suspect you knew that," he says to her, eyes still on me.

Becky, who's leaning forward in the booth, her head propped on her hand, nods. "*I* knew it," she whispers.

Jeremy clears his throat. "Yeah, well. It wasn't fair to you, and for that...well, I'm sorry. But..." He starts edging away from the table, his hand on my waist guiding me to follow. "I'm going to go dance with this gorgeous date of mine now, and when we get back, Freya and I would like some privacy."

My head is reeling, and I don't know if the responsibility lies with the two pints of Guinness I drank or Jeremy's words. Probably both. I wait until he's pulled me into his arms and we're swaying to the music before planting a hand on his chest, grounding myself in the soft cotton of his shirt and the steady *thump-thump-thump* of his heart beneath my palm.

I blink, trying to fight through the fray of emotions bombarding me. The warm, satisfied glow of finally getting back at Tiffany Ebner. The blaring alarms that have my palms sweating. *Danger! Danger! Danger!* The incessant pull I feel toward Jeremy, red hot and pleasant, even as our bodies are pressed together. I should focus on that heat, that sharp bite of attraction. That's where I want him. It's where I'm comfortable. It's where a no-strings-attached, nine-day holiday fling resides. Which is my goal. Obviously.

I lean back in his arms to say something flippant and flirty. Something to deflect from the way the spicy scent of his cologne makes my heart flip-flop and flutter.

So, of course, what comes out is, "It was always me, huh?"

His mouth quirks into a lopsided grin. "Always, Sunshine."

THIRTY

JEREMY

I don't know if my little confession is the right move strategically. And I don't care.

I don't have it in me to play right now. Maybe it was seeing Tiffany and finally understanding my unwitting role in Freya's bullying. Maybe it was the hour of being squeezed next to Freya in that booth, her "ruse" the perfect cover for me to touch and kiss and adore her the way I've always wanted to. Maybe it's the way she's looking at me now, her gray eyes open and soft. Vulnerable.

The song ends, and our feet stop moving, but I keep her next to me, my hand at the small of her back splaying wide and pulling her closer. She can't run away. She can outright reject me, and I'll respect her wishes. She can make one of her snide "Only nine days left" remarks. She can laugh in my face. But she's not running away this time. She needs to look me in the eye and decide how to respond to the truth. Because it *is* the truth, no matter how hard we've both tried to run from it: It's always, *always* been her.

She licks her red lips, and my brow furrows with confusion when she reaches up and slides her fingers along the top of her dress, grazing the pale curve of her breast with her fingertips. Then she pulls out two gold plastic cards like some kind of erotic magic trick and holds one up for me.

"I'm staying here tonight. At the inn. Room 204."

It's a hotel key. It's a motherfucking hotel key. I stare at it stupidly, wondering how on earth this Christmas miracle came to be. Then I remember. Freya stopping at the front desk earlier on her way to the bathroom. Her back had been to me, and all I'd been able to focus on were the seams running up the back of her stockings, over her shapely calves and under the edge of her skirt. I thought she'd just been torturing me with the sight of her legs, but all the while, she'd been setting the ultimate gambit into motion.

Checkmate.

"Thank you for dinner," she says, then stands on tiptoe to press her lips to my cheek. "And for what you did with Tiffany. It was a long time ago, but..." Her grin turns wicked. "It still felt pretty fucking amazing."

"Freya, I—" Her fingers press to my lips, stopping the apology that wants to tumble out. She shakes her head and presses the plastic hotel key into my hand.

"Room 204. No pressure. If you decide not to join me, I'll have Bethany pick me up tomorrow." Then she turns away, pausing only long enough to peek at me over her shoulder. "But I hope you do."

***

My heart beats triple time as I take the elevator to the second floor. An older couple, wrinkled and snowy-haired, rides with me, hands clasped. I keep my eyes lowered, wondering if they can hear the frantic, tripping rhythm of my pulse, like I'm off to my own execution instead of on my way to get laid. But I can't shake the suspicion that sex with Freya might have more in common with facing my own death than with a casual tumble in the sheets. Because I know, deep down, that I'm not walking out of here the same person.

I knew we'd get here. I accepted a while ago that it was inevitable, and the moment she slid that hotel key out of her dress, I knew my little game of keeping things "friendly" was over. Kaput. Finished. Aside from the fact that I don't have it in me to pass this up—I just don't—there's a real possibility that rejecting her invitation might put an end to her seduction. She might feel like she put all her cards on the table and decide to fold. Which is *not* what I want.

She's waiting for me when I open the door, leaning back in an upholstered chair, legs crossed. The lights are dim, but there's a fire burning in the fireplace, the flames casting shadows over each of her delicate features. She's perfection. A fantasy come to life.

And I'm hers. Just like that. I'm hers in a way that—crazy or not—survived almost twenty years apart. Hers in a way that's woven into me, as immutable as my height or eye color or the shape of my nose. I'm not in this for a nine-day fling. I'm in it for keeps.

Which means I'm not playing by her rules.

I know what she's expecting. I know because I know *her*. This sexy, confident, grown-up Freya—a Freya who's not afraid to take center stage—is orchestrating this scene flawlessly. She's framed herself in the center of the room, her gray gaze watching me as I close the door with a quiet *click*. She's still, silent. A siren who doesn't even need to sing to reel me in. She knows that every molecule in my body is begging to give in to her gravitational pull. And I want to. I want to sink to my knees before her, a humble devotee. I want to slide her skirt up the soft, smooth skin of her thighs and spread her legs and worship her with my mouth and fingers and tongue. I want to give her pleasure like a mortal gives a goddess sacred offerings, wholeheartedly and fearfully, with no guarantees of anything in return. I want to kiss and lick and fuck her to every orgasm I've denied her over the past five days, every shudder and moan she bestows on me a holy relic I'll carry with me for the rest of my days.

I can't give her what she wants, though. I have to give her what she needs.

I lean back against the door and crook my finger at her. "Come here, Freya."

One dark eyebrow jerks upward in surprise. *You dare to command me, you frail, foolish man?* I smile, widen my stance, and point at the space between my feet. *Right here.*

For a second, we stare each other down, nothing breaking the silence but the hiss of the fire. Then Freya gets to her feet and crosses the room gracefully, her high heels silent on the carpeted floor. I knew she'd cave. My Freya is a curious creature, and someone who insists on being treated as her equal? That, I'm sure, is a novelty she can't resist.

She stops directly before me, close enough for me to feel her heat. Close enough to make my head spin with her flowers-and-patchouli scent. Her hands are behind her back, the gesture demure and obedient, but her eyes flash silver.

"I'm here...Asshat."

"Only took you twenty years," I quip, trailing the back of my finger along her silken cheek.

WAR ON CHRISTMAS: A HOLIDAY ROMANCE

Her hands, those gorgeous, fine-boned hands, run restlessly up and down my chest, dropping a little further down with every pass. To my abs. My hips. I'm already hard—have been since the moment I walked in and saw her lounging in that chair, waiting for me—but this time when her fingertips graze my cock over my pants, I don't pull her hand away. She pauses for a second, peeks up at me through her long lashes, and bites back a smile before returning to her ministrations with single-minded focus, like she's committing the size and shape of me to memory. Every graze, every press, every pass of her fingers over my length fills me with heat, and I don't even try to hide my reaction to her touch. My breath skipping. My heart pounding.

I love watching her. I love the sexy way she bites her lip as she studies me, discovering the strokes that make me grunt and squirm under her fingers. I love the flush that creeps up her chest, staining her pale skin a warm, glowing pink. I love her smile of triumph when she cups my balls through my pants and I can't hold back a loud, low groan. I rasp out a laugh and tip her head back, my mouth falling to hers for a hard, fast kiss before I pull back.

"Do you still think I hate you?" I ask, my lips nibbling along her throat and jaw.

She snorts. "Umm...ever heard of a hate fuck?"

"Pretty sure that's not what's happening here," I say. I hold her still for a long, slow kiss, and she opens those forbidden-fruit lips for me immediately, no hesitation. The moment my tongue touches hers, all bets are off. It's like the taste of her, chocolatey hops and salt, is the spark that finally sets fire to the tension simmering between us.

"Speak for yourself," she gasps, and I chuckle against her lips between kisses.

"You don't hate me, Sunshine." If her kisses are driving me wild, her hands are driving me *insane*. My hips start pressing forward, seeking out the pressure and friction of her fingers, and I need to stop. Now.

"I don't?" she asks. My hand drifts down to the soft curve of her breast, and she arches her back, pushing herself into me. "Please mansplain some more."

Fuck, I love that sassy mouth of hers. I pick her up, cradling her in my arms, and stride across the room.

"Do you have any clue how many times I've fantasized about spanking that perfect ass of yours?" My hand palms her bottom through her skirt, and she squirms against me.

"See, you *do* get hate fucking." She pats my cheek. "You were always so smart."

God help me.

When we get to the bed, I let Freya's body slide down mine, enjoying every moment of friction. "You're about one smart-ass comment away from ending up over my knee."

She gives me an evil smile. "Promises, promises."

Fuck. Strategy, Jeremy. Strategy.

"Slow down there, Sunshine." I spin her so her back is pressed to my chest, and we're both facing the fire. I keep one hand on her hip, pulling her into me, and rest the other on her breastbone, delighting in the way her heartbeat races under my palm. "Don't you think we should save *something* for the second date?"

She rocks against me, little rolling movements that rub the upper curve of her ass against my cock, and my fingers seek out her breast, dipping inside the neckline of her dress to massage her hard nipple. She whimpers, and I press my lips to her hair, wrapping my arm around her waist to give her more support.

And still, she can't seem to stop that mouth of hers.

"Who said anything about a second date?"

THIRTY-ONE

FREYA

It's not that I don't realize when I'm pushing people's buttons. It's that I *enjoy* pushing people's buttons. So, I'm not totally surprised when Jeremy is suddenly sitting on the edge of the bed and, as promised, he has me turned over his knees, staring at the plush carpet.

Here I am, back in the land of Whoops! I've Gone Too Far, my new favorite tourist destination.

Then Jeremy's big, calloused hand is sliding my skirt up the back of my legs, the material brushing pleasantly along the sensitive skin of my thighs, and Too Far feels more like Just Right. My skirt swishes up, and for the barest moment, Jeremy freezes. He can't see my face, so I allow myself a grin, knowing *exactly* what tripped him up.

"Fuck," he exhales. "A garter belt?" His fingertips trail upwards again, past the tops of my black silk stockings and onto the bare skin just under my bottom, and I can't suppress a little shiver. "Are you trying to kill me?"

"Not gonna lie. There are moments when the idea has merit." I wiggle, giving my booty a little shake. The air on my skin is cool, but it's no match for the rush of heat between my legs. "Do you think I'm going to strangle you with my garter belt? There are worse ways to go, I guess. That would be—"

Thwack!

It's light and playful. There's no sting to it. However, there's no denying the sizzle of dominance in his touch, even now as he soothes and calms my bottom.

For the first time in my sexual history, I'm definitely not in charge. He's not going to let me walk all over him like my Tim/Toms. Jeremy may play nice with everybody else, but with me, he's not going to cede control out of some misplaced urge to be polite or gentlemanly. This is the boy who wrestled me to the ground and tickle-tortured me until I peed myself when I stole all the Reese's peanut butter cups from his Halloween candy. He's never been afraid to challenge me.

And I really, *really* like it.

"Up," he says with one more quick slap to my ass, and I scramble to obey. I sway for a moment as the blood rushes from my head, and he reaches out to steady me. Once I've found my sea legs, he leans back on his hands. His eyes, shadowed in the low light, hold mine. "Now take off that dress and let me see you."

My breath catches, and the heat between my thighs has me squirming with anticipation. When I was younger and less experienced, I felt fear in these moments. Vulnerable and exposed. Now this moment of exposure—this unveiling—is when I feel *powerful*. Because when I'm dropping my costume to the stage, piece by piece, *I'm* not the one being revealed at all. Not really. For every inch of skin I expose, the people watching expose so much more. Desire. Passion. Longing. Envy. Fear.

And I like it. Crave it even.

Just like that, I'm on stage, calculating each movement to entice. I keep my gaze on Jeremy and step between his spread legs, turning my back to him and pulling my hair to the side to expose my neck.

"Unzip me?"

He leans in, his warm lips grazing my neck and shoulders as his hands float along my back, finding my zipper. Every touch, every point of contact, is fire. The sound of the zipper is deafening as it slides downward, each tiny metal tooth releasing its grip to reveal a little more of me. Once the zipper is down, his hands skate up and down my arms, his head dropping to place a soft kiss on my tattooed shoulder before he leans back.

I spin to face him, lowering my eyes in a show of false modesty, my lashes tickling my cheeks. I love this part of sex. The *playing*. The teasing. The performance. I shimmy my shoulders and hips, and with a swish, the dress falls to a pile at my feet.

It's only when I hear Jeremy's deep, ragged inhale that I allow myself to peek up. To take in the color staining his cheekbones. The stranglehold his hands have on the sheets. The obvious bulge straining at his pants.

And I want to push. I want to push him until that considerable—and *annoying*—self-control he's exerted over the past week snaps like a twig.

Because I'm living for every tiny falsehood I can flake away from his polished exterior. Because I know that underneath that happy, agreeable façade—the side he shows everyone else—there's a Jeremy who is every bit as dark and needy as I am.

There's a Jeremy who wanted to fuck me against my bedroom wall and didn't care that my parents were just down the hallway. There's a Jeremy who wanted to shake me until my teeth rattled when I crawled all over Hot Santa last night. There's a Jeremy who wants to tell his boss to go fuck himself when he demands that Jeremy take clients out for a round of golf. And there's a Jeremy who wants to roar with grief over his mother's betrayal. There's a Jeremy who is jealous and resentful and scared. A Jeremy who nobody knows about. Except me.

That is the Jeremy I want. And *that* is the Jeremy I'm determined to get.

Slowly, I bring my hands up to cup my breasts over the black lace of my bra, feeling the weight and shape of them before plucking at my hardened nipples. It sends a shot of heat deep into my core, and I sigh into the sensation, letting my head tip to the side. I do it again, massaging and pinching, but before I can make another noise, Jeremy lunges and hauls me onto his lap, my legs straddling his waist. I'm on my knees looking down at him, and he reaches behind me to unclip my bra with one deft twist, freeing my breasts mere inches from his face.

"Damn, Sunshine," he breathes, reverent, and then he doesn't say anything at all. Then his mouth is too busy with long, deep kisses as his hands explore my body, his strong fingers taking in every inch of me from my neck and shoulders to my legs.

For several breathless minutes, I'm the sole focus of his considerable concentration as he studies me with the same rapt focus he used to apply to a drawing he was particularly engrossed with. No sigh, no shiver, no breath goes unnoticed. When his fingers graze the back of my knee and I give a laughing yelp, he smiles against my lips and moves on. When his touch floats below the curve of my ass and my hips give a jerk, he repeats the motion until I'm moaning into his mouth, my hips rolling needily against his erection. My body is a puzzle he's solving with ruthless precision until we're both shaking and my hands are tugging at his clothes, desperate to have him as naked—or nearly naked—as me.

I give a frustrated moan when I can't pull his jacket over his shoulders, and Jeremy spins us so I'm kneeling on the bed and he's standing, facing me. He shrugs out of his coat, then we're kissing again, my hands tangling with his as we both rush to unbutton his shirt. Because we're really doing this. We're finally, *finally*—

"What the actual fuck, Asshat?" I snap.

I pull back and scowl, grabbing his white shirt and pulling it open so hard the final few buttons fly off like bullets. Because underneath it, plastered to his grown-up, muscular torso, is a familiar dark-gray T-shirt with gold writing.

Dave Matthews Band, Summer 2005.

I smack a hand into his shoulder and receive a deep chuckle in return.

"I just—" he begins, but he's interrupted by me viciously yanking the neckline of his shirt as I try to rip it in two. He laughs harder.

"This *fucking* shirt," I mutter, giving another jerk, but it's like the damn thing is made of chainmail, not sixteen-year-old cotton.

"I just knew you would put so much—Jesus, Frey"—he tries to bat my hands away—"*effort* into what you wore tonight," he says, eyes dancing even as he's getting bounced around by my efforts to destroy his shirt. "And I wanted to…wear something…that would be equally…" He chuckles again, not even attempting to hide his glee at my reaction. "Sentimental."

I lean forward and clamp the neck of the shirt between my teeth. I just need to get a tear *started* and then I can—

"Are you trying to *chew* my shirt off, you harpy?"

We're sparring now, Jeremy laughing uncontrollably as I sputter and gasp, wrenching at his shirt with all my might. When it fails to give, I growl and land one more smack on Jeremy's shoulder before sinking onto my heels, the soft, white cloud of a comforter embracing me.

"Why are you such an *asshole*?"

Now that I'm not in his face, he peels the shirt off and throws it to the ground. "I'm not an asshole." He leans down to remove his footwear, then his pants follow, revealing thickly muscled thighs. "I just really, *really* love—" And there go his boxer briefs, leaving his erection on full display. He wraps a hand around it and gives himself a long, slow stroke. "—driving you out of your mind."

I lick my lips. He's an impressive sight, big and toned, but my head is still buzzing with annoyance. Well, *screaming* with annoyance. He climbs onto the mattress, grinning when I lean back on my hands and scurry away from him toward the head of the bed. He follows, pinning me beneath him, and I sink under the weight of his body.

Gods, he feels good.

My limbs wrap around his, moving restlessly against the prickle of his hairy arms and legs.

"I fucking hate you," I whisper.

"No you don't." He dips his head and sucks my nipple into his mouth, flicking it with his tongue, and my hips try to shoot off the mattress.

"This is definitely a hate fuck."

"Nope." He leans back for a moment and considers what I'm still wearing—high heels, stockings, garter belt, panties—and raises one thick golden eyebrow. Then, before I know what he's going to do, he grabs the top of my panties and tears them straight down the middle before tugging them off and throwing them behind him. It's the exclamation point on my own failed attempt to rip that cursed T-shirt. *Ass.* "I'll buy you new ones," he promises. "As a Yule present." He slides a hand up my leg from calf to hip. "But these stockings are staying."

"Have I mentioned that I hate you?" My hands are on his shoulders, massaging and kneading. Pulling him closer.

"Not true." His mouth is on my breasts now, teasing and sucking. "And it's not nice to lie, Frey."

"What can I say? Sometimes the truth hurts." I reach down, wanting to feel his cock. I want to feel the hard length of him in my hands, skin to skin, nothing between us. But he holds me down and drops lower, out of reach, his kisses trailing down my stomach.

"*Not* the truth." He's between my legs now, spreading them wide and dropping one on either side of his broad shoulders. I can feel his breath on me, warm and intoxicating, and I start to squirm. He looks up at me and winks.

"Oh, I definitely hate you," I assure him, grabbing his hair. He chuckles, even as he lowers his head and runs his tongue along me in one long, firm stroke that leaves me panting.

"Fuck, you taste good," he mutters, pausing long enough to suck gently at my clit before returning to the topic at hand. "If you hate me so much, then why are you going to *beg* me to fuck you?"

I laugh, trying to sound way more confident than I'm feeling. It comes out more like a gasp. "Not going to happen."

"Hmm," he hums against my pussy. "We'll see."

And with a final smile, Jeremy immerses himself in discovering me with his mouth, growling with appreciation when my hands tighten in his hair and I pull him closer. He's bold and unembarrassed in his explorations, trying out different strokes and pressures with lips and tongue. Within minutes, I feel like a code he's cracked that he can read at will, and I hate it.

I hate how I'm melting, completely taken over by heat and wanting. I hate how my legs are trembling. I hate the desperate, needy sounds I'm making in the back of my throat. I hate how I can feel something cracking inside me, a tiny fissure that looks almost imperceptible from the outside but hints at something gaping and huge beneath the surface.

But mostly I hate how empty I feel without him inside of me.

Because while Jeremy has been more than generous with his mouth, he's been holding out with his hands. He's been using them to cup my bottom, tipping me to the angle he wants, or reaching up to massage my breasts, pinching and rolling my nipples. He's even skated a fingertip around my clit and played with the sensitive folds around my entrance. But no matter how much I roll and tilt my hips toward his fingers, he won't put them *inside* me.

A particularly clever swirl of his tongue leaves me teetering on the edge, but when I lift my hips, trying to get that final bit of friction to topple me over, he pulls back, chuckling when I give his hair a frustrated tug. Then he's kissing his way back up my body until his forehead is pressed to mine and I can feel his cock pressed to my core. *Yes.* I squirm, and he kisses me long and slow, letting me taste myself on his tongue.

"What do you want, Sunshine? Say it."

I'm hollowed out. Wanting. He's *right there*, the length of him rubbing against my slick heat, but every time I shimmy, trying to position myself to take him, he pins me with his hips.

"Tell me what you want."

His voice is bossy, but his hands are gentle in my hair, his kisses soft. My hands slide from his shoulders to the round muscles of his ass, and I press him closer, silently signaling where I want him. But he pulls back.

"What. Do. You. Want?"

He's circling his hips now, tiny, nudging movements that press the head of his cock directly against my clit. I'm so close. The heat is gathering deep in my belly, hot and electric, and my head hums. I grab his face between my hands and stare at him, *willing* him to give me what I want.

But still he denies me.

His tongue is in my mouth, and I hate how much I love tasting myself on him. How I can't get enough of it. But goddamn it, I don't *want* to give him this. I stay silent, beseeching him with tiny thrusts of my hips, but he pulls back from the kiss and stares down at me, his eyes full of promise.

"Tell me what you want, Freya, or I swear to you I will meet my maker with the worst case of blue balls this world has ever seen before I fuck you."

He means it. He may have waved the white flag when it comes to us having sex, but he's determined to take some ground of his own. I can tell from the set of his jaw that he will burn this battleground to ashes before he steps down.

"Fine." My hands are back on his buttocks, kneading and pushing. "I want your cock...please."

My tone leaves much to be desired, but Jeremy relents, the tension easing from his shoulders as he drops a kiss to my forehead. "Look at those nice manners."

I tweak his nipple, earning me a laugh, then he tortures me with slow, gentle strokes of his cock along my core while we quickly check in. Birth control? IUD. Testing? Clear. By the time the blunt head of his cock is coaxing me open, I'm biting my lip, my hips moving against him of their own accord. I feel splintered, fractured, on the edge of shattering. Jeremy, on the other hand, is calm, his smile beautiful as he drops his forehead to mine.

"It's just you and me, Frey." He nuzzles my neck, weaving his fingers through mine as he begins to sink into me. "You and me."

I moan into the sensation of him filling me, and he slows, giving my body a chance to adjust to the pressure of him. The stretch. It's hot and torturous and the tiniest bit uncomfortable, but in the best possible way. When that final inch slides home, my pelvis cradles his, and his body gives that familiar, involuntary twitch.

And something behind my breastbone heats.

It grows warm and heavy, *too* heavy, and for a second I can't breathe. Because *this*—whatever it is—is finally happening. Jeremy's head is burrowed into my neck, my legs wrapped around his waist, and he's moving, so slow and steady and tender it makes that thing in my chest *ache*. It's precious and fragile and frightening, and it's balanced on a precipice, a terrifying edge, and I need something to distract me from the breathtaking hurt of it. So, I tighten my legs, the heels of my shoes digging into Jeremy's ass, and breathe into his ear.

"More."

He obeys, thrusting harder, faster, my hips rolling up to meet his, and the pressure is building, the heat too much. I'm gasping for breath—and so is he—but every time I'm close to falling, every time my body begins to tense and prepare for release, he eases back, his thrusts shallow. And every time he does it, I moan with frustration and grab at his shoulders, his hair, his face, and demand, over and over again, "More."

And he gives it to me. Every time. More force, more speed, more *him*. He gives me more until the world has narrowed to us. Just us. Just me and him, his eyes on mine as our bodies work feverishly to erase the final blurry boundaries between us, as if we move fast enough and hard enough, he'll be able to sink into me for good and we'll stop being Jeremy and Freya, and we'll be…just *us*. No single version of us. Best friends. Rivals. Friends with benefits. We're all of them, all the infinite, individual points of our lives that have led to this single moment, sweating and aching and reaching on this hotel bed.

"Freya." His voice breaks as he says my name, his hands shaking as they cup my face, and just like that I come apart. My back arches. My moans turn to screams. His arms tighten around me, pulling me close—but still not close enough—and he breathes my name as he comes. "Freya. Freya. Freya."

And somewhere, beyond the dizzying waves of heat and pleasure, I think to myself that it sounds like an oath. A prayer. A vow.

THIRTY-TWO

JEREMY

8 days until Christmas...

"Where's the Dave Matthews shirt, Sunshine?"

I'm wearing nothing but my pants, hands on my hips, as I pull myself to my full height and shoot a (hopefully) intimidating glower at Freya. Freya, of course, doesn't look the slightest bit intimidated.

"I don't know what you're talking about," she says coolly, sipping coffee from our room-service breakfast and returning her attention to her phone.

The fuck she doesn't.

I sigh as I pull on my white button-down, which is missing half its buttons, but it's all for show. The truth is I'd sacrifice every shirt I own for the night—and morning—I had with Freya. Hell, I'm just happy she's still here.

Because last night was...intense. Hot and sexy and satisfying, but also...really fucking intense. Sure, I made some confessions last night, but there's still a lot unsaid between Freya and me. She knows I want to see where this thing between us could go, but she doesn't know how keenly I ache for it. How clearly I can see the life we'd build together back in Chicago. There's a future there for us. I just need to convince her to *try*, and I suspect that all my longing—all the things I haven't said out loud—came through loud and clear in our lovemaking. I can play her games, the banter and the battles of will. Hell, I *love* her games. But my body...my body can't lie to her.

I'd been afraid to fall asleep, half expecting her to make a break for it in the middle of the night. But when I peeled my eyes open this morning, still feeling sated and a little drunk from the combination of sex and sleeping with Freya in my arms all night, she was still here, already up and dressed. Her waves were gone, due to a late-night shower for two, but her red lips and winged eyeliner were in place.

Clearly, she'd cared enough about the Dave Matthews shirt prank to get up early. I need to give her *some* grief about it, or I'll disappoint her.

"Look at this," I pout, standing in front of Freya and turning to the side as I flap the buttonless bottom of my shirt. It flops open to reveal my abs. (Abs that Freya spent a solid ten minutes licking last night). "And now you're going to send me out in public without an undershirt?"

Freya arches an eyebrow. "Ask my panties how much they care about your shirts."

Ah, the panties...I smirk, then press a kiss to the top of Freya's head and sink into the chair opposite her, our empty breakfast dishes littering the small table between us.

"But think of all the memories behind that shirt," I argue. *Don't you want to show that shirt to our grandkids someday?* But I like my balls attached to my body, so I keep *that* comment to myself. Freya snorts as I grab the last slice of sourdough toast and take a bite.

"Now let's get going," Freya says, then drains her coffee. "Check-out is in ten minutes." I groan and reach out to grab her wrist. I want to pull her onto my lap and stay in this inn until New Year's, living on room service and orgasms. But she slides out of my reach and gives me a happy smile. An alarming smile. "Thad and Sam are home."

***

"How did they get into town so early?" I grimace, pulling at my shirt collar as I eye Thad's orange Honda Civic parked next to us in the Nilsen's driveway. Bethany's SUV is parked in the street.

"Early start," Freya says. "They wanted to get here in time for kickoff."

Kickoff. Packers game. Starting in—I check the dashboard clock—approximately forty-five minutes.

Shit.

I get out of the car and walk around the front to open Freya's door for her. "Well, out you go." I flash her a smile and gesture for her to get out. "I'm going to run home quick and freshen—"

Her fingers fasten around my wrist like a vice as she climbs out.

"Oh, no. No, no, no, no, no." She shakes her head, limp hair swishing. "You think you're going to send me in there for my own personal walk of shame while you go home and 'freshen up' and come back looking like some kind of all-American golden boy? Fuck. No."

"Frey..." I'm whining, tugging against her hold as she pulls me to the front door. "This is awkward. You know what's worse than a walk of shame? A *parade* of shame. Nobody wants to—"

My pleading is interrupted by the front door of the Nilsen's house bursting open. Thad and Sam tumble out shouting a chorus of "Freya sandwich!" and then descend on Freya and squeeze her between them, Freya squealing in protest and trying to push them away.

Thad, in jeans and a thermal shirt, looks a lot like a male version of his twin, with the same dark hair and classic features but with their mother's light-blue eyes. A total goofball, he's worn his hair in every style imaginable. Long. Buzzed. A mohawk most of his sophomore year of college. Today, he's sporting an undercut with the long top pulled into a bun and just enough scruff to call it a beard.

Sam, who insists on being called "fun-size," is petite, not even reaching Thad's shoulders. Her brown hair is tied back into a short, spiky ponytail, and her face scrunches up with glee as she squeezes into Freya.

I smile, taking in the sight. Freya has mentioned that she and Sam get along, but it's different seeing it. And I'm happy for Thad. He and Freya are close—*twin* close—and not everyone is excited about their partner having that kind of connection with someone else. The kind of bond where Thad would drop everything and drive to Chicago at a moment's notice if Freya needed him, and vice versa. Clearly, Sam has figured out that the only way to love one Nilsen twin is to love them both.

I take one step back. And another.

"Well, since you're...occupied...with your sandwich...I'm just going to run next door and—"

"He's getting away!" Freya shrieks, pointing at me.

The next thing I hear is Sam yelling, "Jeremy sandwich!" and then I'm surrounded by all *three* of them, a mass of writhing, tangled arms and bodies pressing into me.

"I need to—*oof*—go change—"

"Ooh," Sam trills, grinning up at me. "Somebody pulled an all-nighter."

"Gross," Thad moans. His mouth twists with disgust, and I want to die of shame right there on the Nilsen's front porch with its garlands and oversized Christmas wreath. They can put the wreath on my casket to commemorate the exact moment of my death.

"What's gross?" Bethany sticks her head out the front door, and the Jeremy sandwich breaks up. I draw in a long, shuddering breath, and she smiles at me. "Oh, hey, Jeremy."

I give Bethany a nod. Because I can't speak around the taste of bile and guilt.

"Jeremy and Freya," Sam croons, reaching out to tickle my rib and make me squirm. "Walk of shaaa-aaaame."

Bethany smirks and reaches out to fist bump Freya. "Nice."

And now I'm blushing.

"Like I said..." I try one more time, even though I've accepted that the universe hates me and all my efforts are doomed. "I need to go home and change—"

"You're not going anywhere." Freya's hand clamps onto my bicep. "Thad, can Jeremy borrow a shirt? His is missing some buttons." *Shoot me now.* "I just need to throw on some panties."

And I'm dead.

Judging by Thad's groan and dramatic gagging noises, he won't be far behind.

THIRTY-THREE

FREYA

My rules for uncomplicated, no-strings-attached sex are lying around me in tatters, blown to smithereens by the surreal circumstances of said sex happening with Jeremy Asshat Kelly.

Rule #1: Don't talk about anything too personal. *Kaboom!*

Rule #2: Once the date is done, it's done. *Bam!*

Rule #3: No meeting each other's families. *Kablooey!*

Because it's Sunday evening, and we're crowded around my parents' dining room table, Jeremy seated to my right wearing Thad's *The Empire Strikes Back* T-shirt. And since the Good Twin does *not* have Jeremy's Thor-like physique, the T-shirt looks in danger of ripping every time Jeremy lifts a forkful of my mom's spaghetti to his mouth, a phenomenon that has kept me staring hopefully at his biceps throughout dinner. So far, the cotton blend is holding up.

Which is more than I can say for Bethany.

Drew is, once again, having a work crisis. Which means that instead of attending our family dinner, he's now at the office. Then Marcy, the shop's weekend employee, called in sick and left Bethany scrambling to find a replacement. Add in Abi's raging teenage angst, which is directed entirely at her mother, and Bethany is barely hanging on. And for Bethany, "barely hanging on" mostly consists of her being more and more positive, trying to *force* the ugly away through sheer will. Or, as I like to think of it, willful ignorance.

It doesn't help that my mom invited Jeremy's mother over for dinner. Janet has been her typical, sweet self, quietly observing the antics of my much bigger, much louder family. She smiles into her napkin when Aiden and August start tossing cherry tomatoes at each other over Bethany's head, challenging each other to catch them in their mouths, but I don't detect any judgment. Just amusement. Still, I can tell that the "audience"—even a small one—is adding to Bethany's stress.

"Knock it *off*," Bethany hisses, reaching out to snatch a tomato midair. Then she turns to Janet with a grimace. "Sorry. Their dad has been spending a lot of extra time at work lately, and I think they're acting—"

A slice of cucumber hits her in the face. I look down at Andy, who's sitting to my left, and he has his little hands clapped over his mouth in horror.

"Sorry, Mama," he says. "I was trying to play the game that Aiden—"

"Look at what you're teaching your brother," Bethany snaps at her two older sons, her cheeks flushed. "You were *not* raised to—"

Which is interrupted, of course, with a rousing chorus of "You *always* blame us for what *Andy* does!" and "Just 'cause he's your *favorite*." and "So unfair."

"Stop it," my dad orders in his deep, stern voice, and I risk a look down the table at Thad, who's staring way too hard at his salad, trying not to laugh. "Listen to your mother. All of you."

"You know," I keep my voice low as I lean toward Jeremy. "The only time I heard that voice growing up was when I ended up in the principal's office. Because of *you*."

His mouth twists into a half smile, and his hand squeezes my knee. "I had to do yard work," he whispers back.

"So!" Bethany claps her hands. *All done! Moving on!* "I would love a slice of that delicious-looking garlic bread. Abi, would you—"

"I'm sorry," Abi snaps, crossing her arms over her chest. "I only take requests by *text*. And since you've grounded me from my phone..."

I love Abi. Not only is she bright and funny and creative, but she's a good big sister, caring and sweet, especially to Andy. But right now...that girl is *pushing* it. Thad looks at me, blue eyes round—*What happened to our sweet little Abi Banana?*—and I shake my head back. *Demonic possession. Obviously.*

"Young lady—" my dad starts, his beard bristling.

"Dad," Bethany cuts in, a smile plastered to her face, at the same time that my mom murmurs "Mike" and places a hand on his forearm. I sneak a peek at Janet, who's calmly chewing her spaghetti and watching the family drama unfold like dinnertime entertainment.

"Let's keep things positive, right?" Bethany says brightly. "We have this delicious food. And nice company." If her smile was any more brittle, it would shatter. "I mean we have so much to be grateful—"

"Oh my god, could you be any more fake right now?" Abi asks, rolling her eyes, and I cough into my glass of water.

Ok, Abi *is* being a little snot. But she's also…a little bit right. Bethany is stressed and overwhelmed—understandably so. If she'd just acknowledge that it's been a hot mess kind of day, it would take the pressure off. Instead, she's creating an emotional pressure cooker by desperately wanting to look like a picture-perfect, magazine ad family. It *is* annoying. And, yes, fake.

Still, the power of being a truth teller comes with great responsibility, a memo that Abi clearly hasn't gotten. (Maybe it didn't come via text.)

I sit back in my chair, lips pressed together, and watch with fascination as Bethany takes three deep breaths, phony smile still in place. She opens her mouth like she's about to speak, then closes it and returns to deep breathing, at which point I lean over to Jeremy, close enough to smell the clean scent of hotel soap.

"Watch," I whisper. "She's going to say 'love and light.'"

Bethany stretches her smile wider and looks around the table, "I think what we all need right now is some love and light."

Nailed it.

Jeremy chokes on his salad as Abi mumbles, "What *you* need is a Xanax and some wine." At the same moment, Aiden sails a cherry tomato over Bethany's head to August.

Tomatoes fly. Abi rolls her eyes. Bethany puts her head down on the table and sobs. And Thad and I look around in astonishment because our family dinner just descended into absolute madness, and for once, I'm not the one responsible.

***

Rule #4: No sex two nights in a row. *Smash!*

Tap-tap-tap. I wait at Jeremy's window, teeth chattering, and pull my sweater tighter around me.

This is a bad idea. An awful idea. A *terrible* idea.

What Jeremy and I need right now is some space. A little room to cool down from whatever the hell last night was. Because nothing about last night—or early this morning—*felt* casual and no-strings-attached. It felt...intense. Too much eye contact that was actually the perfect amount. Soothing touches every time I was coming down from the high of orgasm. Deep, dreamless sleep, like his big Viking body wrapped around mine was the long-lost key to feeling safe in a way I never have before.

Which is ridiculous, because *safe* is the last word I would use to describe Jeremy. Not because he called my bluff on the spanking. I'd straight-up dared him to follow through on that. But because being with Jeremy—whether setting the hotel sheets on fire or watching movies in my parents' basement—feels like tiptoeing along a cliff's edge in high heels. Naked. I want to deny it, but I can't quite shake the swooping, unsettling feeling that at any moment I could fall from a height that will leave me broken and mangled.

But there are only eight days until Christmas. Eight days left to get Jeremy Kelly out of my system for good.

That's what I'd told myself when I woke up early this morning, hand splayed on Jeremy's chest, rising and falling to the rhythm of his breath. The sun had filtered through a crack in the drapes, painting his handsome face—and that impossible chin dimple—gold as I studied him, drinking in details I've never been in a position to notice before. The sandpaper tickle of his morning stubble. The childlike pout of his lower lip while he slept. The way his fingers tightened on my hip, trying to hold me to him when I got out of bed.

I'd felt it then. The urge to grab my things and go. *Run, run, run.*

However, I like to think I'm a little more strategic than I was at fifteen. If I'd run off scared this morning, it would have been the ultimate admission that last night had been...well, special. And *that* kind of concession is a big, fat *nope*.

Which is why I'm freezing my tits off outside Jeremy's window at midnight. I'm proving a point. I can do this. Anything that felt unprecedented or downright fucking magical last night was obviously the result of a hormone-induced frenzy, nothing more. Best to be grown-ups about the whole thing and take advantage of the time we have. (And that, my friends, is what we call "adulting.")

The window squeaks open, and I try to look casual—shivering outside his bedroom window like a stalker in the middle of the night—as he leans out.

"Miss me, Sunshine?"

For the record, it's been ten minutes since I've seen him. After that extremely awkward family dinner, Thad, Sam, Jeremy, and I retreated to the basement to give Sam an impromptu Caves & Conquerors tutorial, and the night flew by in some kind of weird (but fun) middle-school reunion, with surprise appearances from our long dormant C&C characters. Thad had orchestrated and run the short campaign—a quest to search an abandoned cave for hidden magical objects—and Sam, playing as a newly created character, jumped into the merriment. Dice were rolled. Adventure was had. The Nilsen "triplets" (plus Sam) were together again, except we replaced our off-brand soda with a six-pack and two of the "triplets" are having a super-hot holiday fling.

So, not *totally* like old times.

(Come to think of it, I never did love that whole "triplets" thing.)

I tear my eyes away from Jeremy in nothing but boxer briefs and pretend to check an imaginary watch on my wrist. "By my calculations, it's been fifteen hours since my last orgasm." I shake my head. "I have to admit, Asshat, I didn't expect you to be such a slack—*oof*!"

Jeremy pulls me through the window, his arms hooked under my armpits, and I press my hands to my mouth to smother my laughter. I may love grossing out Thad, but I have no desire to wake up Janet. So, I bite my lip, subduing my sigh when Jeremy picks me up and carries me the two big steps across his tiny bedroom to his twin-size bed. He lowers me to the mattress gently, his lips already on mine, and my traitorous body melts into him, craving his heat after the winter cold. I press my icy palms to his bare chest and ribs, and he shudders against me.

"Christ, you're cold," he mumbles against my mouth, but he doesn't pull away. He steadies himself between my bent knees and pulls my hands against him—his cheeks, his neck, his shoulders—like he can draw the cold out of me, absorbing it into himself.

"You could have been a gentleman and come to *my* room," I whisper, my hands now roaming the muscles of his back. He's peeling off my hoodie, my loose T-shirt, my leggings, his lips pressing against my bare skin as it's exposed, and I soak up every touch. "Instead, you made me brave the winter elements, risking life and limb to—"

He brings his lips to mine, silencing me. When he pulls back, he smooths my hair from my forehead, his hand warm against my face. His sheets still carry the faint scent of the Tommy Hilfiger cologne he wore in high school, and for a second, I wonder what my teenage self would think of this situation. A secret fantasy and cavorting with the enemy, rolled into one.

"I wasn't sure if the fair bard was sore after last night," he whispers, and for the briefest moment, my jaw drops open in shock. Because Jeremy is *playing* with me—as in *role* playing—using my beloved bard character from C&C.

He smirks at my look of shock, and I quickly compose my face into bored neutrality, even as my pulse races. Because Roxy Noteleaf, the half-elf bard, is never, *ever* shocked. Roxy has carried the world's most thrilling stories—stories of romance and adventure—hither and yon. Roxy has seen it all. Jeremy looks down at me, considering, and then flips our positions in one smooth motion—no small feat on his twin mattress. Once he's beneath me, he holds my gaze as he slides my panties down and drops them to the floor.

"Or if she was..." His hands grab onto my ass and pull me up his body, positioning me so I'm straddling his face, and my breath leaves my body. I reach out and balance myself against the wall, his stubble brushing my inner thighs. "... *amenable* to me further proving my considerable skills in the bed chamber?"

His hands, firm and commanding, push my legs wider, dropping me lower until his mouth is on me, his tongue running delicately around my clit. My fingers clutch at the drywall.

I struggle to catch my breath as I answer. "Such an arrangement could certainly be...*aah*..." My hips start moving, circling against him, and his deep hum of approval has my eyes rolling back in my head. "...agreeable. I would be happy to tell tales of Ulrik Lightborne's lustful, uh..." Another swirl of his tongue, and I'm pressing my hand to my mouth to stifle my moan. "...appetites, far and wide. Now, dwarf...whether your skills are *considerable*..." He turns his head to nip my thigh, and I jerk, swallowing back a laugh. "...now, that remains to be seen."

His teasing nips turn to soothing kisses. "Sounds like I better get to work."

THIRTY-FOUR

JEREMY

7 days until Christmas...

"I'm just feeling so refreshed this morning. I got such a good night's sleep." My mom stretches her arms above her head before turning to me, her smile bright. "How about you? Did *you* get a good night's sleep?"

I force myself not to blush as I chew my Lucky Charms. I'm pretty sure she's fucking with me. Which means she definitely heard me sneaking in my late-night visitor. Or she heard Freya sneaking out early this morning, while it was still dark.

"Um..." I consider my words carefully. "I'm feeling...great," I hedge before shoveling a giant spoonful of cereal into my mouth. You'd think by the ripe old age of thirty-four I'd have learned how to tell a halfway decent lie to my mother, but nope. I eat faster, crunching so furiously I can barely taste the sugary burst of the marshmallows.

To be fair, it's not a lie. I *do* feel great. Amazing. I want to sprint around Northview like George Bailey through Bedford Falls at the end of *It's a Wonderful Life*, exclaiming to every poor stranger I meet how goddamn fucking wonderful life is.

But I didn't get a lot of sleep.

"And it seems like your date the other night went pretty well." She doesn't bother hiding her smirk as she sips her coffee, and it's game over. My face blazes with a fire hotter than a blacksmith's forge.

"Um, yeah...it was..." Lucky Charms are my only defense. I'm cramming them in now, hoping the spectacle of my overstuffed mouth will distract her from my flaming cheeks.

"Let me guess...great?" Mom asks.

"Um, yeah," I mumble around my cereal. That's me, the silver tongue of Andersen & Sons Architecture. My empty bowl stares up at me, and I release a sigh of defeat along with my spoon. It clinks against the edge of the bowl, and I run a hand through my hair. "Like I said in my text, we both had a little too much to drink. We lucked out that they had rooms available—"

"Ah, *rooms*. Plural." Her brow lifts. "Right..."

Just as I'm hoping for a chasm to break open in our dining room and drop me into the bowels of Middle Earth, the front door gives a loud squeak and Thad pushes inside, covered in a thin layer of snow. He didn't bother knocking—we never knocked as kids because we were back and forth so often—and the sight of him casually letting himself in is oddly comforting. Familiar.

His arrival is also the perfect opportunity to distract my mother from this conversation.

"Coffee, Thad?" Mom asks, getting up from the table and already walking toward the coffeepot. She's still in her pajamas, but so is Thad. He smiles at her as he shakes the snow out of his hair and brushes off his plaid pajama pants.

"Yes, please, Mrs. Cassidy," he answers as he toes off his winter boots, then crosses the living room to plop down next to me at the table. When he sees the Lucky Charms box, he grabs my empty bowl and fills it with cereal. "Could I get some milk too, please?" he asks her.

My face twists. "Gross. We have clean bowls, man."

But Thad just shrugs and grins a thank-you to my mom as she sets the milk carton and a mug of coffee at his elbow. Then, as he pours milk over his giant helping of cereal, he looks up at me, clears his throat, and jumps right in. Because why not? The water's warm.

"So, what's happening with you and Freya?"

I never get snippy with Thad. I'm not, in general, a snippy person. However, Thad is the last person I want to talk to about this. I've tried to be straight-up with him about dating Freya, but it's still awkward as fuck, and I don't know exactly where the boundaries should be. It's my own discomfort that has me leaning back in my chair and throwing Thad's old words back at him.

"I don't know. Why don't you pick up a phone and ask her?"

My mom scowls at me as she settles back into her chair across the table from us. "Jem," she mutters. Thad, on the other hand, throws back his head and laughs.

"I knew it," he crows around a mouthful of cereal.

I run my hand through my hair again—I'm sure I look like a porcupine—and stare up at the ceiling. Apparently, Thad isn't as uncomfortable with the whole situation as I am. Neither is my mom, who leans forward on her elbows.

"Ooh, Jem." Her brown eyes sparkle. "Tell us."

"Tell you what?" I shoot her an exasperated look. "Exactly."

"What's happening with Freya," she says.

I turn to Thad for help. Surely he understands that he and my mom would be my last choice of confidants. Especially since things between Freya and I have escalated in the bedroom. I mean, what exactly does he want me to confess? That Freya enjoys a good slap to the ass as much as I enjoy giving it to her? Or that she has an uncanny ability to maintain her role playing right through orgasm?

But he just blinks at me as he steadily works his way through my Lucky Charms.

"We're dating? I guess?" I shrug, trying to ignore the itch on the back of my neck. "But last we talked about it, which was before our date, Freya was pretty damn adamant that she doesn't want to stay in touch when we get back to Chicago. Whereas I..."

Whereas I'm free-falling into a place where a future without Freya seems downright unimaginable. Coming into this trip, I'd been hoping Freya would shake things up. But instead of bringing chaos, Freya's presence has instigated something altogether different. A fullness, a completeness, that was lacking before. Sure, she may be rearranging all the furniture—things are *different*—but she's also been dragging out all the dusty artifacts I'd packaged up and put away in storage. The parts of me I'd let go of because I didn't know how they worked in my new, responsible, grown-up reality. My sense of adventure and my inclination toward bending the rules. My love of fantasy and art. My urge to compete, to acknowledge a conflict between myself and another person and challenge myself to *win* it. With Freya, life isn't about constantly acquiescing to what's expected of me. It's about truth and integrity. About being the most complete version of me, even when it gets a little messy.

And the thought of going back to Chicago without her...of returning to golf and cookie-cutter office buildings and girlfriends who would, at best, scoff at Ulrik the dwarf? It feels repulsive to me.

"You..." Thad prompts.

I tap my fingers along the worn wood of the table, impatient. "It feels good having her back."

"She hasn't mentioned going your separate ways since the date, though, right?" Thad asks, watching me over his shoulder as he carries the empty cereal bowl to the dishwasher.

"No, she hasn't." I shake my head. I don't have to think about it. My brain has been fixated on sifting through my interactions with Freya, searching for the tiniest hints about her feelings. And she hasn't mentioned the dreaded "Christmas countdown" since our date. I've been clinging to that like a life raft. "Not once."

Thad nods as he rejoins us at the table. "Good," he mutters. "Has she called you 'sport?'"

"What?" Mom asks.

At the same time, I pull back with a grimace and answer, "No. Weird, dude."

"Just a little thing I've noticed," Thad says, stroking his jaw. "The cat! Does the cat like you?"

"Yeah, Hecate likes me fine." I frown. "At least that's what Freya said."

"Excellent."

WAR ON CHRISTMAS: A HOLIDAY ROMANCE

"What is going on?" My mom asks Thad, and he blows out his cheeks as he leans back in his chair, balancing on the back two legs. Clearly, being Freya's twin is exhausting work.

"Freya—also known as the Evil Twin"—he grins—"had a string of bad luck when it came to love." And just like that, I'm *eager* to have this conversation with Thad. I lean forward, hands clasped on the table. Thad takes one look at my sudden interest and his mouth tips into a smug smile. "So *now* you want to have this conversation with me?"

"I've wanted to have this conversation for years," I correct him. "*You* refused to have it."

He rolls his eyes. "Do you know what it was like being stuck in the middle of you two? Both of you nonstop harassing me about what the other person was doing. 'Who's he dating?' 'Where is she working?' It was miserable."

Ok, he has a point.

"So, why now?" I ask. "Why the change of heart?"

"Maybe I got sick of seeing my two favorite people keep making the same fucking—sorry, Mrs. Cassidy—mistakes over and over and dating the wrong fucking—sorry—people." He crosses his arms over his chest. "Maybe it felt—with you coming home—like it was time for you and Frey to finally face whatever happened in high school. *Maybe* when you know that two people are fucking perfect for each other, it gets old waiting for them to pull their stubborn heads out of their asses and reach out to each other."

I stare at him. He stares back at me, unblinking. My mom stares back and forth between us.

"We kissed, Thad." I shrug. "In high school. We kissed. Freya panicked and ghosted me. I started dating Tiffany to make myself feel better. And the rest is history. That's what happened."

Thad shakes his head. "Sounds about right. God, she's stubborn."

"You're telling me," I mumble.

"The bad luck," Mom says, reaching across the table to pat Thad's arm. "You were telling us about Freya's bad luck with love."

She seems almost as greedy for information about Freya as I am, and with my nerves hovering between euphoria and the very real possibility of having my heart broken, a flicker of annoyance burns in my chest. Part of me wants to challenge her with the same question I'd asked Thad: *So, why now? Why the change of heart?* I don't want to sound like a total asshole, though, so I settle for raising an eyebrow at her.

"Grandkids, Jem," she answers, as if the answer had been obvious. As if she hadn't checked out of being a *mom* for the past seventeen years.

Thad snorts, then gives me an apologetic shrug. "Nieces and nephews, dude."

The idea of a miniature Freya, all gray eyes and dark hair, sends my inner caveman into a frenzy, howling at the sky and rattling the bars of his cage. It's exactly the kind of thought I've been strictly avoiding, at least consciously. Those *aren't* thoughts you entertain about a fling. But have I noticed that Freya is amazing with Bethany's kids? That she treats them with the same thoughtful respect she gives adults? Hell yeah, I've noticed.

My foot bounces against the linoleum floor and my hands clench together.

"You're both out of your goddamn—sorry, Mom—minds," I say. Because that little glimmer of hope Thad's words are giving me? It's terrifying.

"Jeremy, if you ever tell Freya what I'm about to say, I will call you a filthy liar. Because I'm too young to die, and Sam would miss me." Thad leans forward. "But Freya has been her own worst enemy when it comes to love, and clearly it's time for her wiser, better-looking twin"— I snort, and Thad grins—"to step in and help."

I narrow my eyes. "From what Freya's told me, it sounds like she's been more than happy sticking to casual relationships."

Thad scoffs and waves this comment away like a pesky mosquito. "Freya hasn't even tried to have a real relationship since her twenties. Do you remember what guys are like in their early twenties?"

I cringe. There are exceptions to every rule, obviously, but most people I'd known at that age were strange, hybrid creatures of adolescents and adults, high on the combination of maximum freedom and minimal responsibilities. No answering to parents, but no mortgage or kids either. It was a time for backpacking through Europe, drinking on work nights, and racking up sexual conquests. Given my drive to create stability for myself, I'd had a more constrained approach, but most of my friends had been sowing wild oats like it was a government-issued directive.

Thad points at my face. "Exactly. They're dumbasses. And Freya had gone through this transformation from Freaky Freya"—his mouth pinches for a moment, and I feel a grim satisfaction about plastering myself to Freya's side in front of Tiffany at the Galway Inn—"to this...well..." He scratches his head, looking bemused. "She's really pretty."

Saying Freya is "really pretty" is like saying Albert Einstein was "really smart," but I take pity on Thad and don't belabor the point.

"Men treated her badly?" I ask, my voice strangled. Mom's eyes widen at my tone, and I force my clenched fists to relax. Because I suddenly want to pummel every sorry asshole who ever hurt Freya.

Thad sighs. "They liked the *idea* of her, right? Her image. But you know Freya. There's a lot of depth there. She has big feelings and big ideas and big ways of sharing them. It intimidated the guys she dated, and whenever things started getting more serious, they'd break it off. There was one guy, Ryan, who I thought might get more serious, but something happened there, too. And Freya had no interest in being less, well," Thad shrugs, "in being less *Freya*. So, she just learned not to go there."

My cereal churns in my guts. I hate the idea of Freya facing that kind of rejection. The idea of men who weren't fit to lick her sexy little boots making her feel less than. I crack my knuckles as I blow a hard breath out of my nose, and Thad gives me an amused half smile.

"There was also their other fatal flaw, of course."

"What was that?"

He smiles. "They weren't you."

THIRTY-FIVE

FREYA

5 days until Christmas...

Leo: So how is the seduction going?

Me: You need to ask? Oh ye of little faith...

Leo: Glad it's shaping up to be a merry Christmas ;-) You said he lives in Chicago...

Me: Yeah. Your point being???

Leo: That you could keep seeing him after the holidays? That you might have someone to comfort you and stop you from living a cold, lonely, miserable existence once I'm discovered and move to LA? You know, basic companionship? The human need for connection? ORGASMS?!?!?

Me: WTF? You sound like my sister. Remember before you started dating Todd? When you used to be cool?

With a sigh, I toss my phone back onto the couch, trusting the fifty-year-old springs to cushion its landing. My parents are both at work, and Thad and Sam went downtown for last-minute Christmas shopping. Which means I have the house to myself.

I thought about sleeping in, but my brain wouldn't turn off this morning after I snuck back into my room. It's swirling with what-ifs. *What if Jeremy and I tried to keep this thing going? What if I let my guard down? What if I trusted him, just a little?*

My brain is also swirling with answers. *One of his coworkers would recognize me from The Sphere and Jeremy would be embarrassed at work. Or maybe I'd shoot my mouth off at a work function and get him in trouble. Jeremy would get sick of me once the novelty wore off. Once I wasn't just a fantasy anymore.*

And the result is always the same: *I would get my heart crushed.*

No thank you.

So, to quiet the hamster wheel that is my brain, I'm taking advantage of the empty house and using the basement to dance. The Sphere's January burlesque will be our first performance after the holiday break, so it will need to come together fast. The theme? "New Year, New Me." It's going to be a full-on satire of people pursuing stereotypical New Year's resolutions. People at an exercise class crashing into each other, an item of clothing falling off with every collision. An enthusiastic dieter who ends her number sobbing into a bowl of lettuce.

It's going to be great. It even distracted me a little, the physicality of it. Working my muscles through the familiar moves. Shimmies and grinds and three-step turns. Then Leo had to interrupt and bring my thoughts straight back to Jeremy.

With a sigh, I towel my face and grab my phone, heading back upstairs. Hecate's waiting for me in my room, butting her head against my legs until I scratch behind her ears. My phone dings, but I ignore it, concentrating instead on the soft rumble of Hecate's purr. I know it's probably Leo, and I don't need his "human need for connection" negativity this morning.

But there's no ignoring the twist of unease behind my breastbone.

Because this thing with Jeremy...it doesn't feel like a fling. The sex is amazing, sure, but it's not the sex that has me on edge. Well, not *just* the sex. It's everything. The way he trails his fingertips down my back while he listens to me endlessly prattle about The Sphere and our upcoming shows. Hell, the way I *want* to prattle to him about work, watching to see which details will make him smile with amusement. The look in his eye when I catch him watching me from across the room. The casual way he holds my hand and plays with my hair throughout our movie nights and C&C sessions with Thad and Sam. Fuck, even his annoying Sunshine nickname has started getting me all hot and bothered.

Seventeen-year-old Freya would be mortified.

And trust me, I've noticed that since our night together at the Galway Inn I haven't brought up going our separate ways in Chicago. The countdown is always on my mind, ticking away with every sunrise, but I don't want to say it out loud. It's like those words—"Six days left...Nope! Down to five."—will burst this magical bubble we've created. A bubble of teasing, and games, and steamy sex. *Poof!* Gone. When it's already going to burst way too soon.

Hecate blinks her golden eyes at me, then, without warning, jumps to the nightstand. I snort when she lands on my tarot deck and slides off the edge of the nightstand onto the carpet. She lands on her feet, then looks at me over her shoulder with a disdainful scowl.

"Whoever heard of a clumsy cat?" I tease, bending over to collect my deck. I shuffle the cards back into place, and I'm just about to put them back when I notice the dark corner of a card poking out from under Hecate's paw. I stretch, reaching for it, and she turns her nose in the air and slinks away, allowing me to pick up the lone card. I flip it over, and my breath leaves me with a whoosh, like I went too fast down a slide.

Because I immediately recognize the lone, bent figure. It's the upside-down Hermit. Of course.

***

"Freya?" Sam's clear, cheerful voice sounds from the other side of the bathroom door, and I frown as I sink further into my bath water, which has long since cooled to barely warm.

"I'll be out in a minute," I call.

"Oh, I just wanted to chat quick. Is the shower curtain closed?"

"Yeah, come on in." I lean back against the smooth porcelain tub and kick my feet onto the teal and off-white wall tiles. I hear the door open and close and the quiet creak of the toilet seat as Sam settles onto it. "Something to talk about you don't want Thad to hear?" I ask.

My guess? She's going to hit me up for Thad's feelings about marriage. They've been together over a year now, and she's obviously The One. But my dolt of twin still hasn't put a ring on it.

"*I* don't care what he hears," Sam says, "but I thought you might be willing to say more without him around."

Aaaaah.

"More about what?" I ask cautiously, even though I already know.

"About what the heck is going on with you and Jeremy."

"You know what's going on," I say, careful to keep my voice even. "We're killing time until the holidays are over. Hooking up. Having a fling. A nine-night stand. Well, a five-night stand, now. Non-friends with benefits. A torrid—"

I'm cut off by Sam's loud, wild laughter echoing off the tiny bathroom's walls.

"Uh, yeah. Whatever." I swear I can *hear* her eyes roll. *Shit.* Why did Thad have to fall for somebody so fucking perceptive? "Now tell me what's really going on."

I sigh, splashing some lukewarm water over my breasts and shoulders as I contemplate how much I'll have to confess to get her off my back.

"The sex..."

"Yeah?"

A groan tears out of me. "So fucking good. Like...*hot.*"

"Excellent."

I bite my lip, hoping she's satisfied.

"And..." she prompts. I should have known better. Sam's sweet, but she's got a conniving side. It's why I like her so much.

"He does this thing, with his tongue, that—"

Sam laughs. *Dammit.* That would have sent Thad sprinting from the room, but Sam is made of sterner stuff.

"You know that's not what I meant, Frey. What's *really* going on? Because he is *in*to you." She pauses. "And I gotta be honest. You seem really into him too."

Damn my moony-eyed stares. I was in a state of post-orgasmic bliss yesterday. Clearly, it made me weak.

ELLE CAMPBELL

I stare at my eggplant-colored toenails against the tiles and reconsider my strategy. Maybe Sam is the perfect person to confide in. She knows both Jeremy and me, but she still has enough distance to be reasonably objective. She wouldn't feel stuck in the middle like Thad, for instance. I decide to test the waters.

"When we were out on our date the other night, we ran into Jeremy's ex-girlfriend from high school. She's the one who started the whole Freaky Freya thing my freshman year. Did Thad ever tell—"

"Mmhmm," Sam quickly mutters, urging me to go on.

"Well, she started it because she was jealous, apparently. Jealous that Jeremy always seemed...into me, I guess? Even though we fought like cats and dogs." I take a deep breath for courage. "And Friday night, Jeremy apologized to her because—and I quote—'It was always her.' Meaning *me*. It was always me." I squirm, sending the water sloshing. "That means like twenty-years-ago 'always,' though. Right? Like back-in-high-school 'always.' Not like *always* 'always'?"

I cringe, pretty sure that made no sense, but Sam just hums, like she knows exactly what I meant.

"Do you remember the first time we met?" she asks.

"Of course." I smile at the memory. "Thad had been in love with you for *years*. I couldn't wait to meet you."

Thad and Sam had been workplace buddies for three years before they ever got romantic. He had fallen for her instantly—"Like a direct kick to the gut, Frey. *Pow!*"—but she'd been in a long-term relationship when they'd met. It had been a big deal when she'd finally broken off her engagement and she and Thad were sent on a business trip to Chicago together. Watching them exchange furtive glances and look for every tiny excuse to touch each other had been downright painful.

And wildly entertaining.

Sam continues, "Do you remember what you asked me, about—oh, I don't know—ten minutes after we met? While we were at that bar across from The Sphere?"

Goddamn it. My face flushes. Powers of perception *and* a good memory? Now that's just fucking annoying.

"Noooo?" I hedge.

Sam snorts. "I'll refresh your memory. It went a little something like"—she clears her throat and drops her voice, so it's huskier like mine—"You must have met Thad's friend Jeremy by now. What's he up to these days?"

And Sam had answered as if Thad had *trained* her (because I'm sure he *had*), "I don't know. Why don't you pick up the phone and ask him?" It had been humiliating. I still haven't forgiven myself for being so utterly predictable.

I groan, pushing my hands into my face. You'd think I would be over it a year later, but...nope. Still embarrassing.

"So," Sam says, a smile in her voice, "a couple nights later we met up with Jeremy. And you know what he asked me about—oh, I don't know—ten minutes after we met?"

My stomach flip flops, and I *hate* the little jig of hope dancing in my belly.

"I don't know. Something about golf?" I ask sullenly, and Sam snorts out a laugh.

"Thad may be the good twin, but you're definitely the funny one. Don't tell him I said that, though," Sam orders. "The second Thad left to use the bathroom, Jeremy leaned over and said, 'You must have met Freya by now.

How is she doing?' And *I* said, 'I don't know. Why don't you pick up the phone and ask her?'"

My traitorous mouth tries to jerk into a smile, but I hold tight onto my resting bitch face. "What's your point?"

"My *point*, oh Queen of Snark and Sass, is that you asked me if Jeremy meant *always* 'always' or just back-in-the-day 'always.' And I think there's a very real possibility that it's *always* 'always' been you for him. And if you were really being honest with yourself..." Sam takes a deep breath, "...it's probably always been Jeremy for you, too."

Oh gods. I breathe through the anxious nausea that smacks me, wondering what on earth I could possibly say to *that*. I mean, it's ridiculous. Ludicrous. Silly. Delusional.

"That's—that's—" I scramble into a sitting position, hoping it will ease the tightening sensation around my chest. Water sloshes onto the floor, but I don't care. "That's—"

True, a quiet voice whispers.

And that one word—*True*—drifts into that hairline crack I could sense Friday night at the inn. That tiny fracture I could feel spreading across my walls, all my carefully erected defenses. That truth is a speck, the tiniest piece of dust, but after all the denials and deflections and dismissals, it's that little fleck of honesty that wrenches the crack wide open, and that ache in my chest escalates to a full-on panic.

I gasp for breath, my hand pressed to my breastbone to soothe the pain, and on the other side of the shower curtain, Sam sighs.

"Well, shit, Freya. I was looking for some fun girl talk. I didn't realize you were in *that* much denial." She sounds worried. Remorseful, even. "Do you need anything? Wine? Chocolate?" Her voice drops to a hush. "Do you have a stash of weed somewhere?"

WAR ON CHRISTMAS: A HOLIDAY ROMANCE

I laugh, because the idea of sweet, innocent Sam rolling a joint is hilarious, but it comes out dull and cynical. Because there's no amount of wine—or weed—that could make it ok that I'm in love with Jeremy Kelly.

THIRTY-SIX

JEREMY

"I mean, don't you think we're a little old for this?" Sam eyes the tablespoon of ghost pepper hot sauce with suspicion and hunches her shoulders against the chill of the Nilsen's basement. "I mean, we're in our *thirties*...Truth or Dare? Come on, guys."

Sam may look innocent, but she's a sneak. She blinks at us, her big hazel eyes wide and doe-like, looking tiny and defenseless in her rainbow-pajama shorts and hoodie. As if she isn't the one who'd suggested playing this to begin with.

"Eat it, Lambert," Thad orders, using a hard, unflinching tone I've literally *never* heard him use with his girlfriend, and Sam's lower lip threatens to tremble. Next to me on the couch, Freya snorts.

Context: For the past hour, Sam has been a hard-ass taskmaster, shamelessly coercing the rest of us into a string of embarrassing (and sometimes illegal) tasks. Thad's lips are still blue from Sam's dare to do a snow angel in his boxers—"Time to prove your manhood, babe."—and Freya could've gotten arrested stealing baby Jesus from old Mrs. Johnson's nativity scene and leaving him on the front porch of old Mr. Pasterski, aka Mrs. Johnson's next-door neighbor and longtime rival. (That one might result in a violent escalation tomorrow, but the possibility of a blood feud only fueled Sam's determination.)

And the ugly truths are pouring out of us like confessions in a torture chamber. Thad secretly dated one of my high school ex-girlfriends for an entire week our junior year. (The betrayal!) Freya is a secret but die-hard Taylor Swift fan. ("I swear, Asshat, if you ever tell *anyone*, I will cut you.") And the truth is finally out regarding my real feelings about Dave Matthews Band. ("Fine! I can't fucking stand them. Are you happy now?")

All of it orchestrated by Samantha.

So, you'll have to excuse us for not buying into her whole "I'm cute and sweet and fragile" bit. It's a sham.

"You know your choices." Freya shrugs. "Answer the question—Who is the first celebrity crush you ever masturbated to?—or eat the sauce."

It's Freya who finally found the key to breaking Sam's reign of terror. Neither Thad nor I would have dared to ask that question, but somehow, Freya zeroed in on it with unerring instincts.

And now the more Sam resists, the more we're all dying to know.

We all watch, riveted, as Sam scrunches up her face, sticks out her tongue, and touches it to the hot sauce. With a yelp, she pulls back. Nobody—not even Freya—has been able to tolerate the sauce. Back in eighth grade she managed to swallow it once, but she immediately threw it up, so it didn't count. We're sticklers like that.

"Fine!" Sam seethes, tossing the spoonful of hot sauce into the mug on the old coffee table. "It was Bill Pullman! Are you happy?"

Stunned silence fills the basement. Even the springs on the ancient couch are afraid to make a sound. Across from me, Thad's mouth drops open in shock.

"Bill...Pullman?" he repeats, and Sam curls into her overstuffed armchair with shame, burying her face in her knees. Freya starts to snicker.

"So, like...*While You Were Sleeping* Bill Pullman?" Freya asks. "Not *Mr. Wrong* Bill Pullman. That would be *too* weird." Then she gasps. "Not *Casper* Bill Pullman?!"

We all pull back with a grimace, and Sam groans. "It was turn-of-the-century newspaper guy Bill Pullman."

Freya considers this, then shrugs. "That's not so bad."

"But wait..." Thad chews at his lip. "If Bill Pullman is like, your *type*...how did you end up with *me*?"

Freya doesn't miss a beat. She turns to Thad and stares hard at his face. "Oh, I can see it."

"What?" Thad looks horrified, and I turn my head to hide the laugh I'm struggling to keep down.

"Oh, for sure." Freya nods, exuding 100 percent confidence. "That whole guy-next-door, super safe and forgettable thing."

"Safe?!" Thad sputters. "Forgettable?!" He turns to Sam. "Tell her how *not* safe I am." Sam, who appears to have given up on life, pulls herself tighter into a ball and says nothing while Freya gives an evil chuckle only I can hear. Thad tries again. "Babe, tell her how wild I can be."

"Dude," I laugh, taking pity on him. And myself. Quite frankly, I really don't want to hear how wild Thad is. "Frey is fucking with you. You're not Bill Pullman."

Not entirely anyway. Thad does have that whole "nice guy" vibe, though. Not that he looks nice right now. Right now he's staring daggers at his twin, who responds by sticking her tongue out at him.

It's all very mature.

Ok, honestly? Ever since Thad got home, it's been a little bit like we've all reverted to our middle school selves. Fantasy games and movie nights and, yes, Truth or Dare. And, sure, maybe it hasn't been very mature, but...it's been super fun.

"Who's up next?" Thad asks. "Oh, that's right. The Evil Twin. What's it gonna be, Frey? The truth or the sauce?"

Freya rolls her eyes. "I have nothing to hide."

Sam unfolds from the fetal position to glare at Freya as well, a question already on the tip of her tongue. "All right, who—"

"Nope." Thad holds up a hand to interrupt her, his eyes staying trained on Freya. "It's time for the big guns." Freya scoffs, but Thad narrows his eyes. He means business. "What happened with Ryan?"

Freya goes still, staring back at Thad with a look of utter betrayal, and a trickle of foreboding runs down my spine. Thad had mentioned Ryan to me the other morning. What the fuck did this guy do to Freya? More importantly, how the fuck do I get my hands on him?

"You really want to go there, Thaddeus?" Freya asks, and Thad takes a few seconds to read her face before giving a jerky nod. He's not looking vindictive anymore, though. His mouth is pinched, his shoulders braced. Freya sighs. "Fine."

She licks her red lips, her eyes flitting to mine, and I realize she's nervous. Alarms are blaring now, but I'm careful to keep my face relaxed and neutral. My fingertips, though, are digging into the bumpy fabric of the couch cushion.

"Ryan, for those of you who *don't* know," Freya nods to me, then Sam, "is a guy I dated in my mid-twenties. Things got serious quickly, and he was planning to propose, but when I met his parents at Thanksgiving, they made it pretty damn clear that I am *not* the kind of girl you marry. They pulled him aside in the afternoon, and when they didn't come back after a while, I went looking for him. I wasn't trying to be sneaky or anything," she explains, shaking her head. "They just ditched me with his sister, who would barely look at me, so I got bored and went looking for them." She raises her eyebrows. "Well, I found them. His parents had cornered him in the living room—sorry, the *parlor*—and as I walked up, I heard them giving him a talk. I believe his dad's exact words were, 'Go ahead and have your fun, but girls like her are *not* the marrying type.'"

"Fucking douchebag," Thad mutters, and Sam nods in eager agreement.

Freya, however, shrugs. "He wasn't wrong, though. I'm *not* the marrying type. Ryan taught me something..." She pauses for a moment, considering her words. "I'm more content on my own. I'm *free*. I don't have to worry about anyone's approval. I have no pressure to compromise who I am. And you know what happened when I stopped trying to settle down? I got *happier*."

She shoots me a sad, lopsided smile, as if she knows how her casual statement is making my heart twinge. Most of the time, if I dared to feel concern for Freya, she'd go all prickly and sharp like a cactus, but she's been different the past couple days. There's an undercurrent. An agitation. The barest crease of a frown pulling down her face when she thinks I'm not looking. Even before this whole Ryan debacle came up.

The whole situation—Freya's quiet unrest and now this "I'm free" business—puts me on edge. Like her unrest is contagious.

Then Freya turns away and throws up her hands. "And, since we're playing Truth or Dare and I'm *not* a filthy liar...that wasn't the only part." She rolls her eyes. "I was super upset, because I *knew* that Ryan wouldn't stand up to his parents, so after dinner I needed a few minutes to myself." Her nose wrinkles as she admits, "I needed to have a good cry before the car ride home. So...I snuck into his dad's study for some privacy."

Aw, hell. I can feel where this is heading, and my leg muscles jerk. Part of me needs to stand up and pace. To move this anger and this fear out of my body. But I can remember too well the late nights I spent in Freya's room as a kid, whispering my darkest truths to her. Freya never made it about herself. She accepted my rambling confessions calmly, her gray eyes serious and steady, and it meant everything to me. The fact that she could listen without turning away, without rejecting the truths I entrusted her with...it's what convinced me I was going to be ok.

She sighs as she sifts through her memories, and I hold steady. For her.

"His dad found me in the study and cornered me. Jesus, it was all so cliché." She scoffs, then drops her voice to mimic a man's. "'Nobody else would need to know. He had the money to take good care of me.' You get the picture." She shakes her head, sending her waves bouncing. "I said no—*obviously*—then he tried to get handsy, so I kneed him in the balls and I ruptured his testicle. And that"—she blows out a noisy breath—"is what happened with Ryan." Her mouth twists as she mutters, "Talk about an awkward ride home."

A long, heavy silence descends on the basement, and my heart starts to pump so hard that dark spots cloud the edges of my vision. My hands, tingling and numb, clench into fists.

"I'm going to fucking kill them," I say at the exact same moment that Thad mutters a furious, "I'm going to fucking hack their computers."

Sam, however, is having a completely different reaction. She's staring at Freya with...admiration. Then her mouth lifts into a cheeky grin and she whispers, "Freya, you are a *literal* ballbuster."

And Freya grins back at her.

THIRTY-SEVEN

FREYA

"Frey?" Thad's familiar voice accompanies a soft knock on my bedroom door. It's late. Our parents have been in bed for hours, and they'll be getting up early to open the shop, so we've been tiptoeing and whispering as we dispersed from our ill-fated game of Truth or Dare to get ready for bed.

"Come in," I say. I was halfway out the window, but I step back inside and slide it shut behind me. Thad lets himself in and flops into the papasan chair in the corner. Hecate immediately jumps into his lap, and he pets her back as he looks me over.

Thad is in plaid pajama pants and an old T-shirt. I'm wrapped up in a thick sweater, a scarf, and my winter boots. He raises an eyebrow at my apparel. Clearly, I wasn't about to get into bed. (Well, not *my* bed anyway.) I raise one back.

"Going somewhere?" he smirks.

"I *was*," I say, but I flop onto my bed, arms outstretched.

I should have known Thad would show up here. My breakup with Ryan is one of the only things I refused to tell him about. Ever. I'm not surprised he leveraged Truth or Dare to finally learn what really happened. Ruptured testicle and all.

"Why didn't you tell me?" Thad asks, the glow of the Christmas lights highlighting the concern etched onto his face. "*You* didn't do anything wrong."

I sigh. "I was embarrassed. Not by the testicle. That was bad ass," I clarify, and Thad chuckles darkly. "I was embarrassed by his parents' reaction to me. Looking back, Ryan and I were obviously all wrong for each other. I know *you* never liked him."

Thad shakes his head. He never said anything to me outright, but he's not a hard person to read. Especially for me.

"At the time, though, I really believed in us. I had this whole fairytale built up in my head, and then to be found so...I don't know...lacking? It was humiliating. And the things is, I'd tried so *hard*, Thad." My nose wrinkles at the memory. "My tattoos were covered. I bought a new outfit to wear that seemed all proper and 'meet the parents.' I didn't shoot my mouth off or say anything controversial—which you know takes some effort for me," I joke, but Thad doesn't laugh. "I was on my best behavior, and it was like they could still tell—and I mean *instantly*—that there was something different about me."

When I close my eyes, it's not Ryan's mother I see, her thin lips pursed into a frown. It's my own mom, her eyes distant to hide her distaste as I browsed at the mall through the dark, dreary clothes I favored in high school. Whenever I did something that didn't make sense to her, which was a *lot*, she never got on my case about it. She just focused on something else. The store, or Bethany, or whatever drama was going on with the PTA. She wasn't *mean* about my sullen nature or the uncomfortable truths I had a habit of blurting out. She's not a mean person. She just…drifted away. Because she didn't know what to make of me.

And let's be real, if my own mom finds me hard to deal with, I'm probably not going to be a dream come true for a mother-in-law.

"Of course there's something different about you," Thad jumps in. "You're braver than the rest of us, Frey. Freer. You know that intimidates people until—"

"Thad." I keep my voice gentle. Thad loves me. Thad sees the good—the strength—in my darkness better than anyone. Except maybe Jeremy. *Nope. Not going there.* I focus instead on my twin, the sweetheart of a guy who's never wanted to admit my faults. "There's a cost to being different. You've seen it."

Obviously, my mom isn't the only person who struggled to understand me. It was teachers and principals and professors and bosses. Over the years, I've learned to temper my strong opinions and my stronger way of communicating them, but the truth is I don't *want* to fit in with all the bullshit. I don't want to be that person who says, "It's not like he's hitting the boy," and turns my back on a kid stuck with an emotionally abusive stepdad because I'm afraid to ruffle people's feathers. People who look away from that *should* have their damn feathers ruffled. Hell, they should be plucked out, one by one, until they wake the fuck up and do the right thing.

Unfortunately, most people don't agree. Most people want to breeze over conflict as quickly as possible, even if that means leaving injustice unchallenged.

I lucked out landing at The Sphere. I fit there, where bold truth-telling and daily drama are the norm, not a horrifying fall from grace. With my artsy little Sphere family, I can live authentically, and I don't have to worry about being punished—aka fired—for being who I am. However, I'm well aware that The Sphere is not the "real world." And it's not Jeremy's world, with golf outings and a company culture of "keep the customer happy." (Or whatever it is those wealthy capitalists say.)

The worst part? Jeremy gets me. I'm pretty sure Jeremy *loves* me. But the world he lives in? It does not, and he needs someone who will fit there. Someone who will charm his boss and smile pleasantly when he takes clients out to dinner. And as much hell as I give him for his safe, stable, 401(k) lifestyle, I understand why he craves that security. Especially now that I know about Gary giving him the boot when he left for college.

"So you're just going to let Ryan and his asshole family convince you to be alone forever?" Thad scoffs, irritated now. Hecate jumps from his lap with a feline huff. "That's not like you, Frey. Why would you give them that kind of—"

I chuckle, rolling to my side so I can face him. "It's not just Ryan. It's a lot of experiences, Good Twin. Experiences that all add up. The Ryan situation just helped me see it all a lot more clearly." I smile, trying to prove to him I'm ok. Maybe trying to prove it to myself, too. "I like me the way I am. And I'll take the hits to be her. It's a price I'm happy to pay, but..." I sigh, "...it makes me a liability to a partner. Eventually, I'll say or do the wrong thing—because to me it will feel like the *right* thing—and the cost of being with me won't be worth it to them anymore. I know you think I'm so brave, but..." *Oh, fuck.* I bite my bottom lip to stop it from trembling, and I can see Thad's Adam's apple bob in response.

Twin emotions are hard. Especially Scorpio twins. Twice the angst.

Because I can't ignore the revelation I had during my little bathtub chat with Sam. Somehow, I managed to fall for Jeremy. My heels slipped, my arms spun in the air with nothing to grab onto, and I tumbled over the edge, all powered by childhood nostalgia, steamy make-out sessions, and orgasms.

Or maybe, like Sam said, I fell a long time ago.

These feelings, though? They don't change the outcome. They don't change the fact that, five days from today, Christmas will be here, and it will be time to go back to the real world. And I don't want to put myself—or him—through the pain of trying to contort myself into something I'm not. Something I could never be.

I love him too much to put him through that.

Which leaves me hurtling toward the ground, about to splat, and the only move left is to figure out how to land so that I might—*might*—have a chance of picking up the pieces again someday.

Right now, my game plan is simple: Make these days count. Have the hot sex and the whispered conversations. Reminisce together. Be in the moment. Make memories.

Then, when it's time, have the wisdom to let go.

"Frey?" Thad asks, and I shake my head, trying to clear my mood. I have the rest of my life to brood and feel sorry for myself. Now isn't the time.

"It's ok." I offer him a wobbly smile. "I'm going to be ok."

"None of this is ok. You're making—"

The soft slide of the window interrupts him, and he snaps his mouth shut, making the room silent as Jeremy pulls himself through the open window and closes it behind him. He spots me on my bed right away and takes a step toward me, but as I sit up, I nod toward the corner where Thad is now sitting with a grimace, his hands held over his eyes.

"Oh, um..." Jeremy clears his throat. "Hey...man."

"I was just leaving," Thad says, stumbling out of the papasan chair with one hand still over his eyes. As if Jeremy might start stripping down while he's still in the room. When he makes it to the doorway, feeling along the wall and furniture with his free hand, he mutters a quiet, "Good night," and clicks the door shut behind him.

"Lock it," I whisper, and Jeremy immediately obeys. Then I hold out my hand and crook my finger in a "come hither" gesture. He's been adamant about not letting me boss him around in the bedroom—and I've enjoyed the challenge—but tonight his feet follow my commands, like I'm a puppet master with his strings twined around my purple-tipped fingers.

He slides out of his snowy sneakers as he walks across the room, and as he gets close, I spread my knees wide to accommodate him. But instead of pushing me back into the mattress like I expect him to, he lowers himself to his knees in front of me and buries his head in my thigh, his arms wrapping around my hips and pulling me close.

"Freya..." he mumbles into my leg, his voice gravelly, and my heart starts skipping at the sound of his distress. Clearly, he was as upset by the Ryan story as Thad was.

"Asshat," I say, trying to lighten the mood. My fingertips sift through the silky strands of his hair. "I'm totally fine. I promise. I swear to the gods—every last one of them—that the second that fucker's fingers touched my skirt, my knee was so far up his groin I probably bruised his spleen." He laughs, a dry, unhappy sound, and pulls me closer. "Come on," I urge, hooking my hands under his armpits and pulling up, as if I could possibly budge him on my own. "That was almost a decade ago. I literally never even think of it anymore."

Except for every Thanksgiving, when I always eat a drumstick in memory of Mr. Taylor's right nut. May it rest in peace.

WAR ON CHRISTMAS: A HOLIDAY ROMANCE

"Don't let that ruin our night," I whisper. Jeremy is letting me win, following along as I tug him onto the bed with me. I scooch backward on the mattress, and he fits his chest to mine. When I make it up to the pillows, he goes limp, pinning me beneath his considerable weight, and I dip my head into the crook of his shoulder, breathing in his scent of crisp night air and laundry detergent. "I mean, for all we know, old Mrs. Johnson and old Mr. Pasterski will burn down the neighborhood tomorrow over Baby Jesus Gate, and we'll spend the rest of the holiday in emergency housing." My hands drift down his back to the round muscles of his ass, and I grab on tight. "We should really take advantage of the privacy while we have it."

He shakes his head against mine and eases my hands back onto the comforter. I pout, but he slides to the side and rolls me toward him, so we're face to face, his nose just a couple inches from mine.

"You're sure you're ok?" he asks, his fingertips floating along my cheek.

"*Yes*," I promise. "Absolutely. Now can we..." My hand trails down his stomach this time, but he catches my wrist and lifts it to his lips, pressing a soft kiss where my pulse jumps.

"Can I—" He clears his throat. "Can I just hold you? Just for tonight?"

My first instinct is to protest. It's not like I was traumatized by what happened. It was the emotional toll of the breakup that hurt the worst. Mr. Taylor's right nut was just collateral damage. However, one look into Jeremy's earnest eyes, and I soften, letting my body go limp against his.

Because I remember. I remember being in this room, listening to Jeremy tell me about the latest incident with Gary. I remember the crushing helplessness. The suffocating frustration that Jeremy, *my* Jeremy, was being hurt, and there was nothing I could do. So, I'd touch him. I'd run my fingers through his hair or let them drift up and down his forearm. I'd connect physically, so he'd know he wasn't alone.

The second he feels me relax, Jeremy wraps himself around me, all hairy limbs and muscle and heavy bones. Our legs intertwine, he tucks my head onto his shoulder, and then, in the twinkling glow of the Christmas tree with its black ornaments, we just breathe.

And for tonight, it's enough.

THIRTY-EIGHT

FREYA

4 days until Christmas...

"Warm enough, Sunshine?" Jeremy bends down to speak into my ear, and I nod as I lean my back into him, delighting in the feel of his tall, hard body supporting mine.

Apparently, over the past four years, Bethany has become cool. Apparently, Bethany is now the type of person who hires hot Santa Clauses and hosts winter solstice parties, complete with a raging bonfire, sparklers for the kids, and mulled wine that is better than mine.

Not that I'd admit that to her.

"Extra cinnamon sticks for good fiery energy," she'd told me, then winked as she'd looked over at Jeremy and muttered, "Not that you need any help with that."

Bethany's large backyard, a half-acre lot that would cost a bajillion dollars in Chicago, is teeming with people, all of them rosy-cheeked and smiling as they chat with casual friends they haven't seen since the winter weather set in. Drew is handing out sparklers, dark head bent toward the small mob of children surrounding him, but even their incessant screaming doesn't bring down my mood. Maybe Bethany's spawn have made me impervious to loud noises over the past ten days. Or maybe, I'm just...happy.

I scowl, and Jeremy's arms tighten around me.

"Our Yule log is holding up," he observes, his warm breath tickling my ear. He smells like cloves, fresh air, and Christmas, and when I catch myself turning my face into his neck to breathe him in, I snap back around to stare at the fire.

Jeremy had taken the day off from helping his mother, who was ready for a break anyway, and we'd spent the afternoon with Thad and Sam making a Yule log. It's a tradition that gets posted every year on *Hope & Stardust*, but when I was in Chicago, I didn't have a place to burn one. This year, Bethany provided the log, a fallen branch from the maple tree on the back corner of her property, and the rest of us went for a cold, snowy hike through a nearby nature preserve, collecting random pine cones, leaves, and dried plants to decorate it with. Then Sam and I had attached the "decorations" with twine.

I'm not sure why the resulting Yule log was so beautiful. It wasn't the type of decoration you'd find back in Chicago. It wasn't shiny or glitzy. There were no lights or polka-dotted bows or curled ribbons. It was rough and poky, the dehydrated wildflowers a stark reminder of the short, fleeting nature of summer.

But beautiful it was. Even Bethany said so, which makes it official.

WAR ON CHRISTMAS: A HOLIDAY ROMANCE

Best of all, Bethany invited the four of us to stay over tonight after the party, so we don't need to worry about a designated driver. Thad and Sam are staying in her guest room, while Jeremy and I get the small apartment over her garage. Which means that for the first time since our official date, we'll get to spend a night together without a relative down the hallway.

There are only four nights left, and I'm determined that this one...this one is going to be special.

"Are you having fun?" Bethany pops up next to me with no warning, and I bite back a squeal of surprise.

"Easy, Sunshine," Jeremy murmurs like I'm a spooked horse, then chuckles when I bump my elbow back into his ribs.

"This is really nice," I tell Bethany. And I mean it. It's not fancy. In addition to the mulled wine, there are giant tubs of popcorn, along with marshmallows and hot cocoa for the kids. Overall, though, it's simple and laid-back. Not Bethany's usual Martha-Stewart-wannabe style.

"Thanks." She dimples at me. "It started with only a handful of people—mostly our family and my Bunco ladies—but it's grown every year into"—she gestures at her yard and the dozens of people—"this. People really like the whole winter solstice theme."

I nod, even though I'm a little salty that celebrating solstice isn't quite as subversive as I thought it was.

Do I "fit in" in Northview, Wisconsin, now?

I push that thought away—like a lot of thoughts lately—and clear my throat.

"I always loved the idea of celebrating the longest night of the year," I confess. "Of really embracing the dark." I turn my eyes up to the smattering of clear, bright stars in the inky black sky. I love Chicago, but we don't get stars like this. When I look away, I catch Bethany staring at me, her brow furrowed in a cute, bemused kind of way. I stiffen. "What?" I ask.

"Nothing!" She blinks, turning her gaze to the stars as well. A long pause. "I guess...I guess I just thought of solstice as celebrating the light. Longer days on their way, and all that."

I snort. "You would," I mutter, then to my surprise, we both dissolve into laughter.

Across the fire, Abi and a few friends are huddled together whispering, and as Bethany's giggles die down, I nod at her daughter. Her nose and cheeks are pink from the cold, her dark hair woven into an elaborate braid that hangs over her shoulder. She looks happy enough chatting with her friends.

"How's she doing?" I ask.

Bethany follows my gaze and sighs. "She'll be ok. Don't worry. You've got other stuff to focus on. *Fun* stuff." She bumps her shoulder into Jeremy's, as if I could have missed her point. "You're good for her," she says, smiling up at him.

Dammit, Bethany. I force myself to stay soft and relaxed in Jeremy's arms. No need to react to a throwaway comment that doesn't change anything. Jeremy, however, chuckles lightly and rests his chin on my head.

"She's already perfect," he replies, his arms squeezing my waist gently. "I'm just basking in her infernal darkness."

A throaty, full-belly laugh bursts out of me—I blame the mulled wine—and Bethany rolls her eyes. "Too fucking adorable," she mutters under her breath, then squeezes my hand as she drifts away to chat up another guest.

Too fucking adorable. The words drop like tiny bombs around Jeremy and me, words that under normal circumstances would be considered casual and sweet. *Oh, look at that. People think we're adorable.* Except there is no *we*.

I inhale through my nose and exhale slowly through my mouth, begging my suddenly pounding heart to ease. Overall, I've been disciplined about staying in the moment. About making every second with Jeremy count. Then there are times, like this, when the dread sets in. Times when my mind races ahead to a future that looks exactly like my past. Getting home late from the theater with only Hecate there to greet me. Grabbing drinks at Joe's with Leo and the crew, exchanging empty flirtations over dirty martinis. Indulging in a hot, steamy bath for one, glass of red wine in hand, with no big, hairy Viking body surrounding me. I'll have my freedom. My space. My independence. All the things I love about my life in Chicago.

I just won't have him.

"Do you think we can sneak away yet?" Jeremy murmurs in my ear, and I nod, even as I swallow the lump in my throat. "Good." His arms tighten around me. "Because I have a Yule present for you."

THIRTY-NINE

JEREMY

"A Yule present?" Freya flops onto the bed cross-legged, leaning back on her hands. She shed her coat and winter gear on the way in, and she's looking barefoot and beautiful in curve-hugging skinny jeans and a black sweater. "You're an overachiever."

We managed to escape to the apartment above Bethany's garage without attracting anyone's attention. Now, I'm standing across the small studio apartment from her, hands stuffed in my pockets. The open concept bedroom, living space, and kitchenette are decorated in soft, hazy shades of gray and taupe, all dimly lit by a small lamp.

"Well, I didn't have to eat nineteen Burger King meals to get it," I tease, "so I can't compete with you circa Christmas 2001. Your title as Greatest Gift Giver of All Time is safe."

Freya fluffs her hair, preening.

WAR ON CHRISTMAS: A HOLIDAY ROMANCE

The moment of levity eases the tightness I've been carrying in my chest all day. I'd tried to keep things light. I'd smiled and joked through our hike, pelting Freya with snowballs every time she turned her back on me. (Which she'd promptly avenge by jumping on my back and stuffing handfuls of snow down my coat.) I'd chatted with folks at the solstice party and played tag with Andy, August, and Aiden. I'd sipped the mulled wine and gazed at crystal-clear stars I'd never be able to see in Chicago. But through it all, those fucking words ran through my head on a loop.

"Go ahead and have your fun, but girls like her are not the marrying type."

Freya—my headstrong Freya who doesn't take directions for shit—had somehow absorbed them until they rewrote the next decade of her life.

Maybe it's because, in a sense, there's a grain of truth in the words. Because that old windbag had probably meant "the marrying type" in a very specific way. He'd meant a pliable, biddable girl who would accept marriage as a hierarchy with her kneeling humbly at her husband's feet.

And Freya sure as hell *isn't*—and never was—that kind of "marrying type."

However, you're never going to convince me that she—the girl who'd nearly swooned with delight when she'd read about Billy Bob Thornton and Angelina Jolie's weird-ass blood necklaces—is a commitment-phobe. It might be her best kept secret, but Freya I'm-a-closet-Swiftie Nilsen is a hardcore romantic.

I just need to remind her.

Following Freya's lead, I slide off my boots, coat, and hat, running my hand through my hair as I cross the small space to my overnight bag and grab my gift for her. After years of spending the holidays by myself, selecting and wrapping gifts this year has been a novelty. For most people, the ritual of gift-giving may be a chore, but the act had felt significant to me. A symbol, hopefully, of a new stage in life. A stage where I'm not alone. A stage where my past, present, and future are more integrated.

Freya reaches out her pretty hand, and I place the rectangular package into her palm as I sink onto the bed next to her. Her side tips into mine as the mattress dips, but it's still not close enough, so I slide up to the pillows and pull her back into my chest, my legs enveloping her.

There's a part of me that wants to drag her so we're face to face, nose to nose, and demand that she admit how we fit together. Naturally. Effortlessly. Like two trees planted side by side as saplings so that they bend and weave and embrace each other as they grow, their roots inextricably tangled beneath the earth's surface.

The wiser part of me recognizes that Freya already knows this. It's what scares the hell out of her.

Her fingers smooth over the wrapping paper, a white background scattered with gold suns, and as she looks at it, her mouth drags into a smile.

"Fine," she says, "I give in. Why did you start calling me Sunshine?"

I chuckle into her hair.

"You fell so hard into your emo stage. It was like you were begging the world to see you as so dark and scary. So, I knew calling you Sunshine would piss you off, which meant you'd pay attention to me." I clear my throat, my face heating.

She twists her head around to narrow her eyes at me, and I laugh as I drop a kiss on the tip of her nose.

"I also think..." I tuck my head next to hers, so it's nestled into the curve of her shoulder. "You were never *all* dark, Frey." My hand trails up her ribs to the soft, sweet-smelling skin of her neck, and I reach across her chest to draw the neckline of her sweater over her shoulder to reveal her tattoo. Her witch's garden. "You've always been the medicine to me." My lips trail along the swirling black lines. "Everyone else kept looking away from my mom and me. They insisted we were ok because Gary put food on the table and didn't smack us around or whatever. And that? *That* felt fucking dark."

I swallow, and Freya's hand snakes up my neck to grab me by the nape. A silent, comforting *I'm here.* I nibble along her shoulder before I continue.

"The fact that you never asked me to deny what was happening? That you listened to me and acknowledged the truth I was living with?" I pause for a moment, trying to find the right words. "That was pure light. You were a—a *star*, Freya, illuminating my deepest, darkest secrets. I never thanked you properly for that, but I should have. I should have—"

She shakes her head.

"Don't you dare thank me for that," she interrupts, and I'm shocked at the vehemence in her voice. "Don't you dare thank me. I should have been there for—" Frowning, I turn her around so she's facing me, rearranging her legs so they wrap around my waist. She's clutching the present to her chest, still shaking her head. "I should have been there for you. You *needed* me, Jeremy. In a big way. And I wasn't there. I—"

"You were always there." I pull back, tipping her head so she's forced to meet my gaze. "Like a little angel on my shoulder, whispering in my ear." She snorts, and my lips tug into a smile. "Well, like a *fallen* angel," I amend, then jerk my head at the present pressed to her chest. "Open it."

She releases her breath in a tiny puff, nodding, and as she starts to unwrap the gift, I slide her next to me, my arm wrapped around her shoulders. My belly gives a nervous twitch. Freya is a notoriously amazing gift giver. She sees people with unerring—and quite frankly, unnerving—accuracy, and she chooses presents that leave the recipient feeling validated and seen. It's like a superpower.

But I know, deep down, that what I'm giving her is pretty damn good.

She tosses the wrapping paper onto the nightstand, covering the digital clock that keeps blinking a neon red 12:00, and runs her fingers reverently over the black sketchbook in her hands.

"Jeremy, is this—"

"From high school, yeah. Senior year." My face warms. "Well, mostly high school. I may have made a few"— I cough—"additions over the past week. But I have to warn you, I'm out of practice. I'm all straight lines and right angles now, so don't—"

"I love it," she breathes.

I grin. I knew she'd love it. There's nothing that Freya craves more than secrets, than the hidden nooks and crannies we hide from the rest of the world, and giving her my sketchbook is the equivalent of handing over my journal. As a kid, I spent hours drawing in these notebooks, and it drove Freya wild that I'd never let her see them. I believe the exact phrase I usually used was, "Over my dead body," to which Freya would always reply, "Gladly."

The cover opens with a creak, and Freya snuggles in closer, her head resting on my shoulder as she peruses the first page. It takes two whole seconds before her sharp gasp echoes through the small apartment.

"It's Roxy!" she squeals, sitting up straight, her legs bent to support the book.

There's no denying it. The sketch staring back at us, a dark-haired, pointy-eared elf with a heart-shaped face, full lips, and a beauty mark next to her pert nose is absolutely Roxy Noteleaf, right down to the bow and arrow hanging casually from one shoulder. Freya's fingers float above the paper, like she desperately wants to touch it, but she won't risk smudging the graphite.

"Keep going," I urge her, excited by her initial response.

They're not all of her. There's an ancient wizard with a distinct walrus-look, who Freya immediately recognizes as our high school trig teacher, Mr. Zimmer. There's Thad as his cleric character, Stromm Godsan, draped in robes. Even her dad disguised as a Tolkien Ent, his beard carefully shaded into the knots and grooves of the tree's bark.

But they're mostly her.

Freya as a sun elf, light emanating from her fingertips and hair. Freya as a menacing fairy with torn black wings and sharp, jagged teeth. ("Pretty sure I drew that one the day you pulled ahead of me in AP U.S. History," I admit with a sheepish grin, and Freya laughs.) Freya as a fairy queen, feminine and lush, covered head to toe in flowers. Freya as a vampire, hugged in skintight leather from shirt to knee-high boots, her fangs dripping blood. ("The day I found out you were dating that skater dweeb." There's no hiding my blush. "I was a tiny bit jealous.")

She loves them all—I can tell from the way she bites her lip to stop herself from smiling—but she loves the dark, creepy ones the best.

When she gets to the last handful of pages, I slap a hand over the book, cringing.

"These are new," I rush to explain. "I haven't drawn anything but buildings in—"

"Move your hand, Asshat," Freya orders, and like the poor, lovesick fool I am, I obey.

Freya falls silent as she studies the new additions, her face focused and serious. I see the drawings with an artist's eye, taking in every flaw. The shading that's not quite right and the smudges from where I had to erase, over and over. But I try to see them from her perspective now. Sketches not based on fantasy, but on moments we've lived together over the past week and a half. Grown-up Freya, her face a little leaner, cheekbones more pronounced. Freya and Andy, with her head tipped toward him, listening intently. Freya's dark eyes peeking at me over a windowsill, a winter hat pulled low over her head. Freya sleeping, her hand resting under her cheek, her thick lashes splayed across pale cheeks.

They're...intimate. The level of detail, the damning accuracy of her face and body and expressions. They're a confession, as surely as dropping to my knees and declaring my undying love for her.

"Jeremy..." she murmurs as her fingertips hover above the paper. My heart pounds behind my breastbone, every beat protesting the rejection I've set myself up for, and I swallow, not sure how to respond. But before I can, Freya turns to the final page and freezes inside the circle of my arm, her breath catching. "How did you find out?" she chokes.

I look down at the final sketch, my sole attempt from a couple days ago at my teenage style of epic fantasy. Freya is front and center, of course, but in this picture, I've depicted her as a sea creature, bold and terrifying and gorgeous. Her stare is direct, her expression fathomless. Myriad limbs snake from a voluptuous body, six of them ending in monstrous, scale-covered heads with sharp, threatening teeth. She's balanced on a jagged rock, and around her, the water rotates inwards, creating a vortex.

My mouth twists with confusion. "Find out what?"

"About Scylla," she whispers. I shake my head, not sure what she's talking about, and her lips lift as she continues, her eyes still glued to the page. "Remember reading *The Odyssey* in eighth grade?" she asks, and I nod. Freya, Thad, and I—as self-proclaimed nerds—had been a little obsessed with it. "Scylla," Freya explains, "was the sea monster that Odysseus had to pass. He lost one sailor to each of her six heads." Her fingers trace the six heads on the sketch. "Scylla—well, Scylla Wilde—also happens to be my stage name when I perform."

And just like that, I can picture her, stripped down and exposed, hips and breasts swaying to a hypnotic rhythm that holds the audience enthralled. Her arms circling, wrists twirling like each person's attention is a string that she's wrapping, wrapping, wrapping around her pretty fingers, pulling them in whether they want to be or not. She's a storm, a hurricane, a force of nature, drawing them to her with a finality, an inevitability, they can't escape.

Scylla, indeed.

She lifts her head so she can meet my gaze, her red lips parted, and these unspoken things between us snap—*thwip*—like a broken guitar string. The longing ache, rooted deep in my chest. The jealousy and the protectiveness and the *mine, mine, mine*. The rightness of cradling her close and the way our bodies fit together.

And for once, she's not denying it. There are no deflections. No sassy, snappy responses designed to make me lose my everlasting mind. Just her clear, slate-gray eyes, open and vulnerable, then the hard press of her lips against mine.

FORTY

JEREMY

I wasn't prepared for Freya to launch herself at me. But I'm definitely not opposed to it.

She's pinning me to the bed, so I'm sinking into the pillows propped against the headboard. Sinking into the sensation of being consumed by her. By her flowers-and-patchouli scent. By the press of her fingers against my ribs under my shirt. By the quick, panting breaths she takes as her mouth captures mine.

I'm drowning in her. And it's glorious.

"Frey?" I ask between long, searching kisses, her face cupped between my palms. I don't know what I'm asking. There's something that's shifted, something disorienting, and I need her to anchor me. To make it all make sense.

"What?" She peels my shirt over my head, and I lean forward to help her.

WAR ON CHRISTMAS: A HOLIDAY ROMANCE

The Henley goes sailing across the room, along with all the questions racing through my mind. *Do you feel it too? This pull? Is the game over now? Have you given up on the whole fling idea? Did you ache for me like I ached for you all those years?*

"Nothing," I mutter against her lips. My fingers clutch her hips and I move to roll her over, to change positions so I'm on top, controlling the momentum.

"Please." Her hand presses into my chest, and I freeze. Physically, it would be too easy to keep moving. I'm stronger than her. But her gaze, so serious and pleading, has me relaxing back into the pillows, my muscles going limp at her single uttered request. If I'm Samson, she's Delilah, rendering me weak and useless, and all it takes is that soft, husky *please*. No haircut necessary.

Freya pushes me back and slowly trails her poison-apple lips down my jaw, my neck, my chest.

"Why did you have to be so beautiful?" she whispers as her tongue flicks over my belly button like liquid fire. My abs twitch in response, even as I choke out a rough laugh.

"I've asked myself the exact same thing about you, Sunshine."

She's taking her time, her lips trailing along every curve of muscle and bone, and I'm trying not to think about her fingers working deftly at the straining fly of my jeans. I started my whole strategy of staying in control to separate myself from the fuckboys she's used and discarded over the years. It was a lucky coincidence that it also allowed me to pace myself. I could slow things down and pull back whenever I felt my passion outpacing hers.

Now that Freya's finally in control, she's having none of that.

She leans back as she lowers my zipper, and I grunt as my cock springs free from the denim, only the thin material of my boxer briefs between her warm hands and my skin. But her fingers barely brush against me before she moves back up, shifting her attention to my collar bones and shoulders and slowly, slowly down each arm.

No inch of bare skin goes untouched, first by her fingertips, then those red lips, and I'm mesmerized by the sight of them trailing over my torso and arms, her kisses as soft as silk. The whole thing is sexy as hell, slow and hypnotic, but there's something else there too. A tenderness. There's no urgency in her touch. Every graze of her fingers or lips is an end in and of itself. By the time she reaches my hand, pressing a kiss to the center then cupping it around her jaw, I'm a mess. A trembling, goosebump-covered mess who's about to punch a hole through his boxer briefs with his erection.

"Can I tell you a secret?" she asks as she presses her cheek harder into my palm.

I swallow. With Freya, I could be signing up for anything. A "four more days" reminder. An "I just want you to know this is still hate fucking." (That would be a lie. Obviously.) But I want it. Whatever it is.

"You can tell me anything, Frey," I rasp out.

"I've always loved your hands." She turns her head and drags my thumb over the sharp edge of her teeth, then nips the pad at the end. My hips jerk underneath her, driving my cock into the cradle of her hips, and she sinks into me, letting me feel her heat through her jeans. "They're the first thing I noticed about you. Noticed like *that*, I mean." She wiggles her eyebrows in case I didn't pick up on her meaning, and I huff out a laugh. "I'd watch you drawing in these books for hours, obsessing about the shape of your fingers. The strength and speed of them as you sketched." She flicks the tip of her tongue over the spot she bit on my thumb, and I squeeze my eyes shut tight at the sheer pleasure of it. "I *dreamt* about them, Jeremy."

WAR ON CHRISTMAS: A HOLIDAY ROMANCE

I've never noticed anything remarkable about my hands. I could draw Freya's from memory—every delicate, fine-boned finger and the freckle at the base of her thumb—but if somebody asked me to describe my own, I don't know that I could. But watching Freya kiss and nibble and torture each fingertip transforms them into powerful erogenous zones. They'd just been waiting for her to wake them up.

"What—" The sight of my pointer finger getting sucked between her lips distracts me for a second, but I soldier on. "What did you dream about?"

She releases my finger with a chuckle, rolling her eyes. "Lots of 'Draw me like one of your French girls fantasies," she admits, performing a flawless impression of Kate Winslet from *Titanic*. Then she nods at the sketchbook lying next to us on the bed, open to the final picture. "*That* definitely would have done it for me. All those years you wouldn't let me see what you were drawing? One peek and I would have spontaneously dropped my panties like a bad habit."

I scoff. "Freya Nilsen spontaneously drops her panties for no one. Especially not for an Abercrombie & Fitch zombie."

I'd meant it as a joke, a little punch of self-deprecating humor, but her forehead pinches and she shakes her head.

"That was never you. Not really."

She slides down the bed, sliding my pants and briefs with her and tossing them to the floor. I'm about to point out how unfair it is that she's still fully clothed, but before I can open my mouth, she's standing at the side of the bed. She shifts her stance, pointing the toes of one foot toward me to turn her waist to the best advantage as she moves to peel her sweater over her head. It's a performance. An orchestrated "big reveal." She lifts the edge of the black sweater, unveiling a smooth strip of pale skin, and her fingers slowly caress it, drawing my eyes exactly where she wants them.

I wet my lips. I would love a private performance from Scylla Wilde someday. But tonight...tonight I just want Freya. As tantalizing as a burlesque-show-for-one is, that performance is a wall. A barrier between us.

And we've had too many of those.

Silently, I slide to the floor before her, my bare knees landing on the hardwood, and I bury my face in her stomach. Her fingers release her sweater, then they're in my hair, pulling me close, and my lips are on her skin, tasting and caressing and savoring. My heart pounds—*More. Faster. Now.*—but our movements are slow as we work together to undress her until she's naked and kneeling on the floor with me, hands in my hair, her kisses deep and desperate. When she pushes against my chest, urging me back onto the bed, I fall back onto the pillows and drag her on top of me.

My hands roam over every curve of her body, drinking in the satin feel of her skin. Skin that plenty of people have seen and longed to touch. But I'm the one who gets to feel it, soft and sleek under my fingertips. Her eyes are on mine, her hands pressed into the muscles of my chest, and the head of my cock strains between her legs. She's hot and soaking wet, and she's *Freya*. The closest thing I can imagine to heaven. But she stays hovering above me, biting her lip.

"What?" I ask, skating my hands from the round globes of her ass to her waist. Everything in my body is screaming to be inside of her, to feel her surrounding me. My hips want to thrust off the mattress, chasing her heat, but that's not what she wants. She wants my surrender. So, I stay still and let her lead.

"You were perfect," she whispers, dropping her hips so the head of my cock slides inside her. *Fuck*. She's slick and warm. Sheer bliss. But her eyes are wide and earnest. What she's saying is important. So, I try. For her.

"Huh?" I grunt.

She lowers herself more, taking another inch of me, and when her eyes flutter closed—as if she's enjoying the sensation of me filling her almost as much as I am—I have to think about baseball so fucking hard I'll never be able to watch the sport again without blushing. Forget bases and bats and home runs. All baseball means to me now is the red-hot sensation of Freya letting her body go soft and supple around my cock until I'm buried deep inside her. My muscles give that subtle, undeniable jerk that only happens with her—just to let her know she owns me—and I grit my teeth, willing myself not to focus on the ache in my balls and how good it would feel to come inside her, right this fucking instant.

She must not want this to be over any more than I do, because she takes pity on me and stills, giving me a moment to absorb the feel of her. When I've regained control, I tip my hips into a soft thrust, and she answers with a subtle rock, a light, gentle rhythm that draws us closer together.

"You were perfect," she repeats, her voice a little breathier now. "I loved your overgrown, shaggy hair. I loved your dorky hobbies and your dorky sense of humor and your dorkier glasses. I loved your secret drawings."

Her eyes are on mine, unblinking as she moves above me, and I'm unraveling under the intensity of her gaze. Because I know her, and my cool, aloof Freya isn't really cool or aloof at all. The distance? The stoicism? They're just walls, defense mechanisms, and finally—*finally*—she's letting them crumble around us.

My fingers dig into her hips, urging her on. Trying to give more of myself, all of myself, even though it feels like it should be physically impossible to be closer. She grinds her hips into mine, and a breath shudders out of me.

"You could have had me." I thrust, trying to get deeper, closer, *more*. "I was always yours. Always."

She shakes her head, her dark waves swinging. "It's like I couldn't recognize you anymore." She rocks on top of me as she talks, and the friction between us has me tightening, on edge. It's too much, but not enough. Her movements quicken, taking on new urgency as I fight to keep my orgasm at bay. "I could forgive them for what they did to me. The Freaky Freya thing. The prom hex rumors—"

"Did you—"

"Never gonna tell," she breathes, and a smile plays at the edges of her lips. Then her eyes are on mine again, pinning me in place, and any hint of humor is gone. "But, Jeremy, I could never forgive them for trying to change *you*."

I take her hands and slide them to my breastbone, where my heart is trying to beat out of my chest. For her. Always for her.

"We're the same, Frey." I keep one hand over both of hers, holding them in place, then rest the other over her chest, between her full, swaying breasts. Beneath my fingers, her heart pumps out a frantic rhythm, and maybe it's my imagination or desperation or magical thinking, but I swear the cadence of it matches my own. I press into her pulse, my fingers spreading. "We're the same. Always were. Always will be. No high school makeover was gonna change that." I shake my head. "No amount of time was gonna change that."

I worry for a second that I said too much. Got too close to the truth. But then her mouth is on mine and she's moving, fluid and graceful, sweeping me under and away in a current so strong I have no chance of resisting.

WAR ON CHRISTMAS: A HOLIDAY ROMANCE

So, I don't.

In the past I felt sorry for the sailors who were lured to their deaths by siren songs. Sad, pathetic puppets who lost all control, all sense of self. Now, though, as Freya rides me closer and closer to completion, I get it. The sweet promise of oblivion, of giving up the fight. Of surrender. This war we've been waging—not just for the past two weeks, but for two decades—crumbles around us, laid to waste by the bright sheen of Freya's eyes and the frenzied movements of her hips. She might be drawing me to my ruin, but I don't even care.

Heat gathers. My balls draw tight. My cock swells. I want to hold back. To watch her tumble first. To let her pleasure send me over the edge. I press a hand to her back, pushing her forward until the hard pebble of her nipple is in my mouth, and I suck, hard. She gasps, her pussy clenching around me, but when she pushes my shoulders back down into the pillows, I follow. I obey.

"*You,*" she moans, her eyes glassy. "I want to feel you come."

And I'm done. Finished. Hers. My body, my heart. My very soul. My hips pump once more. Twice. Then I'm lost, left gasping and groaning through my release. She drinks it in, hungry for my capitulation, the rolling grind of her body on mine relentless as she's seized by her own orgasm. Her eyes squeeze shut, but I reach up and cup her face until she opens them through the wild euphoria. When it passes, she slumps into me, soft and spent, and surrender has never, ever felt so good.

***

She wakes me in the early morning, tugging my hand until I roll closer to her, then on top of her. The longest night of the year is still dark, but the tiny lamp we never turned off casts Freya's perfect face in a soft glow of light and shadow. I sink into her with a groan, still half asleep, and she smiles up at me as she wraps her legs around my waist.

I blink. She must have snuck to the bathroom and washed up. Her face is clean, her lips the soft, natural pink I remember from childhood. Her gray eyes are fresh and unlined. I steady myself on my elbows so I can push her hair back and study her face.

"Hey." My voice is all sleep and sandpaper, but she doesn't seem to care.

"Hey." Her voice is husky and sexy as hell.

Then she gives a wiggle, sending all my blood straight to my cock, and we're laughing, foreheads pressed together until we're desperate and breathless and not laughing at all. When our bodies finally still and settle, I curl myself around her, and she sighs as she presses a kiss to my forearm.

***

When I wake up again to sunlight shining through the apartment windows, she's gone.

Forty-one

FREYA

3 days until Christmas...

"I don't understand." My mom stands in front of me wringing her hands, shifting nervously from foot to foot. "I thought everything was going so well. Christmas is still three days away, and Thad is here, and I thought you and Jeremy—"

"You don't need to understand it." She flinches at the ice-cold edge to my voice. Thank the gods for the numbness surrounding me, or I'd feel like a total asshole. But I can't back down. "You just need to respect it. It's time for me to go home."

Home. The message is loud and clear. Home is Chicago. Home is *not* here. I use that word like a weapon, and, judging by the way my mom rapidly blinks away tears and retreats to the kitchen, it's a direct hit.

It's better this way, I remind myself.

Jeremy isn't the only victim of me letting the lines get blurry. Late-night tarot readings. Helping out at the shop. Christmas festivals and solstice parties. I let myself slip with Mom and Bethany, too. I let them think our relationship can be something it can't.

I'm never going to be what they all want me to be. I'm never going to be *Bethany*. Perfect daughter. Cutesy shopkeeper. The type of woman who looks at a man like Jeremy and says things like, "The man is going to be a fantastic dad." I can't be Bethany any more than I can be the partner Jeremy needs for his golf and gym and 401(k) life.

Something about this fucking trip lulled me. I let my defenses slip. Let myself play pretend, like I could fit in here. With my family. With Jeremy.

And now we're all going to pay the price.

I sit on the living room couch, surrounded by my bags, with Hecate mewing grumpily in her carrier. My knees bounce as I watch the driveway and will Leo to appear. He'd immediately responded to my SOS text at four this morning and confirmed he could borrow Todd's car to pick me up. Depending on how fast Leo's driving, he could be here any minute.

Then again, so could Jeremy.

Fuck, fuck, fuck.

Last night got out of hand. Should I blame it on the mulled wine? That fucking sketchbook? Maybe it's just the natural, way too predictable consequence of reconnecting with Jeremy, my ~~best friend, arch rival, one who got away, friend, lover~~, one who's gonna break me. Whatever the reason, my defenses crumbled, and as I lay in Jeremy's arms this morning, dreading Christmas with all the doom and gloom of an execution, it became clear that the time to say goodbye is right now. Or maybe it was seventeen years ago. Maybe, just maybe, eighteen-year-old Freya got it right.

Maybe the past two weeks have been a mistake.

I thought I had a few days left of the free fall. A few more days of the rush and the wind whipping across my face before I hit the surface. *Splat!* Whatever happened last night, though, it accelerated the impact. I can already feel the pain of it, sharp and jarring. Not just the ache of missing him, that low-grade pulse living in the background that I learned to live with after twenty years, but a splintering. A deep, terrifying knowing that, on some level, I'm never again going to feel totally complete once he's gone.

Todd's boxy blue MINI Cooper rounds the corner onto our street, and I surge to my feet, bags and Hecate in hand. I'm vaguely aware of my mom following me out to the driveway, of her muttered "I just don't *understand*," but my sole focus is on throwing bags into the back seat and getting the hell out of here.

Leo, either totally missing the mood or really enjoying the drama, rolls down his window and slides his aviator sunglasses down his nose, ignoring me completely to give my mom a wide grin straight out of toothpaste ad. (No, seriously. He did a toothpaste ad.)

"And you must be Mrs. Nilsen!" He puts the car in park and jumps out of the driver's seat, gripping my mom by the elbows as he looks her up and down. My mom stops her fretting to stare back at him. Leo is, by all accounts, startlingly handsome. "Freya," he chides, "you didn't tell me that your mother is a dead ringer for June Cleaver. How flippin' adorable is she? Now Mary—can I call you Mary?"—Mom nods, clearly dazed—"tell me *all* of Freya's most embarrassing moments. I mean—"

I'm opening my mouth to shut this—whatever it is—down, but the screech of tires down the block sends an icy chill from my neck to my tailbone. I don't need to turn around to know there's a silver sedan racing toward us and that it's driven by one seriously pissed off Viking.

"Mom. Bye. I'll call soon." I urge her back to the sidewalk, away from the car, and Leo pouts with annoyance. "You," I jab a finger at Leo, "in the car. *Now*. We need to—"

Jeremy's car slams to a halt in his mom's driveway, and I jump at the bang of the driver's side door. I swallow a shriek and grab Leo's hand to drag him toward the waiting MINI Cooper.

"Freya Estelle Nilsen!" Jeremy's voice booms as he tromps through the snow separating our driveways. He's coatless, in his jeans and forest-green Henley from last night, the sleeves pushed up his forearms, his boots untied. Morning scruff dots his jaw, giving him an extra rugged edge. Snow flies with every step he takes, and I race toward the passenger door, but Leo—that goddamn traitor—stands rooted to the spot, his mouth agape.

"Is *he* the emergency?" he asks out of the corner of his mouth. "Because I fail to see the prob—"

"Shut it, Leo!" I snap as I grab for the handle, but before I can open the door, two large, square-fingered hands splay on either side of my shoulders, holding it shut. Caging me in. I tug on the handle. I mean, don't desperate mothers lift entire cars off trapped children? I should be able to open a car *door* with enough adrenaline. But it doesn't budge.

"You are seriously pissing me off, Sunshine," Jeremy growls in my ear.

I close my eyes, digging deep for the willpower to keep my face neutral as I turn around in the circle of his arms. When I open them, he's glaring at me, leaning down so he's just inches away. I glare back.

"Jeremy Kelly!" From across the street, Mrs. Johnson's shrill voice cuts through the frigid air like a blow horn. "Is that Nilsen girl bothering you?"

Fuck me. That old crone always did like Jeremy better than me. It boggles the mind that anyone would look at Jeremy trapping me against a car and ask if *he* was ok, but that's Mrs. Johnson for you. I peek around Jeremy's shoulder to narrow my eyes at her, standing on her porch in her nightgown and winter coat, white hair blowing like a dandelion puff. She takes a step back, like I've just given her the plague with my evil eye.

"I'm fine, Mrs. Johnson," Jeremy calls out, keeping his eyes on me.

"You sure I shouldn't call the police?" a deep, shaky voice asks. Old Mr. Pasterski stands in his driveway holding an ancient cell phone the size of a cereal box, clearly unwilling to let Mrs. Johnson get the edge on neighborhood gossip. "You know that Nilsen girl has it out for you."

I huff out a breath, and a cloud of mist rises between Jeremy and me.

"Believe me, Mr. Pasterski, I know," Jeremy calls out over his shoulder. On either side of me, his thick, tree-trunk arms flex, and I have the distinct impression he's trying not to throttle me. "But I've got it all under control." *Hardly.* "No need for the police. You and Mrs. Johnson can go back inside now."

"Oh my god, Frey," Leo pipes up, "is this like one of those Christmas romances on TV? Is he the one who got away? Does he want you to pop out his ginormous, lumberjack babies and—"

"Honey," my mom, bless her heart, interrupts him, "why don't you come inside for a cup of coffee? It must have been an early morning for you, and there's a fresh pot ready to go."

Jeremy and I stare each other down, the air thick with tension, while Mom herds Leo into the house, both of them chatting away. A quick glance across the street confirms that Mrs. Johnson and Mr. Pasterski are still watching us, of course, but I ignore them, turning my attention back to the real threat. Jeremy towers over me, pain and confusion etched on every line of his face.

"I thought we were past this," he grits out between his teeth. "I thought, after last night—"

"I guess you thought wrong."

He nods, the muscles in his throat working. Even pissed off, he's so beautiful, it makes my stomach flip. The early morning sunshine gilds his sandy hair and golden skin, and the thought that this, right here, might be the last time I ever see him leaves me weak-kneed with panic.

It's for the best. The best for him, I remind myself. There may have been a time when things could have gone differently. *We* could have gone differently. But we were still kids when our paths diverged. The amount of work and compromise it would take to forge a real life together now... I don't change myself for relationships. I gave that up after Ryan, and dammit, I'm not starting again now. Jeremy needs someone tamer, gentler.

Someone who's not me.

"I can't stop you from leaving." His voice drops. "But I'm damned if you're going to ghost me again. If you're going to go, look me in the eye this time and tell me why. At least be fucking honest."

I press my shoulders into the car door, shivering in my thin, gray sweater as I cross my arms over my chest and tuck my hands under my armpits to hide their shaking. That pain, sharp and blinding, is rattling behind my breastbone. I stare over Jeremy's shoulder, trying my best to appear bored. When he realizes I'm not going to respond, he releases a long, thunderous grumble, his hands tensing like he wants to rip off the car door, Hulk-style.

"*Fuck*, Frey!" he hisses, gripping my chin and forcing me to meet his gaze. "Don't do this."

"I'm just doing what needs to be done."

"Bullshit."

"Fuck you!" I snap. "We're too different. Our *lives* are too—"

"No, fuck *you*!" he snaps back, brow furrowing. "And fuck this whole lie you tell yourself that you have so much more integrity than everyone else. That you're so much more honest. That's what you're supposed to be so good at, isn't it? Honesty?"

I rip my chin out of his grasp and stare straight at his chest, a solid green wall expanding and contracting with every labored breath he takes. My throat tightens, and I try to swallow the burning sensation, but I can't, so I choke on it.

"You're scared," he continues. "You try to act like such a bad ass, but you're fucking terrified. Because you love so big and so hard." His forehead drops to mine, and the point of warm, skin-to-skin contact brings back such clear memories of early this morning—his head pressed to mine as he moved over me, inside me—that I lock my knees to stop my legs from wobbling. "You're scared because if we give this thing a shot—a real shot—and it doesn't work out, you don't trust yourself to handle the fallout."

I squeeze my eyes shut. Try to block out the anguish edging his voice.

"I'm done changing myself to please a partner." I make my voice hard. Cold. But even I can hear it tremble. "I *like* myself, Jeremy, and I won't compromise myself for a relationship. I'm done with—"

"When have I asked you to be anything—*anything*—other than what you are?" He pulls back, stares me down. "I love you, Freya. *You*. I loved you then, when we were still practically kids, and I love you now. Exactly as you are. So use your bullshit excuses on someone else, because I have *never* asked you to change."

My eyes sting, and I drop my head to hide my tears, wrapping my arms tighter around myself. Like I can hold the pieces of my breaking heart together if I press hard enough. This, *this* is what I wanted to avoid. This scene. This suffering. Jeremy shakes his head, and his Adam's apple bobs as he steps back.

Away from me.

"I think you deserve the world, Frey. We could have everything. I want to give you *everything*—" His voice breaks, and I swallow back a sob. "*You're* the one who's too scared to try."

FOrTy-TWO

JEREMY

2 days until Christmas...

"Jem?"

I ignore her, choosing instead to focus on Bruce Willis kicking some serious ass as I work my way through a second box of Lucky Charms, the crunch of whole-grain oats almost drowning out the explosions rattling my mom's TV. My sweatpants are stained with milk and red dye 40, my Green Bay Packers hoodie definitely smells like I haven't showered since before the solstice party—because I haven't—and I've been watching *Die Hard* on a loop since late last night, when I slouched onto the couch in a stinking heap of heartbreak and despair.

It's my own 24/7 Christmas marathon.

Just like every Christmas.

"Jem, honey..."

My mom is standing behind me, out of my line of sight, but I know what she looks like. Face pinched. Narrow shoulders hunched with worry. She's been checking on me periodically since I crashed into the house yesterday morning, my blood still pumping with adrenaline from my fight with Freya. I hadn't wanted her to see me like that—pissed off, emotional, too out of control to make myself smaller and less intimidating—so I'd retreated to my room for the rest of the day, where I'd alternated between pacing and lying on my too-small bed, trying to think of anything that would make this all right.

Thad had let himself into my room mid-morning, looking ashen and subdued.

"You ok, man?" he asked. He was sitting at the small desk I'd used for homework, lanky frame folded forward with his elbows resting on his knees. I raised an eyebrow from where I lay sprawled on the bed, and he leaned back with a groan. "Stupid question," he mumbled.

I stared at the ceiling, wondering how the fuck I was supposed to make peace with this feeling in my chest, my guts, my bones. This feeling that things were going to go back to the way they were before. But *worse*. I'd go back to the same routines. The same ass-kissing. The same uninspired work projects. The same relationships that I'd inevitably break off six months in, before she could expect a ring. Except now, instead of having a comforting familiarity, it would all be thrown into sharp relief against this time with Freya. These fraught, battle-filled days brimming with drama and laughter and sex that had reminded me there are entire parts of myself I've been denying. Days that had reminded me that *Freya* is a part of me I'll never feel complete without. Not really.

I swallowed, opened my mouth to speak. Swallowed again.

"I don't *want* to go back to life without her," I confessed, and across the room, Thad groaned and sunk his fingers into his hair.

"God, I feel like such an asshole," he said, his words tight with agitation.

"Dude, it's not your fault your sister doesn't love me like I love her." I lifted my head enough to glare at him. "That's on my shit luck, not—"

"Ok, first of all," Thad interrupted, "that is not what's going on. She loves you, too, Jeremy. We both know it. And so does Freya. I'd bet anything that's why she went off the rails this morning."

I snorted. Part of me could see where he was going with this. Freya wasn't unloving; Freya was terrified. I said as much directly to her face that morning. Well, more like shouted it loud enough for the entire neighborhood to hear.

Another part of me saw something altogether different. Call it a pattern. A series of coincidences. A curse. But part of me couldn't help but feel like there must be something inherently wrong with me. Because I now had a track record of not only being ditched by my girl—twice—but by my own mother too. I kept putting myself out there, holding nothing back, and all I had to show for it was a lonely, sterile life back in Chicago that I now dreaded going back to.

"*Also*," Thad grimaced, "this is kind of, sort of—fine, *totally*—my fault."

I raised myself up onto my elbows to stare him down. "Did you *say* something to her? Something to spook her? To make her—"

"No, no, nothing like that." He shook his head. "But I may have, kind of, sort of—"

"Jesus, Thaddeaus, spit it out."

"I may have given you and Freya a nudge to reconnect for my own selfish purposes?" He scrunched up his face, like he thought I might spring off the bed and punch him, but I flopped back onto the mattress, hands stacked behind my head.

"What are you talking about?"

He took a deep breath. Then another one.

"*Shit*, this feels like awful timing, but..." I could hear his gulp from across the room. "I'm going to propose to Sam. Christmas morning. Well, I *was*," he amended. "And I can't get married without *you* there. And I can't get married without *Freya*. You're my people. Both of you. So, I thought...maybe...it might be time for you two to figure out your shit?"

I sighed, both elated for Thad—Sam was perfect for him—and a little sickened by the punch of jealousy that gripped me. Thad had everything. His ideal job. An awesome, supportive family. The love of his life. All things I wanted and didn't have. Things that whenever I truly reached for them, the universe—or whoever I'd pissed off out there—smacked me down with the proverbial newspaper like a misbehaving dog.

But just because I *felt* that blast of envy didn't mean I had to *act* on it.

"Congrats, man." I forced myself to sit up, consciously ordered the corners of my lips to lift, even though it felt like a mortician trying to get a corpse to smile. "And I get it. You didn't want Freya and me to see each other for the first time at the wedding and have your big day turn into World War III. It makes sense. You didn't know it would turn into...well, whatever this is."

"Well, I kind of suspected," he mumbled, tugging at his hair again. "But I honestly thought you two would work things out. I *still* think—"

"No." I cut him off as I flopped back onto the bed, my stomach roiling at the hope he was trying to give me. "I just—I just can't let myself go there right now."

He left shortly after with a quiet, "Let me know if I can do anything," and a few hours later, I found my way to the couch with a box of Lucky Charms, fully prepared to carbo-load my way through this stupid broken heart.

No, not broken. *Pulverized.*

My heart feels fucking pulverized.

"Jem?" my mom asks again, and when I ignore her—*again*—she doesn't walk away this time. This time she shuffles into the living room and slumps onto the couch next to me, her shoulder sliding against my arm.

She's still in her long-sleeved nightgown, slender legs propped against the coffee table next to mine, and she's here. With me. I clear my throat as I set my empty cereal bowl on the coffee table. I should feel grateful she's finally here, trying to be the mom she should have been all along, but I can't see beyond my own pain. My own bitterness. I can't trust myself right now. I can't trust myself to be polite, smooth, kind. To put her at ease. But I also have to say *something*, so...

"Sorry," I whisper. "I'm just..."

I'm just what? What, Jeremy? I'm just sick of biting back my thoughts around her? I'm just at my limit with stifling the questions that have been burning a hole through me for seventeen years? I'm just tired of pretending that she hadn't hurt me? Really, truly, profoundly hurt me?

The silence between us stretches as she waits for me to collect my thoughts, and suddenly, I don't *want* to protect her anymore. I don't want to hurt her—not on purpose—but dammit, what about *my* feelings? Don't those count? Yes, she's my mom, but I'm her son. Shouldn't she care how *I* feel?

But...I look down next to me, and my mom looks back, blinking expectantly. She *does* care. She's asking me, straight up, to share my real feelings with her. Right now.

And isn't that what Freya would do? Chase down the truth and let the pieces fall where they may?

Dammit, I'm not going back to the way things were. Freya may be gone, and I'll have to learn to accept that. But this time with her? It's not going to waste. I looked her in the eye and told her we were the same, and I meant it. Deep down, under the hurt and the trauma and the lessons we never should have learned, we're made of the same stuff. It's messy and complicated, and it doesn't always look pretty, but it seeks the truth. It craves honesty.

I straighten my back and take a deep breath.

"Christmases," I blurt out to my mom. "In college. I never had anywhere to go." The words tumble out, one after the other, stilted but true. "The first couple years, I had to couch surf. Had to beg to stay at people's houses for the month-long break. I hated every second."

Her eyes go round with shock. This isn't what she was expecting. She was expecting something about Freya. About my broken heart.

I guess she hadn't realized that Freya wasn't the first one to break it.

"I wasn't sure how to explain to people that I had nowhere to go for the holidays." True. I hated the look on people's faces. Not just pity. Although that was bad enough. But suspicions. What was *wrong* with me? What terrible thing must I have done to be disowned by my own mother? "By my junior year, I started telling people that you'd—" I choke on the words but force them out "—that you'd died."

I must be the only person on Earth who felt relieved when family estrangements became more common. By my thirties, a quick, almost painless "I don't have a relationship with my parents" usually sufficed, and people were happy to fill in the gaps with expressions like "toxic relationships" and "generational differences."

"You told them I was dead?" She sucks in a breath, her hand fluttering to her throat. She's clearly distressed, but I forge on.

"For a few years, yeah. It was..." I shrug. "It was easier." The words roll easier now. "I've spent holidays with more families than I can count. Thanksgivings. Easters. Hanukkahs. New Years. But once I was out of the dorms and had my own place, I never celebrated Christmas with other people. Not even girlfriends. This"—I jerk my head toward the screen, where Alan Rickman leers villainously—"this was my Christmas. Every year. *Die Hard* and takeout."

Christmas was different than the other holidays. Everyone's Thanksgiving looked pretty much the same. Turkey, football, awkward relatives. Easter was egg hunts and ham. But with Christmas, each family's traditions were unique. Special. The treats baked. The presents given. The decorations displayed. Every moment was bursting with meaning and nostalgia. With the obscure details and shared history that make...well, that make a family.

And every Christmas was a stark, kick-in-the-ass reminder that I didn't have one.

She listens, head hanging forward, her body still as she takes in my rambling. And I talk, then I talk some more. Not just about Christmas, but about all of it. The anxiety I had in college, always feeling one bad semester—one bad *test*—away from disaster. The desperation I started to feel for acceptance and security. The way I lost parts of myself. My art, my love of fantasy, my drive to push the limits, be at the fringes.

I talk until my disjointed stream of consciousness peters out. Until the credits are rolling on the movie, and there's only one thing left to say. To ask.

"*How*, Mom?" My throat works up and down. I'm not a crier. The last time I cried, I was fourteen years old, and I'd just been ditched by the best friend I was head-over-heels crazy about. Now, in the past twenty-four hours, I've lost count of how many times I've felt that telltale prickle behind my eyes. My stomach jerks as I realize that I'm not going to be able to hold it in this time. I swipe at my face with the back of my hand, embarrassed but determined. "How could you pick him over me like that? How could you ditch me when I was still just a kid?"

The next thing I know, her arms, wiry but strong, are around me, and she's pulling me down, so my head rests on the soft cotton of her nightgown-clad shoulder. She smells like coffee and faint traces of yesterday's perfume, citrus and vanilla. She smells like childhood. Like home.

"Jem..." she murmurs, her hand running up and down my back like when I was little. It's the first time we've touched since I put my arm around her at the funeral, when she shrugged me off, and I soak up her touch. For a long time, that's all she says, just my name, until my tears have run out and I lean back on the couch to drag my sweater over my eyes and nose. Even then, her hand stays on my arm as she watches me, her eyes pained.

"I'm sorry," she whispers. "I thought"—she swallows hard—"well, I thought you'd be better off without me. On your own."

"I was eighteen!" It bursts out of me, almost a shout, and I hate myself for it, but she doesn't even flinch, which almost feels worse.

"You were eighteen," she agrees calmly. "You were eighteen, and you were already exceeding all my wildest dreams for you. Valedictorian. Captain of the football team. College scholarships. You had your whole life ahead of you, and I was just—" She sighs. "I was your tie to Gary. You had a chance to get out, Jem. To break *free*. I didn't want to be the thing that kept you tied here. What did I have to offer? I wasn't even qualified to hold a job. I would have been dead weight. One more responsibility for you to—"

"You're my *mom*. We would have made things work. Figured it—"

"You think that's what I wanted for you? You, who I always loved more than anything? More than *anyone*?" She cups my face, forcing me to hold her gaze. To see the love shining there. "I could bear a lot. God knows I did over the years with Gary. But I couldn't bear to be a burden to you. Not when you had so much going for you. You deserved better than that. So, I tried to give it to you. Even if it did break my heart."

Her answer is so fucked up it makes me want to scream. Scream for what those years with Gary did to her self-esteem. Scream that he made her feel so low about herself, so unworthy, that she thought I was better off without her. Scream for all the time we lost. For all the rejection I felt. The loneliness.

But the bigger message isn't lost on me.

She loves me. She loved me when I was eighteen and she thought—however wrong she was—that she was doing me a favor by sending me off on my own. She loved me when I was twenty-four and she wanted me to be free, unencumbered, as I started my life and career in Chicago.

And she loves me now.

She may have not chosen to be in my life, but in her mind, she had always, always chosen me.

A fresh wave of tears hits—*Fuck me. I blame the lack of sleep.*—and I lean forward to bury my eyes into the heels of my hands, pressing hard. Her hand is on my back again, rubbing up and down my spine, and when I've collected myself, I lean back with a sniff, rubbing the snot-streaked sleeve of my sweater over my nose. Christ, I need a shower and a change of clothes. I turn my head to look at her, and she looks back.

"I'm still angry at you," I say with a sniff, and she nods. "I get that you don't feel great about yourself. I was here all those years. I know how he treated you. How he talked to you." If my suspicions are right, Gary had been directly in my mom's ear, telling her all the ways she'd be a hardship to me. How she'd slow me down. Not only did he love to make her feel small—like it somehow made him big—but he was terrified of her leaving him. "But *Mom*..." I shake my head. "It had always been *us*. You and me. And then you were just *gone* and I was alone—"

"I'm so sorry, Jem." A tear trails down her cheek, but she brushes it away. She takes a deep breath and squares her shoulders. "I wish I could take it back, but I can't. It's done. I want to move forward with you—to be in your life again—but I understand if you just can't. I knew it might—"

"I want to try, too." I pause for a second, letting myself *feel* the words. And they feel...right. "I'm still angry and I'm still hurt, and I really think you need to find a counselor." Mom watches my face, nodding along as I talk. "And I want to figure out a way to be in each other's lives. Even if it takes some time." I blow out a breath. "And Mom?"

"Yeah?" she sniffs, rubbing at her nose.

"I love you, too."

Forty-Three

FREYA

I'm huddled on the couch, surrounded by a small mountain of snotty tissues and an empty bottle of cheap red wine. No wineglass. I did the *Hope & Stardust* "Sorry-Ass Broken Heart Bath" only to change into the same dirty T-shirt I'd put on yesterday. So, the mascara streaking my face has been scrubbed clean, but I still look like shit. My hair is limp, my eyes swollen and bloodshot, my bottom lip trembling. Season two of *Chilling Adventures of Sabrina* is just starting, right along with round 273 of me crying.

I am a hot fucking mess.

Joe's in-laws, who'd been renting my apartment, handled the change in plans well, graciously accepting Leo's offer to spend the last few days of their visit at his place down the block. Honestly? They probably felt like they were trading up. Leo's place is a couple decades younger, and his style is more Swedish minimalism than witchy. The wife was polite as she handed over my keys, but I saw her peek over her shoulder at Frida as if she felt more haunted than encouraged by the painting's heavy stare.

Leo had been uncharacteristically quiet on the ride home, stealing quick, side-eye glances at me as he drove. I knew he wanted to give me a full inquisition, but I'm sure I looked too pathetic to harass with questions like "Was it straight? Or curved?" and "Oral. Does he *really* enjoy it? Or is he just putting in his time?"

He offered to stay with me, but I sent him back to Todd. I didn't want them to miss any more holiday time together, and I only made it until the door slammed shut behind him before the tears started.

I wanted to be alone.

Utterly, totally alone. A-L-O-N-E. All by my freaking self.

"Alone" is my new personal philosophy. It's now my creed, my motto, my way of life.

Because clearly, I am *not* cut out for committed relationships. Not with humans, anyway. (Hecate can stay.)

Because if I were a relationship type of person, this wouldn't hurt so much. Right? If I were a relationship person, I could fall in love with Jeremy without feeling like my entire universe would be pushed off its axis if he decides that I'm "too much." If I were a relationship person, I'd feel resilient and strong, ready to face the slings and arrows of dating and beyond.

But the more I hurt, the more I think, "Thank the gods I left now." Because if it hurts this bad now—when it's been less than two weeks—how on earth would I handle it in another month? A year? A *decade* from now?

I couldn't.

Hence, my new mission statement: Freya Estelle Nilsen shall remain alone. Forever.

WAR ON CHRISTMAS: A HOLIDAY ROMANCE

When that upside-down Hermit card appeared in my tarot reading, I (oh, sweet summer child), had assumed it was a warning. But really it was a *direction*: Isolate yourself.

For a brief period last night—about halfway through my bottle of wine—I'd contemplated a face tattoo of the Hermit card. Just in case I ever manage to forget the marrow-quaking pain I'm in right now. But by the time I sobered up this morning, my plans de-escalated into a wall hanging of the hunched old man instead. I'm hitting "Submit" on my Etsy order when a loud, frantic banging on my door has me flinching.

"Wrong door!" I bellow, holding my throbbing head between my palms. (Wine hangovers are the worst.) The only person who would visit me the day before Christmas Eve is Leo, and he hasn't knocked in years because he has a key. Obviously, whoever it is has the wrong apartment.

But they bang again, harder this time, sending the black and silver beads in my bedroom doorway swinging.

"Freya Estelle Nilsen!" Sam's voice shouts from the hallway. "Open the door right this instant or I'll kick it down!"

I scramble up on the couch, eyes wide. *Sam* is here? In Chicago? Did Thad bring her? This would be the type of thing he'd—

"Freya." Bethany's voice, firm and commanding. Like a mom. *Bethany?* I blink, but before I can wrap my head around it, she says, "I know Sam's tiny, but I'm pretty sure she could do it. Open up before you owe your landlord a new door."

That gets me moving. My landlord is an asshole who would definitely inflate the price. I wrap myself in a quilt and sprint for the door, stockinged feet sliding across the hardwood floor. I pause in front of the gold sunburst mirror to check my reflection. I shouldn't have. I look as terrible as I suspected, but before I can attempt to finger comb my hair, a loud *bang* rocks my apartment, followed by a tortured, "Holy *shit*, that *hurt*! Oops! Sorry, Mrs. Nilsen."

I stagger forward and fling open the door so hard it crashes into the wall behind it. My jaw drops as I take in the trio on the other side. Sam, her foot raised as if she's about to give the door another kick. Bethany, hands on her slim hips, raising a single you've-really-done-it-this-time eyebrow. And—

"*Mom?*"

And my mom, bundled up in her cotton-candy pink parka, looking like a very concerned modern-day June Cleaver.

Forty-Four

FREYA

"What—" I shake my head, as if they're a mirage brought on by a broken heart and too much cheap wine. "What are you all *doing*—"

But they're already pushing their way inside, Bethany leading the way.

"We would have been here yesterday," she says, beelining for the kitchen and digging under the cupboards until she finds a garbage bag. As she talks, she heads to the couch and starts picking up dirty tissues. "But I had to line up people to watch the shop. Last-minute Christmas shopping, you know?" She stops long enough to look around my apartment, then turns to me and raises her eyebrows. "This place is *cute*. Why haven't we been doing girls' weekends down here?"

I gape. In my entire thirty-five years, the idea of a "girls' weekend" with Bethany has *never* come up. It would have been laughable. But Bethany just suggested it so casually—so matter-of-factly—that for a moment I can see it. Taking her to The Sphere for our latest performance. Sambusas at my favorite Ethiopian restaurant. Shopping for fake bags in Chinatown.

"The question isn't 'What are we doing here?'" says Sam, stopping in front of me to frown. "The question is 'Why are you wearing a Dave Matthews Band T-shirt?' You hate them."

Fuck. I'd been so shocked at their sudden appearance that I'd let my blanket sag around my elbows. I snap it shut around me like a cocoon, but it's too late. They've already seen me wandering around in nothing but my knee-high Wednesday Addams socks and one very large, very stolen Dave Matthews Band T-shirt.

Look. I'm not proud of it. But it smells like him, and if I'd taken any of his other shirts, it would have been too suspicious. Also, I know now that this stupid fucking shirt had nothing to do with impressing his football friends and everything to do with getting a reaction out of me.

Which is kind of sweet. In a backwards, immature, seventeen-year-old kind of way.

Before I can start to defend my poor choices, my mom steps forward, her brow furrowing as she grips my shoulders. My back goes ramrod straight at her touch—old habit—but she doesn't pull away this time. Instead of taking a step back and changing the subject, she stills, giving me time to settle into the physical contact between us.

"Of course we're here," she says quietly. "You're *hurting*, Freya. And we love—"

"Hold up." I step away, drawing the blanket tighter around me. "*Of course*? Of course you're here?" I snort, unable to hold back my disbelief. "Mom, I've been in this apartment for *eight years*. And how many times have you been here?"

One beat of silence. Two. "This is my first," she finally says, her gaze steady on mine.

"I've been at The Sphere for twelve years. Twelve. We do eight productions a year." I do some quick mental math. "That's ninety-six shows we've staged since I started working there. How many have you come to see?"

She swallows, but she doesn't look away. "None."

"So, what's up with this '*of course*' bullshit?" It feels good to focus on something other than the burning ache of missing Jeremy, and I throw myself into it, doing nothing to temper my voice or body language, which I know is screaming, *Leave me alone!* "Look, I know you love me—on some level, at least—but can we just not pretend that there's anything 'of course' about our relationship? Because there's not."

My apartment suddenly feels too small, like the 600 square feet can't contain the decades of hard feelings I've let loose. Bethany and Sam freeze, watching me warily. My mom, however, squares her shoulders, lifts her chin, and jerks her head toward the couch.

"Sit," she orders me, then turns to Bethany. "Make some tea." Then she sniffs at me, and last night's wine must be oozing out of my pores, because she asks, "Are you hungover?" At my terse nod, she adds, "Peppermint if she has it."

Ten minutes later, we're sitting around my coffee table like a goddamn therapy circle, me scrunched in the middle of my green velvet couch, bookended by Bethany and Sam, Mom perched on the edge of the secondhand leather chair. Peppermint steam scents the air, herbal and sharp, and I have the unshakeable—and disconcerting—feeling of a teenager about to be called out for missing curfew. It's doing nothing to settle my nausea.

Mom, unlike her usual, chatty self, stares me down, her blue eyes unblinking.

"What?" I finally ask, bristling. I was already tense, but with every second that passes, my spine fills with steel, cold and hard. "Was I *wrong*? What did I say that wasn't—"

"*You*, young lady..." Mom pauses, then swallows. "Were absolutely correct."

I've lost it. I shake my head, waiting for this entire crazy scene to evaporate into a merlot-induced hallucination. Any second now I'm going to wake up on the bathroom floor, face dried to the cold tiles with vomit.

But Mom's still here, hands folded neatly in her lap.

I clear my throat. Sip my tea. "Pardon me?"

"I said you were *right*, Freya. I haven't been there for you the way I should have been." She takes a deep breath. "And I'm sorry."

"Sorry?" I parrot. My head feels thick and slow. Like it can't keep up.

Mom nods, and next to me, Bethany rests a hand on my knee. I look down, and for the first time, I notice that her hands look like mine, fine bones and tapered fingers.

"I'm sorry, too," she says, so earnest her brow creases. "We've never had the relationship I would like as"—she shrugs—"well, as sisters. And I want to do better going forward."

"I'm not sorry about anything," Sam pipes up. "I've been an *awesome* twin brother's girlfriend."

Bethany reaches across me to lightly smack Sam on the leg, but my eyes are on my mom. I was already raw when they arrived. My defenses down. Confronting our dysfunctional family dynamics on top of leaving Jeremy feels like too much. This can't be an easy conversation for Mom—she's really putting herself out there—but for crying out loud. I'm *thirty-five*. It's too little, too late.

I open my mouth to ask them to leave, but what comes out is, "What—*exactly*—do you mean about not being there for me?"

Mom's mouth quirks into a sad smile. "I didn't know how to be the mother you needed. Bethany was easy. She was enough like me that I could put myself in her shoes. Anticipate what she needed. You..." She sighs. "You were harder. So prickly and independent. And so, *so* brave."

"I'm sorry I wasn't Bethany," I snap. "I couldn't *help*—"

"Of course you couldn't," she interrupts, her voice soft. Soothing. "It was on me, Freya. *Me*. We're very different people. Obviously." I wait for her to sneer. To curl a lip at the black crystal chandelier hanging over the coffee table or the collage wall featuring a cow skull bedecked with red and black dried roses. But she doesn't. She just continues calmly. "*I'm* the mom. It was my responsibility to work through our differences. To find ways to connect. I just didn't know what to do, so I...I let you drift. I let you find your way with Thad and"—she hesitates, and I brace myself—"and Jeremy. By the time you were in high school, you didn't *want* me around anymore, and I told myself I was respecting your boundaries. Giving you space."

I *did* want space as a teenager. Or—I frown—I *thought* I did. However, those are two different things.

I chew my lip as I remember my first theater production: *Bye Bye Birdie*, freshman year. Between Jeremy and Tiffany dating and the Freaky Freya thing, life had gone to shit. I was convinced that it was never going to feel ok again. Ever. But working on stage crew for a few hours every afternoon, everything else turned off. Missing my best friend. The shame I carried for deserting him. The stupid nicknames. *Poof!* Gone.

I attacked theater with the passion of a Scorpio discovering her life's work. I started to eat, sleep, and dream that musical until—in my mind—our 2003 high school production of *Bye Bye Birdie* took on the weight and scope of a major, life-changing world event.

It was the big bang of theater events.

The lights, the sound, the sets...they were going to be perfection. They were going to play their own role, however invisible, in giving the audience an escape from the weight of everyday life. By opening night, I'd worked myself into such a frenzy, I was sick with anxiety. Would Bobby Kimble remember to switch the mics between scenes six and seven? What if our spotlight got glitchy again? Would *everyone* on crew remember to wear black?

When Mom told me over breakfast that she and dad would be attending the play, I'd lashed out. Wasn't the pressure bad enough without having to impress my parents, too? And what if they did something embarrassing? I was already sinking myself socially without their help.

"Um, could you just *not*?" I'd asked around a mouthful of Lucky Charms.

Mom's eyes had gone round, and without a word, she'd carried her plate and coffee cup to the sink and left for work. She never mentioned attending one of my theater events again, and I told myself that's what I wanted. Space to do my thing. I didn't do theater to gain my parents' approval. I did it because I loved it.

But in hindsight...it created a rift. At the very least, it exacerbated the rift that was already there. I pushed my mom away in a moment of stress, but as I grew more comfortable in my new role, I felt her absence. I loved the theater so much. How could anyone really understand me, really *love* me, if they didn't understand my passion for it?

"I pushed you away," I admit, worrying at my lip.

Talk about a goddamn pattern.

"Yeah, you did," she agrees. "But you were a teenager, sweetie. *I* was the grown-up. I should have kept trying. And honestly?" Her nose wrinkles. "You intimidated me. You were so smart. So sure of yourself. I didn't know how to push back, and we ended up with this—well, this *distance* between us. And now..." For the first time, her bottom lip trembles, a crack in her armor. "I've missed you, Freya. *We've* missed you. All of us. These past four years since you've been home?" Her mouth twists. "I get that you feel like the black sheep, but you're *our* black sheep. We're not the same without you."

I think back to the new moon and the tarot card I pulled for her: Justice. Karmic balance. Reaping the fruits of past actions. The skittish way she avoided my gaze when I told her the meaning of her card.

"The Justice card," I say, pinning her with a stare. "It was about me. About your regrets with me."

She nods. "I messed up in the past—a lot—and I take responsibility for that." She releases a huge breath. "I also *really* want the opportunity to make it right."

I still feel like shit, the pain of losing Jeremy a wide, gaping hole dead center in my black heart. My head hurts from crying (fine, *and* the wine), and my stomach has more knots than a rope at a Boy Scout meeting. But, to my surprise, I also feel something ease and relax. One of those knots—one I wasn't even aware of—releases its hold.

"How—" I clear my throat, spin my teacup in my hands. "How are you going to make it right?"

"Well, for starters, by being here to support you. When you're hurting." Mom smiles gently, then adds, "And by pointing out that you're making a huge fucking mistake."

Silence descends, all three of us on the couch freezing. Even Hecate, who's sprawled across the coffee table, goes still. Mom does not swear. Curse words, she's always insisted, are unladylike. Curse words show a lack of imagination. Curse words show a lack of decorum.

This f-bomb has been decades in the making.

Next to me, Bethany giggles, followed by Sam. I always thought I'd *love* to hear my mom let loose, but now that it's happened, I'm shook.

"Pardon me?" I ask. The *young lady* is implied, but my mom just stares back at me, unrepentant.

"I said," she repeats, "you're making a huge *fucking* mistake."

Gods help me, she looks downright pleased with herself, her lips curling at the edges like she's just discovered a new favorite dessert.

"I didn't, though." I shake my head, stomach tightening now that the subject has switched to Jeremy. "I can't do it. I just…"

"Just what?" Bethany asks, squeezing my knee.

I stare into the murky green-brown of my peppermint tea, struggling to put my worst fears into words.

"I don't know how—" *Shit.* Here I go again. I shift my gaze to the white plaster ceiling, blinking rapidly, but the tears still spill down my cheeks, hot and wet. "I don't know how to love him a…a safe amount." I'm not sure if that makes sense, but three blurry faces nod, so it must. At least a little. "If I go there, and things don't work out…" I shudder, shaking my head. "It'll break me. I know you all think I'm super brave, but I'm not. Not when it comes to him. And his life and mine? They're too different. He needs something else. *Someone* else. Someone who—"

"He doesn't *want* someone else," Sam interrupts. "He wants you, Frey."

Bethany nods. "Do you have any clue what I'd give to have Drew look at me like Jeremy looks at you?" She fans herself. "Girl, you'd be crazy to walk away from—"

"It hurts too much," I protest. I set my teacup on the coffee table. Wipe my sweaty palms on the blanket. "Even if—for the sake of argument—it works out. What if something *happens* to him?" I know he's a big, burly Viking now, but shit happens. Car accidents. Illness. Cruel twists of fate that pop up out of the blue to ravage people's lives. "I wouldn't *survive* it. I'd fall apart. Crumble. Completely lose my—"

"No, you wouldn't." Mom shakes her head, then amends. "Well, you *would*, but not forever. You're strong, Freya. Trust me, I know."

"How?" I whisper.

"Because you're my daughter," she says simply.

And somehow...I believe her. I don't *feel* strong. I feel like death warmed over. With a hangover. But there's a quiet authority in her voice I respond to. She's known me since my first breath. *Before* my first breath. For crying out loud, she tells ultrasound stories about me putting Thad into headlocks in utero, wrapping my tiny arms around his neck. (Was it a hug? An attempt to kill off my competition? Nobody knows.) She put Band-Aids on my scraped knees and knows how I like an extra pat of butter on top of my mac 'n' cheese. However complicated our relationship has become, she's still my mom, and if *she* knows I'm strong enough for this...maybe I am.

"And," Bethany adds, "if something did—goddess forbid—happen, you wouldn't be dealing with it alone."

"I wouldn't?" I sniff.

"Nope," Bethany responds. "You'd have us." She smiles, her dimple popping. "Your coven."

Even crying, I manage to roll my eyes.

"You'll have us no matter what happens with Jeremy," Sam clarifies, slinging an arm over my shoulders. "But Freya...you and Jeremy?" She smiles. "You belong together."

Three pairs of eyes stare at me, waiting for me to catch up, but I'm already there.

I need to fix things with Jeremy. I remember the frustration in his eyes yesterday morning, the tension that grabbed every muscle in his body. I know how wrong it felt to me, and *I* was the one in control, exerting my will.

Jeremy must feel rejected...powerless.

And just like that, I find myself facing the same question I threw in my mom's face less than ten minutes ago: How am I going to make it right?

Forty-Five

FREYA

The ride back to Northview from Chicago is surprisingly jovial. At least for my companions. Me? *I* feel like I'm going to throw up. At first I blame it on lingering effects of the wine, but my mom—who's riding in the second row with me—shoots me a blinding smile, pats my hand, and says, "That's not the hangover, honey. That's what it feels like to be in *love*."

Her eyes go all starry, and she says the word *love* with an enthusiasm that sane people reserve for cheese and Baby Yoda.

"Love feels like wanting to hurl all over Bethany's SUV?" I ask, wondering if *she* got into some wine too.

But three enthusiastic heads nod back at me.

Fuck.

"So, what are you going to do?" Bethany asks, glancing at me in the rearview mirror. "Not to be a downer, but you fucked up pretty royally. You're gonna have to *grovel*. Like, get down on your knees and—"

She uses her tongue and hand to mimic a blow job in the mirror, and I lean forward to slap her shoulder.

"Freya!" my mom scolds. She's sitting directly behind the driver's seat, so she didn't see Bethany's fancy tongue action. "Don't hit your sister while she's driving."

I stick my tongue out at Bethany, and she winks back. Bethany, I suddenly realize, was never a goody-goody; Bethany, it hits me like a bolt of lightning, is just *sneaky*.

Gods, what is the world coming to?

"So..." I heave a sigh, not believing what I'm about to ask. A couple days ago, I would have sat through a four-hour sermon on the benefits of chastity before I would ask this particular trio for love advice. But desperate times call for desperate measures. "What do I, you know...do?"

"Like, how should you pledge your love to him?" Mom asks, and something inside me dies. Maybe I'll just start with Bethany's advice and see if a really amazing BJ does the trick.

"Forget I asked," I mumble, but all three women squeal in protest.

"That's what we're *here* for," Sam insists, twisting around in the passenger seat to beam at me. "You don't have to do this alone, Frey." She spins back toward the front, already brainstorming. "So, one time when your brother and I got into a fight about something stupid, I apologized by hardcore organizing all the closets in our condo. You know how tidy he is. He was *so* excited."

"That is the fucking nerdiest thing I've ever heard," I reply. "I bet he loved it."

"Oh, he totally did."

For the rest of the ride, they share romantic gestures they've taken part in, sometimes as recipients, sometimes as the gift giver. Fancy dates. Moonlit walks. I get teary-eyed hearing the story of my dad's proposal for the first time: he filled Mom's tiny, rundown apartment with flowers, a promise that even though they didn't own a flower shop *yet*, they'd work toward that goal together. Then Bethany shares a story about Drew dragging her into the utility closet at the shop for some super-hot sex that has *Mom* slapping her on the shoulder.

"*Bethany!* While there were *customers* there?"

"No," Bethany says, sounding offended. But she nods at me in the rearview mirror.

By the time we're getting close to home, a blanket of black is settling over the sky, dark and comforting, and as Bethany turns onto our street, she lets out a squeal.

"Ooh! I've got it!" she shouts, hitting the steering wheel with excitement. "What about *prom*? What if you set up a little prom and go as his date since you hexed—"

"Can't prove it," I say. Prom *is* kind of a cool idea, but prom also feels like it belongs to the world of high school Jeremy. Bright and glittery and a little fake. A world I never *wanted* to belong to. "And I don't know if prom feels quite right."

"Maybe you don't need something fancy at all," Mom suggests. "Maybe you can just, you know, tell him how you feel?"

"Yeah," Sam says, stretching her arms dramatically, "you know—*pledge your love* to him."

Before I can comment, Bethany pulls into my parents' driveway and puts the SUV in park. I peek at the driveway next door—Jeremy's car is still there—and my butterflies come back with a vengeance, fluttering drunkenly. I push the feeling down as I collect my bags and Hecate's carrier.

It's Jeremy. Just Jeremy. Yes, I fucked up, but he'll forgive me. I just need to come clean and tell him how I feel.

It'll be simple.

Right?

FORTY-SIX

FREYA

Tap-tap-tap.

I wrap my arms around myself, teeth chattering, and wish I'd dragged on more than a thin hoodie. I'd considered reaching out to Jeremy in the morning, but I knew I'd be in for a night of tossing and turning, envisioning the worst. My mind wasn't on my wardrobe as I'd thrown on whatever I could grab and climbed out my bedroom window.

So, here I am. Colder than a witch's tit.

I reach out to tap on the window again, eggplant fingernail an inch from the glass, when it slides open with a squeak. I scurry back, nearly falling on my ass in the snow as Jeremy, wearing a plain black T-shirt, leans out the window. Instead of the easy smile I'd been hoping for, he raises a thick, sandy eyebrow, his handsome face inscrutable.

So, it's going to be like that then. I take a deep breath. Press my hands to my stomach.

"Hey," I mumble.

His second eyebrow joins the first.

Damn. Tough audience.

"I came back," I blurt out, then chew at my lip. "Obviously. I mean, I'm here." *Oh gods.* "You must feel like your life has been nothing but drama since we've been hanging out, but—"

"I never complained," he shoots back.

His forehead creases into a V, but even scowling, he's the most beautiful man I've ever seen. The moon is round and bright and nearly full. It highlights the sharp cut of his cheekbones and his long nose, throws shadows on the defined muscles of his arms as his fingers flex around the windowsill.

"You're right," I whisper. Jeremy may love to tease and taunt me. And there was that spanking. But he's never complained about me or the drama I inevitably stir up.

I run my hands along my thighs, trying to dry my sweaty palms on my leggings. How I'm simultaneously sweating and bordering on frostbite, I'll never know, but that's where love gets you, I guess.

Silence stretches between us, Jeremy's eyes glowing silver in the dark, revealing nothing.

This is it. Our moment. The stories from this afternoon's car ride race through my brain, but they all feel so...big. Dramatic. I don't know why that bothers me. *I* am usually big and dramatic. But I don't want drama right now. I want to feel safe. It's like my breastbone has been cracked and pried open à la *Grey's Anatomy*, leaving my beating heart quivering and exposed. I want to make things right, but can't I do that with a gesture that's, I don't know, *smaller*? So that if Jeremy rejects me, I still have a teeny, tiny shred of dignity I can army crawl back to Chicago with?

"I was thinking..." I trail off. Twist my hands together in front of me. "I was thinking that maybe...after Christmas..."

I swallow. *Shit. Why am I fucking this up so badly?* He's not going to reject me...is he? It's Jeremy. It was always meant to be him. Him and me. Even if I didn't want to admit it. Fate wouldn't have thrown us together again just so he could turn me down. I mean, *he's* the one who suggested dating in the first place.

"After Christmas..." he drawls.

Oh gods. Here goes nothing.

I shrug. Try to look casual. Like I don't know I busted his heart into smithereens yesterday morning. Just like mine.

"Maybe we could, I don't know...go on a date?"

There. I said it. My hands are numb, and I don't know if it's the cold or an impending panic attack, but I said it. I exhale and lift my gaze from the snowy ground to his face, expecting to see that summer-and-sunshine smile he shares so easily. Especially with me.

He snorts.

"You want to go on a date?" he repeats, his tone suggesting I requested something truly ridiculous.

"Yes?" I ask. "I mean—that's what you wanted. Right?"

His eyes narrow as he considers me like an especially difficult calculus problem.

Good luck, buddy. Math has rules; this brain is all anarchy.

"You're right," he finally says. "I did." I sigh, releasing my breath with a misty puff, but before I can feel relieved, he adds, "But the terms have changed."

"Changed?" I ask, my voice small. "Why?"

"Why?" he echoes. "Freya, I stood in your driveway and told you I'm *in love* with you. That I want to be with you. That I want to give you *everything*. And your response was to leave—literally flee the city, no, the *state*—and then come back a day later and ask me on a goddamn *date*?"

I cringe, keeping my eyes on my old, scuffed up Doc Martens sinking into the snow. A hoarse laugh escapes him, grating on my last nerve, and I groan.

"Fine." I stick my freezing hands under my armpits. "What do you want then?"

"I want you to acknowledge that what you did yesterday morning can't be fixed with a plate of fucking sushi," he snaps. "What's between us, Sunshine, isn't small. It's not easy. It's not simple. And it sure as fuck isn't safe. It's big and terrifying, and if it goes wrong, it's going to hurt like hell, and *I* need to know that you're not going to lash out every time you get scared." He jabs a finger at me. "So, what are the new terms? Convince me that you're not going to turn coward and run every time things get intense. Because quite frankly, Frey, intense is the only way we know how to be."

And then he slams the window shut.

Forty-seven

FREYA

Christmas Eve

I stare at the boxy brick building looming over me, and even though I know it's abandoned for winter break, I can still smell the ghosts of pencil shavings, body odor, and Axe body spray. For the first time since I stomped out of this hellhole on the last day of my senior year, middle fingers raised in salute, I'm back at Northview High School.

And cue my own personal nightmare.

My stomach cramps around the blueberry muffin my mom forced me to eat this morning. ("You need your energy for pledging your love," she'd singsonged.) I squeeze my eyes shut. Ebeneezer Scrooge only had to face the prospect of a cold, lonely grave waiting to swallow him whole. I would much rather face a dirt-filled symbol of my mortality than my high school alma mater.

"So, a romantic emergency with your sworn enemy..." a soft, familiar voice croons behind me. "How deliciously Shakespearean."

Despite everything that's gone to hell in the proverbial handbasket over the past two weeks, I smile.

"Hey, D.G.," I say, turning to her as she walks up beside me.

Mrs. Davis-Green, cheeks flushed from the cold, stands staring at the building where she's spent the past thirty years teaching the adolescents of Northview about Shakespeare, Arthur Miller, and Neil Simon.

After a sleepless night spent plotting, I knew I needed D.G.'s help. And I knew, just as surely, she would give it to me.

"Sorry to bother you on Christmas Eve." I follow her brisk footsteps to the front entrance, and she leans over to put in the security code that unlocks the doors with a soft click.

"Oh, Freya," she sighs. We walk through echoey hallways, our boots thumping over the tile floors. I peek at her, and she is definitely smiling to herself. "*You* know better than anyone what a thrill it is to play a supporting role in a great love story. And I suspect that yours and Jeremy Kelly's is pretty great."

We arrive at the auditorium entrance, and I mull over her words as she takes out a gigantic set of keys and starts unlocking the wide double doors. Jeremy's and my story *is* pretty great. That's what this whole plan depends on. It's also, as he said last night, big and difficult and terrifying.

"Have you ever noticed that in the greatest love stories, the lovers tend to end up, well...dead?" I ask D.G. That feeling of impending doom rushes toward me, that inevitable collision of my body—my heart—against an unforgiving surface. But D.G. looks over her shoulder at me and chuckles.

When I had her as a teacher, she was in her thirties, so she must be in her fifties now. Her long, wild hair is more silver than brown, and subtle lines crease her forehead. Her eyes are still kind, though, crinkling as she grins at me.

"I have," she affirms as we make our way through the auditorium. My eyes eat up the dark expanse of the empty stage and the rows of wooden seats, scuffed and marked with decades of illicitly carved initials. Her voice ripples with amusement as she follows up with, "Why? Are you planning on killing Jeremy?"

"No." I laugh. "Nothing like that."

"Well, that's good." She opens the door to the costume room and flicks on the fluorescent lights. "I'd hate to end my illustrious career as a public-school teacher by aiding and abetting a murder. Now, what exactly are you looking for?"

I explain my plan. Well, it's more a concept right now. I'd found an old journal last night and spent hours sitting cross-legged on my bed, staring at the blank pages, but all I had to show for it was a series of fits and starts, all crossed out. So, I'd decided to concentrate on the more practical parts of my plan first. Hence, why I'm here.

D.G. purses her lips and nods as I share my idea, then she points me to the back corner of the room. As we start digging through racks of clothes and plastic tubs of accessories, I push her harder.

"So, why do they die?" I ask. "Romeo and Juliet? Antony and Cleopatra? Heathcliff and Catherine?"

She tosses me a pair of faux-leather breeches, and I catch them, holding them up to my hips.

"Maybe it's a metaphor," she says. "On stage, or on the page, it's *literal* death. Star-crossed lovers and gory sacrifices. But figuratively, the best loves *do* transform us, don't they? They push us. Stretch us. Encourage us to dig for the truest, most selfless versions of ourselves."

Like the Death card, I muse, thinking back on my conversation with Bethany. Not an actual death, but an ending, followed by a beginning. Over the past two days, it's felt like my heart's been physically breaking, but I'm not dying. Just the old version of me, so something else can emerge. A new variation of me that's willing to do life a little less alone.

D.G. shrugs. "Then there's the *drama* of it, of course. Death—literal or figurative—is exciting. Especially when it's tragic. Plays and books, they allow people to live the fantasy of something wilder. Greater." She shoots me a sly smile over her shoulder. "*You* were never going to settle for a nice, quiet love story, now were you?"

I glance around the room, where it's easy to imagine the ghost of my teenage self among the gowns and tunics and three-piece suits. She spent more than one late night here, taking in and letting out costumes, fixing buttons and adding sequins. That girl was impulsive and abrasive and naïve. But she was also brave. And she loved the theater because it told big, bold stories.

Stories like she desperately wanted for herself one day.

Teenage Freya never dreamed of a soft, unassuming love. She craved a love story for the ages. A love that moved mountains. Shook the heavens. Parted seas. A love that turned her world upside down. Turned her heart inside out. Rocked her to her very core.

I run my thumbs over the waistband of the pants, smiling to myself. "No," I admit, as the words I'd been looking for all night start to take shape. "No, I wasn't."

FOrTy-EIGHT

JEREMY

"Only one drink, right?" I ask Thad.

"Sure, man," he says, pulling into a parking spot at the Galway Inn. "One drink."

Let's be clear: I didn't want to come out tonight at all. However, when Thad and Sam showed up on my doorstep and invited me to go out, every excuse I grasped at melted away like a spring icicle. First, I claimed it was too late, but my mom had insisted on serving Christmas Eve dinner promptly at 4:30, like a seniors-only early bird special. So, even after eating and doing the dishes, it was still only six o'clock. Next, I told Thad I was planning on spending Christmas Eve with my mom, which was true. Until Mom started to yawn loudly in front of Thad and Sam and informed me she was going to bed. Three hours before her usual bedtime.

I'd grumbled and grabbed my coat.

The Galway Inn is bustling, its lights warm and welcoming, its main doorway bedecked in evergreen boughs, all making for a festive air. I follow Thad and Sam inside, trying not to let my thoughts linger on the last time I was here. As Freya and I had left that morning, I'd held the heavy wooden door open for her, and she'd pressed her hand into my chest and leaned up to kiss me.

I rejected her last night. She'd come to my window with an offer I would have jumped at two weeks ago, and I'd turned her down flat.

Do I regret it, though?

Hell, no.

As I'd looked out at Freya standing in the snow, trying to play things as small and safe as possible, I'd known I needed to be honest with her. And not my make-sure-you're-still-the-nice-guy kind of honesty. Because I can't love Freya in half measures, and if I try—if I hold back how I truly feel—I'll end up resenting her. It will be death by a thousand cuts, every time I swallow my feelings another tiny wound, and I won't do that to us.

I know in my gut it was the right call, but that doesn't make waiting for her next move—if she has one—any easier.

I'm barely inside, the door still swinging shut behind us, when Sam trips to a stop beside me and slaps a mittened hand into her forehead.

"Shit," she mutters, already pivoting to leave. "I forgot my purse in the car."

Thad grabs her hand and twists toward me. "We'll be back in a minute. Grab us a table?"

I jerk my head in a nod, and they disappear into the night, leaving me to navigate the crowd. I keep my head down to avoid eye contact with anyone—I don't need another run-in with Tiffany Ebner or the like—but before I can reach the hostess stand, a firm, clear voice I haven't heard since high school reaches out from the hum of small talk in the bar.

"Ulrik Lightborne."

I freeze, hands still stuffed in my pockets, and slowly turn my head to where a tiny, middle-aged woman is standing from a wooden bench, smoothing her long, brightly colored skirts. I blink, trying to shake off the topsy-turvy feeling of two distinct worlds—the academic world of Northview High School and the fantasy world of Caves & Conquerors—colliding.

"Mrs. Davis-Green?" My shock turns my voice into a croak, and I clear my throat. "Um…how do you know about—"

She straightens her back, her posture rigid, and rests her hands on her hips. She always could command a room. "Ulrik Lightborne, Dwarf Paladin of Tradepass. Welcome, crusader, to our fair town of Palribe." My eyes widen, and it takes considerable effort to stop my jaw from dropping. Mrs. Davis-Green, ever the professional, keeps right on going. "I would invite you to quench your thirst with a pint of ale or mead, but unfortunately, time is of the essence. A quest awaits, and you, brave warrior, are the only one who can complete it."

My heart thunders in my chest, and my eyes flick around the crowded bar, scanning for bold winged eyeliner and poison-apple lips. A few curious onlookers stare back at me, obviously noticing Mrs. Davis-Green's theatrics, but Freya is nowhere to be found.

My cheeks heat. Playing the role of Ulrik Lightborne in the safety of Thad and Freya's basement is one thing. Letting my nerd light shine in the middle of Northview's most popular bar is another. But I don't care. Because whatever this is, Freya *must* be behind it.

I was waiting for her to make a move and *this*...this is it. Which means Freya is all in. She is finally saying yes to *us*.

"Thank you for the warm welcome," I rush to say, my tone formal as I tuck my hands behind my back. "And thank you for considering me for this quest. If time is of the essence, please continue."

She jumps back into her monologue, all business. "You have heard, I'm sure, of the half-elf Roxy Noteleaf, one of the great bards of our time. She's known not only for her ability to weave an entrancing story, but for her cunning as well." I nod, keeping my face solemn. "Noteleaf was supposed to arrive in Palribe yesterday to provide holiday entertainment for the townsfolk, but she never arrived. A Druid who passed through the tavern heard rumors she was being followed by a band of orcs. Do you, Ulrik Lightborne, accept the quest to locate and protect the bard? She was supposed to bring a magical tale to Palribe—a tale of romantic love that would make other love stories pale in comparison—and the townspeople have been highly anticipating her visit. Will you save her, dwarf?"

I know I should be staying in character, and Ulrik would be deadly serious in this moment. But I can't keep the grin from my lips as I lay my fist on my heart.

"I accept this quest. I will give everything—sacrifice anything—to bring Roxy Noteleaf safely to Palribe."

To my surprise, there's a smattering of applause from the people surrounding us. My face must be fifty shades of embarrassed, but I nod my head magnanimously in acknowledgment. Just like Ulrik would.

"Thank you," Mrs. Davis-Green says, then reaches into the quilted purse hanging at her hip and draws out a small velvet bag, handing it to me. I know without having to look inside that it contains Thad's dark-green dice with faded gold numbers that we've been playing C&C with since fifth grade. "Best of luck to you, Ulrik. The Druid who saw Noteleaf on his way to Palribe said her last known whereabouts were at Roosevelt Park. Best to begin your search there."

***

"Come on, Sam," I wheedle from the back seat. "You know you want to tell me what the hell is going on."

She twists around to glare at me over her shoulder from the passenger seat.

"I told you, dwarf, my name is Luliana."

From the moment I threw myself into Thad's car, nerves dancing with anticipation, Thad and Sam have refused to break character.

"Come on, Luliana," I try again, giving her my most charming smile. "Not even a hint?"

"You're usually known for your patience, Ulrik," Thad scolds. "Let the adventure play out as it will."

When we arrive at the parking lot of the Roosevelt Park pool, there's a lone car waiting. I squint into the darkness. It's Bethany's black SUV. As soon as Thad pulls to a stop next to it, I fling open my door and jump out, half-sprinting to where I can see Bethany's willowy shadow standing against the pool fence.

"Welcome, Ulrik," she says with a wide smile, holding a small stack of index cards in front of her. My chest tightens around something warm and hopeful.

Thad and Sam, Mrs. Davis-Green, and now Bethany? How many people has my notoriously independent Freya asked for help?

"This is the local swimming hole," Bethany explains, sweeping her arm toward the empty cement pool behind her, "and the bard Roxy Noteleaf's last known location. As a youngling, Noteleaf spent much time here in the fair summer months. It's here that Noteleaf first noticed her most trusted companion, the young dwarf Paladin Ulrik Lightborne"—she pauses to raise an eyebrow at me—"looking at her a bit...differently than he used to. Was his gaze...lingering? Was he taking a little bit longer to rub that sunscreen into her shoulders?"

I reach up to rub at the back of my neck, which is growing hotter by the second. My middle-school self would be mortified to be called out like this by Bethany, of all people, but it's impossible to feel judged by her happy, delighted giggle.

"My gaze was definitely lingering," I admit with a wince.

Bethany nods and steals a quick glance at the cards she's holding. "The young Roxy Noteleaf certainly *hoped* Ulrik was taking notice of her because *she* was taking notice of *him*. And because Noteleaf is brave and bold of heart, she decided to push things just a bit further. She decided to test Ulrik's true feelings using the"—she pauses dramatically—"Polka Dot Bikini attack."

I throw my head back and laugh—I *knew* she wore that bikini to torture me—and I'm still chuckling as I follow Bethany's instructions to roll the twenty-sided die to see if Roxy Noteleaf's attack was a hit. Spoiler alert: It was. My roll with the ten-sided die to determine the damage of her attack is equally devastating. A nine out of ten.

"From here, Ulrik, you must go on an expedition to the District of Flowers, where Noteleaf's family keeps a small shop. The cleric Stromm Godsan and his companion, Luliana Nimblefingers, will take you."

WAR ON CHRISTMAS: A HOLIDAY ROMANCE

***

Thad and Sam—excuse me, *Stromm* and *Luliana*—spend the next hour driving me hither and yon across Northview. It's not, by any means, a real game of Caves & Conquerors. It's more scripted, and rolling the dice is for show rather than function. Which is good, because I'm pretty sure that, given the effectiveness of *most* of the attacks, Freya and I would both be goners.

At the flower shop, Mrs. Nilsen tells how, in eighth grade, Freya called me to rescue a giant spider she found in a flower shipment. She was terrified of it but didn't want it to get killed. So, I rode my bike to the shop, gently captured the spider, which we named Aragog after Harry Potter, and released it outdoors. It was the Flower Power attack, Mrs. Nilsen explains, and according to Roxy Noteleaf, it was a direct hit, regardless of how the dice fall.

Drew and the three boys are at the high school, and Andy giggles his way through some stories about Freya's and my trips to the principal's office. Best of all, he's wearing a familiar Dave Matthews Band T-shirt over his winter coat. (I knew she nabbed it.) Not surprisingly, the Annoy-Her-Into-Liking-You attack is an epic fail, and I roll a measly two.

At Freya's bedroom window, Abi waits for me, reminding me of the nights I spent next to Freya's bed, soothed by her quiet, steady presence. The Best Friend attack, it turns out, is a doozy, and combined with First Kiss, it's a knockout blow.

As I pick up the dice from the windowsill and return them carefully to their bag, she points over my shoulder at my house.

"That way, Ulrik McHottie."

I snort—like mother like daughter—as I turn on my heel and tromp through the snow toward home, where my mom is waiting for me on the front porch. She's changed from the dress she wore for Christmas Eve dinner into jeans and a thick green cardigan, which she's holding wrapped around her thin frame. Without thinking about it, I step close and wrap her in a hug, and she hugs me back without hesitation.

"So, you were in on this all along?" I ask, stepping back and holding her shoulders. "Dinner at 4:30 and all that?"

"I sure was."

She smiles then, a real, honest-to-goodness smile like I haven't seen since Gary came into our lives. It's bright and open and warm, and for the first time, I start to suspect that she's going to be ok. Things will take time between us, but we'll get there. And, of course, she'll have a lot of work—and therapy—to do to address the trauma from Gary. But she's strong and resilient. She really, truly is going to be all right.

My throat tightens, and I blink away an unexpected burning behind my eyes. *Shit.* Maybe it's the sudden hope I feel for my mom. Maybe it's the turn my relationship with Freya seems to finally be taking. Probably, it's a combination of the two. Because after years of spending Christmas alone, I'm having a Christmas Eve filled with people who seem to, well...*care* about me.

"She loves you," Mom says as she looks up at me. "I know she hurt you, but she loves you so, so much, Jem."

I clear my throat, trying to push down the emotions that are threatening to overwhelm me. Because I *feel* loved. I don't know what's going to happen tonight. I don't know how it's going to end or what Freya is going to say or not say, but it doesn't really matter. Because this impromptu campaign she's staged says it all.

"I love her too," I whisper. "A lot."

Mom pats my cheek and blinks away some shining eyes of her own before pulling back.

"Well, Ulrik, you're in luck. Because Roxy Noteleed—"

"Noteleaf," I automatically correct, and she laughs.

"Yes, *that*. Roxy Note*leaf* left a final clue for you."

I let out a deep breath, relieved to hear that I'm nearing the end. As much as I've loved reminiscing about my decades of history with Freya, the answers I'm looking for aren't in the past. The stories I heard tonight are the stepping stones that got us here, to this moment, but there's no roll of the dice that can change any of it. The love we felt, the pain we caused, the time we lost…it's all done. The future, though, is a game still left to be played, full of possibility. And I don't want to wait a second longer to go after it.

Mom digs into her jeans pocket for an index card, but she doesn't even glance at it as she recites, "Every journey must come to an end, but the end of one journey is, by necessity, the beginning of another. To find your bard and close out tonight's journey—so that you might start another—you must return to the beginning."

"The beginning?" I ask, already backing off the porch. "Back to the Galway Inn?"

At her nod, I bound up the porch to give her one last hug, then sprint for Thad's car.

"To the Galway Inn, trusty steed!"

Forty-Nine

FREYA

*W*hy does love have to feel so much like a hangover?

It's one of several questions I contemplate as I get ready in my room at the Galway Inn, my stomach tossing and tumbling every time I get a text update from Sam.

Sam: At the shop. He and your mom are hugging :-)

Sam: At the school. I see them all laughing.

Sam: OMG, Frey, he is SOOOO into this. You nailed it!

And finally...

Sam: Leaving his house now. Will be there in ten.

My hands shake as I bustle around the room, doing a final sweep to make sure everything looks perfect. Or as perfect as it can, given that I pulled this whole performance together in less than a day.

I lucked out, getting a room here due to a last-minute cancelation, and I've spent the past two hours setting the stage with props I borrowed from

WAR ON CHRISTMAS: A HOLIDAY ROMANCE

the Northview High School theater department. A bow and some arrows lean against the wall next to the fireplace, where a fire crackles merrily. Heavy golden candlesticks of various sizes trail across the room, holding LED candles that throw off a soft, golden glow. On a small table under the window, a large, aged-looking map is spread out, its corners pinned with a compass, an elaborate silver tankard, and several shining coins. A cloak drapes over the back of the wingback chair I dragged in front of the fireplace, giving the deceptive impression of being casually tossed, even though I spent a solid ten minutes making sure the folds were just so.

It's a scene straight out of our middle-school imaginations, a Caves & Conquerors fantasy come to life.

When the knock comes at the door, I jump, like my nerves are a lute string he just plucked. Jeremy and I have seen each other every single day over the past two weeks, but never like this. Never without the games or the walls or that stupid countdown looming over us. I take a deep breath to settle the swimming sensation in my stomach and square my shoulders as I swing open the door.

Real talk: I didn't think I'd ever be in this position, standing here with my heart in my hands, asking someone else to accept it.

And I definitely didn't think I'd be doing it dressed as an elf.

Yet here I am.

Before I launch into the script I prepared, I give Jeremy a second to take me in. The faux leather breeches and knee-high boots molded to my legs. The dark-red tunic cinched around my waist with a thick belt. The prosthetic pointy ears. My subtle makeup, my lips a soft pink close to my natural color.

When his eyes start making their way back up my body, I try to begin. "Welcome, Ulri—"

"You led my on a merry chase, bard," he interrupts, and *gods* the way his blue-green eyes burn into mine. The heat of his stare settles low and heavy in my belly, and I lick my lips, greedily taking in every perfect, windswept inch of him, from his long legs to his high cheekbones, flushed from the cold.

He stalks forward, shutting the door behind him, and for every step forward he takes, I take one back. His expression is downright hungry—*predatory* even—as he peels off his winter coat and tosses it to the ground. My heart rate quickens in response.

"A song," I blurt out, scurrying toward my planned position in front of the fireplace. We always called Roxy's stories "songs," but they're just spoken, not sung. I gesture toward the wingback chair in front of me and inject some authority into my tone. "Rest, weary traveler, and let me entertain you."

For a long moment, I think he might chase after me, magical song be damned, but he takes a deep, shuddering breath and slumps into the chair, legs spread wide. If I didn't know any better, I might mistake his fiery eyes and curt body language for anger or grumpiness, but I recognize it for what it is: impatience.

Impatience for me.

I hold back my smile as that knowledge warms me, my chest straining with the effort it takes to contain my happiness. Jeremy wants me. Not only that, he loves me. Even after all the walls he had to scale over the past two weeks, he still loves me. Honestly, I'd prefer to forget the song and fling myself into his lap, letting the C&C-style campaign around Northview speak for itself. But if anyone deserves to hear these words—proudly and unmistakably—it's Jeremy. He deserves everything, and I'm going to give it to him.

WAR ON CHRISTMAS: A HOLIDAY ROMANCE

It's time to pledge my love.

"In every great love story," I begin, my voice soft but clear, "the stars align when a soul meets its match. Across the galaxies, the planets and moons and asteroids shift, and the stars—just flaming balls of light until that moment—flare with more than fire. For a single moment, they burn with magic. They blaze with the knowledge that out there, somewhere in the universe, one soul has met another, made just for them. Not identical, but alike in substance, values, and heart. So it was when Romeo met Juliet's gaze across the Capulet's party. When Heathcliff first saw Catherine across the Yorkshire moors. When Aragorn encountered Arwen in Rivendell."

Jeremy's mouth tips into the barest of smiles at the *Lord of the Rings* reference, and I fight to hold back my own grin. I know him so well.

"And so it was when Freya first saw Jeremy," I continue. "They began as playmates and friends, but as adulthood neared, they felt a draw to become more than that, until one fateful evening in her fifteenth year, not long after Yuletide, they..." I pause for a dramatic beat. "Kissed."

Right on cue, Jeremy utters a scandalized gasp, his eyes dancing in the firelight. He always did enjoy Roxy's ballads.

"Now, one would think that a kiss—especially a kiss as sweet and perfect as the one shared by Jeremy and Freya—could only be a harbinger of happy things. It was, after all, exactly what the stars foreshadowed: a bond fated by the heavens themselves. Except," I bow my head, "in the wake of the kiss, Freya was beset with a terrible fear. Jeremy was already Freya's best friend. Her trusted advisor. Her keeper of secrets. If he became her sweetheart too..."

I let the sentence trail off, feeling an unexpected surge of compassion for my teenage self. I'd been paralyzed with fear, unsure how to venture into a romantic relationship with Jeremy while also protecting the friendship that meant so much to me. I would have done anything to keep him in my life, and then it was my own indecision that tore him away.

"If he was her sweetheart too…" Jeremy prompts quietly.

"He would have become her everything," I answer. "And if the epic romance between them went down like a bad roll of the dice—as teenage romances are wont to do—she would also have everything to lose. Her fear drove a wedge between the would-be lovers, and the intimacy they'd once enjoyed descended into pettiness, rivalry, and jealousy, all ruthlessly spurred on by the popular girls of Northview High School, with whom Jeremy sought…" I tap my chin, pretending to consider my words carefully, "much comfort."

He swipes a hand down his face, clearly exasperated, and I grin back at him.

"When Jeremy and Freya reached the age of majority and left their small hamlet to pursue bigger adventures, the two parted ways, and the stars that aligned so meticulously to prophesy their romance shone a little dimmer, until"—my lips curl into a smile—"one fateful Yule, many years later, when their paths crossed again."

"Is that right?" Jeremy asks, and I nod, my gaze never wavering from his.

"It is," I confirm. "Because Jeremy and Freya shared a bond so strong and true—a genuine meeting of hearts and minds and bodies—that the stars didn't align for them once, but *twice*."

"*Twice*?" He lets out a slow whistle. "That sounds pretty serious."

"Serious as an orc attack," I respond, prompting Jeremy to emit a sigh that borders on a groan.

"Fuck, I love it when you speak nerd."

Abi twisted my hair into Roxy's signature braids, and I pat them now as I shrug a shoulder. "It's one of my many talents. I'm also fluent in both Please-Forgive-Me-Because-I-Really-Fucked-Up and Groveling-by-Blow-Job."

I'm not sure what springs him into motion, the mention of blow jobs or the extreme rarity of me admitting I've made a mistake, but the next thing I know, he's out of the chair and pinning me to the wall. My hands are above my head, his fingers circling my wrists, and my eyes roll back as his hips press into me.

He's already hard, and I go molten at the feel of him, heat rushing between my legs.

"I'm not done," I whimper, giving an obligatory but weak tug at my wrists. He grips tighter and dips his head, running his nose along the sensitive skin of my neck, and I hate the way I shiver in response.

Except I actually totally love it.

"Then finish, Sunshine," he whispers back. But his free hand is roaming over me, gently pushing a braided loop from my forehead then dropping to trace the line of my collarbone. And every brush of his fingertips is fire, a meteor trailing heat and stardust in its wake.

"I can't—" My breath hitches. "I can't *think* when you're touching me like that."

"Mm." He nods, like he's mulling over my dilemma. "Can't be that important then, can it?"

His smile is teasing as he leans in to kiss me. He knows what he's doing. He knows what I still need to say, and it's like he's going to make me *beg* to say it.

Ha! Just because I'm crazy about him doesn't mean I'm going to give up my favorite pastime. Which is, of course, driving him out of his mind. I mean, what would be the fun in that?

I shrug my shoulders. "You're right," I say, my voice airy as I lift my face to press my lips against his. "Nothing important at—"

"Say it," he laughs, dropping my hands so he can cradle my face. He's smiling that unabashed, megawatt smile that warms me from the inside out. "Please, Frey..."

"Sorry." I stick my nose in the air. "I can't seem to remember what I was about to—"

"Say it."

He's gone from laughing to growling like a beast, and I've never in my life been so delighted.

"What is wrong with my head? I just really can't recall—"

"Say it."

My snarling beast of a Viking changes tactics, and my eyes widen with glee as clothes start flying off me. The belt. The tunic. My lacy red bra. They fly across the hotel room, one after the other, like the frenzied shower of wrapping paper flying across a living room on Christmas morning. He's unwrapping me like I'm the present he's been waiting *forever* to open. By the time he's kneeling in front of me, tossing my boots over his shoulder and peeling the breeches down my legs, I'm shaking, my fingers digging into his hair to steady myself.

He just makes the land of Whoops! I've Gone Too Far so damn...exciting.

His eyes never leave mine as he slides my panties off then lifts my leg, hooking it over his broad shoulder. I'm completely naked, spread and exposed before him, while he hasn't removed a stitch of clothing, and something about the drag of his cotton button-down shirt against the bare skin of my thigh feels dirty and wrong and so very, very right. His fingers rest on my stomach then drift down, over the hill of my pubic bone and into the slick folds between my legs. His eyes flare at how wet I already am, and he plunges two fingers inside me, stroking slow and steady and ruthless, and goddammit I'm going to come. I'm going to come, and I haven't even said what I need to say because we get caught up in these games, but fuck it feels so good and—

"Say it, Sunshine." His mouth is so close to my pussy his breath heats me as he speaks, and my thigh muscles start to tremble.

"Sorry—say what exactly?"

Never say I'm not a glutton for punishment.

Jeremy smiles as he reaches out his tongue and laps at my clit, one firm, lazy stroke that has my orgasm barreling down on me. I gasp, tightening my fingers in his hair. Me teasing him isn't *that* bad, right? It got me here, with his head buried between my legs, finger fucking me toward an earth-shattering orgasm. And I'm going to spend the rest of my life telling him that I love him. Every single day. I'm quite affectionate once I've decided someone's mine. I'll tell him right after I—

Without warning, he turns his head and nips at the secret ticklish spot on my inner thigh, and I squeal as my legs seize around him.

"Say it," he whispers, his tongue tracing swirling patterns along the soft skin he bit. "Say it, Frey."

And when I finally, *finally* do, it feels like the most natural thing in the world. Like my first time walking out on a darkened stage, my scuffed-up Vans echoing across the wooden planks, my stomach falling with the uncanny sensation that I'd done it countless times before.

"I love you." I use my grip on his hair to tip his head back so he can see my face. So he can see every ounce of affection and desire and love I can feel pulsing through me. "I love you, Jeremy. I know I got scared, and I know I fucked up, but it's always been you, even if I haven't—"

"I know, Freya. I love you, too." He stands, toeing off his shoes as he unbuttons his shirt. My fingers are already at his belt, fumbling to unbuckle it. "Now say it again," he rasps.

"I love you."

He lowers his head, his lips brushing against mine. His shirt drops to the floor, and I press my chest to his, melting at the friction of his chest hair against my hard nipples.

"Again."

"I love you."

He demands it, again and again and again, and I give it willingly. After all, honesty is what I'm known for, and honestly? My love for this man is a part of me, spun into every fiber of my being. No more games, no more teasing, no more denying it. He's my best friend. My biggest fan. My occasional tormentor—but always in a sexy kind of way.

My lover.

When he's finally naked, he reaches around to grab my ass, his big hands firm and possessive as he lifts me. I wrap my legs around his waist, greedy for the sensation of him filling me. I'm drowning, gasping for breath, desperate to feel him inside of me, but he controls every movement. He notches himself against me so I can feel the blunt head of his cock at my entrance, then stops.

I bat at his hard, muscled shoulder.

"Stop teasing me," I grind out, squirming my hips to try to take more of him.

He shakes his head. "Never." Then he leans forward to nip my bottom lip. "Now tell me you're mine, Sunshine."

I grab his face between my palms.

"I'm yours," I breathe, and he rewards me with a small thrust, giving me the first inch of his cock.

We both groan, but he's not done yet. "And this pussy?" he demands.

"Yours," I answer, whimpering as he pushes further, stretching and filling me.

He demands ownership of every part of me—my ass, my breasts, my mouth, my hair, my neck—and for every concession I make—"Yours, yours, yours"—he gives me a little more of himself, until he's fully seated inside me.

Then he starts to move. He starts to move, and that tenuous grasp on his self-control snaps, the slow, easy glide of his hips quickly escalating into hard, determined thrusts that push me into the wall behind me. If the night of winter solstice was a surrender, this is a claiming.

And I am here for it.

It's rough and sweaty and raw, the slap of our bodies loud and uneven as he drives into me. His hands grip my ass too hard—there will probably be bruises tomorrow—and I love it. I love every single second of it. That smooth, cautious man who calculates every action, every word, is gone, replaced by a creature who is as dark and greedy as I am. A creature who only I get to hold and love and fuck like this. My nails dig into his scalp, his shoulders, his back, claiming him as surely as he's claiming me, and every stroke of his cock inside me ratchets up my need, until I'm straining against him, back bowed and head thrown back.

"And you're mine," I moan, rolling my hips against him. "You're mine, Jeremy. Say it."

"I'm yours, Freya." He's panting, muscles laboring with the force of his thrusts. "Always."

And with a final push, I'm falling, my body shaking as I tighten around him and he jerks against me, every muscle in his body going rigid as he comes inside of me. But I'm not scared of the fall anymore. I'm not scared of the rush of air against my face or worried about the impending doom of a rough landing. Because nothing—and no one—could ever feel as right as this. As *him*. If I'm falling, he's right next to me, hand in mine, holding on as long and as tight as he can.

Yes, I'm going to piss off his stodgy old boss at some point. And I'm pretty damn sure my ragtag, artsy Sphere family will manage to shock and surprise him. He'll be too neat. I'll be too messy. Hecate will pee in his favorite shoes, and Jeremy will do a double take when I hang my flower-bedecked cow skull in his ultra-modern, ultra-boring condo someday.

But we're in this thing now. In this big, complicated, messy relationship. And regardless of how the dice land, we'll figure it out. Together.

FIFTY

JEREMY

Christmas

I do my best not to blush when we arrive at the Nilsen's on Christmas morning, but it's hard not to when it's obvious that everybody crowded into the tiny, familiar living room knows exactly how we spent last night. Thad avoids looking at us altogether—thank Christ—but Sam and Bethany, who are chatting in the corner, wiggle their eyebrows then burst into giggles when my face turns redder than the maroon Christmas dress Mrs. Nilsen is wearing.

I rub at the back of my neck. I guess this is what having siblings is like. It's kind of...nice. Embarrassing, but also nice.

"Merry Christmas, Jeremy." Mr. Nilsen approaches carefully, a Tom & Jerry in each hand, threatening to spill.

He hands them off to Freya and me with a relieved sigh, and the sharp scent of brandy assaults my nose. The cups, clear glass shaped like moose, remind me of the cups Chevy Chase uses in *Christmas Vacation*, and they're almost enough to make me forget that his daughter is standing next to us sporting obvious whisker burn across her chest.

"Merry Christmas, Mr. Nilsen." I clear my throat, careful not to look at Freya. "Nice cups."

And then I proceed to down the Tom & Jerry, which contains enough brandy to give me a plausible excuse for my permanently blushing face.

"Thanks," he says, leaning back on his heels with a smile. "Freya gave them to me. They're my favorite."

Andy runs forward, arms outstretched to Freya for a hug, and she's crouching to fold him in her arms when my mom wanders in from the kitchen, balancing a plate of Christmas cookies on one hand.

"Mom?"

I'd called her this morning to let her know I'd be spending some time with the Nilsens before heading home, and she'd said it was fine. But here she is, looking pretty and made-up in a long plaid skirt and green sweater, her eyes shining brightly as she leans up to kiss me on the cheek.

"Merry Christmas, Jem," she says, patting Andy's glossy black curls. "And Merry Christmas, Freya."

To my surprise, Freya—who has so far been completely nonplussed by her family's presence—blushes as she leans forward to give my mom a hug.

"Merry Christmas," Freya says quietly, her voice husky and sweet. A little hesitant.

We talked a lot last night, naked and twisted around one another in the hotel sheets. Freya insists that she's the "forever" type—at least where I'm concerned—but she's still not sure if she's the marrying type. Which, I assured her, is fine. I don't need my relationship with Freya to look traditional; I just need her to be mine. However, as I watch her with my mom, shy and a little unsure of herself, I can tell that at least part of her hesitancy is rooted in doubt that Mom would want her as a daughter-in-law. Luckily, I know my mom will be thrilled to fold Freya, tattoos and all, into our tiny family.

We'll see how it goes.

Mrs. Nilsen steps next to my mother, and they exchange a smile. "I didn't want you to have to choose between spending Christmas with Freya or your mom," she explains, handing me a small plate loaded with breakfast pastries.

Before I can say thank you, Bethany's boys start to chant for presents, and everyone scurries to grab seats.

Bethany's crew claims the couch, with Bethany on one end, Drew on the other, and the four kids squished between them, elbowing and jockeying for room. Our mothers share the loveseat, both watching the commotion with satisfied smiles. Thad and Sam choose spots on the floor next to Freya and me. Mr. Nilsen, on the other hand, barely sits down at all, running from one corner of the room to the other with a giant garbage bag, collecting each stray piece of used wrapping paper.

I'm fascinated watching the Nilsen's big, loud family as the kids tear through a mountain of presents. I'm so fascinated—and let's face it, also sleep deprived—that I completely forget about a certain event that's supposed to be taking place until Thad stands up and grabs a small paper bag from under the tree. Without thinking, I squeeze Freya's hand. She's twisted around talking to Bethany, but she turns to me and raises an eyebrow. I jerk my head toward Thad, who's blowing out a breath as he sinks in front of Sam, cross-legged, and takes her hands in his.

"Sam," he says, his voice thick, and the room goes silent. Which, given the volume ten seconds ago, feels like a Christmas miracle. Next to me, Freya freezes.

"For the first three years I knew you, I loved you from a distance, never thinking we'd get to be anything more than friends. Then, one fateful birthday—due to desperation and one too many drinks—I did a...well..." Thad's face turns neon pink. "I did a love spell."

Everyone laughs, their teasing happy and good natured, and my eyes flit briefly to Freya, who's smiling broadly. If Thad did a love spell, I'd bet anything that Freya was there, egging him on.

Thad, who never hesitates to laugh at himself, joins in before continuing, his attention focused on Sam. "For the love spell, I had to write down what I was looking for in a partner, and ever since I told you about it—super early in our relationship—you've wanted to see what I wrote. And I've always told you—"

"Absolutely not," Sam finishes for him.

"Absolutely not," Thad repeats, then lets a long pause build. "Until now."

"Yes! Best Christmas present *ever*!" Sam raises her arms with a triumphant shout, and we all watch with interest as Thad peeks in the paper bag and pulls out what looks like a spice jar filled with a mishmash of herbs and other random objects. He twists off the top, which appears to be covered in melted wax, and as he pulls out three green leaves—bay leaves?—I lean down to Freya's ear.

"This wasn't *your* doing, now was it?"

Freya chuckles, not taking her eyes off Sam, whose hand is fluttering over her heart as she reads the writing on the leaves.

"I merely *facilitated*," Freya replies quietly. "Thad did all the important parts."

"Well, what's on them?" demands Mrs. Nilsen.

Sam looks to Thad for permission, and he nods. So, she takes a deep breath and reads loud enough for everyone to hear, "I want someone who's my best friend. Someone who understands me. Someone who isn't afraid to be a dork with me…" And the list goes on, Sam growing more and more emotional with each item. By the time she gets to the last item, "Someone who gets my goofy side, but also know I'm *more* than that," her voice is shaking with every word, and Thad doesn't look too dry-eyed either.

"You're all of it, Sam," he says. "I honestly don't know if I believe in the spell or not, but we've been together for over a year now, and…" He swallows hard, and my own throat closes around a knot of emotion for my friend. "It's been amazing. Better than anything I ever, ever could have dreamed up in my cubicle during those three years as just friends. You're it for me."

Sam has her arms around his neck before he can pull out the ring, her enthusiastic, "Yes!" filling the living room.

We're already laughing and clapping and hooting when Thad pulls back far enough to say, "Babe, I was just going to ask if you wanted to sell the condo and go house hunting."

Sam, not fooled for a second, tackles Thad to the ground—I'm not surprised; she's stronger than she looks—and starts grappling with him for the bag.

"Let me see the ring!"

"What ring?" he asks, grinning, at which point, Sam crawls over him to snatch the paper bag from his hands and pull out a velvet box.

All hell breaks loose as everyone rushes over to see the ring and offer their congratulations, and next to me, Freya sighs, the sound a little sad and heavy.

"What is it?" I ask, tightening my arm around her.

"Thad got Sam a freaking diamond ring for Christmas, and here I am with nothing to give you." She pouts, her forbidden-fruit lip sticking out so delectably I can't stop myself from leaning over to kiss her. Just for a second. Freya, however, won't be deterred. "It's our first Christmas officially dating and I'm already failing as a girlfriend."

She told me this morning while we were in the shower that the presents she ordered for me wouldn't arrive until after the holidays, and I assured her it was fine. Given how tumultuous the past few days have been, I wasn't honestly expecting anything. But Freya being Freya, she's less than thrilled about not having the *perfect* gift for me on Christmas morning.

I look around us, desperate for the words to explain how *wondrous* this all is to me. The brightly decorated tree, topped by a homemade tissue-paper angel who's so abstract it resembles a creepy Salvador Dalí imitation. The laughter and shouts of Bethany's kids. The affection between Mr. and Mrs. Nilsen as they hug each other tightly, watching Thad and Sam with misty eyes. Even my mom's here, smiling quietly on the loveseat, hands clasped in her lap as she takes in all the happy chaos.

And, of course, there's Freya, curled into my side like she belongs there. Because she does.

Nothing she ordered online could come close to this sense of belonging. Of family.

I open my mouth to tell her again that I'm not upset—that as far as I'm concerned, this is the best Christmas ever—but then I get an idea. I'm not going to talk Freya down from her disappointment. I know her well enough to know *that*.

But I can always distract her.

And nothing distracts Freya like getting riled up.

I bite back my smile as I drag Freya onto my lap so she's facing me. She raises a sassy eyebrow, and I cup her heart-shaped face, smoothing my thumbs over the silken skin of her cheeks.

"Freya Estelle Nilsen." I keep things chaste, dropping kisses to her nose, her cheeks, her forehead. We are surrounded by family, after all. "All I want for—"

"Don't." She pulls back and plasters a hand over my mouth, but I just talk around her fingers, my voice muffled.

"All I want for Chris—"

"Do not say it," she orders, gray eyes flashing dangerously.

I love it. I love the little furrow between her brows. I love the way her nose scrunches up. I love the scary curl to her lips.

I love *her*.

I pull her hand away and speak as quickly as I can, before she can cover my mouth again. "All I want for Christmas is you," I finish with a grin.

"I hate you," she whispers, but her hands are already behind my neck, pulling me in close.

"No you don't," I whisper back.

And then we kiss.

EPILOGUE

FREYA

Six months later...

"Now *that*," Jeremy says, unbuttoning his shirt, "was a fun wedding."

He's right. The beachside ceremony. The seafood dinner. The private dance afterwards, with the stars and crescent moon shining overhead. It was perfection. Exactly what Sam and Thad had been hoping for.

But I don't want to be too agreeable. Best to keep him on his toes.

"Don't let it go to your head that he chose you as his best man," I respond, kicking off my strappy sandals as the hotel room door swings shut behind me. The mai tais at the reception were free flowing, and they've left me feeling as light and airy as the tropical breeze outside. It's a sexy drunk.

The kind that makes my skin notice every swish of my silky dress across my thighs. "It was sexism. Pure and simple."

Jeremy snorts, taking a moment to pull my back into his chest and drop a kiss to my bare shoulder.

"That decision was a hundred percent Sam," he says. "I'm pretty sure they both wanted you, but Thad's a sucker and always gives Sam what she wants. Hence, you ended up the maid of honor, and Thad was stuck with me."

I smirk. He's not wrong. The Good Twin is well and truly smitten, and it makes my heart happy to see it.

Besides, my grumbling to Jeremy about not being best man is all for show. I enjoyed being Sam's maid of honor. I already liked her before the engagement, but our friendship leveled up with wedding planning. We exchanged daily text messages about what flowers she wanted in her bridal bouquet and whether she was obligated to invite her cousin who always hits on Thad. Then, when the cousin situation became a "whole thing" and Sam decided she'd prefer a small ceremony at a remote, tropical location, I was there to reassure her that, no, she wasn't being selfish and, yes, it was her and Thad's day and they should do what they wanted. Which meant cutting the guest list down to twenty, finding a resort, and handing over all the details to an onsite wedding planner.

Once the entire wedding was delegated, Sam and I switched to daily texts about *Chilling Adventures of Sabrina.*

It was a bonding experience.

When Jeremy pulls away to slide out of his white linen shirt, my eyes follow, eating up every inch of his golden torso and arms. He lost no time acquiring a tan. He's dripping sunshine.

The man is always handsome. (So annoying.) But after half a year together, I'm almost used to it. Perfectly groomed and put together for a date? Traditionally handsome. Rumpled and spikey-haired first thing in the morning? Adorably handsome. Puzzling his way out of a rat swarm in the C&C club he formed with coworkers? Nerdy handsome. Sweaty and mussed after a workout? Makes-me-feral handsome.

However, I was *not* prepared for Jeremy-at-a-Bahamas-wedding handsome. I've seen him in a tux, and it's impressive. Swoony handsome. Today on the beach, though, the sea breeze tousling his hair while he watched Thad and Sam exchange vows, a wistful tilt to his full lips?

I-want-to-grow-old-with-you handsome. Marry-me-like-yesterday handsome. Put-your-babies-in-me handsome.

I'd blame it on the mai tais, but honestly? This isn't the first time my thoughts have strayed down the aisle. I know Jeremy's game for it. He told me so when Hecate and I moved in with him a few months ago. Maybe it was his quiet, "Just so you know, I'd marry you in a heartbeat, Sunshine," murmured into my ear while he spooned me that first night. Or maybe it was the wedding planning with Sam and the way my mind continually slipped into thoughts of what I'd choose if it was Jeremy and me getting married. A crisp autumn day. A black, figure-hugging dress. Dark, witchy flowers with Bethany's signature accents. Black Baccara roses, burgundy dahlias, chocolate cosmos, eggplant calla lilies, and a giant chunk of smoky quartz.

It's much more fun to contemplate a tradition like a wedding if I plan on making it as *un*traditional as possible.

I grin to myself, watching Jeremy strip out of his pants. I wait for the perfect moment, when he's just kicking off the first pant leg and still connected to the second.

WAR ON CHRISTMAS: A HOLIDAY ROMANCE

"So, do you think *we* should get married?" I ask.

He goes down like a felled tree, losing his balance and dropping to his knees on the carpet. My laughter bubbles out of me as he curses, kicking at his light-khaki pants, and I press my hands to my mouth. He's usually so athletic and graceful. It's impossible not to enjoy a moment of him being less than perfect. With a grunt, he flings the pants off his foot then grabs me by the ankle, toppling me down on top of him.

I make Jeremy's tumble look positively graceful, going down with a shriek while windmilling my arms. Luckily, there's a large, scowling Viking to catch me.

"Did you just propose marriage, then *laugh* at me when I fell over in shock?"

I blink up from where I'm sitting on his hard thighs. "Yes?"

He narrows his eyes, like I'm setting a trap for him. "You, Freya Estelle Nilsen, want to get married?"

"I don't know if I'm the marrying type in *general*..." I shrug, winding my arms around his neck. "But I think I'm definitely the marrying-Jeremy-Kelly type."

He stares down at me, still suspicious.

"You know it would be really mean to take this back, right, Sunshine?"

I gasp. "I wouldn't take it back. I'm chaotic, but I'm chaotic *good*, not *evil*."

Apparently, I've put it into terms my dreamy nerd understands. I play by my own rules, but I have a moral code, and it's not intentionally cruel.

In one smooth motion, Jeremy rolls me onto my back and settles between my legs, pressing me into the floor. I wrap my limbs around him and pull him tight.

"You want to marry me?" His lips tug into a smile, wide and bright and warm, that reaches up to his blue-green eyes.

"I mean, if you want to. I'm not saying we *have* to do—"

"No takebacks," he blurts, then his mouth is on mine, his big hands already peeling my dress down my arms, and we're laughing. Because he's my person. He's my person, and I'm his, and we're in this thing together.

However, much to my surprise, he is not my everything. Not only do I have Thad, the goodest twin ever, but I have Sam and Bethany now, too. Video chat tarot readings with Abi and my mom. Weekly spooky story time with Andy and his invisible monster. Regular calls from Aiden and August to update me on their latest video game achievements. And, of course, my theater family at The Sphere.

But Jeremy? Jeremy is my favorite, and I've finally found the perfect category to put him in:

~~Best Friend~~
~~Crush~~
~~First Kiss~~
~~Guy I'm Awkwardly Avoiding~~
~~Arch Rival~~
~~Sexual Conquest~~
~~Boyfriend~~
My forever

THE END

Want more Freya and Jeremy? Go to authorellecampbell.com to access a FREE bonus epilogue. (Hint: It's steamy...and there is burlesque.)

Acknowledgements

When I started writing again in fall of 2020, it was a lonely endeavor. There were a lot of late nights clicking away at my computer with only my cats for company.

It turns out *publishing* a book is radically different from writing one. Sharing your work publicly requires a vast network of support, and I'm humbled every time I think of the people who showed up for me—over and over again—to make it possible.

First of all, to my beta readers: This literally would not have happened without you.

Rough Draft Book Club, you came through in such a big way. Savannah, your immediate and enthusiastic love for Jeremy and Freya is what I continually circled back to whenever this process became overwhelming. It was my touchstone during the scariest moments. Laura, your email about Freya gave me the courage to keep her edges. Angie, you are the best all-around cheerleader a witch could ask for. The way you support and uplift the women around you is the best kind of magic. Kate, I would keep writing just so we can exchange Google doc messages . Reading your reactions to my stories is one of my happy places.

Amanda, I appreciate you so much as a reader. Your love of books and stories *shines*, and I'm so grateful that you're willing to lend that experience to me so I can benefit from it as a writer. Thank you.

Lauren, I'm sorry I used the word "cock" so many times. I feel like I stole your innocence. However, we've been friends since we were twelve, so you're officially stuck with me, steamy books and all. I don't make the rules; I just live by them.

Mom, I'm sorry I traumatized you with this book. Don't worry: You never missed a tennis match or an extra-curricular activity; it's ok if you skip out on some steamy romance novels.

Romance Writers Club? Gah. Get out of here. You all are the best. Kat Sterling, when I sent out my first novel to beta readers and was wondering *What the heck do I do next?* you were the one who encouraged me to follow this crazy idea I had for a witchy, Big Scorpio Energy holiday romance. Rylie Keen, you immediately understood who Freya was as a character, and that gave me so much drive to push through the hard parts of this process. Lisa Troy, you were so generous with your thoughtful, detailed feedback. It helped so much as I was doing revisions!

Elise Kennedy, you absolute chaos monster, you throw your love of the romance genre around like magical pebbles, and I don't think any of us can truly conceive how many ripples you're creating. Your generosity with the support you provide to other authors is unmatched, and I *love* to think of all the readers who will get to enjoy and fall in love with stories that you encouraged in some way, from beta reading to offering endless (solicited!) advice about the technicalities of indie publishing. I cannot thank you enough for being such an amazing resource as I navigated this process for the first time. I honestly don't think I would have made it through this crazy experience without your help.

WAR ON CHRISTMAS: A HOLIDAY ROMANCE

Tom, thank you for your help with the Caves & Conquerors characters. Ulrik, Roxy, Stromm, and Luliana will be forever in your debt.

To the Dungeons & Dragons group that let me crash your Wednesday night gathering for research purposes, thank you! I could do all the online research I wanted to, but none of it came close to experiencing it for myself. I hope that the spirit of DND came through in Caves & Conquerors, if not all the rules and technicalities.

Chelsea Kemp, illustrator extraordinaire, thank you for capturing Freya and Jeremy so perfectly in your illustration. I've received so many compliments on the cover, and it 100 percent comes down to your illustration! In addition to being super talented, you were sweet and lovely to work with.

Kristin Verdin, I entrusted you with writing my wedding ceremony...but this was so much scarier! Thank you for lending your bad-ass copy editing skills to this project even though enemies-to-lovers romance novels are not your usual jam. And thank you for liking this story despite its "I hate you...but I love you" energy. I know you would have given Freya and Jeremy your typical care and attention to detail regardless, but it made me feel a lot less guilty about begging you to take on this project knowing that you didn't hate it.

To my ARC readers: Thank you for taking a chance on a debut indie author and spending your precious time and energy with Freya and Jeremy. And for those of you who shared reviews and posts about this book, you have my gratitude. I want this story to find all the readers who will find joy in it, and it's not possible without people willing to leverage social media to spread their love of books and stories.

To #bookstagram, #booktok, and all the online book-loving communities out there, thank you for helping me see the good in social media again. It can be a fickle beast, but knowing that there are always other book nerds out there excited to talk about stories makes this big world seem a little less lonely.

To my three boys. Thank you for your patience as I sat at my laptop for hours at a time, usually staring off into the distance. I could write an entire book just about the Mom Guilt that went into writing this one—The time spent on my computer! My preoccupation with made-up people! The floors that never got cleaned!—but I don't want to teach you how to be perfect. I want to teach you how to chase your passions with single-minded purpose, and I don't know how to do that except for modeling it. I hope someday you all have homes that are as messy as ours and hearts that feel as full as mine right now.

To my husband: Thank you for always encouraging me to pursue this dream of mine. Thank you for being my first reader. And thank you for always answering "No" when I ask "Does this go too far?"

ABOUT THE AUTHOR

Elle Campbell is a Wisconsin-based author living with her husband, three sons, two dogs, and cat. It is absolutely as loud and chaotic as it sounds. And she loves it. When she's not writing or dodging Nerf darts (Sometimes she does both simultaneously!) she's usually reading.

Visit authorellecampbell.com and sign up for her newsletter to stay current with her upcoming projects and free bonus content. You can also follow her on Facebook, Instagram, or TikTok.

Printed in Great Britain
by Amazon